ONE

The surgeon removed the perfumed handkerchief from his nose and tipped his head forward to let the night rain pour from the brim of his hat. Another fellow stood silently alongside and together they watched two sextons labour thigh-deep in a muddy hole to excavate quantities of wet earth on to a growing mound beside them. Six Metropolitan Police bullseye lamps around the exhumation site cast a yellowish light upon the proceedings, reducing all to a grimy *tableau* in sepia and charcoal.

'Forgive me for insisting, Inspector, but are you absolutely certain that we have the right place?' said the surgeon. 'There is no gravestone, no record of interment and generally not the least indication of a known casket here. Frankly, I am not certain I can tolerate a minute longer in this . . . this confounded Gologotha.'

There came no answer. Apart from the labourers' grunts and the glutinous suck of their doubled shovels, the only other sound was of the ceaseless downpour upon the reeking, corpse-clogged enclosure of Portugal-street burial ground.

'And I need hardly relate to you the nature of what we will find if this is indeed the body you seek,' continued the surgeon. 'Recognition will be virtually impossible – the corpse will have passed beyond the fermentation phase and entered the foetid stage of gaseous swelling. At best, you will behold a cloth-bound ammoniac soap of margaric acid: eyes gone, nose collapsed and body bloated. At worst . . . well, nothing much more than a mass of green pultaceous matter in the mockery of human form. It might be anyone at all. I say, Inspector Newsome – are you even listening to me?'

The other gentleman showed no sign of having heard his interlocutor. Rather, he watched with unblinking eyes as the gravediggers worked their way down through the endless strata of London's mortalities: those uncountable victims of plague, typhus, pox, cholera, poverty and murder stretching back beyond memory. His coat was now quite saturated, and the wild red hair escaping from beneath his hat dripped steadily inside his collar. If his face bore a scowl, it was due to his natural disposition rather than the early hour and the rain. If he seemed somewhat wiry of build, it was in the way that a rapier is deceptively slender. And if he seemed to be wilfully ignoring his medical colleague, it was because Inspector Albert Newsome was well known to be the most irascible and least personable member of the Detective Force. He was also grudgingly acknowledged to be its best.

'Only two hours to dawn. Put your backs into it, men,' said Mr Newsome, returning his pocket watch beneath his coat and casting a grimace into the black cloud that smothered the city.

'This would have been easier for everyone if we had waited for daylight and fair weather,' muttered the surgeon. 'The casket – if there is one – will still be there. I feel that this haste and secrecy is really quite disproportionate.'

'Would you have us conduct the procedure with dozens of local people crowding about us, doctor, turning this scientific endeavour into one of gruesome titillation? Did you also not tell me at great length how the ground hereabouts is utterly poisoned with human putrescence and that its miasmic exhalations might veritably throw a man – let alone a crowd – into fatal insensibility?'

'That is true, but—'

'And might not this d_____ rain actually aid us in restraining the exhalations you so fear?'

'To some degree, yes, but—

'Very well, so there is nothing more to say on the matter.'

The surgeon cast a sidelong glance at the profile of Mr Newsome. 'I cannot help but wonder, Inspector, whether you were able to secure the requisite parochial authority for this exhumation at such short notice. I know that such permissions can be difficult to—'

'Allow me to worry about such things, doctor. Might I suggest, instead, that you apply some of the lime chloride solution? The grave seems to be quite steaming.'

And the hole containing the mud-splashed sextons had indeed begun to emit a foul breath of heated decomposition into the late October night. The surgeon tutted to himself, held the handkerchief over his lower face and approached the grave holding a zinc can fitted with a spout and a rose so that the disinfectant could be distributed around the sides of the shaft. In cross-section, the oozing earth walls dimly revealed countless fragments of long-rotted coffins, splintered bone ends and assorted scull shards as plentiful as the fractured crockery to be found in Thames mud.

'Take care not to get this in your eyes or on your skin, gentlemen,' warned the surgeon.

Now rib-deep, the two diggers heedlessly continued their rhythmic labour even as the solution trickled down around their sludge-bound boots.

Then came a hollow shovel thud.

Mr Newsome was jerked back from his reveries and seized a bullseye lamp from a tombstone to better see what had been found.

'A coffin? Is it really a coffin so shallow?' he said, directing the beam into the pit.

'In this place, they no longer bury in virgin earth,' said the surgeon, himself taking a lamp. 'Only in the mulch of other bodies. An unmarked grave like this has no need of a deeper shaft.'

'Clear it, men!' said Mr Newsome. 'Is the wood still whole and strong? An extra shilling apiece if this is the one I seek!'

The shovel-wielders drew new strength and cleared around the coffin top until its outline became clear. Even in the poor light of the lamps, the wood seemed to retain patches of its original lacquer where it showed through the mud.

'Thur's a rope!' shouted one of the diggers, holding up a filth-clotted length of hemp.

'Good,' said Mr Newsome. 'They must have been left beneath the casket when it was lowered. This will aid us no end. Dig out the others and we will see if they will still bear the weight after soaking in the ground.'

Four heavy lengths were uncoiled from the abominable nooks of the hole and handed up to the surgeon, who took them with double-gloved hands and an unrestrained expression of horror at their provenance. When all were laid out on the surface, the sextons were aided out of the mire and each of the men took an end, winding it around their forearms for purchase. Or rather, three of them did so.

'Inspector – this is quite intolerable,' said the surgeon, beholding the glistening black serpent at his feet. 'It is beyond my remit as—'

'Take it, doctor! We cannot do this without you, and we are all quite saturated in any event. I feel sure that these two burly gentlemen would be most disappointed if I was unable to pay them on account of your intransigence.'

The sextons may not have gathered the finer elements of the vocabulary, but they seemed to perceive that their payment was in some manner of jeopardy and glared at the surgeon with mud- and sweat-streaked expressions of threat.

'Very well, very well, but I will be making a formal compl—'

'Pull!' shouted Mr Newsome.

The ropes tautened and cut into the soft earth walls of the shaft. Four sets of boots struggled for purchase in the puddled mud.

'It is the suction,' said the surgeon. 'I fear that we will not be able to pull the casket free of that liquid grasp.'

'Nonsense,' said Mr Newsome. 'We are four strong men and it is just a box. We must establish a rhythm as sailors do when they hoist a mainsail. Pull! Pull! Pull!'

They co-ordinated their efforts, and within seconds there was a sickening gurgling from within the shaft. It was followed by a resounding viscous suck and Mr Newsome half slipped backwards, losing his hat to the mud, as the coffin began to rise upon the ropes.

'It is holding, men!' shouted Mr Newsome, the rain plastering his curly red hair to his forehead and his face set in a maniacal mask in the light of the bullseyes. 'Bring it up slowly; keep it steady now.'

The slightly domed top of the coffin emerged from the hole, running with rivulets of mud, rain, lime chloride and the composted remains of London's timeless dead.

'Everyone take one step to the left!' called Mr Newsome as they shuffled the coffin towards solid ground. 'And another . . . keep the ropes taut.' Then, when it was barely half balanced above the shaft, he raced towards the land-bound end and hauled on a discoloured brass handle to slide the full length of it to safety. 'Some help, men! It is a heavy one – lead-lined by the feel of it.'

Together, they dragged the coffin fully away from the shaft and stood panting around it, the two sextons bending over to rest fatigued palms on tired knees in a fine dumb-show of persuasive acquisitiveness.

'It is rather a fine casket,' said the surgeon. 'I thought you said it was a common criminal you sought.'

'A criminal, yes, but a thoroughly *un*common one. The box does not surprize me.'

'Well, I suppose we should attempt to transport it to a more suitable—'

'No. We will open it here. Rain will do the body no harm, and the only evidence I seek is its identity. Then we can return it to that vile abyss and fill in the hole before dawn.'

'This is most irregular, Inspector. I am not at all comfortable conducting the procedure in the open.'

'Then you must direct any blame at me in your subsequent complaints. Meanwhile, I hope you will prevent any harm coming to us from infection by fulfilling your duty as a medical man. Please – let us get the casket open.'

7

'I should have listened to what people told me about you, Inspector. Very well – if you insist, I must first rinse the entire surface of the thing with the chloride of lime. It is utterly virulent with miasmic particles and we must not breathe its odour.'

The surgeon worked his way methodically around the casket, pouring the solution particularly over the handles and the join between the two parts. As he did so, he could not help but conjecture on the possible contents. Even with the blooms of moisture that had variously permeated the lacquer to damage the wood, it was indeed a handsome specimen of its kind and evidenced a budget far beyond that granted by parochial or police finances.

Mr Newsome was looking at his pocket watch again. 'That is enough, I think. Let us tap it.'

With pursed lips and a held tongue, the surgeon went to a leather bag he had been attempting to keep dry under a leaning tombstone. He withdrew a gimlet about 12 inches in length and the thickness of a finger, handing it to the sexton nearest to him:

'Here. Bore this into the wood until you feel no further resistance . . . no, not through the top – there is very likely a glass inner lid in such a casket. Enter through the side."

The dirt-smeared gravedigger forced the point of the tool into the wood with a grunt and twisted the handle with some slight exaggeration of effort until his face showed he was through to whatever horror lay within. Was the tip of the gimlet resting now against a jellied limb or yellowed mass of ripe adipocere?

The surgeon nodded and approached with a thin steel tube that was tapered at one end and had a small stop-cock at the other. He indicated that the gimlet should be slowly withdrawn and, with a slightly trembling hand, quickly inserted the end of the tube into the freshly bored hole before anything could escape. A tap of a carpenter's maul secured it in the aperture.

'Is this pantomime strictly necessary, doctor?' said Mr Newsome, again looking from his watch to the still gloomy eastern horizon.

'It is necessary if you do not want to be party to a horrible eruption, Inspector. The body is very likely hermetically sealed in a lead box that is itself laid inside the wooden casket. While the lead prevents corruption from without, it also encourages corruption within – corruption that creates a quantity of combustible and poisonous gas.'

'Yes, yes – I bow to your expertise. Do what you must, but quicker.'

The surgeon took a box of Lucifer matches from an inner pocket and struck one before holding the quivering flame to the tiny mouth of the stop-cock and minimally turning the key. He flinched in anticipation of the emerging gas . . . but none came.

'What is it, doctor?' said Mr Newsome.

'There . . . there appears to be no gas.' The surgeon turned the key further but still no gas emerged. He moved towards the stop-cock and made a tentative sniff. 'Nothing.'

'So there is no body inside?'

'Not necessarily – perhaps it is a body that has not yet passed into the putrescent phase . . . but I thought you told me it has been interred for a year or more. Atmospheric conditions play a part, of course . . . it was a cool summer, then a cold winter . . .'

'There is only one way to solve this mystery. Sextons – to your pry bars! We will open the box.'

The two men took up their bars from the mud and made to splinter the fine wood.

The surgeon continued to be ill at ease. 'Very well, Inspector, but I would remind these gentlemen to be particular in their pryings. If there *is* a glass top, a violent strike against its edge might cast fragments into the body and impair your evidence.'

'A pertinent observation, doctor. Take care, men.' Mr Newsome nodded his assent to the men, who set about forcing their irons into the join as they worked their way around the casket.

'It is heavy enough to contain a body,' muttered Mr Newsome, 'even taking the weight of the lead into account. Do not some coffins intended for vaults have tiny holes bored in them to allow the safe escape of gas? That would explain it . . .'

'Sorry, Inspector? Were you speaking to me?'

'No. It was nothing. I was just . . .'

There was a rending of wood and the two sextons looked to Mr Newsome for further instruction.

'Fetch the lamps. Fetch all the lamps,' said the inspector. 'Bring them close. You two men – carry the top away.'

The gravediggers each took an end and carried the coffin top a few paces into the darkness beyond. There, they lingered, seemingly unwilling to participate further in the desecration.

'Just as I thought: a glass top,' said the surgeon, stepping forward and setting two lamps upon the surface. 'That should make your identification less problematic.'

But as Mr Newsome swiftly joined him, it became clear that their view of the coffin's interior was obfuscated by the raindrops from above and by a quantity of beaded condensation from the inside. The inspector smeared a muddy glove over the smooth glass and pressed his nose almost to its coldness, tilting the lamp to pick out any detail. All was indistinct.

'Is that a burial suit? Do you see it, doctor? It looks like black cloth . . . possibly a hand, but I am not certain I can distinguish a face. There is *something* . . .'

'Perhaps there is some structural defect in the base . . . moisture may have entered from there and condensed on the underside.'

'Sextons!' called Mr Newsome. 'Come here and take the bottom end of the coffin. Come – do not be afraid of its contents. I will not make you reveal the body.'

'What are you doing, Inspector?' said the surgeon.

'If we tilt the coffin, the inner droplets will run down towards the head and clear the view momentarily.'

'Ah yes – very good. Let us stand back.'

The gravediggers slipped meaty fingers into the mud beneath the wood and hoisted together. Just as predicted, the water began to run along the underside of the glass panel, washing away the opacity in lucid streaks.

'All right – let it go, men!' charged Mr Newsome.

The raised end of the casket fell with a squelch and a corona of mud that splashed their trouser bottoms. Its handlers retreated uneasily, but both detective and surgeon bent immediately towards the top and angled their lamps to see what lay within.

'*My G__, Inspector!* What on earth is it?'

'I am no medical man, but it appears to be a face.'

'But . . . but there is no decomposition! The eyes are whole and seem to glisten . . . the lips have not withered. He looks . . . my G__, he looks alive!'

'He is assuredly not alive, doctor.'

'And what is that curious deformation of the skin? It appears to have bubbled or melted quite horribly . . . and yet the wound appears fresh, without scabbing or scarring. What is happening, Inspector Newsome? What manner of atrocity has been perpetrated here? You seem neither shocked nor surprized. Is this what you expected to find?'

'We must remove the glass and gain access to the body.'

'*What?*'

'As you have stated, doctor: all the evidence points towards no decomposition having taken place. There is, therefore, no danger to our health.'

'But what is this . . . this *unholy* thing? It is surely not a human body. It cannot be.'

'That is what I intend to discover.'

Mr Newsome withdrew a dagger from within his coat and began to prise the leaden lip away from the edge of the glass. Within minutes, he had

11

removed enough of the seal to slip the blade under the top and raise it enough to grasp the edge with a gloved hand.

The surgeon stepped back in expectation of a putrid exhalation, but there was none and he soon returned. Instead of decay, there was something else.

'Wait, Inspector! There is some manner of strip attached beneath the glass here at the side,' he warned Mr Newsome. 'It looks like . . . like a length of sandpaper.'

Even as the Inspector continued to lift the glass cover free, he understood with a chilling dread what the sandpaper must mean. His legs froze in terror and he let the heavy top fall from his hands.

But it was already too late.

The narrow strip of sandpaper descended into a waxed box within the coffin. Wound into the end of the strip was a Lucifer match, which had been struck when the coffin cover had been raised sufficiently. And surrounding the flame in that waxed box was a quantity of fine-milled gunpowder.

'*Get to the ground!*' screamed Mr Newsome, leaping face first into the quagmire around the grave.

The surgeon perceived the merest glow inside the coffin and likewise fell dramatically to the pestilential earth with his hands over his ears.

There was a colossal cracking boom and a flash of yellow-orange light as the gunpowder ignited. The casket erupted into a shower of splinters and the glass top was shattered instantly into a vitreous hail that fell upon them even as they lay coiled in the sludge. It was an explosion that echoed even as far as Southwark and along the Thames to Wapping.

'Are you unhurt?' said Mr Newsome, rising. His own voice came to him but distantly through stunned ears.

'I ... I think so,' said the surgeon.

The coffin and its contents had been all but obliterated in its lower half, but the body remained from the hips upwards, albeit severely charred and tattered. It smoked still and Mr Newsome patted at an ember with his glove.

'That charge should have destroyed the whole thing, doctor. The condensation within must have dampened a proportion of the powder. We are very fortunate.'

'"Fortunate", you say? Look at me – I am a veritable effigy of filth. We were almost killed!'

'As I say: fortunate.'

Not everyone had escaped unharmed, however. A groan from where the sextons had been loitering drew the surgeon's attention.

''Enry is 'urt,' came a tremulous cry from the darkness.

Mr Newsome and the surgeon splashed towards the call and beheld the one called Henry leaning against a tombstone, a jagged stake of wood jutting from his left shoulder. The blood was copious even in the darkness and the man's face was quite pale.

'Can you do something with this injury, doctor?' said Mr Newsome in an even voice.

'Here? Amid the mulch and reek of one hundred thousand rotted corpses?' replied the surgeon with a tone of rising incredulity. 'Of course not! This man should be brought to a hospital with all haste. There must be constable on his beat hereabouts – I must go for help.'

'No – I believe, we can manage the situation ourselves,' said Mr Newsome.

'You are a lunatic, Inspector, if you believe so. I should have listened to what they told me about you. It is no business of mine what you hoped to achieve here tonight, but my purpose is to preserve life and I will do so now by going for a constable.'

Mr Newsome found that he was reaching for his dagger, but a baleful look from the unhurt (and well built) sexton forced him to stay his hand and resign himself to frustrated inaction as the surgeon made his way purposefully towards the iron gates of the burial ground.

At the corner with Carey-street, the medical man squinted through the rain but could see no constable beneath the gas light at the opposite corner.

He turned and ran instead in the direction of Clements-lane, where there must surely be help at hand.

On arrival at that place, he saw the blessed *silhouette* of a PC standing under a distant lamp post – the only figure in a bleak and deserted street.

'Ho! Constable!' called the surgeon. 'Hello? I need help at Portugal-street burial ground. Ho! You there!'

The figure made no move in response, but remained quite immobile.

Cursing at such lassitude, the surgeon ran towards the lamp, all the while shouting: 'Did you not hear me? A man is dying! We need a conveyance to move him to hospital. Ho! You there!'

Finally, out of breath and in no mood to discuss matters reasonably, the surgeon came to a halt before the constable, who had not even deigned to turn his head at the noisily approaching man.

'I say – what kind of policing do you call this?' began the surgeon.

But the words dried in his mouth and his eyes started in horror at what he saw before him.

The constable was frozen quite immobile: eyes unblinking, open mouth partially filled with rainwater, one arm raised with his rattle grasped in a rigidly unmoving hand. The oilskin cape about his shoulders glistened under the illumination of the gas, but the rest of his clothes were utterly soaked through as if the fellow had not moved for some time. And as the surgeon glanced down at the constable's boots, he saw with a tremor of nauseating terror that the whole body was seemingly affixed to a board to keep it from toppling over. If the policeman was not technically dead, it was because he was also not entirely human.

'G__ have mercy,' whispered the surgeon, suddenly chilled beyond tolerance by the relentless rain. Bile rose hotly in his throat and he fought the urge to vomit.

TWO

Commissioner of the Metropolitan Police Sir Richard Mayne sat alone in his office at 4 Whitehall-place, known more colloquially as Scotland Yard. A freshly stocked fire crackled in the grate and a sturdy mantle clock tocked venerably below an imperious portrait of Her Majesty allegorically attired in the robes of Justice. All else was silence as Sir Richard – perpetually pale, but with his dark eyes tirelessly attentive – opened the dossier on the broad oaken desk before him and addressed the first document.

FITNESS-FOR-DUTY REPORT
SUBJECT: Detective Inspector Albert Newsome

The inspector remains, as ever, in rude health and has lost none of his corporeal vigour. Indeed, it seems he is able to sustain himself on the very slightest provision of both sleep and sustenance, though he would no doubt benefit greatly from an increase in each of these. In his work, he is utterly tireless and shows a dedication that is exemplary while bordering on the fanatical (more of which below).

The inspector's recent experiences cannot be overlooked, however, in considering his overall – that is to say, his temperamental – fitness for duty. Interviews with Mr Newsome, along with testimonies gathered discreetly from his colleagues in the Detective Force would seem to suggest that his erstwhile entombment within the city's sewer system for a number of days (while investigating a case, I understand) has adversely affected his mind.

It is well documented that extensive periods spent utterly alone, in darkness and in danger can affect the equilibrium of a man's sanity. Add to this the likely presence of mephitic gases in those unspeakable tunnels, and it is not difficult to imagine how that period may have warped his senses. In fact, the evidence would

15

seem to suggest that the cumulative effect in this instance has been to magnify certain of the less measured elements of the inspector's character – those negative elements, in short, which may unfit him for duty.

While Mr Newsome remains capable of reasoned judgement (and lethal with an incisive jibe), he nevertheless shows occasional instances of poor judgement in regard to his duties that may almost be termed "maniacal". Rather than risk hyperbole, I here append an academic definition of the state so that you may make your own judgement when next you see him: "*Mania: a ferocity of language and deportment; a wild expression and protuberant eyes; an insensitivity to cold and a neglect of food, but also an indiscriminate voraciousness. Reasoning is impulsive, absurd or incoherent, though may seem normal when steered away from the subject that agitates the patient's mania.*"

In conclusion, my judgement is that Inspector Newsome is operating at the very edge of rational tolerance. Though he remains unerringly effective in his duties, he risks damage to himself in the short term and damage to the Force in the more distant future if his extreme characteristics are left to develop further.

MY VERDICT: The Police Commissioner to make a personal decision in this case.

Dr Benedict Norman
Surgeon, Division A

Sir Richard shook his head, perhaps in negation or perhaps in regret. The next item in the folder was the inspector's disciplinary records, documenting any infractions of police regulations dating back to when he had first joined the force at its inception in 1829. It was, notoriously, the longest and most detailed such document kept in the Scotland Yard archives.

Willing himself not to read too closely, the commissioner glanced quickly through the pages. Here was the incident in which the sailors' bar in the Minories had been destroyed; here was the theft of a cab in pursuit of a thief; here was the assault upon the eminent politician; here was the time he had been arrested by the men of his own division; and here, more latterly, was the occasion on which he had left two men to drown in a subterranean room. Indeed, some of his misadventures of recent years were too sensitive even to feature in this already highly confidential document. Any one of them might have seen him ejected from the force, and yet each had somehow redeemed him when his impetuosity had resulted in an outrageous solution or the prevention of a greater crime. It was almost as if the inspector was akin to one of those warriors of ancient times – an Achilles perhaps – who was invaluable in the thick of battle but a liability in times of peace.

The dossier provided sufficient evidence, arguably, to either honour or hang its subject. There was one further sheet, however, that Sir Richard wanted to read before facing Inspector Newsome over this latest incident at Portugal-street burial ground. Complementary to the medical report of Dr Norman, an additional study had been made of the errant inspector by one of Scotland Yard's lesser known experts: one employed periodically as consultant physiognomist, craniognomist and pathognomist.

CONFIDENTIAL ANTHROPOMETRIC REPORT
SUBJECT: Inspector Albert Newsome

Physiognomy – Mr Newsome remains largely unchanged in organic constitution since his last examination. That is to say, his form and visage exhibits strong traits of biliousness, energy and inquisitiveness, combined with a formidable stamina and quickness to react.

Craniognomy – Once again, the scull is broadly identical to previous studies that have shown arrogance, diligence, competitiveness, pragmatism and firmness of purpose. The only significant change appears to be a slight development of the contours suggestive of the carnivorous instinct, which is to say that associated with single-mindedness and aggression.

17

Pathognomy – It is in this respect that I see most alteration in the posture and gestures of Inspector Newsome. Of late, his gesticulations have become more jerkily erratic and the set of his spine marginally curved forwards in its upper regions. Together, these traits indicate a likely increase in both anxiety and impatience.

(NOTE: This is, as requested, merely a synopsis. See my full graphical report for detailed analysis of my specific measurements and judgements. Edward Figgs)

Sir Richard closed the dossier slowly and looked to the mantle clock. As he had been reading, the subject of those sundry reports had no doubt been waiting impatiently in the anteroom for his interview with the commissioner. Now, as the clock began to chime, there came a knock at the connecting door and the uniformed clerk was jostled aside even before he could announce the visiter.

Inspector Newsome entered as if borne upon a gust of wind. Though he had changed his ruined clothes since the events at Portugal-street, it seemed he had not slept in the meantime. His manner may have been brisk, but his eyeballs were veined and dull with fatigue.

'You requested to see me, sir,' was his terse salutation as he adopted the accustomed stance of attention, hands clasped behind his back, before the commissioner's desk.

'Indeed I did,' said Sir Richard, wilfully maintaining composure. 'Perhaps you could explain to me on whose authority and with what aim you thought it prudent to flout good sense and all regulations by exhuming a body last night?'

'Sir – I tendered a formal application to the parochial authorities of St Clement Danes as specified by procedure, but—'

'But you did not have the patience to wait for it, knowing, no doubt, that it would be passed on to me and queried.'

'It was a matter of ... of some urgency, sir, that I investigate a particular avenue—'

'What "avenue", Inspector? I fear even to ask because I am sure I know the answer.'

'Lucius Boyle, sir.' Mr Newsome's jaw flexed in anticipation of the response.

Sir Richard sighed and clasped his hands before him on the desk. 'Have not we discussed this at great length? The man is dead. You saw his fire-blackened corpse yourself over a year ago. Even his most ferocious enemies have accepted his demise. But you ...'

'I have seen him alive since then, sir. You have seen my report. I was not mistaken. I saw his eyes, his burned skin. It was undoubtedly Boyle. How else do we explain that no other perpetrator was ever caught in that recent smuggling enterprize? And the man's survival is made manifest in so many other ways—'

'Except in the realms of the physical and temporal, Inspector. You were trapped in the sewer system for days. Any man's judgement would be affected by such an experience. It was a difficult case for all involved and you had the worst of it.'

'I know what I saw, and now I have proof of it.'

'Proof? What possible proof could there be? Surely you have not disinterred a corpse to prove to yourself that a man remains alive?'

'It was Boyle's grave that I found, sir.'

Sir Richard thought of the dossier notes he had so recently read and looked doubtfully at the ember stare of the inspector. He sighed again, this time more deeply. 'What makes you think it was Lucius Boyle's grave?'

'I made some enquires, sir. It is common knowledge that the police will occasionally bury victims or perpetrators of crime at Portugal-street if no parish will pay for their interment. Knowing this, I checked the records around the time of Boyle's death and found that there had indeed been a burial at that time. All names had been omitted: the corpse, the funerary agent, the gravediggers and even the payee – all entries had been either crossed through as blank or purposefully smudged beyond recognition. Nor was there a tombstone. Such secrecy was highly suggestive, was it not?'

'Why, then, would the burial be recorded at all, Inspector? It makes no sense.'

'Merely because the burial ground must have accurate knowledge of where fresh coffins lie. A sexton cannot dig where hard wood prevents him, particularly in that over-filled earth.'

'I think you overstate both your case and your cause. Many bodies are buried without name or stone. And even if you did find a body, all you can show is a nameless, featureless wreck which is quite useless as evidence.'

'It was not a body in the coffin, sir. At least, not a human form.'

'I beg your pardon?'

'If I may demonstrate . . .'

Mr Newsome went briskly to the main door and opened it, calling out to someone in the corridor beyond. A number of footsteps could then be heard approaching and he held the door open in anticipation of their arrival.

Sir Richard began to stand. 'What is this, Inspector? I will not tolerate . . .'

Two clerks entered, manoeuvring a board round the door jamb and into the office. Upon it was a long box covered in a white sheet.

'This is outrageous!' expostulated Sir Richard, coming from behind his desk.

Now fully inside the office, the clerks released long spring-mounted legs from the board (which was akin to a battlefield operating table) and settled it upon a large Persian rug in the centre of the room so that the veiled box was presented at waist height. Mr Newsome thanked the men and they left swiftly, grateful that the commissioner had been too shocked to address them.

'Sir – may I present Lucius Boyle,' said Mr Newsome, whisking away the sheet to reveal the charred and splintered remains of the coffin from Portugal-street.

'Inspector Newsome! This is quite beyond tolerance. I will not . . .'

But the sight before him quite robbed Sir Richard of his ire, replacing it with a sickening jolt of incredulity.

The lower half of the coffin was gone, along with the legs of its inhabitant. All that remained here was split wood, jagged edges of lead, burned cloth and fragments of glass. But where the tattered trouser legs should have presented a gruesome stub of putrescent matter, only a trickle of fine sand seemed to emerge.

The figure within had evidently been clothed for burial in a fine black suit and showed no sign of decomposition. Rather, the chest remained full, the arms whole and the hands utterly untainted by death at the sides of the body. Though they were preternaturally pale, the fingers were perhaps more perfectly formed and graceful than those of a living man.

As for the face, it was at once fascinating and repulsive. The smoke-grey eyes – though quite immobile – were indeed bright and full, suggesting that they might blink at any moment. The countenance as a whole, however, was akin to a freshly skinned animal: all raw muscle, sinew, bone and peeling skin that seemed to glisten with a hideous necrotic vitality. A large patch of hair had also been apparently burned off so that the forehead extended unnaturally back as an expanse of mottled pink flesh. There was no stench of death – only the sharp smell of the consumed gunpowder, the fustiness of the long-interred coffin and something more that was oddly unidentifiable.

'Wax,' said Mr Newsome by way of explanation.

'What . . . what is this thing?' said Sir Richard, still mesmerized by the oddity of it.

'It is an effigy in wax, sir – an effigy of a man who might have been badly burned about the face. It is very skilfully executed, sir, so that anyone looking in through the glass coffin-top could not tell it apart from a real man prior to burial.'

'What does this prove, Inspector? There is no human body here. My patience is at an end.'

'Sir Richard ... why would anyone bury an effigy such as this? One designed to look like a burned man – like the very image of Lucius Boyle himself? And why would it contain a bomb intended to kill anyone foolhardy enough to exhume it at a later date? And why is the casket such a fine one? I am quite certain that the Metropolitan Police finances do not extend so far. You are right in one critical respect, sir: none of it makes the least sense ... unless Boyle is alive.'

'I cannot see how ... how this could have happened.'

'Forgive me any impertinence, sir, but it seems to me that one conclusion is inescapable. Just as you are required to authorize an exhumation, surely you also have oversight of any burials drawing upon police finances. Was Lucius Boyle buried anonymously at Portugal-street?'

Sir Richard looked at his inspector and saw that he was barely suppressing the triumph he must have felt. An impetuous lunatic Mr Newsome may have been, but he was a detective to the very core.

'Inspector – did I not make it clear you were not to investigate the continued existence of Lucius Boyle?'

'I saw him living, sir. Now I have proved that he is not dead – or at least not interred where he is supposed to be. I respectfully request that I be assigned to the ongoing case until I can apprehend him.'

'There is no ongoing case, Inspector.'

'The smuggling case, sir: the theft of the brig *Aurora*. Nobody has been caught, and Lucius Boyle is a key suspect.'

'There are indeed some unsolved elements of that case – certain characters we would like to question – but I would not call it an ongoing case. And Lucius Boyle has never been an official suspect.'

'Then what of the body found last night just a few hundred yards from the burial ground – that macabre representation of a constable?'

'What of it, Inspector?'

'Well, does it not seem a colossal coincidence to you, sir, that the two bodies would be found in such close proximity? We know from experience that Boyle is prone to audaciously conspicuous murders.'

'As you say: a coincidence. Even if the body of the constable does match the *modus operandi* attributed to Boyle, I see no possible or logical connection.'

'That is precisely why I should investigate that crime, sir: to prove the connection. Furthermore, I assume you are aware of certain recent reports from around the city concerning a "masked man" . . .'

'I have of course heard of such reports and consider them nothing more than the fancy of a gullible populace. It matters not whether a fellow in a mask is stalking the streets – no crimes have been committed and there are none to be investigated.'

'Yes, sir . . . but do you not find the reports somewhat suggestive in light of my discovery at Portugal-street?'

'Not at all.'

'I mean to say, sir, that a man such as Lucius Boyle might not walk freely in London with a face so disfigured. All current reports of the "masked man" note that he is glimpsed only at night: a ghostly, pale-faced countenance. Now we have a suggestion that Boyle is acquainted with the use of wax to create a likeness. Might the "masked man" not be Boyle himself attending to his criminal activities?'

'Or a student playing a prank, or a man wounded in battle who is ashamed of his face, or a naturally pale man whose real face is taken for a mask . . . Your suppositions are too tendentious, Inspector.'

'The clues point persuasively towards—'

'Let me make myself absolutely clear: you are forbidden from investigating further this nonsense with the effigy in the coffin. Nor will you ask any questions about the death of this constable. It will be dealt with by others.'

'Which others?'

'Moderate your tone, Inspector. It is not your business to whom each case is assigned. There are other inspectors in the Detective Force.'

'I . . . with respect . . . may I be given the opportunity to at least make just a small number of further enquiries into this wax figure – merely to prove beyond any reasonable doubt that Boyle is no longer alive. I will be discreet.'

'I wonder if you still posses that ability. Of late, you have been rather too . . . spirited in your duties. There is a private matter in Brighton that requires a good man—'

'No! Rather, I . . . I mean to say, sir. That I am quite sound of mind, no matter what these head-measurers may tell you. Judge a man by his actions, not by his eyebrows – that is my "science".'

Sir Richard returned to his desk, using the opportunity to conceal his smile at Mr Newsome's robust gainsaying of the anthropometric arts. Once seated, he clasped his hands on the desk's leather top and looked down at them, his lips compressed in deliberation.

'You are impetuous, Inspector. Your actions say that about you.'

'I . . . I do not mean to embarrass the Force, sir.'

'I am sure you do not. It has been suggested to me that you are afflicted with a mania and that your mind is unbalanced. What do you say to that?'

'I call it a passion for justice, sir. I cannot leave a case when I see there is more to discover.'

Sir Richard cogitated further, his eyes settling upon the closed dossiers containing the assessments of Inspector Newsome. 'If I were to allow you a short period to satisfy your curiosity . . . to purge yourself of this mania, or passion as you call it . . . could you promise me—'

'Yes, sir!'

'Could you promise me, Inspector, that you will cause no more chaos — and that if you *do* disgrace the Force in any way, you will stand down from your position?'

'Sir Richard – I seek only justice. I accept your conditions.'

'Very well. I give you one week – not an hour more. Speak of this matter to nobody at all. There are certain people – you know precisely who I mean – who would become crazed with a vengeful phrensy if they thought Lucius Boyle were still alive. We must avoid that at all costs. Conduct your investigation with the utmost subtlety, involving as few civilians as possible. I am thinking particularly of that young doctor from the College of Surgeons who you managed to cajole into your scheme. He has been quite upset by the whole experience and faces a disciplinary interview with his professor. If you have turned up nothing conclusive within the next week, you will cease this *charade* and take a more serious case.'

'Thank you, Sir Richard. There is just one further matter. You will recall that a diary was recovered from a previous investigation. It seems to have belonged to Boyle and may prove instrumental in—'

'Absolutely not.'

'I . . .' Mr Newsome saw that the commissioner's expression allowed not the slightest latitude. 'Very good, sir.'

'And remember, Inspector: stay away from the case of the constable.'

'Yes, sir.'

'Now – please have this waxen abomination removed from my office. And keep it covered with a sheet – I do not want everyone in the building seeing it and spreading gossip.'

Mr Newsome nodded a silent assent and leaned out of the door to call back the two coffin-bearers, who re-covered the box with the sheet and bustled it from the office with downcast eyes. He followed them with vigour.

Alone again in his office, Sir Richard shook his head and sighed heavily. He opened his top left-hand drawer with a dry scrape and took out a dossier marked "Newspaper Office".

On turning the string-bound cardboard cover, he saw a number of cuttings from the previous few days' newspapers and periodicals. The uppermost was from a common scandal sheet printed in the Seven Dials:

THE MASKED MAN IN WESTMINSTER

The mysterious false-faced fellow stalking our streets has been sighted once again, this time in the environs of Tothill-street, Westminster. Milliner's assistant Fanny Jones fainted quite away on seeing him, but not before she beheld the full terror of his phantom pallor. Her testimony: "It was the face of an innocent, but with evil in its eyes . . ."

Sir Richard put the excerpt to one side with a look of disdain and a quick pencilled note to the Newspaper Office that they cease to bother him with such inconsequentialities. The next two pieces were more significant and were immediately identifiable as being from his nemesis in print: that satirical rag named *Punch*. The excerpts were brief enough, but they reddened his face and ensured that the morning would be very much longer for certain people at 4 Whitehall-place:

POLICEMEN IN PLAIN CLOTHES

Mr Nathan of the Masquerade warehouse begs to inform the Commissioner of Police, that, in consequence of the prevailing practice of dressing up policemen in plain clothes, he has added to his wardrobe an extensive stock of disguises, suited to every class of society. For the purposes of political spying, Mr Nathan has a variety of fustian jackets of all sizes, with working-men's aprons and brown paper caps en suite. Baskets of tools can also be had if required. Sporting suits always ready for race-grounds.

THE DETECTIVE FORCE

From the inefficiency of the Detective Force in discovering the perpetrators of crime, it is the intention, we believe, to alter their title to the more appropriate one of the "Defective Force".

THREE

In truth, very little was known beyond the corridors of Scotland Yard concerning the existence and duties of that aforementioned Newspaper Office. Certain newspaper editors would no doubt have been intrigued to learn that their outpourings were sifted daily by a permanent staff of four uniformed clerks, that every mention of the Metropolitan Police and its men was carefully noted, excized, categorized, filtered and delivered to Sir Richard Mayne himself so he might keep a constant view of how his organisation was perceived by the public at large.

There, in that small office at the end of a second-floor corridor, great piles of newsprint were delivered each day, massing into leaning piles of the *Times,* the *Morning Chronicle,* the *Standard, Lloyds Weekly,* the *Morning Post, Punch,* the *London Monitor* and a variety of provincial titles amongst whose blotchily amateurish typography could be found stories that might perhaps warrant the (lucrative) aid of a London detective. Accidents, incidents, observations and interventions – all were neatly scissored in that office, and pity the constable unfortunate enough to have his name or number appear in a context contrary to the commissioner's expectations.

Certainly, few have the authority to pass through its door and gaze upon the four column-strewn desks, the four squinting gentlemen, the four hissing gas lamps and the irregular snip-ticking of the blades as stories are hewn angularly concise. Few, that is to say, have earned sufficient trust to be welcomed to this odd anteroom of police power, this whispering chamber beside the very ear of Sir Richard Mayne himself.

I have.

Call me what you will: penny-a-liner, fire-engine-chaser, poetaster, scribbler or hack – I have been accused of all and deny none. I am a writer of uncommon merit but of common means: a journalist for my supper, a playwright for my lunch, a proofreader for my coffee, and an author for my sins. You may have read such of my titles as *The Pirate King*, *The Detective's Curse* or *The Gypsy Prince* – although very likely you have not. It seems nobody has. Between the Scylla of lost copyright and the Charybdis of unfavourable reviews, my endeavours come often to nought. Under such circumstances, what other avenue is left to the poor writer but fraud?

Thus, as Mr Newsome left Sir Richard's office, I found myself reflected in the distorting spectacle lenses of the Newspaper Office's chief clerk, one Mr Parker. Before him on the desk was my exemplary application under a false name, along with a number of skilfully forged references. For a man charged with professionally wielding blades, he had an undoubted flair for verbosity and unattributed quotation.

'It is not just any man,' he said, 'who is invited to write for this office – do not allow yourself to be fooled otherwise, sir. It is not just *any* man, I say, but rather man who has a "*way with words*": a man who always "*crosses his T's*" if I may speak both figuratively and metaphorically. The man who writes for this office represents the entire edifice of Justice and of the Metropolitan Police. Yes, I have read your letters of referral – all very fine, very impressive, very good – but, I ask: are you "*that man*"?'

I acknowledged soberly that "*I was*".

'You understand, of course,' continued Mr Parker, 'that this role is not what you may be used to in the "*common press*". I will tolerate none of that penny-a-liner prolixity, that column-stretching tautology, that "*synonymorrhoea*" to which some of you fellows are prone. Concision is the thing. Concision, I mean to say, and a "*positive representation*" of the force. When a constable aids a lady, when a detective solves a crime, when Sir Richard speaks in the Commons (as he will in a matter of days), it is *your* copy which will express the facts clearly and concisely to the editors in Fleet-street so that they need not concern themselves with those other inky-fingered "*rapscallion reprobates*" of the gutter press.'

I nodded sagely – clearly not a rapscallion reprobate – and slipped my hands into my jacket pockets.

'You must understand, sir, that despite my acuity and diligence as a reader, I – that is, *we* four gentlemen here – are not writers. We do not "*aspire to it*", have not the patience for it – are, in some senses, *above* it . . . but we know it when we see it. Most assuredly we do.'

I did not doubt it, and (concisely) said as much.

'Very well,' continued Mr Parker. 'Might I suppose that you have any further questions concerning the position of Newspaper Office reporter?'

I had not. Or, more precisely, I had no interest in the job whatsoever other than to the extent it would allow me access to those private offices of Scotland Yard where the choicest stories lurked. Surely, in these murky *bureaux*, I would learn more about the so-called Masked Man who had been selling papers. And, though it was perhaps not ten hours since those two bodies had been discovered near Portugal-street, the telegraph wires of rumour had already begun to thrum around the city's coffee houses (where every starving scribbler knew it to be the story that would lift him from penury). I was myself but one more publishing failure from another spell in the debtor's gaol, and I would use this opportunity to pry beneath the police silence on these incidents if it was my final act on this earth.

'No? No questions?' said Mr Parker, his eyes like two spirited black fish through the lenses. 'It seems I have "*enunciated the particulars*" with sufficient comprehensiveness and brevity to negate any further necessities of clarification. As you see, there is not space in this office for you to share a desk with any of us fellows. Rather, you will report here each morning and I will inform you what stories are to be covered for that day. It may be that you need to visit certain other constables or courts about the city to question them further and "*accumulate the facts*" pertaining to your story.'

I asked if that day's stories might include the discoveries of earlier that morning.

'Portugal-street, you say?' Mr Parker's swimming eyes reflected convex vexation. 'I have seen nothing about it in last night's bulletins. Perhaps there will be notification later from the Detective Force. No – you must not concern yourself with such coffee-house tattle. Only the stories given to you in this office carry the "*stamp of veracity*". In fact, your story for today is something rather out of the ordinary. You have heard, no doubt, of François Eugène Vidocq: he who was once the chief of the Parisian Secret Police?'

I admitted that I had been reading the newspapers for the past few weeks.

'Then you will know that the "*esteemed gentleman himself*" is here in London with his fascinating exposition at the Cosmorama. A piece is required from you that celebrates his character and his visit, while also subtly noting that the French appetite for *espionage* is quite against the spirit of our own Detective Force, which is quite, quite a different thing altogether. I have some guidance notes for you on precisely how different. And you will also refrain from mentioning Inspector Albert Newsome in any way. This latter point is a matter of . . . well, it is something Sir Richard has personally requested.' Mr Parker here pointed a knowing finger upwards as if to indicate that the commissioner might be peering down upon them from his office above. 'Otherwise, it remains, sir, only for me to welcome you the Newspaper Office! I await your story with interest.'

And so I was given my liberty, which I exploited in order to roam – as if lost – through the previously unknown and endlessly tantalising corridors of Scotland Yard. What had once been to me but a stately *façade* of imperious windows would now lift up its petticoats and reveal its innermost secrets.

On my immediate left, according to its brass plate, was the Theatre Office, whose special constables are chosen for their stature and accent so that they may pass invisibly among the finer people and observe the pickpocket dandies from the anonymity of their plain-clothes guise. Stroll past this room at any time of the day, and you will invariably hear somebody whistling a tune that has maddeningly invaded their head during the seventeen orchestral performances of *The Sultana's Dowry* or whatever other show they have been obliged to attend.

On the same side, one also finds the dreary abodes of the Dangerous Structures Office, the Criminal Returns Office, the Carriage Office and the Police Dismissals Office, across whose desks every document spells trouble for someone and cost for all. It is police work by paper and number – the slow attrition of crime by administrative drudgery alone.

The ground floor is the place for stories. Here, for example, is the office of the Detective Force: a rather forlorn and silent space consisting of a worn leather sofa, a cold fireplace and a number of desks so barren as to suggest that they are never used. In fact, these most independent of policemen are seldom be found inside the walls of their headquarters while the criminals they seek operate as far as possible from its walls.

Next door is the Foreign Detective's Office: that oddity and virtually unknown diplomatic courtesy extended by the British government to policemen of other nations in pursuit of criminals who have fled their native shores into the ramifying shadows of the world's greatest city. In this smoke-filled room, on any representative day, one might find a Frenchman with his waxed moustache and gaudy scarf, a brooding German, or perhaps an American whose manners did not fit him for the presence of ladies. Only Sir Richard knew the particulars of their respective cases, but no indications of these would ever be seen in the pages of the *Police Gazette*.

Then there is the varnished herringbone parquetry of the Examination Room, where new recruits are subjected to the rigour of a written test and physically examined for any taint of deformity. Let us look through the open door as we pass to see perhaps fifty men standing nervously to attention before the penetrating stare of Mr Edward Figgs, who weighs configurations of shoulder, forehead and finger to calculate the arcane algebra of his anthropometric science. An ocular streak of vanity, a homicidal temple, an arrogant jaw or a rhinal propensity to incest – none can escape his unerring gaze.

And, of course, we cannot omit that great ramshackle treasury of the misplaced: the Lost Property Office. Can one even conceive that, in this city of two million souls, every item left on every seat of every cab and omnibus will find itself – sooner or later, on pain of a ten pound fine for non-compliance – to this lofty and dim-windowed hall at Whitehall-place? How many umbrellas reside here? How many canes, gloves and hats gather dust? What might be found inside that brown-paper parcel left two days ago? And what of that empty infant's carriage that has long forgotten the warmth of its accustomed cargo?

More to the point, what might be the contents of the large leather bag now being deposited? From the exertions of the porter, it must be a weighty one. It might indeed be a carpenter's bag but for its large size, though it makes no noise as it is lowered respectfully to the ground to join the dozens of other bags in that part of the room. If there are tools inside, they must be expensive, for only the most specialized instruments are habitually cushioned with horsehair stuffing or woollen blanket. No doubt the owner will soon realize his loss and remember that his property was last seen on the bus service from Blackfriars-bridge.

As for the below-ground space of Scotland Yard, it would not normally deserve our attention with its storerooms, unused cells and surgery. But on that day, the surgery was locked from the inside and voices could be heard within. An inquisitive sort might have pressed his ear to the cold iron door and discerned the commissioner's voice. And a journalist of exceptional acuity might have understood that the muffled discussion very likely concerned the repulsively transformed body of a certain constable found earlier that morning.

Fortunately, I had my pencil and paper perpetually to hand.

FOUR

'How did he die, doctor?' said Sir Richard, ardently desirous of removing his eyes from the undead figure before him while seemingly unable to do so.

The surgeon of Division A, a luxuriantly bearded gentleman with amused eyes, also seemed quite fixed upon the body. 'I believe that there are other questions more immediately pertinent, sir. Among them: was this ever a man, and is he one still?'

'You are making no sense. Is this, or is this not, the corpse of a constable?'

'It is indeed the *likeness* of a constable in every way, sir, but I believe it is not biologically a complete man. From the perspective of forensic medicine, therefore, I would hesitate to term it a corpse.'

'Doctor – my morning has been one of considerable irritation. Perhaps you will come to the point. What is this . . . thing we see before us?'

The constable stood exactly as he had when found: one arm holding a rattle as if to set it going, and the other reaching under his oilskin cape for his truncheon. The pose might have been entirely natural, except that it had remained quite rigid for many hours. Even when brought to Scotland Yard in a covered wagon, its form had remained unchanged. Now, it remained fastened to its wooden board, surrounded by a small puddle of the rainwater that continued to drip from it. The eyes were healthy, the mouth still open and the pale skin uncorrupted, while the expression was one of curious dullness – an approximation of humanity quite devoid of mind. In short, it seemed to bear all the marks of life but for warmth and movement.

'It cannot be *rigor mortis*,' muttered Sir Richard, extending a finger to nudge the constable's outreaching arm.

'Indeed it is not. Let me show you something, sir.'

The surgeon took a steel pen from his inner jacket pocket and tapped the left eyeball with a dull *tink*. 'Enamel, sir – very fine quality. They are used to replace real human eyes, and also in the figures one sees at Madame Tussaud's.'

Sir Richard leaned closer. 'I would never have guessed it. They are the very image of genuine eyes, and set so naturally in the sockets . . .'

'I might also add, sir, that the body is very light – nothing like the weight of a man of this size, even taking into account the board. In fact, the principal reason it cannot be *rigor mortis* is because there are no muscles, no blood, and indeed no internal organs.'

'Are you telling me that it is merely an effigy, doctor? That simply cannot be true: the body has been positively identified by a number of his colleagues at Gardener-lane station in Westminster. Not only that, but this particular constable vanished from his beat a week ago and has been listed as missing for all that time. His own wife has not seen him since his sudden disappearance.'

'As I say, sir: it is a mere representation. I do not know if you have visited the waxworks recently, but one might accidentally begin a conversation with some of the lesser-known figures at Madame Tussauds' before realising one's mistake. The mimetical arts have become exceptionally advanced and—'

'This is clearly not a wax figure, doctor. What *is* it?'

'I would need to perform a full *post mortem* to be certain, but I believe we are looking at a unique example of human taxidermy – a very skilled example.'

Sir Richard did not reply immediately. Rather, he looked again at the figure – at its hair, its lips, the tone of its skin. 'Is it really possible, doctor?'

'In theory, quite so. Other large mammals have been prepared and mounted. No doubt you have seen them at the British Museum. Only, an animal's furry hide is presumably easier to work with because it masks minor inconsistencies of modelling. Human skin is much thinner and sits closer to the bone.'

'Are you saying, then, that this is ... this is the actual skin of PC Taylor?'

'Was that the fellow's name? Yes – his skin, his hair, no doubt his clothes and boots. Inside, however, all that remains is his skeleton. That is why I cannot give you a cause – or even a time – of death. There is nothing for me to examine but the *dermis*.'

'Why? Why would somebody do such a thing, doctor?'

'I am afraid that is your question to answer, sir – you and your detectives.'

'Have you practised taxidermy yourself?'

'In an amateur capacity, on small birds. One of my professors suggested to me that it might be a useful addition to my studies, as well as a pleasure. It is certainly an interesting diversion for those with an appreciation of animal life.'

'Why, then, do you think PC Taylor has been posed thus? It seems a wilful mockery.'

'Not necessarily, sir. The prepared specimen should be arranged in its natural manner so that it will seem alive to the casual observer, and the constable here certainly seems vivid enough at first impression.'

'I suppose so. What has been the extent of your examination of the body so far?'

'Only the most cursory, sir. The eyes, the skin on the hands and face. Your instructions were—'

'Very good. I did not want you to examine it in any detail at this stage. Hereafter, the body will pass into the hands of the detectives, who will no doubt examine it in their own way. You may be required to provide a medical opinion should they find something unusual within.'

'Yes, sir.'

'I will ask you to discuss this with nobody, not even with your medical colleagues. I am sure you understand that the nature of this discovery is such that a veritable storm of newsprint would occur if the full details became known. I would not like to imagine the resulting phrensy. No doubt you recall the nonsense that erupted around the Lucius Boyle case.'

'I do, sir. A terrible business with the two-headed girl.'

'Quite. I thank you for your time, doctor. Please ensure that the body is kept locked here in the surgery until I order it to be removed. In the meantime, you must forgive me my haste – I have another appointment to attend.'

It was not, however, the customary police carriage that Sir Richard took that afternoon, but rather a quite anonymous conveyance stripped of all official identification. Nobody might have guessed the eminence of its single passenger as it rounded Trafalgar-square in its progress west along Cockspur-street and up Haymarket, and even those of a curious bent could have spied no face through its dark curtains.

Inside, the commissioner – never one to waste a journey in mere idle thought –frowned at another recent story from *the Times* that the Newspaper Office had excised for his interest. In itself, the tale of a minor arrest made by a simple constable appeared thoroughly innocuous. What made it contentious was the newspaper's insistence on remarking that the constable in question had made the arrest while "dressed in plain clothes" – as if that simple fact annulled both the crime and the apprehension of its perpetrator. It was no idle comment; seemingly every single arrest made by a plain-clothes policeman in recent months had been thus signalled in *the Times* and repeated in the many other journals that cribbed from it.

He folded the piece of newsprint into his pocket with a stern jaw and withdrew a more yellowed piece that he had requested from the archives in anticipation of his imminent appointment. This scrap dated from almost two decades previously: a notice from the *Westminster Review* concerning a certain publishing sensation of that year:

These memoirs are in fact the morbid anatomy of crime; but then how dextrously does the surgeon detect the peculiarities of his monstrosities; how nicely does he handle the part affected; how ably does he conduct an operation; how brilliantly does he picture the various stages of the disease . . .

The bibliophilic reader will perhaps recognize it as a description of the *memoirs* of that illustrious scoundrel, the notorious Parisian *Chef de la police de sureté*: M. François Eugène Vidocq – the very gentleman whom Sir Richard was to visit at the former's temporary private residence at Regent-street.

What can be said of the man that has not already been said more colourfully by himself? This soldier, thief, convict and arch-dissimulator – this man who associated in the dungeons of France with the country's most dangerous assassins, tricksters and malcontent masterminds – had not only become the police's most formidable agent, but had also (while still formally a wanted man) single-mindedly established a 'secret police' of like-minded felons to infiltrate the criminal gangs of the city.

Was there any truth in the rumour that Sir Robert Peel himself had dispatched men to observe Vidocq's men shortly after the formation of the Metropolitan Police? And could it really be conceivable that Sir Richard had also sent certain officers to Paris in the infant days of the Detective Force so that they may learn from the master? Certainly, proof of such occurrences would have lit a conflagration beneath the tinder accusations of *espionage* currently at large – and any hint of the meeting about to occur would have further sparked a controversy to scorch reputations.

The carriage came to halt and the driver rapped upon its top: 'We have arrived, sir.'

Sir Richard gathered himself but waited for another knock at the carriage door that would signal his opportunity to alight. It would not be advisable for him to be seen entering the address of this particular Frenchman.

The knock came just a few moments later, followed by the carriage door being whisked open and Sir Richard stepping quickly across the wet pavement to take the few steps up through an open street door that closed rapidly behind him.

'May I tek your 'at and coat?' asked an immaculately attired servant standing to attention in the hallway. That procedure effected, the liveried young gentleman – who had the incongruous scarred and battered face of a street ruffian – gestured towards the house's dark interior: 'Zis way, if you pliz, *monsieur* Meyne.'

Sir Richard followed to the end of a corridor and was led into a drawing room that must once have been decorated in an understated style. Now, however, it was an absolute chaos of mess and curiously incongruous objects. Here, an enormous quantity of wax fruit spilled from a reading table onto the carpet around it; here, a number of books had been scattered and lay open with their fine bindings cracked; here, a great stack of apparently filthy clothes had toppled from the seat of a leather wingback chair. A thin, blued-steel dagger stuck vertically from the dark wooden top of a beautiful *escritoire*.

'Ha! I suppose I should apologize for the . . .'

Sir Richard turned quickly towards the origin of the deep, hoarse voice and beheld Vidocq himself leaning against the end of a bookshelf, smiling like a naughty schoolboy and waving a vague gesture at the state of his rooms.

Though now purportedly seventy-three years old, the Frenchman looked no older than fifty. Broad of shoulder and apparently six feet tall, he emanated a kind of animal vigour that might switch between threat – his deeply-lined face was a mass of scars – and the geniality expressed in his sharp grey eyes. Here was a man who had charmed both governments and thieves.

'I hope Jacques performed his duty with the correct *etiquette*,' said Vidocq. 'I am training him to English manners. Two years ago, he would have taken your hat and coat at the point of a knife! Ha!' His English was only minimally accented and he spoke with plentiful gesticulatory aid.

'He was perfectly civil, *monsieur*,' said Sir Richard.

'Good. Good. I must thank you greatly for agreeing to see me. I know from experience that a police commissioner is a very busy man. Let us sit, eh?'

Vidocq tipped a pile of books from a dining chair and dragged it across the carpet towards where Sir Richard was himself looking awkwardly around for somewhere to sit.

'Take this one, commissioner,' said the host, tossing the accumulation of old clothes over the back of the wingback chair and waving a thick hand at the seat.

Sir Richard paused briefly at the profligate scattering of garments, but sat as bidden and clasped his hands on his lap. 'I must admit, *monsieur* Vidocq, that I am uncertain what we might discuss. I know that you have long been retired from active duty and . . . and you must know that the policing of this nation bears little resemblance to the French system. Intentionally so, I might add with all respect.'

'Cognac, Sir Richard?'

'I beg your pardon?'

'Men should drink cognac when they speak of important things, no?' Vidocq hooked open a desk drawer with his foot and bent to withdraw a crystal decanter half full of dark amber liquid. 'From before the Revolution!' he winked, reaching for a stray glass and cleaning it with a spittle-wetted finger.

Sir Richard shifted in his seat. 'To which important things are you referring? I agreed to visit you as a sign of respect: an acknowledgement – shall we say – of a certain shared history. I was not aware we had something particular to discuss.'

Vidocq's eyes crinkled with some secret mirth. He swirled the cognac in the glass and inhaled the aroma appreciatively with his oft-broken nose. 'It seems that you are having some troubles with your London police.'

Sir Richard crossed his legs, then immediately uncrossed them when he saw that his interlocutor had noted and interpreted the defensive gesture. 'Troubles? To what troubles do you refer, *monsieur* Vidocq?'

'I speak "unofficially" of course. Officially, there are no problems. Your Metropolitan Police is the envy of the world – even of France. Your men are honest, righteous, diligent, and yet . . .' Vidocq gave a shrug and a *moue*.

'And yet what?

The Frenchman held up his hands. 'Commissioner, I say only that I read recently of a change in name: from the "Detective Force" to the "Defective Force".'

'You, of all men, should know the wiles of the press, *monsieur*. A slanderous jibe or a whispered rumour is not a fact – at least not in England.'

'True, this is true, Sir Richard. Only . . . well, perhaps it is not my place . . .'

'I have read that you were a master of disguise, demeanour and accent in your time with the *sureté, monsieur*. I see now that this obfuscating subtlety extends to your conversation also. I wonder if you might respect my courtesy in attending this meeting by actually saying what you mean.'

'Ha! Excellent! I have fractured your English reserve!' Vidocq gave a single, resounding clap. 'So – to the point: I asked you here today, Sir Richard, to offer my advice, my experience, my help.' He folded his arms and looked down in an admirable show of modesty.

'Your help? In what respect?'

'In any respect you like. I will, of course, be totally discreet.'

Sir Richard looked again at the almost mask-like face before him. The eyes, though smiling, gave no sign of senility or of delusion, and Vidocq had apparently not drunk enough of the cognac to be intoxicated. The fellow might have been old and French, but he seemed as lucid as any other man.

'Monsieur Vidocq – is there some matter in particular upon which you believe I might require your aid?'

'Allow me to say only this, Sir Richard: most police forces are established along military lines, yes? They have uniforms, drills, divisions and strategies. Everything is planned to the minute; everything has its time and its place. I go on duty at this time and am relieved at this time, yes.'

'Of course. It is the only way to maintain an effective force.'

'But, alas, the criminal is not so military, eh? He wears no uniform; he changes his strategy; he keeps his own time and does not reveal his place. On the same chequered board of London, you play chess and he plays draughts – but it is not the same game, eh? And he is winning according to his rules, no?'

'I have read your book, *monsieur*. I know your methods. However, we do not tolerate *espionage* in England. We find criminals through investigation: through the application of intelligent deduction and just procedure. If your "help" involves violence and duplicity, entrapment and coercion, then I must politely refuse. The Metropolitan Police has no place for it.'

'Indeed?' Vidocq winked and returned his nose to the glass.

'What do you mean by that, *monsieur*?'

'I have heard of a fellow named Dyson. Is he not an agent of the police?'

'Where . . . where did you hear that name? I must insist on knowing.'

'I cannot recall. You know how policemen talk. Perhaps I was mistaken. It might have been a different name: Williamson, perhaps?' Again, the shrug and the impenetrable *moue*.

Sir Richard glared. 'I rather suspect that you *are* mistaken. On both counts.'

'Yes, that must be the case. Although I am curious – what is this I read in the newspapers about certain constables wearing "plain clothes"? Perhaps my knowledge of English . . . but are not the uniforms quite plain? I know that your detectives wear no uniform, but the constables? And also this strange piece I read in *Punch* about Mr Nathan's Masquerade warehouse and its disguises for policeman? I am confused . . .'

'You spoke a moment ago about games, *monsieur*. I do not like them and I will not play them. If you have nothing further to—'

'Sir Richard – forgive me. I mean only to suggest that you *do* engage in *espionage* of a particularly English character. That is, you say one thing and you do another; you show one face to your Home Secretary and another to the criminal. There are rules, and there are exceptions to the rules.'

'I am not sure I like your tone, *monsieur*.' Sir Richard made to stand.

'I do not criticize your methods, commissioner! I praise them. Nobody need know what is said here today.'

'Nothing has been said that need concern me,' said Sir Richard, standing.

'Ah – then I will ask about the unnatural corpse of a policeman that you have locked in a Scotland Yard cellar.'

'What? How did you—?' Sir Richard sank back into the chair.

'And your reaction tells me it is true. How might I help you with *this* case? I am in London for only a few months and it would please me to be part of such an investigation. My retirement . . . well, it sometimes bores me. And the name of "Vidocq" has currency only when it is associated with a certain shrewd intelligence, a certain flair, a certain notoriety. I have read of a mysterious "masked man" and now I hear of this new outrage. Let me aid you.'

'I must demand that you tell me how you know of this.'

'It is my skill, my job, my life – I learn things that are of benefit to me. It matters not how well hidden they are. But fear not, Sir Richard – your secret is safe.'

'I admit nothing. I ask for nothing.'

'Eh . . . how, then, might we approach the problem in a different way?' Vidocq swirled his cognac meditatively, watching its thick oils play around the glass. 'Let us *suppose* that a strange body is found – yes, that is the way forward. Let us *suppose* that it is murder and that the method is something quite out of the ordinary. Let us further *conjecture* that if the newspapers were to get hold of the story, pressure would increase a hundred-fold upon the investigating officers – officers who, *possibly*, were already held in some questionable regard by those same newspapers. Well . . . it could all become quite political, no? The official at the head of the investigating body in question might soon find his position untenable. This one case could be the difference between his lasting glory and his downfall at the hands of an angry session at the House of Commons. Eh?'

Sir Richard's expression had changed from anger to mere consternation, from grudging attention to engagement, and thence to an unspoken acknowledgement that this fellow Vidocq was indeed the very embodiment of those traits attributed to him, both good and ill. It would be difficult to say whether slyness or vanity was the stronger trait.

'Very well. You present an interesting hypothetical case, *monsieur* Vidocq. I wonder what *you* would advise in your capacity as retired chief of a secret police?'

'Ha!' The Frenchman drank off his cognac at a single gulp, winked theatrically and rubbed his hands together with enthusiasm. 'This case that we have imagined together is a curious one indeed, commissioner, and I believe I already know the key to it: your perpetrator is vain.'

'How so? And how might this knowledge help me?'

'I need hardly tell you that every criminal is vain – this much is known to every agent of the law. The pickpocket thinks himself better than the common burglar; the cracksman thinks himself above the pickpocket and so on. But the murderer – if he retains any vestiges of sanity – is the proudest of all in his sordid deeds. His is the unassailable summit of crime. He is its Apollo, and his infamy is his immortality. His name lives for eternity. Greenacre, Rush, Good, Courvoisier, Lucius Boyle – even I have heard of your great English murderers.'

'I believe you have not yet answered my question, *monsieur*.'

Vidocq's eyes crinkled again with the pleasure of leading his esteemed audience. 'Well, this particular criminal – the killer of the constable – appears to have a powerful theatrical impulse, no? He craves attention. He says "Behold: my art!" This is his weakness, and *your* advantage. Here, we have a man who screams to be seen. It is a dangerous game for a murderer and you must play it.'

'This is all very well, *monsieur*, but there is not the slightest indication as to who the murderer might be.'

'Indeed, indeed – but you have his art, no? One may know the artist by his work, by the nature of his brushstrokes, by the mark of his hand in the clay, by his colours. I speak metaphorically, you understand?'

Sir Richard merely pursed his lips and offered a cold stare.

'Of course you understand. I mean to say only that one must understand the criminal as the hunter knows his prey: his lairs, his tracks, his hair, and, yes, his droppings also. What manner of animal do you hunt? Where can he be found? What does one use to bait him? Do you see?'

'I see that you dress in metaphor and allusion what my men already do as their daily duty: read clues, follow them, and apprehend criminals.'

'Or not, as the case may be, eh? To whom might you assign a case such as this?'

'To one of my excellent detectives.'

'One such as Inspector Albert Newsome, perhaps?'

'You have heard of—?' Sir Richard caught Vidocq's knowing smirk. 'No, not he.'

'Then who? Hypothetically, of course . . .'

'There are many in the Detective Force who are equally capable.'

'Perhaps, perhaps. But, as I say, the police operate along military lines – along predictable and conspicuous lines.'

'I assume that you would advocate the use of an agent, *monsieur*. You are going to tell me, no doubt, that I should recruit somebody from the lower parts of London: an ex-convict, a thief or a confidence trickster as you yourself did.'

'Ha! I see that you have indeed been reading my *memoirs*.'

'You are not the first person to suggest this path to me. The fact is that the Metropolitan Police does not, and will not, condone the use of spies.'

'It is a matter of mere definitions, commissioner. When a fellow tells a constable that he has seen another fellow leaving a house with blood upon his sleeve, is this *espionage*? When your off-duty constable sees a man entering a building at night through a window and effects an arrest while out of uniform, is this *espionage*? Justice does not always wear her robes, no? Sometimes she leaves her scales at home, but she still knows how to balance the accounts.'

'Much as I may enjoy your sophistry, *monsieur*, it cannot change the law of this country. Hypothetical or not, this case will be dealt with in accordance with that law.' Sir Richard stood once more, smoothing his trousers and looking to the door for his coat.

Vidocq remained seated and appraised his guest with a half-smile. Had the commissioner's last statement been rather too forceful? Had Sir Richard's eyes avoided his own as the words had been spoken? And might not a master liar catch out a lesser one if the lie were inexpertly produced? The half-smile became full.

'Very well, commissioner – I capitulate. There is but one more thing I might ask you.'

'I am afraid I am quite busy. I must attend to—'

'It is just a trifling thing. There is a countryman of mine currently working at Scotland Yard: a detective following a Paris case. He is named Bissonette.'

'In the Foreign Detectives' Office? I believe I may have heard the name. What of him?'

'He is seeking a gentleman who evidently went missing while on a visit to London a year or so ago – quite a wealthy young gentleman who simply never returned. Bissonette seems to have found nothing at all and I wondered if – as a favour to me – you might look at his case and see if there is anything you can do.'

'It is really not my place to—'

'Just to prove to him that I asked you. I made a promise, and the word of Vidocq is one that is always kept.'

'Very well, very well – I will see that he is told of your intervention, but I promise nothing more.'

'You are too kind, commissioner.'

'Quite.'

The young servant Jacques had, by some hidden signal, now arrived with Sir Richard's coat and hat. Before his master, his posture was rigid with formality and his expression a study in deference.

'I remain in London for some weeks if you wish to discuss the case further,' said Vidocq.

Sir Richard smiled and held out his hand, which the Frenchman took with a grip that gave lie to his seventy years. Later, in the carriage, the commissioner would rub life back into his assaulted hand and cogitate upon the curious interview – notably on the matter of Vidocq knowing more than any foreigner should about the secrets of the Metropolitan Police.

And as the wheels rattled back to Whitehall that rainy afternoon, certain of those people referred to by Vidocq were moving unwittingly towards an appointment with a case that was far from hypothetical.

FIVE

Is there a more dolorous metropolitan prospect than a rain-lashed London-bridge? Its unceasing procession of tilburies, phaetons, omnibuses, drays, cabs, coaches and carts churn mud and dung against trouser and skirt as the faceless multitudes trudge multifariously umbrella'd on stonework slick with sooty puddles. Gas lamps sigh at an obstinately sunless sky, while sodden smuts drip inkily against collar, cuff and downcast face, turning all to weeping grime. Here are the rich in their liveried *equipages*; here are the pieceworkers of Bermondsey carrying canvas for sacks; here are bedraggled magdalenes, glistening tarp-wrapped wagon drivers, hopeful merchants, hopeless beggars, and haranguing constables directing shadowy *tableaux* of wheel, rein and whip amidst the cacophonous throng.

And here is a curious fellow moving among the shuffling pedestrian masses. He might be a merchant or a manufacturer from his attire, though he carries no papers or produce. He might be a senior clerk or a young lawyer from his bearing, though his face has not their supercilious cast. He might even be one of those refined criminals who attend the races and opera to turn their artificial manners into pickpocketed profit, but he pays little notice to the opportunities presented by the accumulated humanity within reach. He is one among many, but a man unlike any other.

Indeed, as he passes one of the bridge's recesses, he steps quickly within and disappears momentarily from view. The absence may be brief enough, yet the man who re-enters the crowds is not quite the same. His top hat is now a peaked cap, his dark *surtout* a similar garment in bottle green, and he carries a black cane where before he carried none. Perhaps the gait is different, too: a slight hunch to the back and shorter steps as if he had miraculously aged ten or twenty years inside the pedestrian recess. Transformed, he seems a retired man about town, possibly visiting his bank or meeting a fellow in a Fleet-street coffee house.

Were we to see beneath this mendacious mantle, we might observe an elaborate tattoo upon his left shoulder, a literature of scars across his back and similar evidence of past shackles on both wrist and ankle. The face beneath the cap's peak is intelligent and alert, with an oft-broken nose suggesting he is no stranger to violence. And, while passing the mid-point of the bridge, he is stirred by the wind-borne smell of the shipping in the Pool: that complex aroma of oakum, rope, bilge and timber that can intoxicate only one who has lived with it for years on end.

His name is Noah Dyson and he has come recently from Lambeth.

At the next recess, he again ducks inside and remains there for longer as the hundreds move inexorably across the bridge. When he emerges, it is only to the slightest degree. His light grey eyes scan the faces approaching from both directions and he assesses each in a moment, dismissing one after another as they bob and eddy through the grey pluvial scene.

Finally, and with a sudden decisive lurch, he leaps aboard a passing cab that thereafter makes halting progress northwards through the chaos of traffic of Gracechurch-street before turning west along Cornhill. His destination that afternoon was Golden-square and the stately pale *façade* of one its grander buildings.

Noah Dyson rapped the brass knocker three times and waited. There was a twitch of curtain to his right, then footsteps approaching from within.

'Yes, sir?'

She was perhaps twenty years old and, for an instant, he was rendered dumb by her unalloyed beauty: dark hair and eyes set off by skin as pure as milk. In that same instant, she saw and knew she had the claimed power of her sex.

'You are Charlotte?' he said.

'It rather depends who is calling, sir, doesn't it?'

'He told me you were pretty; he understated the case.'

Charlotte, as she was sometimes known, smiled. 'Who said I am pretty?'

'Mr George Williamson.'

She smiled again – a secret one, without the previous coquettishness. 'I don't believe I know the gentleman. I'm afraid you have the wrong address, sir. Good day.'

Noah wedged his foot into the closing door and offered his own grin. 'Charlotte – let us avoid games. I know what you are and I know that you know Mr Williamson. I come to you because I seek to help him.'

'If you truly know "what I am", sir, you'll also know that I'm unashamed – and that I do not discuss my gentlemen visiters.' She stood boldly, no fear in her level houri gaze.

'Very well. I understand. I will pay for your time: a sovereign to help me help a friend. If you feel anything for the man – anything beyond the strictly mercantile – you will speak with me.' He held the coin between thumb and forefinger.

Charlotte looked past the coin into Noah's eyes. 'Mr Williamson, you say? Perhaps I do recall the fellow. Won't you enter?'

With a final look backwards into the street, he followed her into the apartment, which was decorated in the fine taste of a lady with style rather than great wealth. No doubt the rent was paid by an older "regular" who chose not to understand he was one of many.

'Please, take a seat, sir' said Charlotte. 'Would you like a sherry? Or I have brandy if you prefer – it is French.' She reached towards an upper shelf, allowing the hem of her dress to reveal a delicate ankle and lower calf. If she did not actually wink, it was because her movements had adequately made the gesture.

Noah, sitting, merely laughed. 'You are very good. I can see why you would steal his heart. And let us be frank: love has taken hold of him like a ripped mainsail at the whim of a storm.'

Charlotte frowned lightly as she brought the brandy to the table. The word "love" meant no more to her than "bread" or "shoes".

'Tell me about him,' said Noah.

'What would you like to know? He pays to see me. I think a man of your experience can guess the rest.'

'A man of my experience knows that a man like Mr Williamson does not easily consort with magdalenes, even one of your charm and ability. Tell me truly: has he consummated his desire?'

She held out her hand and he dropped the sovereign in it.

'What would you say, sir, if I told you that I have in my closet copaiba capsules and an astringent lotion of zinc?'

'Ah – I would say that you likely use the lotion each day . . . afterwards. But the capsules tell me you have recently been betrayed by one of your gentlemen visiters. I am sorry – you have the clap.'

Charlotte lowered her eyes in answer. 'So you see, your Mr Williamson could not have consummated any desire – even if he possessed it.'

'What do you mean by that?'

'You've suggested it yourself: he's quite strangulated with guilt and melancholy. Some deeper part of him wants me as any man wants a woman – but that part is bound tight with religion and doubt and contempt for himself.'

'I see that you know him well.'

'I know men, and I like him, sir. We talk, or rather he talks and I listen. I mend my dresses or send a boy for food and he tells me how I should resign from this "sinful" life – can you imagine!'

'I can. And I suppose that he is tortured to know that he shares you with so many other men who worry less about your honour.'

'Did I not tell you that I am presently unavailable?'

'Do not think me so *naïve*, girl. There are other pleasures you can offer.'

She would have blushed if she were capable of it. 'Well, I dare say he *is* tortured, sir. I have told him it's ridiculous. But what am I to do? I catch him looking at me: *here*, and *here*, and *here*. I pretend not to notice, of course, but it's what he truly seeks from me. He must speak morality even as he challenges it with his eyes. I don't judge him for it. Every man has his letch, doesn't he?'

'It is true, and the tragedy is that you know it better than he.'

'I do wonder, sir, why you come to me if you know Mr Williamson so well.'

'The fact is that I cannot find the man. I have been to his home in Lambeth, to the coffee houses he is wont to frequent, to the Monument . . .'

'Ah yes – he told me about Katherine, his wife. A very sad tale.'

'Yes. Has he told you also about his own past, about how he was once a lauded detective in the Metropolitan Police?'

Charlotte merely nodded, her face set in a faintly bemused expression.

'Well, I have had cause to worry about his behaviour of late. Have *you* seen any change in recent weeks?'

'I suppose he is a little darker in mood, though it is hard to tell. I wonder – have you sought him at St Bride's on Fleet-street?'

'No. Should I? Has he mentioned it to you?'

'I believe it was one of his wife's favoured churches. He goes there occasionally after he sees me – to seek forgiveness, no doubt.'

'I see. Thank you.'

'I am happy to help you, sir. If you had another sovereign, I might offer you other, more pleasurable, services . . .'

'I think not.' Noah stood. 'Save your hands for making him tea and your mouth for telling him what he needs to hear. The rest of you, he will likely never need. I would tell you not to see him again, but it would harm him much more than you.'

Charlotte acknowledged this truth with a smile: the universal matron, muse, Madonna or maenad according to another's desire. The last he saw of her was her large dark eyes watching from the door through which so many men had passed on the way to the chamber where so much innocence had been lost.

And as Noah later stepped out of the insensate rush of Fleet-street, he reflected that St Brides was an oddly apt choice for George Williamson. Despite its pre-eminent spire, it offered a utilitarian and unpretentious exterior to the world: more prose than poetry, more asceticism than Divine celebration. Its tall north-facing windows were but sombre glass-black eyes amid smoke-streaked masonry.

Inside was a different story. Noah closed the door gently behind him and entered a space that was well lighted, airy and mercifully quiet. Twinned pillars bore the weight of the structure with grace and strength, while the groined aisle ceilings with their decorous arches suggested a complexity of minor gothic proportions. The place was a sanctuary of calm amid the city's rage.

A creaking bench echoed about the stonework and Noah moved silently towards the nave to behold a single seated figure gazing up at the murky altar scene of the dead Christ descending from His cross. From behind, the lone congregant showed slight, rounded shoulders and a bare head of dark hair. He might have been one of the local typesetters passing a reflective moment as his meticulously assembled plates ran off a few thousand copies on the presses. Or he could equally have been an ex-detective: one of the Metropolitan Police's most celebrated and gifted investigators until forced by inimical circumstances to leave its ranks.

'I thought you might come for me here, Noah,' said Mr Williamson without turning. His voice was strong but with a heavily resigned tone.

Noah smiled and walked down to take a seat beside his friend. 'How did you know it was me?'

Mr Williamson turned his face to reveal the minor scarring of childhood smallpox. 'Most common visitors let the door bang behind them, so it was likely a tourist or someone particularly sensitive to announcing their presence. The fact that you dawdled before fully entering might have suggested the former, but it could also have been the hesitation of the atheist finding himself on consecrated ground.'

'Very good, George. But hardly conclusive.'

'There is more. As you approached the door, you stepped on the broken flagstone that unleashes a jet of muddy water against the legs on rainy days.'

Noah looked down at the dark stain on his trousers.

'And you uttered an oath that no Christian would express in the shadow of a church.' continued Mr Williamson, looking dully ahead at the altarpiece. 'An elaborate oath that is one of your particular characteristics.'

'I see that you have lost none of your sharpness.'

'Why do you seek me here, Noah? I expect you have exhausted all of the other possibilities, but few people know that I sometimes come to St Brides.'

'I went to see her, George.'

'Hmm. Hmm.' Mr Williamson stared grimly forward, his cheeks reddening. His jaw flexed. His fingers worked at the brim of the top hat that lay on his knees.

'I felt I had no choice, George. I could not find you at home and have not seen you for days. I admit I feared the worst. This melancholy of yours . . .'

'You should not have . . . I will not have you seeing her.'

'Anybody may see her, George. You know that. Any man with a sovereign may—'

'Do not say it!'

The shout reverberated about the church and was followed by a profounder quiet. Beyond the lofty windows, the city's roar was a distant storm. Dusk was approaching quicker beneath a glowering slate sky.

'George – I apologize. Come with me. We will go to my house at Blackfriars and Ben will make us tea. There are things we must all discuss. It may not be safe for you to return to Lambeth. I believe that someone has been following me.'

Mr Williamson nodded. 'I, too, have sensed it.'

'Then let us go. The rain has lately stopped and we might take the opportunity.'

'You will not speak of her or see her again.'

'If that is truly your wish, I will not.'

Noah stood, causing the bench to creak. His friend followed him wordlessly out of the church towards the damp tumult of Fleet-street, where, still unspeaking, they stepped aboard the dim and cloying dampness of an omnibus whose exterior advertising board proclaimed that *Babington's Elixir of Rhubarb gives tone to digestive organs, cures indigestion and eradicates gravel of the bowel.*

Mr Williamson avoided Noah's eyes for the entire journey – easy enough as the light faded and the half-dozen passengers stared assiduously at feet or at newspapers rather than acknowledge the presence of each other. Noah, meanwhile, cast surreptitious glances at all to assure himself that none was paying the slightest attention to these two most recent fares.

In this way did they pass jerkily through Ludgate-circus and south along Bridge-street to the corner of Earl-street, where the oilskin-clad "cad" swung open the rear door and called 'Blackfriars-bridge! Out 'ere for the bridge!' into the passenger cabin.

Mr Williamson followed Noah down the steps and sniffed at the darkness that had descended during their journey. Rain pattered on his hat. 'There is a fire somewhere.'

Noah smelled it too and nodded. 'It is all these fireworks of late. One seldom knows where a rocket will land.'

And as they proceeded down Earl-street, the extent of the nearby conflagration became more apparent. The sky towards the river showed billowing exhalations of orange-tinted smoke and the sound of multiple fire engine bells could be heard along with the cries of massed volunteers.

Noah looked nervously at the rooftops as if gauging the location, then quickened his pace.

'What is it?' said Mr Williamson, hurrying to follow.

But Noah did not answer. His trot became a run and soon he rounded the corner down an alley where he beheld a scene to chill his blood.

Perhaps fifty men were engaged in a phrensy of activity attempting to extinguish a colossal fire at one of the riverfront properties. A tangle of hoses about the wharf seemed to writhe amidst a great quantity of surface water that had evidently done nothing to abate the flames roaring ferociously from the upper windows and thick smoke pouring from the lower ones. The engineers in their grey uniforms and martial helmets might almost have been soldiers laying siege to a castle rather than acting as its saviours, while the ghastly burning light made the entire scene an infernal shadow play.

'You there!' called an engineer dragging a hose. 'Help me to straighten this! Two shillings for every volunteer!'

Noah stood immobile, his face a flickering red mask. 'It is my house! There may be somebody inside!'

'We have a man looking. Don't just stand there – take the hose, won't you? This b_____ fire just won't be put out!'

'Benjamin? Was he at home?' said Mr Williamson, standing beside Noah.

Multiple water jets arced into the upper windows and became hissing steam that reeked of river water even as it ascended with the smoke. A terrible crash was heard within, followed by a renewed eruption of sparks and flames.

'The floors are going! Get him out!' yelled the engineer at some men closer to the house's open door.

One of these men bent to take hold of a thin tube passing close to his feet. He tugged on it three times and Noah observed its path into the doorway. Within moments, an unearthly figure emerged from a vortex of angry smoke and made its way towards the shouts and cooling spray of the engineers. Its head was encased in a cephalopodic hood of leather that seamlessly continued into a baggy suit of the same material, cinched tight at wrist and ankle. Two glassy green eye pieces reflected fire back at its observers as if it were a demon that had stepped forth from Hell.

'Anyone inside?' called the engineer nearest Noah and Mr Williamson.

The creature shook its head and was led away by colleagues.

'The property is lost,' said the engineer, largely to himself. He dropped the hose he had been wrestling. 'We might have saved the structure if we had had the river engine, but . . .'

Noah watched numbly as great tongues of destruction curled from every aperture of his home and caustic gusts buffeted his face with hot ash.

'Noah! Mr Williamson!'

They turned and saw two figures splashing towards them through the twitching hoses: one a burly fellow named John Cullen, the other a formidably tall and broad Negro with one eye a dead, milky orb. Both were dressed for an evening at the theatre, albeit mired now with the mud and water of the scene.

'O! O! I am so happy to see you both unharmed!' said a breathless Mr Cullen. 'What has happened here? Everything was perfectly fine when Ben and I left earlier.'

The imposing Negro Benjamin made a number of complex gesticulations as if describing words and phrases in the air. Bereft of tongue, it was his only means of expression.

'I am not sure, Ben.' said Noah gravely. 'But what you say is highly likely.'

Mr Williamson, meanwhile, seemed preoccupied. He called to the Laocoönic engineer: 'You there – why did you not have use of the river engine tonight?'

'Eh? What? The river engine is down at Lambeth – big fire started there first. All these b_____ fireworks, no doubt!'

Noah and Mr Williamson exchanged an ominous glance and together they looked south-west, where it seemed an orange-tinged plume of smoke rose high into the night sky.

'I think it is time we spoke to Sir Richard Mayne,' said Noah.

'Hmm. Hmm,' said Mr Williamson, his face suffused with heat.

SIX

Deep in the cellars of Scotland Yard, Mr Newsome beheld the face and wondered: was this truly the face of Lucius Boyle – he who had notoriously murdered a man amidst a crowd of 30,000 people before the walls of Newgate? He who had tortured and killed the infamous *bon vivant* Mary Chatterton? The same who had overseen the murder of a two-headed girl and a priest? The same, also, whom Inspector Newsome believed to be the mastermind behind a recent smuggling case involving a number of grisly murders?

The wax effigy now lay inhumanly impassive on a tall stone bench, removed from the splintered coffin but still dressed in its black funerary suit. And yet its existence defied all good sense. Lucius Boyle's true dead body had been seen by a number of witnesses, including his avowed enemy Noah Dyson. Had they not all observed the corpse: limp, charred and flayed by flames into a contorted, blackened thing? Certainly, no formal identification had been made at the time, but there had seemingly been no doubt of his identity and he had been buried with customary administrative efficiency in an unmarked grave to avoid any further interest from a public that had become quite intoxicated with the man and his misdeeds.

If Boyle *were* still alive, was this how he would appear? No doubt there would have been injuries from the balloon crash which had precipitated him to the earth: melted skin, burned hair, exposed bone. Mr Newsome touched the contours of the cool wax and the realisation came to him in an instant: this effigy may have been modelled from a cast of the man himself. Where living fingers now stroked, Lucius Boyle's own face had once been: twisted by the fire and smarting in agony as the liquid plaster poured. It was the closest that criminal and investigator had yet come. This body – this unholy corporeal fabrication – was the key to the capture of Lucius Boyle.

Mr Newsome stepped back and took off his jacket, hanging it on the back of a chair before putting on a pair of thin kidskin gloves. The unused storage was cold, but he felt warmed by his purpose as he began to undress the body, mindful of any potential traps such as the gunpowder that had almost killed him and the surgeon. A man who would leave a bomb in his coffin would not hesitate to sew a razor into his clothes or rinse their buttons in poison.

There was no such occurrence, but neither were there any discoveries in the pockets or in the construction of the garments, which might have been made by any tailor. The material was common enough and the seams stitched in a wholly conventional manner. Meanwhile, the newness of all seemed to suggest that the suit had been made expressly for this burial.

As for the torso beneath, it was evidently not wax. Mr Newsome saw that canvas had been stretched tautly over a wooden frame in order to suggest a ribcage and shoulders beneath the masking suit. He palpated the fabric and felt it flex against his gloved hands. The explosion at Portugal-street had already revealed this flimsy shell to be filled with sand to approximate the weight of a real body – but was that all?

Taking a knife from a workbench, he carefully cut from the neck to where the body had been destroyed at the hips and peeled back the canvas to reveal the chamber within. Sand of the same type filled the cavity and Mr Newsome inserted his fingers through the wooden slats, combing slowly through the length of the organ-bereft space for any trace of an object within. It was only when he came to where a heart might sit that his index finger brushed something small: a mere filament or needle of matter.

Cupping both hands under the place, he lifted the granular heart and trickled it between his fingers until the object alone remained in his palm: a single Lucifer match. Was it some mistake, perhaps, that the match had fallen there while the body was being filled or the bomb prepared? Or was it the grim whimsy of a lunatic incendiary to endow his ceroplastic twin with a phosphorus heart?

Mr Newsome carefully placed the match in his jacket pocket on the chair and regarded the face once more. *Somebody* had made it. Somebody had cast the living face, made the mould and poured the wax. Possibly someone else had painted it to mirror the injuries of the original, while another had supplied the artful eyes, the full set of teeth and the hair that adhered but patchily to the scalp. Assuredly, the hands were a work of art and must also have been made by some rare master of wax modelling. Such people and products were rare enough even in London. They would have to be sought out.

Working again with the knife, Mr Newsome beheaded the figure and lifted the scull clear with a few tatters of canvas still adhering to the inanimate neck. It was not as heavy as he had expected – at least, not the eleven pounds that a normal brain-filled human head would weigh. A quick glance showed that the neck was hollow, presumably leading to a similar void in the scull. He placed it into a hessian sack and tied the top with twine. It was time to take the gruesome artefact to someone who could tell him more.

Omnibuses made him nauseous at the best of times, and there was simply nothing worse than taking an omnibus west along Oxford-street at any time of the day. The constant stopping and starting, the sour reek of the horses, the endless chatter of the cad and the yearning anonymity of the passengers – all conspired to sicken him. The inspector would have taken a police carriage under other circumstances, but Sir Richard would clearly not countenance it in this particular investigation.

The journey was made still more unpleasant by the hessian bag on his lap, for it reminded him of a worrying precedent. Had not the murderer James Greenacre travelled across London in exactly this way – in an omnibus, in daylight hours – carrying the real head of his female victim in a bag? Not only the head, but the other limbs also at various times, reasoning that a policeman might stop him at night but not during the day when many people were carrying parcels of some description. If Mr Newsome's bag were to slip from his knee and spill forth its ugly secret, there would have been uproar among the passengers and endless unwanted questions to answer. Accordingly, he clasped it tightly between sweating palms and stared with an affected but perspiring *nonchalance* through the opposite window.

Perhaps for this very reason, he did not notice the presence of another very recent police employee sitting just a yard to his left. Naturally, I had determined to follow this most catalytic of detectives whenever the opportunity presented itself – especially since discerning the mysterious presence in the cellars of Scotland Yard. If there was a story to be told, he would lead me to it.

And, indeed, the shoots of rumour were already emerging from the fertile urban fabric. Seemingly each time the omnibus lurched to a halt, the voices of the patters could be heard shouting their fragmentary revelations above the racket of the street: "Strange discovery near Lincoln's-inn!" "Explosion at Portugal-Street!" "Grave robbery in the heart of London!" Only the finer detail was lacking, though someone – some keen-minded reporter, no doubt – would assuredly soon wheedle out the facts.

'Out 'ere for Portman- and Manchester-square!' called the omnibus cad. 'Out 'ere for Madame Tussaud's!'

Mr Newsome grasped the bag firmly and climbed awkwardly out of the passenger chamber. But as he was stepping down to the street, his attention was caught vividly by something perceived almost unconsciously amidst the swirling crowds: a momentary yet galvanic jolt of recognition.

Had that been Mr Williamson among them?

It had been a pox-scarred face, a top hat and that customary black attire, but most of all there had been that distinctive metronomic walk acquired from years on the beat. And Mr Newsome's mind was a-whir. Why would Mr Williamson have been on Oxford-street, where only shoppers, merchants and tourists strolled at that time of day? Was he, perhaps, engaged in an investigation?

Sir Richard had said nothing about Mr Williamson and his quasi-criminal *troupe* during the recent meeting at Scotland Yard, and yet they had all had personal dealings with Lucius Boyle in the past. Could it be that they were working a case illicitly and in secret for the commissioner? Surely not – for none of them had the slightest inclination that the villain may still be alive. Only he – Albert Newsome – was the man with that certain knowledge.

All trace of Mr Williamson had now vanished in the roiling pedestrian flood – just another hat bobbing on the human sea – and the omnibus had departed, so the inspector cut up Baker-street towards that world-renowned exhibition of illustrious personages modelled in wax.

A sign was appended to the street entrance advising that the galleries were closed until seven that evening, but he pushed open the doors and entered the lobby all the same. There, a grand double staircase curling gracefully left and right invited him to the upper floor where he was momentarily surprised by his own approaching image reflected in the two mirrored doors to the main chamber. The wild-haired and purposeful fellow emerging from the stairs was not, evidently, how he saw himself. He paused briefly and observed how a slight distortion in the glass rendered him a suggestive but ultimately flawed facsimile of the true Inspector Newsome.

Passing through these doors, he made to address himself to the lady sitting at a small table in the passage before realising that she was not real. Rather, it was the likeness of Madame Tussaud herself, allegedly fashioned by her own hand and dressed respectfully in black silk cloak and bonnet. He frowned at the artifice, and at his having been fooled by it, then continued unobserved to the large hall where the permanent exhibition was laid out.

And what a magnificent spectacle it was. In that long, lofty chamber of scarlet and gilt, of freshly cut flowers in vases and stately plaster mouldings, almost two hundred figures were arrayed for the pleasure of the visiter. Here was Louis Phillipe of Russia, Henry IV of France, Charles II in armour, Shakespeare seated, Byron frozen in conversation with Scott, and the marriage group of Her Majesty (Prince Albert holding out the ring). Here also was

Luther in funereal black, Calvin, Voltaire and a martial gathering of Napoleon, Wellington, and the king of Naples – all swords and ribanded insignia.

Seeing them thus, as one massed population, Mr Newsome not help but feel conspicuous as the single vivid figure among them, as if all had paused at a given signal to draw attention to the fleshly interloper. The detail of their clothing, of their hair and of their faces was quite astoundingly true to nature. Cromwell might almost have blinked indignantly, or Queen Mary bemoaned her sorry fate.

'Hello? Is anybody here?' he called into the curiously peopled silence.

Nobody replied, so he continued through the gallery and turned towards the so-called Room of Horrors, passing through a doorway into the dimly lit anteroom that had caused such controversy in recent months for its glorification of blood and profiting from infamous deeds.

Here could be found those unfortunate regal victims of the *guillotine,* but he recognized also the faces of some he had seen with his own eyes: the murderers Good, Rush, Greenacre and Courvoisier – each portrayed in a sanguineous *tableau* of their most hideous acts. And there was Lucius Boyle himself, misrepresented standing behind the two-headed girl Eliza-Beth with a razor in his hand. It was but an approximate likeness, evidently taken from descriptions or distant observation of the living man: a caricature rather than a faithful representation. The red jaw was quite the wrong shade.

'*He* is one of our most popular exhibits,' said a voice.

Mr Newsome jolted in surprise and looked about him for the origin of the comment.

A young gentleman was looking into the Room of Horrors from the main chamber, where he was standing on a stool to comb the beard of a foreign monarch.

'You must be Inspector Newsome,' said the fellow. '*Madame* received your note, but apologizes that she cannot see you herself. I will help in any way I can.'

'Lucius Boyle did not kill Eliza-Beth,' said Mr Newsome, leaving the Horrors to their glistening stillness. 'The murderer was actually an accomplice of his: Bully Bradford.'

'O, I do not know the stories, sir. I just work on the figures.'

Drawing closer, Mr Newsome made a brief examination of his interlocutor, about whom there was something indefinably amiss: perhaps the voice, whose tone was not quite masculine, or possibly it was the incongruous swell of the hips in his trousers. 'It seems you know my name; may I learn yours?'

'I am Bill: Bill Smith.'

Mr Newsome studied the youth as he descended from his stool. He might have had the face of a young man, but there was not the slightest indication of a beard. The hair was cropped short and the shirt sleeves were rolled up for his duties, though the arms were thin and hairless.

'How old are you Bill?'

'Nineteen, sir – but why do you ask?' Challenge flashed briefly in his eyes. Had he marginally lowered his voice to reply?

'And "Bill" is short for William, I suppose?'

'Of course, sir. Isn't it always the way?' Again, the slightly deeper tone.

'No matter. I thought for a moment ... but, no, it is nothing. As I wrote in my letter to *Madame* Tussaud, I was hoping to elicit an expert opinion on something pertaining to a certain police matter – quite confidential.'

'Yes, sir. Let us go to the workshop.'

Bill Smith picked up the stool, tucked it under an arm with a grunt and led the way through the main chamber to a closed door. As he did so, Mr Newsome again took the opportunity to look surreptitiously at the hips and the gait, still uncertain of what he saw.

Through the door was an unadorned room that was chaotically packed with the tools of the ceroplastic art. On one shelf sat dozens of differently coloured wigs, while another was crowded with labelled boxes filled variously with eyes, teeth, ears and loose eyelashes. A number of 'retired' heads tumbled over each other in a large wicker basket (a younger incarnation of Dickens staring blindly uppermost) while partial plaster casts seemed to litter a workbench beneath a large sash window. The whole was permeated with the subtle aroma of wax.

'So – what have you got in the bag, Inspector?' said Bill Smith, placing his stool behind the door. 'Won't you empty it on to the central workbench here?'

Mr Newsome pushed a number of tools to one side and carefully extracted the head, supporting it face up so that it could be seen more clearly.

'O, it's quite horrid, isn't it?' said Bill. 'I don't recognize the face, though. Is it an illustrious person from history, or rather a work of the imagination?'

'Perhaps you can tell me. I would like you to examine the head and give me all information you can discern from it.'

'May I?' Bill took the head and felt its weight in his hands. He sniffed at it, parted the hair on the scalp, palpated the scull, pressed the eyes with his thumbs and inserted a finger into the slightly open mouth. Then, taking a corkscrew-like tool from the bench, he drilled a shallow hole in the neck and rubbed the loosened wax between his fingers.

'Well?' said Mr Newsome.

'It's pure beeswax. I thought it must be – all of our figures are. It may also have been mixed with a little resin to keep it pliable. The work is really first rate. I couldn't have done it better myself.'

'Could it have been made here? Is it possible to identify who made it?'

'Well, there are no distinguishing marks if that's what you mean. We usually mark ours with a number, which admittedly can be easily removed. Anyone could have made it – at least, anyone with sufficient skill. We do occasionally take private commissions, but I can't imagine anyone would want to be portrayed like this.'

'Do you keep records of such commissions?'

'I suppose *madame* might release them for a police matter. I could—'

'Very good – you must obtain them for me. What about the parts? For example, where does one procure the eyes for these things?'

'Ah yes – the eyes are extremely good: very lifelike, very expensive. In fact, they are mostly used by people who have lost their real eyes. We have ours made to order in France or Austria, but I believe there's a shop on Holborn that sells them and which will match the colour to your living eye.'

'Indeed? What of the hair, the colouring, the modelling?'

'It's human hair for the scalp and the lashes as far as I can tell. Only the best modellers use it. The colouring is rather vivid, but expertly applied – not just painted, but added as pigmented liquid wax. It would have taken hours. As for the modelling, the eyes, ears and mouth are true to nature, but I couldn't say if the likeness is good because I haven't seen an original.'

'Might it have been made from a cast of the living face?'

'O, sir! Do you believe that any *living* face could look like that? It's just a nightmare: a mask to frighten people.'

'I am not attempting to be humorous. This might have been the face of a man who was badly injured, perhaps burned.'

Bill Smith caught the manic glare in Mr Newsome's eyes and swallowed. He looked again at the wax head and, as if recognising something for the first time, he seemed to pale.

'Might it have been made from a cast? From life?' said Mr Newsome sternly.

'I ... I ...' With tremulous hands, Bill bent to re-examine the neck, beneath the chin, below the nose and around the ears. 'Ah ...'

'What? What is it?' said Mr Newsome.

'Do you see these lines here: near the ear lobe and again just under the jaw? They're very, very faint, but you can just about discern them.'

'Perhaps – I am not sure I see anything. What does it mean?'

'Let me show you.'

Bill quickly gathered some pieces of plaster from the table below the window and brought them to where the monstrous head lay. 'When a face is cast, it is done with one large piece of plaster, but when the dried cast is removed, it is cut into pieces like this – in case we ever need to make another nose or chin, you see. For the wax casting, the plaster impression is fastened back together into a whole, but the joins will show in the wax. We normally smooth these away, but if a piece is made in a hurry . . . Most of the lines on your specimen have been erased, but these are the ones most commonly missed.'

'Yes, I see. So this head *was* cast from life.'

'Not necessarily. It might have been cast from a clay bust of the real person, as happens with historic personages.'

'Is there a way to tell?'

'Not really – not if the wax modelling is good.'

Mr Newsome cogitated on the destroyed face before him. Was it really likely that the horribly burned Boyle would have sat patiently while a likeness had been prepared by a sculptor in clay? It would have been faster to submit to the cool plaster poured directly on to his tortured skin.

'This is indeed his face,' muttered the inspector, touching its forehead.

'Well, it may be his face at one remove, sir. The plaster takes the living likeness while the wax takes the likeness of the plaster form. It's more a reflection.'

'It is he.'

'Do you mean . . . ?'

'That is not your concern and you will speak of it to nobody.'

'Yes, sir . . .'

A hand bell tinkled distantly and both looked up at the sound.

'That is *madame* calling for her tea. Pardon me a moment, sir,' said Bill, evidently pleased to leave the room.

Mr Newsome nodded and thought distractedly about the long, slender fingers and delicate wrists of "Bill Smith". He was pondering it further and looking about the room when his attention was taken by a row of unadorned white wax heads upon an upper shelf.

Bereft of their eyes, hair and colouring, they had the look of ancient sculptural busts: some gods or heroes unearthed from the preserving strata of millennia and catalogued for a museum. But as he continued to stare, something about the features of one particular head stirred some vague recognition in him. If it was an illustrious poet or general or politician, he could not quite place the features.

Reaching up to the shelf, he carefully took hold of the head and carried it to where the boxes of eyes were stored. He rattled around for two of an approximate colour and deduced that these had to be inserted from within the hollow head by reaching up through the neck. Then, with his hands beginning to shake somewhat at the presentiment of what he would find, he selected a curly wig of crimson hue from the relevant shelf and placed it atop the smooth white skull.

And it was his very own countenance that looked back at him, albeit with crossed eyes and an asymmetric peruke. Correctly coloured, it would have been an alarmingly persuasive likeness.

Fear and confusion assailed his mind. There was no reason at all for his figure to appear at this gallery – his name was known to appear only occasionally in the newspapers and his exploits were little known to the general populace. He looked at the other heads on the upper shelf and pulled them down also, phrenziedly selecting wigs and eyes to bolster their anonymous features with personality.

And by the time Bill Smith returned from his tea-making duties, four hastily assembled heads lay beside that of Lucius Boyle's on the table, their hair askew and eyes crazed. They were the very images of Inspector Newsome, George Williamson, Noah Dyson and Mr John Cullen.

'What are *these*?' challenged Mr Newsome with an edge of creeping mania.

'I . . . I have no idea, sir. Where did you find them?'

'On the shelf up there! I know these men. I am one of them! Why are they here?'

'That's the shelf for private commissions, sir. They're made for—'

'The records – where are the records? I must see them now.'

'I must ask *madame* . . .'

'No. Show me now. This is a police matter.'

Bill hesitated briefly before going to a set of drawers and opening the uppermost one to take out a ledger. 'Is there a label on the underside?'

'Wait . . . Yes, this one says 147. The other three are consecutive increments.'

'O.'

'What is it?'

'There is no name – only a price and a note that some masks were made from the heads. They were to be collected.'

'When? Who made them?'

'The collection was three weeks ago and paid in full. It says that Mr Varney made them, but he has recently left us – in the last week or so.'

'His address – where can I find this Varney?'

'Perhaps *madame* knows where. I . . . I have no idea. I . . .'

'Well, there is no need to start blubbering, girl. Just get me that address.'

'I am not a girl! I am . . . *Bill Smith.*'

Mr Newsome stared at this defiance of natural emotion. She was not a remotely attractive girl, he thought, but neither an entirely convincing boy. 'Very well, *Bill* – might there also be a record of this head I have brought to you in that ledger?'

'It . . . it is possible, but how could I look for it if I have no identifying name or number?'

'Do you make many private commissions?'

'Not so very many.'

'Then look for entries about a year ago. Are there any that look suspicious through lack of detail?'

'I . . . I should ask *madame*'s permission to reveal . . .'

'Give it to me! I will look.' Mr Newsome snatched the ledger and flicked back the pages to the date he sought. Nothing, however, looked immediately deceitful. Short of visiting every single name and address listed, there was little he could gain from the information. 'Very well. If you will procure that address of Mr Varney for me, I will take my leave.'

Bill offered a malicious look and stamped out of the workroom, leaving Mr Newsome to take the opportunity of ripping the relevant pages from the commissions ledger before putting it back in the drawer. Thoughts boiled in his head, and he glared with unease at his own malformed likeness lying cheek-down on the central work bench. Its inanimate lactic purity and its lopsided gaze made it seem the most disturbing of all the heads arrayed there.

SEVEN

Standing at the eastern end of Fleet-street, one cannot help but have one's attention arrested by two imposing structures rising loftily out of the city's fabric to claim immortality. The first is, of course, the towering grandeur of St Paul's, while the second is the blank curtain wall of the disused Fleet prison, stretching north along Farringdon-street. Between salvation and infamy, is it not always the latter that tells the better tale?

Barely a doorway or window punctuates the prison's long fortress-face of stone, and those few orifices that do exist have long been boarded against idle interest. Its rusting *chevaux de frize* rake the sky four storeys above, guarding an acre of echoing emptiness within: the "perfect town in miniature" according to the auctioneers' pamphlet that has reduced the great gaol to its component three million bricks, fifty tonnes of lead, and 40,000 feet of paving prior to demolition.

And what a curious place it is beyond that vast, expressionless wall. Where once a thousand voices rang, now only mice run in corridors condemned to silence; where cooks, butchers, carpenters and clergymen once laboured at their daily contribution to prison life, now hearths, seats and ovens stand cold. At the very centre of our seething metropolis of two million souls, it is a pocket of emptiness that remains unseen, unheard, unconsidered and uninhabited.

Or, rather, there was one.

Old Adam paused on the stairs down to the inner cobbled courtyard and cocked an ear. He squinted up at the walls and heard snatches of life on the outside: carriages, voices, the intermittent *chough-chough* of a river ferry carried on the breeze. With his straggling white beard, his rheumy eyes and his staff-supported misshapen legs, he might almost have been an obstinate spirit haunting the abandoned Fleet – but he was its longest resident and terminal caretaker.

He made his way awkwardly over the cobbles with the aid of his staff, brushing his free hand eastwards along the perimeter wall until he came to a stairwell and descended to a dank chamber containing nothing but a wooden bench and an arched door banded with iron. Here, he sat and waited with the patience of one who has spent a lifetime purposelessly suspended until there came a sharp rapping on the other side of the door.

'Adam – I am glad to see you well,' said Sir Richard Mayne, entering with a quick backward glance down the passage that had brought him circuitously to this covert entrance.

'Aye, I will outlast the gaol yet!' croaked Adam.

'No sign of our other guests?'

'No, sir, but the Ludgate door is difficult to find if you don't know it.'

'Quite, quite.'

They looked at each other: the commissioner of police and the half-blind superannuated debtor. Time seemed to ossify.

'It is the end of October, is it not?' said Adam.

'Yes,' said Sir Richard. He looked at his watch.

'And a Friday?'

'A Wednesday.'

'Ah . . . at least I had the month correct. One loses track.'

'I am sure.'

The door resounded with a double knock and Adam turned the key to open it, revealing four gentlemen crowded at its narrow jamb: Noah Dyson, George Williamson, John Cullen and the enormous Negro Benjamin.

'Gentlemen – please enter,' said Sir Richard. 'I trust that you were discreet in your approach.'

'We had little choice under the circumstances,' said Noah.

'Well, we will discuss that,' said Sir Richard. 'This way if you please.'

Adam led the way, trailing a hand against the walls as he went, and the unspeaking group finally entered the vast gallery hall, where a plenitude of encircling iron railings and staircases ascended through four floors of yawning cells to a huge skylight filmed with grime.

'I have prepared this one,' rasped Adam, indicating that they should all enter an open cell to the left.

Inside, five rough wooden chairs had been arranged around a stained oak table upon which there was a pewter jug of water and five porcelain mugs. The windows were barred and the floor just bare flags. None of the men had removed his gloves, coat or hat.

Adam scrabbled at the hearth and attempted to rekindle a fire of logs as the others stood exchanging glances. When finally the flames were licking up the chimney, the old debtor hoisted himself up with the staff and whispered, 'I will leave you gentlemen to your business.'

Sir Richard waited for the door to close and scraped a chair across the stone to sit at the head of the table. 'Very well – please be seated. Let us begin'

The others settled themselves and Mr Cullen poured water into each cup. To his left, Benjamin observed the iron bars nervously with his healthy right eye and looked to Noah for reassurance. It was not the first time these two had found themselves in a cell together. Noah gave a slight nod and himself turned to Mr Williamson to ascertain who would speak on behalf of their group. The latter, evidently as uncomfortable as Benjamin, waved a dismissive hand.

'Sir Richard – you have no doubt heard what has happened to our houses,' said Noah. 'Both utterly destroyed. And since the perpetrator is, in all likelihood, the same who has been following us since we last aided you on a case, it falls to you as police commissioner to aid and protect us.'

'So that is why you made so much fuss to seek an appointment with me,' said Sir Richard. 'I am indeed sorry for your unfortunate losses, but tell me: what makes you think it can be any responsibility of mine?'

'Because it was you who involved us in that case,' said Noah. 'Involved us, I might add, and then denied we had played any part in its solution. As ever, Inspector Newsome takes the credit.'

'Hmm. Hmm,' said Mr Williamson with a weighted glare at his erstwhile employer.

'Were it not for that involvement, we would not be marked men,' continued Noah. 'Does it not strike you as an unlikely coincidence that both of our houses would be burned on a single evening in two separate parts of the city? Our lives are clearly in danger and we would like to know what you plan to do about it.'

Sir Richard held up his hands. 'Let us remain calm. It is indeed odd that your homes would be destroyed simultaneously in such a way, but oddity is not in itself a case. What else do you have? What evidence?'

Noah turned in outraged wonder to Mr Williamson, whose face was as sombre as a tombstone.

'Is this the thanks we receive?' said Mr Williamson. 'We risked our lives to help you in that smuggling case. Benjamin and Mr Cullen were mere moments from death. You *know* that the perpetrator was never caught; you *know* that he knows who we are and where we live; you *know* that he wishes us destroyed. What have you done to address the problem?'

'The Metropolitan Police does not exist for you alone,' said Sir Richard with an icy tone. 'Nor do I, as commissioner, have any responsibility to concern myself with – or be summoned to address – the issues of private citizens. Be assured that men are working on the remaining questions of that case.'

'Which men?' said Mr Williamson. 'Inspector Newsome, who would wish us dead?'

'And how should we be assured when we have nowhere to live?' said Noah. 'We "private citizens", as you term us, have acted as unofficial police agents under the direct control of the police commissioner. That is *espionage,*

Sir Richard. I wonder what *the Times* might make of it? No doubt there are already rumours, and with that Commons hearing approaching . . .'

'Enough,' said Sir Richard, with a firm placing of his palm on the table top. 'I agreed to see you – that should be confirmation enough that our fates are disagreeably bound.'

'Then what will you do about our situation?' said Mr Cullen, who had been waiting for his opportunity.

Sir Richard stared hard at this burly six-footer who had never risen above the rank of common constable and yet who now sat at the same table as a commissioner, questioning him.

Benjamin smiled with a broad show of ivory and threw a sightless wink at Mr Cullen. Noah covered his smirk with a hand.

'Mr Dyson – is it strictly necessary that your associates be here?' said Sir Richard.

'Their lives are also in danger. If you will just answer the question . . .'

'Very well, very well,' sighed Sir Richard. 'It might seem to you that I have done nothing to help you, but it has proven more difficult than you might think to gain access to the Fleet prison. It is supposed to be entirely closed.'

'I am not sure I follow your meaning,' said Noah, feeling nauseously sure that in fact he did.

'Why, I mean to say that the Fleet will be your residence while these sundry matters are resolved.'

Benjamin's eye sought Noah's with an urgent stare and he described a complex gesticulation in the air. Mr Williamson meanwhile spluttered and half stood to respond:

'Are we to understand that our reward for losing our homes is to be imprisoned like so many criminals?'

'No – not imprisoned,' said Sir Richard. 'The prison has been decommissioned and is now the property of the Corporation of London. It is, therefore, just another building. You are free to leave at any time, but why would you? Nobody but Adam knows you are here, and nobody can gain access. You have food, fire, beds – it is a perfect castle in the very centre of the city.'

'And we are to remain "not imprisoned" here at your convenience, is that right?' said Noah.

'Not at all. You may go at any moment and take your chances, but I cannot protect you if I do not know where you are.

'If we leave, we risk death each day,' said Mr Williamson.

Sir Richard merely shrugged.

'You have us exactly where you want us,' said Noah with combined contempt and respect.

'Understand the situation as you will, gentlemen,' said Sir Richard. 'I do not say that you must remain here every moment of the day. There are numerous covert entrances known to Adam and you are in a position to investigate the destruction of your properties if you wish. I warn you only to be discreet in your comings and goings. As soon as the case is closed and the criminal caught, you can all return to your normal lives.'

'So you advocate our doing your work for you?' said Mr Williamson.

'Police detectives do not investigate house fires, George.'

Noah rubbed his chin in cogitation and a sly smile came to his lips as he considered the commissioner's ambiguities. 'Tell me, Sir Richard – if we were *independently* to investigate the fires and their cause, would the Metropolitan Police offer any support?'

There was an almost imperceptible nod and Sir Richard's eyes went to the table top. 'Certainly, no *official* help would be available. I would have no personal involvement in such a scheme.'

'I see,' said Noah. He looked to Mr Williamson and saw that he had also understood.

'There is ... one more matter,' said Richard with a tone that set the others more attentive still. 'It is something that ... well, perhaps it better if I show you. Please –will you accompany me down to the basement?'

The four gentlemen stood and, exchanging ineffable glances, followed Sir Richard through the gallery chamber, down murky stone steps that had been worn into bows by a century of incarcerated feet and along an even dimmer vault to a closed iron door. Here, Sir Richard paused and withdrew a key. But before inserting it into the lock, he looked gravely at each man:

'I must swear each of you to absolute secrecy about what you are about to see. You may not feel that you have reason to trust me, but let us agree this much: only I know where you are resident, and only you have the power to cause me trouble if the contents of this room were to become known. Do I have your word?'

'Yes,' said Mr Cullen.

'It seems we have no choice,' said Mr Williamson.

'If *our* secret remains safe ...' said Noah.

Benjamin nodded.

'Very well.' Sir Richard unlocked the door and pushed it open with a dry creak to reveal a dusty and long-disused kitchen. 'Gentlemen – may I present PC Taylor of Division A.'

O L___!' said Mr Cullen.

The body looked just as it had in the surgery at Scotland Yard, the skin uncorrupted, the face forever frozen and the rattle still raised in preserved alacrity.

Noah leaned close to inspect the face and Mr Williamson walked around the figure observing the uniform and the board on which all was fastened. Benjamin – no stranger to articulacy of gesture – merely looked on with fascinated horror.

'This policeman was murdered and rendered into his unnatural form *via* the art of taxidermy,' said Sir Richard. 'That is all we know. He was found exactly like this near Portugal-street burial ground yesterday morning.'

'That is not the beat of Division A,' said Mr Cullen.

'Indeed not. We have no idea why, when or how he was moved there.'

'It is certainly mysterious, but why is it any business of ours?' said Mr Williamson. 'You have the Detective Force for crimes of this kind.'

'That is true, but . . . but the nature of this body is something quite out of the ordinary and –'

'The commissioner means to say that the common press would make spectacular theatre of this crime,' said Noah. 'Another highly visible murder following so closely on the heels of those recent grisly crimes at the London Dock . . . and with the police under such scrutiny these days.'

'*Ahem* – what I mean to say,' said Sir Richard, 'is that there would seem to be certain superficial parallels between this body and those recent murders to which you refer.'

'What parallels?' said Mr Williamson.

'Well, merely in its oddity, conspicuousness and gruesomeness. It would appear to be the work of a madman who evidently wishes to taunt the police. Is this not the same kind of fellow you sought in that previous case?'

'So, you offer us this body as a further clue in our pursuit of whoever burned our houses?' said Noah. 'Or as an additional case that you do not want your detectives to mishandle so near to the Commons debate?'

'A little of both, I suspect,' said Mr Williamson.

Sir Richard maintained composure with difficulty. 'This fellow PC Taylor was a policeman as you were, George, and you, too, Mr Cullen. For some reason, he was taken from his beat and reduced to this parody of humanity by an evil mind. He had no enemies of which we know and he was, by all accounts, a long-serving, popular policeman in his community. I do not compel you to investigate this case, but I ask whether you might.'

'And, of course, you ask us to do this without official sanction, without uniform and without the shield of Justice to enforce our actions,' said Noah. 'I have one overriding question: why would we?'

'Well, quite apart from the fact that I have provided you with personal safety at the Fleet and a possible further clue in the search for your collective nemesis, have you given any thought to your accommodation after you finally leave this place?'

'Go on,' said Noah.

'If this case of the stuffed body is solved quickly and to my satisfaction, I will see to it that you are re-housed. I accept that your present misfortunes are partially caused by your involvement with the Metropolitan Police and I herewith agree to make restitution.'

'Hmm. You should do that without imposing any further task,' said Mr Williamson.

'I am sorry to see you so bitter at your previous employer, George. You have always been an exceptionally gifted investigator and—'

'Why is Inspector Newsome not assigned to this case?' said Noah.

'It is none of your concern, of course, but Mr Newsome is engaged upon . . . another important police matter.'

Benjamin indicated the current rumours with a circling finger at his temple and a farcical expression that made Noah and Mr Cullen smile.

'Will you take this case or not?' said Sir Richard somewhat irritably.

'Let us discuss it together this evening,' said Noah. 'We will stay in the Fleet for one night and see how it suits us. Then we will send word through Adam if we are to accept your offer. Are we all agreed?'

The others nodded, albeit with some evident reluctance.

'Very well, very well,' said Sir Richard. 'I have borrowed a set of surgical tools if you wish to examine the body. I will leave them here. And if you do choose to pursue the killer of PC Taylor, you might talk to this fellow.' He handed a card to Mr Cullen, who was nearest. 'All being well, we will not meet again for some time. Gentlemen – I bid you good evening and I await your response.'

With that, the commissioner of police walked out of the kitchen and could be heard echoing away through the stone corridors until his footsteps faded entirely.

'What do you think?' said Mr Cullen.

'I think I am becoming tired of the regularity with which my life is entwined with the business of the Metropolitan Police,' said Noah, regarding the frozen constable before him.

'I mean, will we take the case?' said Mr Cullen. 'It seems we have little else to do if we are obliged to reside here at the Fleet. And, as Sir Richard suggested, the perpetrator might be the same.'

Benjamin let forth a brief flurry of digital sweeps and curlicues.

'Yes, Ben – perhaps I *do* want to investigate this case,' said Mr Cullen. 'It seems an interesting one does it not?'

Noah looked in sharp surprize at Mr Cullen. 'You understood what Ben said? I thought only I could read him.'

'O, yes, I suppose I did. I must have been paying attention without realising.'

Benjamin grinned, his audience apparently doubled.

'Hmm. Hmm. It is coercion and I don't like it,' said Mr Williamson.

'Well, we have little choice,' said Noah. 'Where else can we go? A hotel? There is Mr Cullen's house, but it will likely be in flames as we speak.'

'O, do you think so?' said Mr Cullen, paling.

'At least the Fleet offers us a degree of invisibility,' said Noah. 'I suggest that I slip away and examine the ruins of the houses tomorrow for any clues.'

'And PC Taylor here?' said Mr Cullen. 'What do we do with him? I hate to see a brother officer so ill treated.'

'I hate to agree with Sir Richard, but the appearance of this body is somewhat reminiscent of those other unsolved murders. It cannot hurt to take a close look at the corpse of the constable here. George – will you examine the evidence?'

'Hmm. I suppose I might look at it.'

'And I?' said Mr Cullen. 'Should I pursue this name that Sir Richard gave me? It appears to be a Doctor Hammerton at Westminster hospital. Is he a taxidermist, do you think?'

'I have heard the name,' said Mr Williamson. 'He is apparently a doctor of the criminal mind. The Detective Force sometimes consults him when no other clues are available. It is said that he has interviewed a number of genuine murderers in the condemned cells at Newgate. I could go to see him.'

'But Sir Richard gave the card to *me*,' said Mr Cullen, holding it up as evidence.

'Good – then it is you who should go and see him, Mr Cullen' said Noah with a disguised smile. 'And Ben – how would you like to attract some attention?'

Benjamin made an interrogative gesture.

'Someone has apparently been following both Mr Williamson and I for days, though we have never been able to catch or even identify them. You are the most visible of us all. While we are engaged in our other duties, perhaps you can acquire one of the fellows who has been trailing us and waylay whoever it is. I would very much like to speak with them.'

Benjamin grinned and massaged a large fist of scarred knuckles.

'And let us all proceed with the utmost care. However safe this temporary eyrie may be, we do not want anyone to follow us here. Is that understood, Mr Cullen?'

'Yes, Noah. Quite clear.'

'Well, I hope old Adam has a functioning kitchen somewhere in this penitential sepulchre. I believe it is time for tea.'

EIGHT

Even in London, few names in the annals of duplicity and deception can rank with that of Perkin Mullender. He was seldom, however, known by that name – least of all by his victims.

To the wealthy people of Portman-square, for example, he was more readily known as the clergyman who came knocking at their doors asking to see the ladies of the house before launching into an impassioned sermon upon his work at a certain ragged school. Naturally, only a significant donation would be sufficient to rid them of the turbulent priest.

Or perhaps the reader will recall the case of the false luggage clerk of Custom House wharf, who came collecting half a crown from each foreign visiter waiting as their suitcases were being examined within. How were they to know that no such charge was levied and that the fellow's insignia were mere worthless badges?

And let us not forget how many lives were ruined by the fellow masquerading as a shipping clerk for Carter & Bonus, taking a large sum in advance for the promise of a familial emigration certificate to the Antipodes. The paper and ink may have been real, but the permission was not, and the consequent wails of despair at dockside were truly lamentable to hear.

But while it is true he had been arrested and served a few months for each of these particular adventures, his unlikely escape from certain transportation was due to Mr Perkin Mullender being tried under a different name and before a different judge each time. Thus could he have been found strolling at liberty along Cinnamon-street, Wapping, that very afternoon. He is an interesting man; let us watch him as he goes.

His clothes are new and well made, his face has a certain dark handsomeness and his freshly shaven chin is fragrant with the aroma of some expensive emollient. But is he a lunatic that he seems separately to smirk, squint and frown in the space of an instant? What inner turmoil must make him both nod and shake his head so, make him arch his eyebrows like an actor in Bardic throes and juggle his hands before him with such unselfconscious abandon? Could it be – fantastical as it may seem – that he is actually engaged in conversation with the sundry pieces of *himself*?

Indeed. Listen closely and one might even hear their individual voices: spoken in breathless *sotto voce* and each with its own discernible accent: 'O, I could not possibly accept your gift, madam! . . . I must insist, your Highness . . . But a diamond? It must be worth a clear thousand . . . Two thousand, your Excellency! . . . Well, if you are quite certain, my sweet child . . .'

'Hoi – Bedlam boy! Oo yer talkin' to?' came the cry from a group of laughing crossing-sweepers.

Perkin Mullender started from his unilateral dialogue and threw a look of proud disdain at the grimy lads. The chattering cast of characters fell immediately from his features and he turned purposefully towards the great rotunda entrance of the Thames Tunnel.

Here, he queued to pay his penny, passed through the brass turnstile with a click that registered him the 1,352,456th visiter and began to walk down and down staggered staircases through the earth to Brunel's world-renowned double bore. Not for him, however, the attraction of the gaudy wall paintings or the echoing organ music that so enchanted his fellow descenders. Rather, he considered this wonder of modern construction just another metropolitan drain, albeit one with a single alleviating feature.

'Hallo, Mr Winchester!' she cried when she saw Perkin Mullender reaching the bottom of the stairs. Her little stall was set with all the usual tasteless rubbish one associates with the tunnel yet he approached with an expression as convincingly joyful as it was fraudulent. In the blink of an eye, he had become the attractive regular customer of her romantic dreams.

82

'Why, Jane – you've become even prettier since I last saw you.'

'O, Mr Winchester. You flatter me so!'

'Nonsense. You are quite the prettiest thing about this dreadful hole.'

'O, ha ha! You do make me laugh, Mr Winchester. I have saved that postcard you wanted: the image of the miners we spoke about. It is the last one.'

'I'm so glad, Jane.'

Perkin Mullender dropped the coin into her hand and examined the card with a flawless show of fascination. He would likely later toss it in the river: another minor investment in her trust that would pay dividends in her eventual ruination.

'Will you take your customary stroll along the tunnel?' bubbled the girl.

'I suppose I must if I am to remain young and healthy for you.'

'O, Mr Winchester!'

He made a little bow, flashed his dark eyes at her for good measure, and turned to enter the right-hand arch, his smile dropping as soon as his back was turned.

The tunnel proper seemed to vanish into dark oblivion, its gas lights too weak and too few to penetrate the considerable distance to the Rotherhithe shore. And with every further step, the infernal atmosphere of the place seemed to permeate one's nose and clothes: that foetid smell of populous expiration combined with the heat of the gas and the ever-present aroma of the river. It might have been seventy-five feet above their heads, but its pressure was as irresistible and as patient as time. Might it not crash through the brickwork at any moment, a deluge of stinking, icy water bringing instant destruction to the hundreds who mocked its power below?

Perkin Mullender walked purposefully on, paying no heed to the numerous ladies tending their stalls in the arched alcoves between the two shafts, nor to the old organ grinder with his apathetic monkey, nor to the coffee seller whose steam hovered at the tunnel's ceiling like a spelaean mist.

Massed voices reverberated dankly: trapped spirits condemned forever to flit about the pie-crust blocks of this engineering folly.

Having passed the halfway point, he glanced behind him to see if anyone was walking close. A couple was strolling and pointing about them in wonder, so he bent as if to tie a shoelace and felt for the iron key in his coat pocket as they passed. Then, when he felt sure he was unobserved, he stepped into an alcove that had not been adopted for the retail of worthless trinkets.

Inside that shadowy space was a rusting iron door cut into the masonry. It should not have led anywhere, but more than one visiter had remarked on how the alcoves thereabouts gave way to artful *trompe l'œil* representations of their form for about ten yards of tunnel. Evidently, there was some manner of storage room or chamber reserved for the workings of the gas or for ventilation.

Perkin Mullender turned the key and pushed the door open with a metallic scrape, his nose immediately beginning to twitch at the chymical smells within: sulphur, saltpetre, nitre and charcoal, along with the more familiar atmosphere of men in illicit confinement. He quickly closed and locked the door.

Though there were pipes and nozzles for the use of gas, the interior was brightly illuminated by a number of Davy lamps hanging from hooks in the bare stone walls. To the immediate right, a singular gentleman was bent over a workbench that appeared to be littered with dozens of lock mechanisms separated into their various parts. The fellow's skin was of a sallow hue and a long horsetail of greasy black hair hung down his back. A single gold earring – that hallmark of the Italian in London – glinted dully, but he did not look up from his work or acknowledge the new arrival in any other way. Rather, he continued to probe a complete lock using a thin strip of steel held in his slender fingers more delicately than any pen.

'Is he here?' said Perkin Mullender with a bold show of boldness.

The "Italian" merely jerked his head backwards and sideways, indicating an interior door upon which a number of haphazardly overlapping engineering diagrams had been adhered.

'Thank you so much.'

A brazen liar and pretender he might have been, but in the next room Perkin Mullender could be none other than the one person he would rather not reveal: himself. His face momentarily flickered like a thumbed picture book through a dozen borrowed emotions and he turned the handle to enter.

This smaller space was also darker. A single Davy lamp shaded with a piece of scarlet cloth cast a sickly light over a workbench cluttered with materials suggesting firework manufacture: the bored wooden block and ramming pole used for packing rockets, a selection of clay bungs, a pot of glue, a mortar and pestle, a set of brass scales. Consumed Lucifer matches – each one burned down to a warped black exclamation point – littered the bench and the floor around it. There appeared to be nobody within.

'You are late, Mr Mullender.'

The voice was somehow corrupted: smothered as if spoken by a ruined mouth through some distorting barrier. The utterance was followed with a liquid suck of breath.

'I . . . I had to be sure that I wasn't being followed.'

'So you were not passing romantic nonsense with that idiot girl at the entrance?'

'I may have bidden her good day, but it was merely—'

'Do not be late again.'

The speaker emerged from behind a wooden partition beyond the workbench. Some past injury had evidently damaged his figure so that he stooped slightly and held his left shoulder higher than the right. But it was his face that both fascinated and repelled.

Or, rather, it was his lack of a face. Where one would expect to see skin and hair, there was only a carapace of blank white wax fashioned into the semblance of a human countenance: simultaneously benign and baleful, characterless and yet exuding menace. Not the merest trace of emotion could move it, though its light grey eyes were intense and the open mouth was a blackness emitting compromised breaths.

'I have heard that you performed your task to perfection,' said the masked man, seating himself with some apparent difficulty at the workbench. 'Did you encounter any obstacles of which I should know?'

'There was a constable snooping about, but I don't think he saw me. In any case, I was wearing the likeness as you instructed.'

'Do you have it with you now?'

Perkin Mullender reached into his coat and withdrew a mask with a peruke attached to its upper forehead. The face had been coloured and textured with such artistry that one might not have told it from human skin. He rested it carefully on the workbench.

'And did you follow my instructions to the letter?' said the impassive white face. 'The positioning? The means of discovery?'

'Everything to the letter, yes.'

'I will learn the truth if you are lying to me.'

'I wouldn't tell a lie.' A smirk involuntarily wrestled for predominance on Perkin Mullender's serious mouth.

'Of course you would not – at least, not to me. I have another task for you.'

He extended a gloved hand across the workbench and Perkin Mullender took the piece of paper. It was a list and he automatically scanned the first few items:

Bécour's arsenical French soap

Gum Arabic solution

Powdered chalk

Four yards of No. 4 wire

Selection of badger-hair brushes, sizes 1-12

'You are to procure all of the items on this list and bring them to me here as soon as you can,' said the masked man. 'I have made clear on the other side of the sheet where you might find them.'

Perkin Mullender nodded, folded the paper and made to take back the lifelike mask.

'No – not that one.' The featureless man reached behind him to where five highly realistic likenesses were arrayed on a shelf, each one with its own hairpiece. 'Wear this one when you buy the items.'

'Very well, but I fear the shop keepers will discern it is a mask when I speak. It is one thing to wear them at night when—'

'No matter. It is enough that your wear this face. Use whatever justification is necessary to explain it – which I am sure it will be no difficulty for you – but wear the mask when you buy these things. And be sure to duplicate his gait and manner exactly. Do I make myself clear?'

'Completely. I wonder if I might ... might raise the question of payment?'

'You will be paid in full when the fullness of the scheme is realized. You are of no use to me if you simply abscond with a portion of your payment. Be assured that you will receive your due.'

'I'm not generally a trusting man ...'

'But you will trust me.' The *tabula rasa* of the waxen face said nothing, but the tone was clear and the unblinking grey eyes might have been enamel for all the humanity they betrayed.

'Yes, yes – of course.'

'Then go. If young Tobias is outside, please tell him to enter.'

Perkin Mullender nodded a good-bye and attempted to exit in the manner of a man not the least intimidated by turning his back on such an interlocutor. Though there was no fireplace in the chamber, it had seemed somehow hotter – as if, indeed, a great fire had previously occupied the space and consumed the majority of its good air.

The Italian-looking fellow was still in the outer room and still entirely engaged with his locks. Standing beside him was a boy who could not have been more than eleven: a grubby, scrappy, tatty, sort of street boy wearing a greasy corduroy cap and an incongruous school uniform which had been so abused by fate that its provenance had now become quite obscure. If he was a scholar of anything, young Tobias Smalletts was an ardent student of fighting, theft and vulgarity.

'Good day to you, Toby,' said Perkin Mullender, tipping his hat in mock respect.

'I tole yer afore, it's _____ "Tobias", not _____ "Toby",' replied the young man.

'Of course it is. I trust you are well? Out and about in the city, I suppose?'

'Well, I ain't got no _____ 'ome, so 'course I'm _____ out 'n' 'bout, aren't I?'

'You're certainly a logical young fellow.'

'_____ ____'

'Yes, well, he told me that you should go in to see him. I would say it's been pleasant to meet you again, but . . .' Perkin Mullender gave a wink and tipped his hat once more before letting himself out into the tunnel.

Master Smalletts wiped his nose on a sleeve and put his cap in a pocket. With a deft glance to see if the Italian was looking, he puffed up his chest and drew himself as tall as his tender years would allow. Then he, too, passed through the other door into the masked man's room.

'Tobias – how are you?' said the man, unmoved since his last guest had left.

'Can't complain, gen'ral. Lifted a nice gold ticker last evenin' and spent the pennies on five meat pies.'

'Then you sold it at too low a price, boy. You must learn ambition. But see that you do not get caught – I have further need of you.'

'No bluebottle can pinch Tobias Smalletts, gen'ral.'

'I hope not. What have you found at Westminster?'

'It's all as yer said: the entrance, the grates an' the rest.'

'Very good. I have more work for you there. Look at this diagram – tell me if you recognize it.' The masked man unfolded a building plan on the workbench and watched carefully as the young man leaned closer to examine it.

'Palice o' Westminster ain't it. Here's the place yer tole me to look.'

'Good boy. Now look at this plan.' The man opened the pages of a journal.

'Don't know what that is, gen'ral. Is it a buildin' too?'

'No – it is a map of *under* a building. Under *this* building – in fact under this room here. If I give you both maps, do you think you might find your way to that place? It will likely be a small, confined place; not any boy would be able to—'

'Tobias Smalletts can do it. I ain't no ordin'ry boy.'

'Indeed you are not. I think I see something of my younger self in you.'

Master Smalletts puffed out his chest until he thought his buttons would pop, but maintained his stern expression lest he be judged too soft.

'In fact, I have a gift for you, Tobias: something you might need to use in the course of your work.' The masked man opened a drawer beneath the workbench and took out a narrow wooden box, which he pushed across to Master Smalletts. 'Open it.'

The boy snatched at it and unlatched the hinged box top with eager fingers, revealing a fine Sheffield penknife with horn scales. He opened the single three-inch polished blade and tilted it so that it caught the scarlet light of the covered Davy lamp.

'Use it to cut your bread or whittle a stick . . . or to mark your enemies,' said the masked man. 'They will remember and fear you every time they touch their scars.'

'I never 'ad no present before,' said Tobias, stroking the smooth scales and testing the blade's edge with his thumb.

'You are with me now. Serve me well and you will receive further rewards. I have been failed too many times in the past. I need certain allies. Can I trust you, Tobias?'

'With me life.'

'One way or the other, yes. So – try to gain access to that place on the plans and bring your full report to me. What does it look like? Is it the same as the diagrams? Do you understand?'

'Yes, gen'ral.'

'And what should you do if you see any of those fellows we have talked about?'

'Follow 'em. Don't talk to 'em. Tell yer where they went.'

'Good. Then go.'

The door closed gently and the masked man waited until he heard the second door scrape before he reached behind his head and loosened the ribbons that held the false face. Taking a fresh handkerchief from his breast pocket, he dabbed the moisture away from his own ruined countenance and called out to the Italian in the adjoining room.

The long-haired fellow appeared at the threshold and raised interrogative eyebrows.

'Are you ready?' said his master.

A shrug. A nod.

'Very well – you will do it tomorrow night.'

A steam ferry passed over the surface of the river many yards above them. The thrashing of its twin paddles sent a deep bass note throbbing down through the water, through the mud, through the chalk and the harder strata to the stones of the walls and ceiling. When it had passed, the renewed silence seemed tomb-like.

NINE

An unmarked goods wagon sat driverless in the rear yard of the Fleet prison, its horses busy with their nose bags and the wagon bed empty but for a large black tarpaulin. At an upper window, two faces appeared surreptitiously above a window ledge: old Adam and Noah Dyson.

'He comes once a week to take measurements or check that nobody has taken the lead from the roofs,' croaked Adam. 'He only stays half an hour or so. You can slip under his tarp and he will carry you out of the gates unseen.'

'Does he not know of your existence?' said Noah.

'O, yes – but we have nothing to say to each other. He and his men will be demolishing my home and I will not thank them for it.'

Noah glanced at the hoary face and depleted eyes of the caretaker but said nothing. Instead, he made his way down the stone stairs and across the courtyard to the wagon, where he carefully secreted himself beneath the tarpaulin so that his contours might not be too obviously revealed.

Minutes later, the driver returned. Noah heard the rattle of bridles and reins, felt the nosebags land on top of him, and noted the change in weight as the fellow climbed aboard. There followed some brief manoeuvring around the yard, the rattle of the gates, and then they out into the city along the narrow road leading to Old Bailey.

Beneath the tarpaulin, Noah attempted to find a position where his knees and elbows would not be jarred by the rattling timbers. He had not the slightest idea where the wagon might take him – only that he should remain unseen for a time sufficient that anyone observing him alight could not guess his origin. It would be necessary to gauge his location only by nose, ear and an ex-sailor's natural sense of the compass.

After a brief distance, they turned left on to the main road and proceeded north, evidenced by the multiple percussion of stonemason's hammers at the corner with Skinner-street, where a handsome new *façade* was being made. The swirl of traffic thereabouts then caused the wagon to make a jerky turning and Noah smiled unseen at the next clue: the reek of the tallow chandlers drifting from the alleys above Paternoster-row meant they were heading east.

Further along Newgate they went, until the unmistakable racket of wheels and hooves indicated that they had reached the swirling storm centre around St Paul's and the junction with Cheapside. Evidently they proceeded straight on, for Noah distinguished the cries of omnibus drivers, the rattles of constables trying to separate the lines of traffic and the discordant calls of the street vendors taking advantage of that thoroughfare's width to clutter the pavement with their barrows. The distinctive scent of pekou souchang wafted aromatically from Mansell & Co's tea warehouse at the end of Friday-street, and, yes – there was the less appealing smell of Sweeting's oyster emporium just down Bow-lane.

But where next? As the wagon swerved haltingly in and out of the flow, Noah could not be entirely sure whether they had turned or not. He strained his senses to reconfigure the sensory map and heard a regular rasping cough that seemed to echo from down an alley: the steam-powered blades of Moggach's saw mill. The sweet smell of resin assured it – they were now moving south along Queen's-street.

Would the driver continue south over Southwark-bridge, or would he turn right along Upper Thames-street and head for the docks? Neither option suited Noah, who wanted to reach his own home at Blackfriars. It was time to get down from the wagon.

As they slowed in the bottleneck of traffic flowing from all sides towards Southwark-bridge, he peeked out from the tarpaulin and assured himself that the driver was thoroughly engaged with the horses. It was just a matter of easing himself from under his masking cloak and dropping to the road, where he winked conspiratorially at a lady observing him open-mouthed from an omnibus. Within seconds, he was just another body in the crowds, moving west towards the ruin of his house.

He was not alone at the site of the destruction. A small group of people were standing around to observe the sooty frontage, whose roof had partially collapsed so that daylight could be seen up through the ravaged windows. There was a powerful smell of burned wood, and a single uniformed fire-engineer was using a long iron rod with a spiked hook at its end to probe among the scattered detritus on the street.

'It is not safe to enter,' said the engineer as Noah approached.

'It is . . . it was my house. I was here the other night as it burned.'

'Then I am sorry. It will have to be demolished, I'm afraid. The floors are beyond repair.'

'What are you doing looking among the ruins?' said Noah.

'In cases such as this, we look for evidence of incendiarism.'

'What do you mean by "cases such as this"?'

'If you were here the other evening, you may have noticed the amount of water on the ground. Well, it was not due only to the quantity of hoses being used.'

'Sabotage?'

'It seems so. A hose may receive the occasional cut or abrasion, but there were numerous holes in many hoses. I suspect that somebody wanted this house to burn.'

'Is there anything else to suggest incendiarism?'

'I am still looking. Some witnesses reported seeing rockets shooting over from the other side of the river. It is a likely cause of fires at this time of year, whether purposeful or accidental. But as I say, it is dangerous to go inside. The whole structure might come crashing down. Better to wait for it to do so and then look.'

'I will go inside,' said Noah. 'It was my home. What else do I have to lose but my life?'

'I cannot stop you – only warn you.'

'Then tell me – what are the signs? How does one prove arson? Does not the fire destroy all evidence?'

'Well, it depends on the criminal in question. Each has his ways. One might start the blaze with a hay bale while another may prefer oil or volatile chemicals. If you cannot find traces of these, look at the damage. Is it more profound at one place than another? If so, that is likely where the fire started. And if you must enter, take care on the stairs. They will be greatly weakened.'

Noah nodded, already stepping through the soot and fragmented charcoal to pass through what had once been his door. The scene inside was one of utter chaos: blackened beams hanging askew, furniture reduced to frail skeletons, upholstery (where it remained) rendered into withered papyrus and everything covered in a thick ash. Finding anything probative amid such a holocaust seemed impossible.

He picked his way carefully through the fallen forest of timbers to the staircase, which was intact and which retained patches of its original carpet. It creaked alarmingly as he ascended to the study and library, but it bore his weight and brought him to the first clue.

Between the library door and the corridor was a broom handle that had been only partially consumed by the flames. There was no evidence of a broom head. Since the only broom in the house was generally kept in the kitchen, and since there was no reason for it be lying headless where it currently was, Noah's assumption was that it had been placed there – perhaps as a purposeful conduit for the flames.

On peering inside the room, he saw what he feared he might: at least one other door standing open and a broom stick leading to the space beyond. He looked down at his feet. Did there seem to be some kind of pattern emerging through the layers of ash: an apparent fan shape extending from the end of the stick? Kneeling, he brushed away the debris and knew immediately what had been arranged there.

Oakum – the thin, tarry strands of unpicked rope used to waterproof the gaps between planking on ships. He sniffed his fingers to confirm it and

94

recalled half a lifetime at sea. Strange how, even amongst the oppressive aroma of smoke, the smell of oakum could transport him to a deck, to the crack of the sails and a sensation of salt on skin. There was not the least reason why oakum should be in his house, unless it had been laid there with the express purpose of aiding, transporting and prolonging the fire. No doubt there was a network of it across the floors, partially consumed or otherwise hidden beneath the wreckage.

Noah stepped into what was left of his library and took a volume from a broken shelf. Its leather spine had been reduced to flaky brittleness and its pages charred illegible two or three inches inwards from the edges. Even as he held it open, the back cracked and it fluttered in pieces to the floor. Anger began to build within him. There had to be more clues.

He looked around the walls for the telltale calligraphy of the flames. Where had they burned hottest? Where had they swirled and blossomed in the flues of the domestic furnace? Where had hot gases expanded, erupted, exploded?

There – above the fireplace. The space had once held a large mirror whose glass now lay in shattered smoky fragments on the floor. The frame itself, however, had somehow remained on the wall, its silvered surface replaced by a seeming blast mark: a curious area of combustion that seemed to radiate from a specific centre. Noah pressed his finger there and felt a clear conical indentation. Had something exploded in the room and *ricocheted* to destroy the mirror? Or had something come in from *outside*, through the opposite window, and stopped with devastating impact against the chimney breast? Something, perhaps, with great velocity – something like a rocket.

Noah began to throw aside the larger pieces of rubbish surrounding the fireplace, stopping occasionally to examine some fragment that did not look like wood or glass. He knew enough of warfare to recognize a squib or a Congreve rocket when he saw one, though the latter's iron cylinder would have been easier to find.

And gradually he found the few pieces. First, a circular clay bung, then a fragment of pasteboard cylinder, and finally an exploded shard of metal cone: presumably the rocket's head. If this was the weapon that had struck the chimney breast, it was not something one could purchase in the shops. No, this rocket was much bigger and more lethal than the simple fireworks sold for the amusement of the common man. Nor, reasoned Noah, could its trajectory have been at all accidental.

A rocket striking the window would have been deflected in any number of directions – no use to an incendiary who had been so careful to set out the rooms in such a way that they would burn well. The deduction was clear: the window would have to have been broken first, either by another rocket or by a stone so that the explosive device could find its target without deflection.

Noah walked to the window and gazed out over the grim chimneys of Southwark on the opposite shore. Somewhere amidst those *façades* had to be a frame to fire a rocket of such size with the requisite accuracy. If he could find that launch site, he might also find more clues leading him to whoever had destroyed his house.

But something stopped him as he was leaving the library: a mark on the wall above the door that did not exhibit the typical patterns of smoke and fire. Rather, there seemed to be some human design that suggested an image or writing. Noah squinted at the indistinct letters and figures. Could it be that someone had daubed them on the wallpaper with a flammable substance and waited for the conflagration to incise them in flame for posterity?

He could not be sure, but the conundrum seemed to spell out: *Jer VII 20.* A Biblical quotation? Retracing his steps over crunching remains, he went to a bookshelf and reached for a large volume that besmirched his hands with soot as he leafed intently through its crumbling pages.

Most of each page had been partially burned inwards, but the book had been pressed tightly by others each side and the central portion was still legible. He read the passage – and a horripilating chill took him: the kind of intuitive sense one gets when an inimical force or implacable enemy glares at one from his predatory vantage.

Noah ripped the brittle page from the spine and dropped the book among the ashes. In his mind, rationality wrestled with instinct amid fearful impressions that made him question what he had long thought to be the truth.

Mr Williamson paused in the terrace gallery of the Fleet prison, his footsteps giving way to a four-storey semi-silence. Alone now (but for the creeping elsewhere spirit of old Adam), he reflected that the vast ramifying edifice was a veritable Aeolian harp that seemed to thrum and echo with the sounds of the city beyond its walls. Here a distant bell . . . there a puffing train . . . here an infant's cry . . . there an indistinct crash of cargo or demolished slum . . . and beneath it all, a constant rumbling roar like an ocean raging at a far-off shore. Was not this strange structure (he may have pondered) akin to the mind itself?

Dismissing such aural illusions with a scowl, he continued with a firmer step into the cool cellar regions and to the dusty kitchen inhabited by unfortunate PC Taylor. Here, Mr Williamson discovered that the velvet-lined surgeon's instrument case left by Sir Richard contained a bewildering array of scalpels, tweezers, grips, scissors and other inexplicable tools in gleaming nickel-plated steel. He hoped he would not have to use any of them. Instead, he would attempt to use an incisive mind.

The victim's uniform seemed genuine enough, but exhibited no unusual marks or stains that might reveal its journey between abduction and exhibition. Indeed, it was in remarkably good condition considering how long most constables waited before cleaning their official garments. The shoes also were unremarkable and showed no abnormal wear on the heels or sides that might have proved the fellow was dragged while unconscious. A deduction, then: PC Taylor went uncomplainingly to his end because he was either surprised or because he knew the man who took him?

Mr Williamson removed the fellow's police helmet and felt around the scull for any sign of damage, of which there was none. Nor had the hands been lacerated in an attempt to fight off an attacker. If there was a fatal injury to be found, it was likely to be under the uniform. And since the body was evidently frozen into its position by some rigid internal structures, the clothing would have to be cut from it with surgeon's scissors.

Within ten minutes, the clothes had been removed, and, as suspected, closer examination showed that the upper garments had necessarily been sewn back on to the body after its positioning. The seams were all but invisible from the outside and could be detected only by looking at the linings. No further evidence, however, presented itself and the body now stood quite naked on its wooden plinth: a humiliating parody of a man stripped not only of garments but also of dignity and soul. Here was Man in his basest, his most mortal state – nothing more than a dermal bag bereft of flesh and feeling. Mr Williamson hung his head and found himself unable to pray for the mocking effigy before him. Was this God's image? Was this man saved?

He forced himself to continue the examination and soon discerned how the operation must have been effected. The incision that stretched from the pubis to where the collar bones met had been neatly sutured closed, but there were no other obvious cuts on the body. The only logical conclusion was therefore that this initial opening had been to allow the entire hide to be peeled from PC Taylor as a stocking is peeled from a leg. Presumably, the hip and shoulder joints would have been necessarily dislocated and certain other cuts made to remove the skin where it formed orifices, but a taxidermist could be consulted later to confirm such details.

The question remained: how did the constable die? The only visible wound was the large incision itself, which suggested two likely causes of death. Either PC Taylor was rendered insensible through the ingestion of some poison, or his cause of death was having his skin removed and his organs replaced with stuffing. Mr Williamson hoped it was the former, though forensic proof would likely be impossible without the contaminated viscera. Certainly, no smell of chloroform remained about the mouth.

He sighed at the realisation he had been trying not to make. If the body were to reveal anything at all about its murderer, the evidence would probably be inside it: in the stuffing materials used, in the chemicals applied, in the wood or wire holding the limbs in place and in the particular techniques of the taxidermist in question. These were the clues that might bring them closer to a solution.

With a heavy heart, Mr Williamson took a hooked blade from the surgeon's case and began to cut away the stitches that ran down the chest.

Noah brushed his hands down his thighs to rid them of the gritty grime accumulated during his climb up the back of the warehouse. Having already ascended two other buildings in this manner, he was quite smeared with filth and sweatily unkempt with the efforts of his search.

Even before beginning this latest examination, however, he saw that this was very likely the right place, for a set of recent footsteps was clearly visible through the carpet of soot, smuts and pigeon carcases atop the flat rooftop. Perhaps the rain of the other night had liquefied the surface into a kind of carbonaceous mud that had simultaneously preserved the prints and fixed their time. He tried to recall: had it not stopped raining while he had been with Mr Williamson at St Bride's, shortly before the fire at Blackfriars had started? If someone had been on the roof earlier in the day, their footsteps would likely have been erased by the downpour.

He followed the shoeprints towards the lip of the roof and looked across the Thames to see the dark smudge of his own home directly opposite. If there had been some kind of launching frame here, it was now gone . . . but the imprints in the dirt showed where it had stood, its four widely-spaced feet suggesting something of sturdiness and weight. Nor were these the only clue.

There was also a single sodden Lucifer match lying on the stone parapet. Whoever had lit the fuse on the rocket must have inadvertently dropped it here as they stood back for the eruption. Or had it been less simple than that? Noah took the brittle black splinter delicately between thumb and forefinger. It had burned along its entire length as if held until the last possible moment. Surely if had been merely dropped against a wet surface it would have been only partly consumed?

He sniffed at the match's familiar sulphurous tang and again felt that irrational sense of unease. The preponderance and positioning of the footprints hereabouts suggested that whoever had fired the rocket had also lingered for some time afterwards to watch the resulting blaze. Perhaps they had been observing at the very moment Noah had been standing on the opposite wharf watching his possessions destroyed.

One thing was certain: somebody had gone to a great deal of trouble to start the fire. They had entered the empty house and prepared it for burning, fashioned an explosive rocket and calculated its angle, built a launch frame and somehow carried it to this rooftop – and all of this without any discernible benefit to themselves. Nothing seemed to have been stolen. No secret had been uncovered. The only result was to make Noah and Benjamin homeless: homeless and more exposed to the ire of one who wished them ill? So it seemed.

Anger was building inside Noah – the kind of anger that he not felt for over a year: a festering, taunting anger whose only relief was revenge. He turned and strode back to where he had ascended the wall. Mr Williamson's house had also to be examined.

PC Taylor was no more. At least, his recognisable effigy was now reduced to so many inanimate parts: the dangling flaps of skin, the chopped flax wadding, the twirled wire that had held his limbs in position, and the stained pine beam that had stood in place of a rigid spine. The eye sockets now gaped empty, offering only wisps of the cotton that had held their sightless orbs in place. The face itself had become shrunken and drawn as its stuffing had been gradually removed. No Prometheus would ever make this constable whole again.

But now there were possible clues to follow. The enamel eyes might be traced; the particular unguents used to preserve the skin might be identified; the methodology of the process might be examined to pinpoint exactly who could have performed the grisly operation. Then, of course, there would be further questions to ask about the locations of abduction and exhibition and the previous cases of PC Taylor.

Mr Williamson bent to retrieve a pair of surgical scissors, and something caught his attention. The rather yellowed fingernails of the constable's right hand were right before his eyes, and there appeared to be some pale substance trapped under two fingers.

Using the end of one scissor blade, he scraped out the soft matter and held it beneath his nose. The smell was mild – almost neutral – and yet it was reminiscent of something familiar. He took the substance between thumb and forefinger, squeezed it and smelled again. If he was not mistaken, it had all the identifying features of beeswax.

TEN

Mr Cullen walked purposefully along Dean-street, trying not to fall into the rhythmic gait of the beat policeman he had so recently been. It was something Noah had warned him against, and Mr Cullen was assiduous in following any advice either Noah or Mr Williamson had to give on the investigative arts. That they had allowed him to conduct this element of the case alone was clearly something of which to be proud – provided he could pursue his duty without discovery, disappointment or disgrace.

He paused at the corner with Tothill-street and glanced around for any sign of an observer, but the few people in this airy corner of Westminster seemed to be more concerned with their own business. The grand soot-smeared frontage of the hospital stood before him, its elaborate gothic entrance putting one in mind more of a cathedral or an exclusive club than a place for illness and death. Behind one of those windows, perhaps, was the illustrious Doctor Hammerton.

Mr Cullen took the central flight of stone steps and crossed the rather dim reception hall, whose unnerving hush and distinct smell of vinegar immediately caused in him that suspicion common to all hospital visitors: that one might fall ill merely by entering one. A severe-looking lady in a frilled cap glared at him from behind the marble-topped counter.

'Fever?' she said by way of a welcome, casting diagnostic eyes about his person.

'Excuse me? I . . .'

'You are perspiring and your face is suffused. The fever ward is to the left and up the staircase. First floor.'

'No . . . I have just walked here and this coat is rather warm . . .'

'Smallpox?'

'No, I am here to—'

'Bodily injury, then. The dressers' ward is to the left.'

'I am here to see Doctor Hammerton.'

'Then why didn't you say? There are people to cure and I can't be talking all day. Go to the end of the corridor there and take the stairs to the second floor. His name is on the door but I suspect you'll hear him.'

Mr Cullen thanked her and proceeded as advised, reflecting that neither Noah nor Mr Williamson would have tolerated such ill manners from a Cerberus in a frilled cap.

Despite hundreds of people being resident in the hospital's various wards, there was barely a figure to be seen in the shadowy corridors and stairwells. Occasionally, he would catch indistinct whispers carried through tiled passages and ventilation shafts, but the loudest sound remained his own obtrusive footsteps moving up through the building.

On reaching the second floor, however, he heard odder sound: a sort of dull thudding that seemed to be emanating from the corridor he was to visit. Mr Cullen walked as delicately as he could towards the door marked "Dr Hammerton" and listened. Again, there came a heavy, muffled blow from within – slightly different from the previous sounds, but evidently from the same place. He took a breath and knocked.

'Who is it?' came the cry from inside.

'Mr Cullen . . . that is, I come at the recommendation of Sir Richard—'

'O, yes. Come in, come in!'

Mr Cullen pushed open the door and started in alarm at what he saw. The doctor – his shirt sleeves rolled up and with exertion flushing his cheeks – was paused with his arm in the air and a long dagger in his hand. On a wooden bench before him was a human leg detached at the hip, naked and lacerated with many bloodless wounds.

'Close the door, Mr Cullen. I would rather the nurses did not see this.'

'What . . . what are you doing?'

'It is really fascinating … excuse me – will you take a seat? Yes, quite fascinating. The leg was retrieved from the Thames this very morning. No way to identify it, of course, unless somebody turns up at lost property for it, what? So the police let me keep it; they know I am always on the lookout for a fresh one, and this is really a prime specimen.'

'But … what are you doing?' Mr Cullen was glad to sit, but could not take his eyes from the knife and the leg.

'Well, do you see the knife?' The doctor plunged the weapon with considerable force into the calf of the leg. 'Now I am able to study the wound and make judgements on it so that I might recognize similar injuries in the course of my future work. It would be better to have a living limb, of course, but volunteers are scarce, what?'

'I …'

'I am sorry – did nobody explain to you that I am a forensic surgeon? It is my task to identify physical evidence of death or injury in matters of jurisprudence. You must forgive me my flippancy about the leg – I have ascertained that its unfortunate owner is a dark-haired gentleman of about five feet and seven inches in height and most likely with a sedentary job. I can tell the police nothing beyond that, so the limb is mine to experiment upon. A knife, a hammer, an axe, a piece of glass – each makes its own distinct mark, what?'

'I see.'

'But I will not bore you further with my studies. I understand there is a particular case you would like to discuss – one which may call upon my other area of interest. Allow me to wash my hands, but please do continue.'

'Well, I admit I am not sure where to begin. Sir Richard advised me to see you, and a fellow investigator remarked that you are a doctor of the criminal mind. I am afraid I have no evidence to show you – only information on a particular criminal.'

'That should be sufficient,' said doctor Hammerton, drying his hands. 'But I would not call myself a "doctor of the criminal mind" – that would imply a level of study I cannot boast in an area that is barely scientific. No – it is rather an intellectual challenge – or a game of logic if you prefer.'

'A game?'

'I am being flippant again. Forgive me. Think of it in this way: when I examine a body, I conduct a series of tests. These are visual, chymical, tactile, nasal *et cetera* by which means I establish how, where and when the injury occurred. But what of the "why"? Might not that avenue also be pursued with similar processes? The scene of the crime, the method of attack, the weapons used, the identity of the victim and the time of the incident – they all tell us something of the perpetrator, what?'

'I suppose that is true.'

'Of course it is true, Mr Cullen. My fellow physicians consider me eccentric in such studies, but I say the approach is wholly appropriate for a forensic surgeon. A crime is more than just a weapon and a victim, what? It is a tangled story that science may unravel – or, at least, philosophy.'

'Is it true that you have spoken with real murderers at Newgate?'

'It is an aspect of my work I do not like to advertise (can you imagine the newspaper headlines?), but I have indeed spoken with certain fellows in the condemned cells. How else can one understand the mind of the murderer? His motives may be far from rational – in fact, he may not know them himself – but he has motives all the same.'

'Are you not afraid?'

'Not at all! There are iron bars between criminal and I, and a turnkey remains close at all times. Besides, a man under sentence of death is a wounded dog who recognizes his end. But perhaps we can move on to your case. What is the crime, or the criminal, we are to consider? What clues has he left us?'

Mr Cullen straightened himself in the chair. 'Well, we suspect there are multiple bodies, but I will begin with the most recent: the stuffed corpse of a policeman left under a lamp at the corner of Carey-street and Clements-lane, Lincoln's-inn.'

'Taxidermied, you say? Most interesting, what? Was the figure life-like and well executed?'

'Extremely. It . . . he even had glass eyes. You could barely tell he was dead except by his unmoving state.'

'Yes, yes – it all follows. What of the pose? Was he lying, standing, sitting? And did he wear a uniform?'

'He was standing with his rattle raised as if to call for attention. In fact, his mouth was open. And yes, he wore a uniform. He was also fastened to a board to keep him upright.'

'Tell me, Mr Cullen – was the unfortunate constable from a different division than where he was found?'

'Why, yes! From Westminster. How did you know?'

'I did not, but the evidence suggests it. Consider what we know: the perpetrator in this case made no attempt to hide his crime. Rather, he actively exhibited it. The pose, the uniform, the illumination from the lamp – here is a proud criminal who wishes his work to be seen. Why? I suspect it is a statement of power and defiance. He is saying, "Look what I can do to your policemen. They are as ineffectual as puppets to me".

'And what of the fact that he was taken from another division?'

'I cannot be sure, but it would seem to indicate a certain degree of forethought and caution by dividing the investigation. Consider – it would be natural enough for the detectives to suspect their murderer of residing or working near either of the two places when in fact he most likely lives somewhere else entirely. He offers an "either/or" question to a "neither" solution. It is pure obfuscation and it makes for a very interesting character.'

'Interesting how? What kind of man is our perpetrator?' Mr Cullen took out a small notebook and poised his pencil ready to write.

'Well, he shows two faces to the world. On the one hand, he calls for attention with his conspicuous victim, while on the other he is cunning in hiding his location. Such a criminal is, of course, highly dangerous. I admit, however, that I cannot ascribe any particular significance to the discovery

106

point near Lincoln's-inn. The variables are too numerous. Were there any obvious injuries to the body?'

'It is being examined as we speak, but I saw none. Is this significant?'

'I suspect that you will find nothing as conspicuous as a crushed scull. If our murderer is concerned with presentation, he will not be so impatient to spoil his work with a wound. Chloroform or ether is the likely tool of a careful and well prepared killer – at least, the sort of fellow who might be adept at taxidermy. I have done a little myself on smaller mammals and the skin must be preserved as perfectly as possible. Tell me – were the other bodies you hinted at also found in a highly public manner?'

'Indeed, doctor. Do you recall the recent discoveries at the London Dock? The seamen in the barrels of rum and the ship-owner half-cooked in the furnace? We suspect it is the same fellow.'

'Ah, now that is very interesting, what? Here is a man with a strong sense for the dramatic, and yet his *modus operandi* is not precisely consistent. Were not the rum-soaked mariners clubbed on the head before their embarreling? I am sure I read as much in *the Times*. That differs from the undamaged corpse of your policemen, though it is possible that someone else committed the actual murder and your criminal merely conceived its exhibition. It is really a most fascinating conundrum: a killer who luxuriates in the visibility of his crimes but who is himself invisible. Have you considered that he might be a detective himself?'

'What? I am sure that is not the case,' said Mr Cullen.

'Do not be so certain. Who better to commit a crime than the man who would investigate it? It takes a special skill to leave a body so conspicuously – to leave so many apparent clues – and still not be caught.'

'Is it not important that the fellow has escaped capture for so long? I mean, even the most famous murderers were caught.'

'Well said, Mr Cullen. He is certainly atypical in that respect. Despite what you may read in the penny novels, the murderer is more often careless than methodical. Let me return to the idea of two faces. My feeling is that

107

your perpetrator is likely one of two things: he is either a person right before your eyes who you would never normally have cause to suspect, or he is a person you have never seen – indeed, a person who almost nobody has seen. The former may be a colleague, the latter almost a phantom. Which seems more likely?'

'I . . . I really could not say. Where would one begin to look for such a person? How might they reveal their character in other ways?'

'Another pertinent point. It goes without saying that your criminal is intelligent – not necessarily a university man, but one with a sharp mind all the same. He notices the finer details; he is always watching, waiting, thinking a few steps ahead. This is a man who is also prone to flashes of anger or violence, though his habitual temperament is probably calm because he knows that inadvertency could land him on the scaffold. Mmm, what else? Well, I would guess that he does not commonly associate with other criminals and that few know his true identity – perhaps just a handful of close cohorts. Secrecy is his weapon, you see, just as many of the more successful cracksmen or pickpockets seem to be respectable citizens. His outrageous shows are possible only because he remains in the darkness. Is any of this useful to you? I fear I am being rather imprecise.'

Mr Cullen hastily finished jotting the doctor's words into his notebook. 'Perhaps. I must discuss it with my colleagues.'

'Of course. I think I should also re-emphasize that this fellow you seek is a deeply dangerous one: not only violent, but also lacking in any sense of the morality or empathy common to a civilized man. To subject a fellow human to taxidermy or entomb him in a barrel is the work of a diseased imagination. I rather suspect that such a person has been raised from the earliest age without love or respect. He sees only his scheme and his advantage.'

'So he is evil?'

'Ah, perhaps a clergyman might say so, or a common newspaper. I am inclined to believe he is a victim: a victim of birth, of experience, of the city itself, which makes every one of us less human. It is no excuse, of course, and

108

this criminal should not be part of our society. But it is unfortunate. The man who kills and the man who is killed are fatefully bound by mutual misfortune, what?'

'I suppose so.' Mr Cullen made to write this latter comment, but seemed to think better of it.

'Fascinating business. Do you have any further questions? I would like to spend another hour with the leg if—'

'I . . . there is one final thing I would like to ask. It does not concern this case, but is more of . . . of a private matter related to the mind. I will be brief.'

'Well, do not be afraid to ask. The mysteries of the brain are endlessly engaging, what?'

'A gentleman of my acquaintance . . . a colleague . . . has of late become quite melancholic. His is an unfortunate story: his wife was murdered, he lost a respectable job, and now it appears he has been consorting with . . . well, a magdalene. He seems to value his life at such little cost. He is a proud man, formerly a moral man . . . I wonder if such a state might have a cure, or if there is something I might do to help him?'

'Ah, Mr Cullen. May I offer the view that you are a simple man? Your work, your meals, your acquaintances – these are sufficient for your happiness, what? Perhaps you have faith in your salvation. If you are not already married, you look forward to a day when a wife will bring you bliss.'

'Well, yes, I suppose that is all true and I am unashamed to admit it, but . . .'

'You are fortunate. Your colleague likely has a darker soul, or perhaps we might say a more restless mind. Happiness is not our due as humans; contentment is not our right. Men carry their prisons inside them. Some escape, others acclimatize, and a few remain incarcerated to their end. Is he a religious man?'

'I believe he attends church.'

'Well, that might explain it to a degree. Melancholy is often stirred by religious anxiety. One compares one's sin-soaked soul to the perfection of our Saviour and it opens a blackness of guilt and unworthiness inside us. Our animal instincts prove stronger than our faith, and so we continuously fail. It is the paradox of goodness that it feeds upon itself.'

'Is there nothing I can do to . . . to help him?'

'You might advocate atheism to him, what?'

'That does not seem . . . I mean . . .'

'I am being flippant again. In truth, you can do nothing more than provide him with company. Solitude will consume a man as surely as small doses of poison.'

'I see.'

'I hope I have been of some help to you, Mr Cullen. Do let me know if you capture the fellow you seek. It would be fascinating to interview him prior to his hanging. Close the door on your way out, will you?'

The two shook hands and Mr Cullen returned whence he had come, trying not to hear the renewed sound of fleshly thuds receding down the corridor. And as his footsteps echoed through the cold, vinegary halls, he found he had an inexplicable desire for a meat pie.

Even amidst the thronging carnival of the London streets – with their beggars, their vendors, their thieves and their ladies of pleasure – Benjamin was a man not to be ignored. With his formidable height, his muscular shoulders and his ominous galactic eyeball set off against a dark African hue, he would attract the attention of most, whether he chose to or not. Today, however, he had opted to exaggerate the effect somewhat by exhibiting the horrible gallows striations about his neck and by wearing his finest theatre-going attire of mirror-polished shoes, finely tailored black suit and a top hat at a quirky angle.

Closer inspection might also have shown the many coalesced scars across his knuckles, the facial damage of the prize ring, the long-healed wounds of a brutal youth in American slavery, and the knife tracks of an early manhood aboard the ocean-raking vessels – but on this day he was quite resplendent: a king among commoners.

Yet though many stared, nobody seemed to be following.

He had strolled Oxford-street, down Regent-street and along Piccadilly without any sense of a shadow. He had ambled the Strand and Fleet-street, made a circuit of St Paul's and loitered about also on Haymarket, giving every opportunity for someone to note his presence or telegraph it to others. But he had sensed nothing.

Nor, despite his eye, could he be accused of impaired visual acuity. As Noah was wont to do, Benjamin carried a small circular mirror in his palm, by which means he might innocently scratch a cheek or reach out for something while covertly looking behind, ahead or above. Every shop window was likewise a looking glass, every passing omnibus a glassy purview, every puddle an oracle to be consulted as he bent rather too frequently to adjust a shoe. After some hours of this, he was quite dizzy with refracted perspective.

It was on Holborn that he allowed himself to relax for a moment, standing quite unintentionally before an emporium specialising in mirrors of endless variety. Such an opportunity would not pass him by and he paused by a full-length dressing frame to admire the effect of his suit. A small adjustment to the hat, a flick of the trouser hem, a lapel unskewed, and he was once again pristine.

But something had caught his eye – something that had flickered silvery among the many-angled facets of the shop, repeated and reflected and made manifold in the multiple panes: a face he knew well, but one that should not be on Holborn.

Mr Williamson?

Benjamin turned to the street and stared about him. Had not the detective agreed to stay at the Fleet that day and to examine the body? It was hardly conceivable that he would be out alone without the knowledge of his colleagues . . . unless some emergency had forced him to seek aid. If that was the case, where was Mr Williamson going now?

Benjamin flashed his monocular gaze about the crowds for a sign of the detective's familiar bowlegged walk and slim shoulders, but there was no sign. It was not possible. Mere seconds had passed since the face had appeared in the looking glasses: the very likeness of Mr Williamson's pockmarked, lugubrious countenance set in perpetual reflection. Yet he was now quite vanished.

Perhaps it was time to return to the Fleet and make a report. Benjamin began to walk south, still scanning heads and faces for a sign of his colleague. And as he did so, there was a movement at the very edge of his vision – a quick jerk of action on his blind side that he would have missed had he not looked momentarily down at the mirrored palm for a rearward view.

He continued without giving any sign he had seen the pursuer, who had been somebody short: a boy. There had been a cap and, incongruously, an instant's glimpse of a dark school uniform.

Something itched in Benjamin's immediate memory: some nagging teleoglossal impression that flitted from cognition even as he chased it. Then the capture – had that same boy not been eating an apple on the corner of Bouverie-street? Had he not been leaning against a lamp at the end of Bread-street? In fact, the grubby lad had been with Benjamin for the last hour or two, always carefully on the periphery of sight and casually invisible as part of the streetscape. Only the jerky movement had finally given him away.

Benjamin walked on, trusting that his shadow was still following. At the corner of Castle-street, however, he took his opportunity to turn right and rapidly right again so that he could hide behind the jutting brickwork of a chimney flue.

Moments later, the boy appeared in all of his grimy splendour and Benjamin stepped silently behind him to wrap a sea-serpent arm around the dirty neck. But the young fellow reacted in a second and the bite of Sheffield steel sliced through the Negro's sleeve to lacerate his skin beneath.

Benjamin instinctively relaxed his grasp and the boy wriggled away, racing down the street with a whoop and an indistinct cat-call that sounded like, 'Ain't nobody gets the better o' Tobias Smalletts!'

Blood trickled into his palm and Benjamin palpated the cut on his forearm. He had had worse. Indeed, he could not help but smile at the boy's spirited pursuit and escape. No doubt Noah would also be interested to hear about the young fellow – and also about the curious sighting of Mr Williamson. It was time to return to the Fleet.

ELEVEN

The man who stepped from the wherry on to the viscous mud bank between Whitehall and Hungerford stairs was dressed entirely in black: some manner of tightly-fitting woollen cloth that seemed to absorb the darkness around it and render him a living shadow. He made not a sound as he stowed the oars, lashed the boat to a rotting pile and made his way across the mud to the coal wharf where Scotland Yard bordered the river.

It might have been a city enclosure of quaint retail activity during the day – its tailor, bootmaker, dressmaker and wine-seller drawing their custom from the larger streets around – but the yard was quite a different place in the evening when the offices and businesses had closed. Then, as a well of darkness insufficiently explored by gas, the only sign of life was the Rising Sun public house with its raucous din of four dozen grit-smeared coal-heavers spending their day's wages in a single chaotic session.

Remaining for a moment at the extremities of the yard, the black-clad man took a sack from his back and withdrew a pair of shoes, which he exchanged with the muddy ones on his feet. The latter then went into the river with a mild plop. Next from the sack came a tight woollen cap into which he pushed his long dark hair before bringing it down low over his forehead in a way that also covered his gold earring. The empty bag followed the shoes into the river and he was ready.

He seemed to move around the yard with the fluid silence of a cat, inconvenienced not a jot by the broken stone paving and the glittering dust of the coal merchant's. And, like a cat, he stayed close to the walls so that no light could cast him as a *silhouette*. If someone emerged in a billow of beery smoke from the Rising Sun, or if an impatient pedestrian walked through from Whitehall-place to Whitehall, he stopped – just another shadow – until they had passed.

Finally, patiently, he arrived at his goal: the rear of 4 Whitehall-place. Only a single upper-storey window was illuminated, the police office having closed at five-thirty. A solitary tree grew close beside the walls, and though it wore its winter branches naked, the trunk was of a sufficient thickness for him to step behind it so that his existence there was utterly blocked from almost every point in the yard. The window before him, he knew, was a ground-floor water closet.

With black-gloved hands, he withdrew a nail from a specially-sewn pocket and took a short-shaft hammer (its metal head smoke-blackened) from a loop at his belt. The tip of the nail was then positioned a half inch from the lower left corner of a pane and the hammer used to make a tiny crack: a mere silver spider in the glass. With the hammer stowed, he then pressed the nail tip against one slender leg of that spider, using just the requisite pressure to tease and trace the crack into a large arc of his choosing so that the pane was silently fractured in a neat oval.

Next, he used a similarly blackened blade to strip the withered putty from the frame until the pane was loose and could be levered outwards. Thereafter, it was merely a matter of reaching round to unlatch the window and clamber though, replacing the pane behind him with a few carefully-placed pieces of putty along the crack's interior. It would stand for a solid window in the darkness, and barely a noise had been made.

Inside the unlit water closet, he accustomed his ears to the silence and heard only echoing cistern drips. He unfolded a map inscribed on a silk handkerchief and oriented himself – a left turn into the corridor and then the second door on the right: the Lost Property Office, where he had an after-hours collection to make.

Intriguing as it was in daylight, that repository was quite fantastical in the dim half-light of a grimy midnight window. Umbrella handles offered curious avian heads, shelved hats formed a faceless audience, tethered canes sprouted as frozen foliage, while a line of coats on hooks formed a patient queue of limbless figures. The Italian was untouched by such impressions. Rather, he sought a large leather bag that had been "accidentally" left on a Westminster-bound omnibus some days previously – a bag of significant weight and contents, but which made no noise when hoisted.

As expected, the heavy bag had been left within a few feet of the door and he was able to unlatch it to ascertain that the contents were still what he required for the job. And he must have smiled to himself, reflecting that only in England, in London, could one rely on the honest clerk to receive one's cumbersome tools of criminality and thoughtfully transport them at no cost to the very scene of one's crime.

The cartographical handkerchief now indicated he should ascend a floor to the room marked "Newspaper Office".

Upstairs, the single illuminated window indicated that Sir Richard Mayne was still at work in his office. The desk was spread with a profusion of newspaper cuttings reflecting the spectrum of opinion upon "plain clothes" policing – from the matronly disdain of *the Times* to the more supportive (if less literate) rants of the notorious *London Monitor*. Like Thames sediment, it would all be stirred up when he faced the forthcoming Commons hearing.

He rubbed his eyes and leaned back in the chair. The hiss of the gas was the only impairment to the blessed silence of the hour. Standing, he walked stiff-legged to the window and saw his own pale reflection looking back at him in black glass whose rippling vitreous surface distorted his face into a liquescent play of light and shadow.

Then came a thud. Another. And another.

It sounded like a stonemason working with a chisel, but in some indistinct part of the building. Perhaps in a cellar or in an adjoining structure. Sir Richard found that he was holding his breath to distinguish the exact origin.

A further thud. Another. Three more in rapid succession.

He looked down into the yard and saw nothing suspicious, no sign of workmen or their lights. During the day, he would barely have registered such noises or considered them suspicious, but at this hour . . .

With a frown of commingled cogitation and concern, he walked over to the large portrait of Her Majesty and opened the ornate gilt frame on a pair of hinges as if it were a cupboard door. Behind the picture was a small cavity concealing a locked iron trap and some manner of winding mechanism featuring a curved arm with a wooden handle.

Sir Richard set to work with the handle, cranking it clockwise for a few moments until there was a clank in the vicinity of the iron trap. He then took a set of small keys from his breast pocket and unlocked the trap so that he might lift the iron lid to reveal a shaft beneath. This, in turn, contained another iron box which required another key. It was, all in all, an ingeniously secure contraption known as a "well safe": a conventional safe attached to a long chain and kept invisibly within a cavity beneath the very walls.

Having opened this box, he reached inside to withdraw its contents: a dark ledger of modest dimensions, and a smaller volume that might have been a personal diary. Evidently, both were still safely where he wanted them, so he replaced them, secured the locks and returned the items to their masonry depths.

The thudding of before had apparently ceased, so Sir Richard once more settled at his desk and took up his pen to continue his work. But the remembered noise would not let him rest.

In the Newspaper Office, the Italian watched as the safe descended on its chain to settle again in the rough aperture he had hacked out of the brickwork with his hammer and chisel. At his feet was a ragged yard of carpet (through which he had muffled the blows) and a set of locksmith's tools displayed in an open leather craftsman's roll. The Davy lamp beside him offered no threat of discovery from outside owing to the length of black damask he had laid across the bottom of the door.

As he waited to be sure that there would be no further movement of the safe, he pondered the significance of Sir Richard's presence in the building. It could be none other than the commissioner, since he was the only one with access to the shaft. Had he perhaps removed the contents in response to the hammering of before? If so, the Italian's choice was a stark one: return to the Tunnel without the prize, or ascend to the office and kill Sir Richard for it. And if the latter option were not selected, it was the Italian who would surely face extinction.

Silence continued, so he set to work on the lock, calling upon many months of tedious probing, dismantling and manipulating of Chubb's famously "unpickable" Detector Lock. Even when one knew the year of manufacture and the exact dimensions, the slightest fraction on an errant inch would bring down the self-locking mechanism and effectively render the safe a solid iron box. Accordingly, he proceeded with the care and delicacy of a boy pulling legs from a spider.

Time seized. Perspiration formed upon his brow. Each micrometric adjustment was timed to coincide with a hiatal breath, while each halation came through clenched teeth. Ten minutes passed. Twenty minutes. Thirty minutes. His fingers seemed to cramp with the rigidity of tension, and every infinitesimal click of pick in lock was the potential knell of failure.

Then a sound outside in the corridor.

His hands froze and sweat trickled beneath his woollen clothes. A shadow disturbed a single point of light through the key hole: watchman carrying a lamp?

He extracted the picks from the safe with agonisingly slow exactitude and quickly extinguished his lamp. His dagger was close at hand.

'Hello? Is anybody inside? I am sure I heard a banging noise.'

The voice was one of authority and breeding: Sir Richard Mayne.

The doorknob rattled, though the Italian had locked it from within and withdrawn the key . . .

Sir Richard removed his hand from the doorknob of the Newspaper Office. He did not have keys to all of the offices at Scotland Yard, though it was at least some minor consolation to find the door locked.

Even so, it seemed he had seen a faint light through the keyhole as he approached with a single candle in its holder. He bent to peer through the keyhole, but could barely make out any shapes among the windowless night within.

Feeling somewhat foolish, he next pressed his ear to the wood to finally rid himself of the vague suspicions that had been plaguing him for the last half an hour. If there was nothing to be heard, he would fetch his coat and go home . . .

The Italian had by this time crawled out of sight of the keyhole and worked his way around the journal-stacked desks – their every precarious pile a potential alarm – to pause kneeling behind the door. Was Sir Richard still there?

He pressed an ungilded ear to the wood and listened.

And thus they paused in an *obelus* of expectant silence: the killer and commissioner, head to head, breathless each side of the door, hearing only the unfathomable muteness of each other's thoughts – one just two inches from discovery, the other just two inches from death.

Mere seconds passed in that way, though it must have seemed minutes: a handful of heartbeats, four airless lungs, two invisible, inaudible presences straining to hear the rustle of clothes or crack of an ankle that would justify their fears. But each remained noiseless.

Sir Richard moved first, shaking his head at his own relentless caution and making his way back upstairs to the office with a mumbling that receded into the darkness.

For his part, the Italian let forth a breath loaded with the heat of relief and went back to his lamp with a renewed impetus for success.

Within another five minutes he would have the safe lock sprung, the contents stolen and the tools returned to the bag. Within another ten, he would replace the loose bricks with the gentlest of scrapes, sweep up the debris with his small hand-brush and pan, and return all to the carpenter's bag, which would itself be returned to the Lost Property Office – there to remain uncollected in perpetuity.

Thereafter, it was as simple as retracing his steps to the water closet, replacing the pane and making his way back across the yard to his wherry in time for a propitious tide.

It would have been a perfectly executed crime but for two minor mistakes.

The first was that, in his haste to leave, the Italian had forgotten to lock the door of the Newspaper Office behind him, so that Sir Richard would find it suddenly open when he passed by about fifteen minutes later to try the knob for a final time.

The second meant that, in his subsequent state of radically increased suspicion, the commissioner would spot a small patch of unswept brick dust on the skirting board below the large portrait of Queen Victoria that hung in the Newspaper Office.

By then, of course, it was far too late. Scotland Yard – the very centre of the Metropolitan Police and the Detective Force – had been robbed. And the items stolen could prove catastrophic to the very apparatus of justice and government.

TWELVE

Mr Newsome bent closer to examine the exposed muscle and glistening connective tissues of the figure before him. Bereft of skin, it provided a remarkable study in the minutiae of fibres, strands, vessels and unnameable cavities beneath every human form. He found himself at once repelled and compelled.

'*Ligamenta glottidis,*' said an elderly voice inflected with the faintest Germanic accent.

Mr Newsome looked up from the anatomical study in wax. 'Mr Schlöss?'

The diminutive gentleman in the brass-buttoned jacket and the half-moon spectacles made a little bow of introduction from the counter. 'The other models on that shelf are, of course the *nervi superficiales, osteo-sarcoma* of the lower jaw, and – an especially fine representation, is it not? – the *feminae partes obscenae.* Are you a medical practitioner?'

'I am a detective pursuing a case.'

'I see. Is it a case pertaining to anatomical models?'

'Perhaps. I was hoping you might tell me.'

Mr Newsome approached the shopkeeper and looked around the cramped space that appeared more like an old apothecary with its many drawers behind the counter and its ranks of shelves stocked with earthenware pots. It hardly seemed possible that the man could make a living from so rare and specialized a stock.

'I was informed that you sell artificial eyes,' said the inspector, finally.

'Indeed. I have the finest eyes in London, for purposes ophthalmological and aesthetic – provided for both human and ceroplastic requirements. Are you looking for something in particular? I can match colour and size to your living *oculus* . . . though I perceive you have no need of a replacement.'

'No. I am seeking identification on a particular specimen. I have it here.'

Mr Newsome withdrew the head from its hessian confines and rested it on the counter.

'Ah, an interesting piece of work,' said Mr Schlöss, pushing his spectacles into place for a more precise look.

'Have you seen the face before?'

'It is a real person? I would not have guessed from the dramatic skin texture.'

'I have reason to believe so. I have been unable to discern where it was made. Madame Tussaud's records are ambiguous on the matter, but they told me the eyes may have been purchased here. Do you think so?'

'Let me see . . . Well, they are certainly very fine quality: most likely French enamel. If I were able to extract one of the eyes from the head, I might find a maker's mark and be more sure.'

'You have my permission.'

Mr Schlöss reached inside the head and concentration showed upon his face as he groped for the back of an eyeball. He tipped the head so that it was facing the counter top, and then popped the orb out of the lifeless socket into his other palm. In a moment, the likeness of Lucius Boyle had become even more ghoulish.

'Just as I thought,' said Mr Schlöss with a lens-glinting smile. 'Do you see the engraved mark there? It is a product of the Argus manufactory near Paris. I have a number of them in stock. Would you like to see?'

'I wish only to know if somebody bought the eyes in this head from your shop, and, if so, whom. Do you keep records of your sales? Perhaps they were a bespoke colour request.'

'No, no – the colour is standard "light grey". No flecks, you see? Anybody might come into the shop and buy them.'

'But surely you must recall such customers, Mr Schlöss. How many men come in to buy light grey eyes each week?'

'Ah, you would be surprized. Only last Thursday, a fellow came to collect forty seven pairs of assorted colours, and one odd piece.'

Mr Newsome glared at the shopkeeper. Was the benign old Teuton mocking him with such fantastical sales? Who could possibly need so many? But the real eyes beneath the half-moon glasses remained earnestly hospitable to interrogation.

'What of deliveries, Mr Schlöss? I feel sure your market is not confined to passing trade.'

'Well, of course I make deliveries – either by post or by boy. Wait a moment – here is the log . . .'

Mr Newsome leaned towards the open book. 'Look for deliveries of standard light grey eyes dating from around this time last year. Just small deliveries to individual customers . . . possibly to unnamed recipients or unusual addresses.'

Mr Schlöss traced a finger down the goods column, stopping at those entries detailing eyes and muttering to himself: 'No . . . these are green. Mmm . . . too large a delivery . . .'

'What about that one?' said Mr Newsome, jabbing a finger lower down the page. 'I cannot quite make out all the words,'

'Ah, yes. 'A pair of light-grey Argus standard. And the delivery address was . . . O – that is rather odd.'

'Your hand is quite illegible. What does it say?'

'The package was to be delivered to someone waiting on the stairs at the front of St Paul's. Very unusual. You know – I think I remember the day . . .'

'Who was the customer? Is there no name? What did the fellow look like?'

'I admit I have no idea. I received an anonymous letter containing half the money for the eyes and instructions to deliver them to St Paul's the very next day. The boy would receive the rest of the money there.'

'And what did the boy tell you?'

'Merely that he met the gentleman in question and made the exchange.'

'Was the customer disfigured in some way? Perhaps with his face disguised?'

'The boy said nothing of that sort and I had no reason to ask him. It was unusual, but payment was made. I cannot further question the boy, unfortunately, as he no longer works for me.'

'When? When did this occur? Let me see.' Mr Newsome took the sales log and turned it on the counter so he might read the entry more exactly. The date of the sale was one day after the balloon crash that had allegedly claimed the life of Lucius Boyle, and one day before the burial of that unnamed corpse at Portugal-street burial ground.

'Is it what you are looking for?' said Mr Schlöss.

'Perhaps. Do you still have the letter that you received from this customer?'

'Very probably, but I would need to find it in my records of last year. They are in boxes upstairs and I fear it would take some time.'

'Then do not let me delay you. I will wait here and intercept any customers who come in search of eyes or waxen organs.'

'I . . .' Mr Schlöss felt the full force of Mr Newsome's glare and opted to go quickly upstairs rather than debate the matter further.

The inspector's fingers drummed on the counter and he turned the facts over in his fevered mind. The over-cautious means of delivery, the coincidence of the dates, the colour of the eyes – it had to be Boyle.

Of course, the mystery of the wax head still remained unsolved. Madame Tussaud's ceroplasticians had apparently not made it (if their records were to be believed), but someone, somewhere in the city, had evidently been fashioning that grisly effigy on the date when Mr Schlöss's boy was walking up Ludgate-hill with a box of eyes in his pocket. All of the evidence so far pointed to that single conclusion.

His concentration stuttered at the sound of the shop bell and he looked up to see a uniformed constable filling the doorway.

'Excuse me, sir – are you Inspector Newsome?' said the fellow.

'Yes?'

'Sir – you are to come to Scotland Yard immediately on the orders of the commissioner, Sir Richard Mayne.'

'I know who the commissioner is . . . but how did you know where to look for me?'

'I was told to find you here, sir.'

'Told by whom . . . ?' Mr Newsome's keen intellect made connections it would rather not make.

'It is very urgent, sir. I was told to stress that the order is immediate.'

'I am in the middle of an investigation. I am waiting for the shopkeeper to provide me with important—'

'Yes, sir. I was told if you said that, I should make clear that this concerns "the ledger" and its security.'

'The ledger?' Mr Newsome paused to understand what it might mean – and his legs seemed to root themselves with leaden fear. 'Have you been at Scotland Yard this morning, constable?'

'Yes, sir. Terrible fuss there. They have closed part of the building – a water leak apparently.'

Mr Newsome interpreted the look of dubiety and understood well enough that it was no water leak. It was something immeasurably more serious than that.

'Let us take the next omnibus to Whitehall, constable.'

The atmosphere around 4 Whitehall-place engendered yet more dread in Mr Newsome's chest as he approached. Small groups of clerks and uniformed men who had apparently been turned out of their offices stood sharing heated gossip on and around the steps – a hum of conspiratorial muttering that became even more agitated when they saw this most notorious of detectives arrive at velocity.

He was escorted directly up through the building to Sir Richard's office, which presented a scene that did little to relieve the fears of his frustrating omnibus journey. The large portrait of Her Majesty was open on its hinges, while two locksmiths were bending over a dusty iron safe on the commissioner's desk. Sir Richard himself paced around them and, on seeing Mr Newsome enter, his look was one of commingled anger and trepidation.

'The men from Chubb have just this moment taken my personal safe from its shaft' said Sir Richard. 'The wall down in the Newspaper Office was broken through last night.'

'Do you mean to say that . . . that Scotland Yard has been robbed?' said Mr Newsome.

'Exactly that. Or, at least, the locksmiths are examining the safe now for signs of forcing or picking.' The commissioner's face seemed quite drained of colour.

'So we do not yet know if the . . . the contents are secure?'

'I looked in it myself just this evening and all was correct. However, I wanted you to be present as the box was opened. It may prove necessary to identify clues.'

Mr Newsome nodded and turned to the locksmiths. 'Gentlemen – what can you see?'

The older of the two held up a bulky magnet. 'See that, sir?'

'I see nothing but a magnet.'

'Precisely, sir. There are no metal fragments from the mechanism that would indicate amateur picking. Nor have we found any traces of gunpowder. It means the robber had a key, or that his technique was highly assured and his tools top quality.'

'Is there no damage to any part of the box? I can see none.'

'No external damage, sir. Nor are there any marks from a cracksman's "jack-in-the-box" forcing off the back plate. It is, after all, case-hardened wrought iron with fire-proof layers of mica. You might drop it from the roof and barely cause a scratch.'

'I understand your urge to defend the quality of your company's product, but it was clearly not dropped from the roof. Why not just open it?'

'Yes, sir – we were waiting for you to arrive.'

The locksmith held out his hand for Sir Richard's key and inserted it delicately into the lock. With a tense look to his colleague, he then turned the mechanism. Nothing happened.

'Aha!' said the locksmith with a look of palpable relief. 'The regulator latch has dropped.'

'Please do not make me ask what that means,' said Mr Newsome.

'This is one of our illustrious patent Detector locks, sir. If someone tries to pick it, or use the wrong key, it essentially locks itself so that nobody but the owner can open it with his reset key. Nobody has ever successfully picked one of these locks, though many have tried.'

Sir Richard passed the reset key to the locksmith, who used it to unlatch the hidden lever. He then used the first key again and opened the mechanism with a click that sounded entirely normal to the ears of all.

'I will leave the honour to you, Sir Richard,' said the locksmith, standing back so that the box could be opened.

Still looking profoundly uneasy, the commissioner opened the latch and reached within. And his face paled so that he might have been an unpainted wax figure, the dark eyes just scorch marks of horrible realisation.

'What? It is empty?' said Mr Newsome.

'It is not possible!' said the locksmith. 'The only way for this to happen would be if the robber had successfully picked the lock, taken the contents, relocked it and then purposefully tripped the latch. Even ignoring the remarkable difficulty of the procedure, why would he do something like that?'

'To humiliate us,' muttered Mr Newsome.

'But ... this model has never been picked – not in decades of production. We have tested it on the greatest cracksmen of our time,' said the locksmith in stupefied awe. 'It will be a disaster for sales.'

'Gentlemen – let us have an agreement, 'said Mr Newsome. 'You will say nothing of what you have seen or heard in this room, and we will say nothing about the security of your illustrious patent mechanism. We four are the only ones who know. Now – if you will leave Sir Richard and I alone, we have much to discuss.'

The locksmiths exchanged another glance and quickly bundled their tools so that they might leave the room as soon as possible. When the door banged behind them, commissioner and detective shared a wordless look of mutual discomfort.

'Do you understand what this means, inspector?' said Sir Richard, almost at a whisper.

'*Ahem* – let us try to remain calm and er ... examine the facts.'

'Remain *calm*, inspector? A ledger containing the immoral and depraved misadventures of London's important people has been stolen – from the very offices of Scotland Yard itself! "Remain calm", you say? There are judges and politicians listed in that poisonous tome; there are clergymen and noblemen listed alongside the tabulated details of their unnatural lechery at brothels across the city ... and you ask that we "remain calm"? I must say ... I must say that I hold *you* responsible, inspector.'

'*Me*? I ... I ...' Mr Newsome had now attained a comparable pallor to his superior.

'Yes – you. Was it not you who instigated this vile catalogue while acting under some distorted illusion of your role as a detective? Was it not you who had your men reporting these entirely private matters to you like schoolboys tattling to their housemaster? Was it not you, indeed, who have only recently been allowed back into the ranks of the Detective Force for your hubris? And now the ledger is stolen.'

'As you say, sir, I have paid my debt in uniform with the Thames Division. I ... I felt sure that you had destroyed the ledger. Why ... why did you keep it?'

'That is a rather moot point now, inspector. One might imagine that the office of the commissioner of the Metropolitan Police might be the safest place in the kingdom to store something, but apparently not.'

'Sir Richard ... who could have known of the ledger's existence, or of its location? Even *I* did not know where it was kept.'

'I dare not wonder. We must certainly investigate. Clearly, the aim is blackmail. Whoever owns that ledger has the power to wield terrifying influence, to destroy reputations and to control the very mechanisms of government. The worst thing is that we have little idea precisely who might be blackmailed first. I have not read the ledger in any detail, and I suspect that you cannot remember every entry, inspector.'

'The entrants are all ... highly significant people. That was, after all, the reason for their being documented. Perhaps we might contact some of them – anonymously, of course – and warm them that—'

'What? That a secret ledger of their grossest immoralities, compiled illicitly by a serving detective, has been stolen from Scotland Yard and that they should expect to be blackmailed at some time in the immediate future? Can you imagine what a stir that would create these days, when accusations of *espionage* are cast at every irregularity in police procedure?'

Sir Richard took his seat at the desk and glared at the blued-metal safe before him. He looked like a man who had not slept for days.

And Mr Newsome's keen investigative sense perceived something further. 'Sir Richard – was there anything else in the safe? Anything else that might have provoked the robbery.'

The commissioner gave but a heavy nod, his eyes still on the safe.

'The diary?'

Another nod, heavier still.

'Then it is proof that Lucius Boyle is alive! It was not the ledger that the robber sought, but the diary which contains incriminating evidence concerning the recent smuggling case. Evidently, the monster has discerned that I grow closer in my investigations and he has taken the boldest of steps in retrieving this major evidence of his recent crimes. If you had only allowed me to take it when I asked you—'

'Inspector! I think that your mania concerning Lucius Boyle has gone quite far enough. We have no way of knowing whether it was the diary or the ledger that was the goal of the robber. In either instance, the criminal has won more than he sought.'

'But do you not see the grander plan, sir? It *must* be Boyle.'

'I have had enough of this insanity and it will end now. The more pressing investigation is this robbery, so you will cease all other trivialities concerning your phantasy that Lucius Boyle is still alive and—'

'I have proof.'

Sir Richard sighed and hung his head.

'Sir – I ask only that you allow me to present my evidence. If it is not compelling, I will indeed forget the case as you demand. I will be brief.'

A tired nod and a wave of the hand from the commissioner: proceed.

'Very well. I have discovered from records here at Scotland Yard that the body recovered from the burned balloon was delivered to Joseph Brailsford & Sons funerary agents in Bell-yard, with instructions for it be buried at minimum cost at Portugal-street. Thus was the body despatched, in a plain deal box, to the burial ground. *However* – it did not arrive. Rather, the box received by the sextons was the rather grander one I showed you – the one containing the wax effigy and the bomb. *That* coffin had been ordered on the day after the balloon crash and delivered to a house which now – as then – stands untenanted. On the very same day as the expensive coffin was ordered, a shop on Holborn received an order for two light grey eyes: the same kind of eyes found in the effigy, the same colour eyes of Lucius Boyle himself. Again, the delivery was highly unusual, leaving no trace of identity . . .'

130

Sir Richard had revived somewhat from his slump and was now looking steadily at Mr Newsome, evidently trying to keep the growing interest from his face.

'But you will perhaps say to me, sir, that the body recovered from the balloon can have been none other than Lucius Boyle, that he was its only passenger. Well, I have quite coincidentally come into some knew intelligence regarding that evening at Vauxhall-gardens. I wonder if you are aware of a French investigator who is staying with us in the Foreign Detective's Office – one *monsieur* Bissonette?'

Sir Richard blinked, remembering his promise to Vidocq. 'Perhaps. Go on.'

'He is investigating the disappearance of a young man called Louis Chiveot who was last seen at Vauxhall-gardens. It seems this fellow Chiveot had been telling friends it was his great ambition to take a balloon trip from the gardens before he returned to France. Indeed, he was last seen in the vicinity of the tethered balloons in the moments prior to Lucius Boyle's escape and my pursuit of him. What if the Frenchman had climbed covertly into one of the baskets to satisfy his youthful curiosity? What if – when Boyle leapt into the balloon in his homicidal rage – he had rendered the fellow insensible or dead? When the balloon crashed, it would have taken a matter of seconds to drape the burning body over the basket in the knowledge that the flames would erase its true identity. We could never have guessed there was another in the basket because we were looking at it all the time through a telescope. In the minutes that the descending balloon passed out of our vision, Boyle must have made his escape – badly burned, assuredly, but alive.'

The fire crackled in the grate and the hissing gas seemed to increase in volume as Sir Richard studied the red-faced zeal of his inspector.

'And now there is the diary,' said Mr Newsome. 'We know that Boyle and his associates are skilled in the criminal arts. Is there anyone else who would even attempt to enter Scotland Yard to commit a robbery? Is there another criminal with his audacity? Does not all the evidence point to the obvious conclusion? All the evidence, and the fact that I have seen the man with my own eyes – seen him alive.'

Sir Richard, the barrister, weighed what he had heard: that agglomeration of coincidence, inference, supposition and dubious fact poured forth by the inspector. Before a judge, it would be unlikely to convince – but before a commissioner staring at an empty safe, it was compelling in its way. The decision he had already taken now had ever greater impetus and significance.

'Inspector Newsome – I am charging you – and you alone – with the solution to this crime of the stolen ledger. I have had the apparent route of the robber completely emptied of staff and closed for all further business on account of a "water leak". You will examine whatever evidence remains and you will pursue it until you reclaim or destroy that ledger. If, in the course of your investigation, you come upon Lucius Boyle, you will take him into custody.'

'Yes, sir!'

'And I need hardly stress the importance of secrecy. It is bad enough that the ledger is lost, but can you imagine the reaction if Noah Dyson should hear even a rumour of this? The man would wreak havoc in his search for Boyle.'

'Of course, Sir Richard. Might I enquire about the other body he found near the burial ground at Portugal-street? I maintain that the method is highly suggestive of Boyle.'

'No – that case is in other hands. I will inform you if I see any parallels.'

'Then might I ask if you are aware that the street patterers are shouting about it? I do not know who your investigators are, or who else has the details, but it would seem there is a leak. Perhaps somebody in the Newspaper Office? I know that they receive bulletins on what they are *not* to tell the press . . .'

'Yes, I have heard that the news is abroad. It is a matter to which I shall attend.'

'Indeed, sir . . . but I do have one further question.'

'Make it brief.'

'I have had the distinct impression recently that somebody has been following me, and today a constable knew exactly where to find me. There was no way anybody could have guessed my location.'

'That is not a question. Perhaps you will therefore allow me the pleasure of not answering directly. Trust is earned, not given blindly. Now – the evidence is waiting for you, inspector. It will not wait for long.'

'Yes, sir.'

THIRTEEN

From the fourth floor of the Fleet prison, twilight London was little more than what could be glimpsed above the walls: spires made ship's masts against a fading sky, the great breaching leviathan of St Paul's dome, chimneys giving out their final spouts, and impatient rockets bursting with faded colours in the dying daylight. Mr Williamson, alone in a cold cell, leaned his palms against a gritty lintel and watched the darkness come. Soon, the only indication of the city beyond the gaol would be its ceaseless groan.

'Are you coming down, George? Adam has made dinner.'

It was Noah's voice that came distorted through angular passages, stone stairs and railing gills. Somewhere downstairs was a healthy fire giving out light and heat and the sound of crackling wood. But with the smell of PC Taylor's chymical composites still upon his fingers, Mr Williamson could not feel hunger.

'It is a very fine piece of lamb,' added Mr Cullen through the prison's emptiness.

A moment's pause, then:

'Ben says he agrees,' shouted Noah.

And Mr Williamson smiled despite himself, imagining Benjamin's grease-glistening fingers spelling out his seemingly unassailable enthusiasm for all varieties of pleasure. Perhaps he would, after all, be persuaded to descend and join them for a cup of tea.

The kitchen was warm and the table full with laden crockery. Old Adam tottered bow-legged with a tray of steaming potatoes and nodded a sub-audible greeting to the latecomer.

'So, it appears we all have news to share,' said Noah, helping himself to the potatoes even before Adam could set them down.

Benjamin swirled a meat-clogged fork at his friend: 'You first.'

Noah waited for Adam to take his leave, closing the door behind him. 'Very well. As I suspected, it was arson. Not only that, but arson of a highly creative and effective form. It was started by a rocket – a hand-fashioned explosive rocket – fired from the opposite shore. Oakum and birch broom handles had been laid about the house to ensure a thorough blaze.'

'Wait – you mean to say that the house was broken into prior to the blaze?' said Mr Williamson, eyeing the succulent pink core of the lamb.

'Exactly that. Of course, any evidence of that was lost in the chaos. I have some pieces of the rocket, but they are burned almost beyond worth.'

'But why?' said Mr Cullen. 'Why would somebody do such a thing?'

'That is the question,' said Noah. 'I can think of no better reason than to cause us inconvenience and misery. And perhaps also for the spectacle of it. If – as we suspect – the perpetrator is he who has escaped capture after the smuggling case, this is exactly his *modus operandi* – to mock as he attacks.'

'What of my house?' said Mr Williamson.

'I am sorry, George – it is completely destroyed. I was able to find some minor evidence of oakum, but your home is reduced to a pile of ash.'

'Hmm. Hmm. Hmm.' Mr Williamson reached for a knife to cut some lamb.

'And yet we have an advantage of sorts,' said Noah. 'Our adversary is angry.'

'I cannot see any advantage in a man's anger when it results in the destruction of my home,' said Mr Williamson.

'Anger shows a loss of control. Perhaps he fears that we are too close to him.'

'How do you know he is angry?' said Mr Cullen. 'Apart from the fires, I mean.'

'I found a biblical reference burned into the wall of my house.'

Noah unfolded the charred Bible page and pushed it into the centre of the table. The verse was circled in black pencil:

20. Behold, mine anger and my fury shall be poured out upon this place, upon man and upon beast, and upon the trees and the field, and upon the fruit of the ground; and it shall burn and shall not be quenched.

The sound of cutlery stopped for a moment as each of the men read and digested the lines. If they all had the same thought, they did not voice it, for to think thus made no sense.

'All it really proves is that we are still targets of a criminal,' said Noah solemnly. 'Though, naturally, the choice of quote would seem to point to a literate man – a man whose sense of self-worth is such that he adopts the words of God as his own. I hate to admit as much, but we are safer for the time being here in the Fleet – at least until some further clue can be found to pick up the trail of this man. George – did the body of PC Taylor tell you anything?'

Mr Williamson grimaced. 'The cause of death remains unknown. Most likely the fellow was rendered insensible with some vapour and killed later after his skin had been peeled back. I rather suspect that he was simply bled dry prior to the operation. Any other course would likely contaminate the hide, though I admit I know little of the practices involved.'

'Was there any indication of a struggle?' said Noah.

'The clothes were perfectly intact and the hands unmarked. The only oddity was a tiny amount of beeswax beneath a fingernail.'

'That could be anything, of course – most likely from a candle,' said Noah. 'Although one might expect someone with a constable's income to buy tallow candles if he bought them at all.'

Mr Cullen made to raise his hand as if in a classroom, but thought better of it and simply spoke: 'What about the Masked Man?'

136

'What about him?' said Mr Williamson. 'He is a figure of fancy whom the common classes have adopted as their demon of the moment. Once it was Spring-Heeled Jack; now it is the Masked Man. No sober, respectable person has glimpsed him.'

'But I was thinking ...' ventured Mr Cullen, '... if there were such a fellow, his mask might be made of wax, might it not? Many of the masks sold in masquerade warehouses are wax. PC Taylor might have tried to tear the false face from his assailant.'

'Or helped a parlour maid to carry a box of candles down to her kitchen. Which seems the likelier?' said Mr Williamson.

'Well, we will bear your idea in mind, Mr Cullen,' said Noah. 'I myself have previously given little credence to those reports of a masked man, though recent events have made me reconsider. In the meantime, let us stay with what we know. Were there no other clues, George?'

'It is possible there are many, but I do not know how to read them: a white powder that may be chalk; silk twine to seal the incision; some manner of glue; a faintly aromatic balm on the inner skin; cotton and flax to pad the form; wire to bind the joints – no doubt it all tells a story if one is a taxidermist. It will be necessary to take samples to such a specialist and ask their advice. Only then, I believe, might we learn more about who might have done this.'

'Yes, but *why* was it done?' said Noah. 'Why, for example, was he moved from his beat in Westminster to Carey-street? What significance does that place have? And why this particular constable?'

Benjamin put down his fork to offer a gesticulatory oration.

'That is interesting, Ben,' mused Noah, chewing lamb.

'Hmm. Might it be shared with us?' said Mr Williamson after some seconds had passed.

'Ben wonders whether it is simply a warning of sorts: a demonstration that the police are powerless. In this case, the identity of the constable is irrelevant. It matters only that he is a serving policeman.'

'If that were the case, would not Oxford-street be a better place for display?' said Mr Williamson. 'Carey-street is hardly a populous location. Indeed, Sir Richard has been able to keep the details of the body almost a secret.'

'Then there must be something specific to the place of discovery,' said Noah. 'A message to somebody in particular, perhaps? Or something related to the past of the killer? I fear there is no way of knowing.'

Mr Cullen cleared his throat somewhat theatrically.

'Ah, yes – you have been consulting an expert, Mr Cullen,' said Noah with a wink to Mr Williamson. 'Will you tell us what you have learned?'

'Doctor Hammerton is a fascinating man, though somewhat flippant. His suggestion was that the location of the discovery was a ruse to direct the police either to Westminster or Lincoln's-inn – to provide a false choice between the two when in fact evidence might be found elsewhere.'

'There is a certain logic to the thought,' said Noah, pouring tea into his and Benjamin's mugs.

Ben sketched a digital thought, triangulating lines on a notional map: points of reference, equivalent distances.

'You might have a point, Ben,' said Mr Cullen, gleeful at his ability to understand. 'If the killer chose these two points as distractions, might they not exist in similar relation to the point they omit? The third point of the triangle?'

'That would put the area of focus roughly about Oxford-street if the triangle were equilateral,' said Noah.

'Hmm. I am suspicious of such mathematical detection,' said Mr Williamson. 'Should we not also consider that the choice of Carey-street was entirely coincidental? Or that the killer chose a less populous area purely to disguise his own identity? Oxford-street is all very well to advertise his work, but how could he possibly deposit the body without being seen?'

'It still does not explain why he chose that particular area,' said Noah. 'Why not near another burial ground? Do we even know that the burial ground is relevant at all? Perhaps there is a library or shop thereabouts that has significance. Without further evidence, we are merely flailing in the dark.'

'Well ... we might consider his pose and the nature of his exhibition,' said Mr Cullen.

'What of it?' said Mr Williamson.

'Dr Hammerton asked specifically about the positioning and uniform even before I told him. He said that the raised rattle, the clean uniform and the lamp above mark it as an exhibit in itself. Not so much a body as a piece of work. That is why there is also no obvious wound. The fellow is evidently proud of his taxidermy. After all, the figures at Madame Tussaud's do not simply stand with their arms by their sides.'

'That makes sense,' said Noah, 'though it does not necessarily help us.'

'Perhaps it does,' said Mr Williamson. 'Our murderer is meticulous. I looked inside that body and I found it to be the most careful, well executed work. Such efforts are accomplished without haste and without the thoughtless abandon common to most murderers. Our criminal respects the body of his victim as a perfect object.'

'Respect enough to kill a man only for his hide and bones?' said Noah. 'The killer is a lunatic, even if he is a calm one.'

'Doctor Hammerton said the fellow will be a keen observer with a sharp mind,' said Mr Cullen.

'That much is evident even to a fool,' said Mr Williamson.

'And ... the doctor also said the murderer might be a detective.'

The other men looked up from their food and at each other.

'That is, he said it was odd that so conspicuous a crime should yield no obvious clues,' added Mr Cullen. 'A detective would know what not to reveal.'

'An interesting thought,' said Noah after some moments of reflection. 'A serving policeman might also have useful information on the beat route of PC Taylor – where best to ambush him – as well as the beat routes around Carey-street.'

'Hmm. The idea is nonsense,' said Mr Williamson. 'Any common criminal also knows the beat of his local constable. A detective would not lower himself to such an outrage as this, for he is ethical by training and moral by inclination.'

Noah sought Mr Williamson's eyes, but found them averted.

'Well … doctor Hammerton also said that the fellow we seek is very dangerous,' said Mr Cullen. 'Very likely he has two distinct elements to his character: not only the calmness of which we have spoken, but also an uncontrolled rage during which he forgets his customary reserve. This could be his downfall.'

Ben leaned back in his chair, his plate wiped quite clean with a piece of bread, and offered a fluttering of palms to the table.

'I could not catch all of that,' said Mr Cullen.

'Ben says that we should consider more exactly whether or not the killer of PC Taylor is indeed the same who murdered those seamen and the ship-owner at London Dock,' said Noah. 'I admit that there are many similarities, but the corpses in those previous cases were clear warnings. Where is the warning here? What are we to understand from this taxidermied body that has no personal connection to any of us?'

'Unless the connection is that Sir Richard has asked us to investigate it?' said Mr Williamson, surprising even himself with the obtuse ramifications of the suggestion.

'You will have to explain that thought further, George' said Noah.

'Hmm. It seems absurd, I agree, but might not the criminal in question provide a crime so purposefully odd, so grimly unpleasant, that the commissioner could not risk giving it to the Detective Force for fear of a leak to the press? Naturally, such an idea also assumes that the murderer knows of our existence and our past collaborations with the Metropolitan Police. Could it, therefore, be some manner of lure?'

'But to what end?' said Noah. 'And depositing the body in a public place risks the very publicity you talk of avoiding.'

'Hmm. Hmm. I do not know. The whole incident is very perplexing. I can see no motive at all.'

'Is there, do you think, any possible connection between the fires and this body?' said Mr Cullen. 'I mean to say: without the fires, we would not be in need of sanctuary and the protection of Sir Richard, who in turn would not have the opportunity to ask our aid.'

Again, silence briefly gripped the kitchen. Then Benjamin slapped his thighs and began to laugh, expressing with a vortex of arms that their situation was as convoluted as could be.

'Ben is right, of course,' said Noah. 'So much supposition without evidence is futile. We need more information. Ben – will you tell the gentlemen what you told me?'

Benjamin signalled that Noah should relate the story for the sake of expedience.

'Very well – Ben spent some hours walking about London while we were engaged in our own activities. He was followed by a dirty street boy dressed in what appeared to be an old school uniform. When grabbed, the grubby little chap cut Ben's arm.'

Benjamin partially uncovered the bandaging beneath his sleeve in illustration.

'So *somebody* is following our progress,' continued Noah. 'I half expected that curious Italian of our recent experience to be the one, but I applaud the use of the boy as a shadow. A London boy is, after all, the best candidate for the job if he is trained. He knows the alleys and all the cuts; he knows that an adult seldom looks down to his level; he knows that there are sufficient numbers of his ilk to make him virtually anonymous.'

Another interjection from Benjamin.

'Ah yes – and we have a name. Evidently the fellow has a sufficiently elevated opinion of himself to speak in the third person: one Tobias Smalletts. Do you know the name?'

Misters Williamson and Cullen did not.

'And there is one other thing worth mentioning,' said Noah. 'Benjamin saw *you*, George, walking near Holborn.'

Mr Williamson blinked as if he had not quite heard. He stared, unspeaking, at Noah.

Mr Cullen looked nervously between the two.

'It is quite impossible, of course,' said Noah, 'but Ben is not one to say things unless he is absolutely certain of himself. He saw your face reflected in a mirror, George. And forgive me for saying, but it *is* a distinctive face.'

'Hmm. Hmm. If you are expecting me to defend myself, I have nothing at all to defend. I was here all day working on the body of PC Taylor, as you all know.'

'I do not doubt it for a moment,' said Noah. 'But I find it both unnerving and intriguing that Ben is so adamant in what he saw. I trust his single eye as I trust two of my own. I do not pretend to understand how it was possible – I only ask *why*.'

'It is said that every man has his double,' said Mr Cullen. 'There used to be a butcher in Stepney who was my very image when I was younger. Apart from his having one less finger, I mean.'

'I would hazard to guess there is not another like Ben,' said Noah with a smile.

The Negro lolled back in his chair, firelight playing over the tortured skin of his neck. He winked a dead eye at Mr Cullen and again broke into laughter, which the latter could not help but join.

'Mirth is all very well,' said Mr Williamson, 'but we are in gaol as the criminal walks free. I have no idea who is using my face, but I would very much like to discover him. I would also like to return to . . . to my life beyond these walls without fear of observation or death. What are we going to do to expedite that state of affairs?'

'We can only continue as we have started,' said Noah.

'Does this mean we are to accept Sir Richard's challenge?' said Mr Cullen.

'It would seem – would it not – that we already have,' said Mr Williamson. 'We might do well to assume for the time being that the body of PC Taylor is connected to our own fates in some inexplicable manner. If it proves otherwise, we can forget it.'

'There is a taxidermy emporium on Wych-street,' said Mr Cullen. 'I have never been inside, but the window display shows all manner of birds and mammals. I can go there and ask about the materials used for PC Taylor.'

'That is an excellent idea,' said Noah. 'For my own part, I am going to further examine the remains of the rocket I found for any clues it might yield. The pasteboard tubes are often made of old newspaper and it might be possible to discover at least a date of manufacture.'

Benjamin brandished his bandaged arm and unvoiced his intention to seek young Tobias Smalletts – either for a rematch, or to discover the lad's paymaster. It would be easier now he knew to look for the soiled uniform.

The three with new purpose now looked to Mr Williamson, who seemed preoccupied with some memory or thought of another place.

Noah winked at Benjamin. 'Ben – did you not say you wanted to watch the fireworks from the fourth floor? Perhaps you can take Mr Cullen with you.'

The two larger gentlemen understood immediately and left the table without further word, closing the door gently behind them. The fire blazed momentarily with the draft of their exit.

'That was not necessary,' said Mr Williamson. 'Am I frail old lady to be given bad news by the solicitous doctor?'

'We have had this conversation before, George. You will tell me only what you wish me to know, and I will not ask more than that. Have you anything to tell me?'

'Hmm. I have not.'

'I speak of the case and of our residence in the Fleet – not of your other . . . complications.'

'I discern, Noah, that it is *you* who have something you wish to say. You did not excuse the others for my benefit, whatever you may pretend. What is plaguing you?'

'Very well. Does not this case suggest to you certain things that cannot be? I have a creeping sense ... a familiar sense I have not had for a long time. The fires ... whoever started them *enjoyed* their spectacle. I found the footprints of him who fired the rocket. I found a match burned completely through. And that biblical quotation. And the way that the criminal in the smuggling case seemed to know so much about us, how particularly to hurt us ...'

'Say what you mean.'

'Lucius Boyle.'

'Hmm. Hmm. I have thought it myself. But he is dead. I saw his corpse; you saw his corpse. Even he could not cheat death. His continued existence is simply not possible. Perhaps ... perhaps someone wishes us to believe that he is still alive – purely to unnerve us. I believe the strategy is working.'

'I have also heard a rumour about Inspector Newsome, George.'

Mr Williamson's mouth turned down at the mention of his erstwhile superior and continued enemy. 'What of him?'

'They say he was conducting an exhumation on the same night PC Taylor was discovered. It was at Portugal-street: just a stone's throw from Carey-street. Does that not seem a colossal coincidence? And for whom was he digging? Information is scarce, even to me.'

'Hmm. Mr Newsome is a serpent at the heart of Justice. There is little of which he cannot be suspected. It would do us well to learn more about that when Sir Richard next pays a visit. Until then, you must calm your fears about Lucius Boyle. The man is a ghost who haunts us all. He must be exorcized.'

Noah merely stared at the table top.

There was combination of loud bangs outside and Mr Cullen's voice came down through the building:

'I say – you fellows below are missing a treat!'

Mr Williamson went to the window and twisted his neck to see the sky above the walls. A number of piercing white flames seemed to hang in the sky, casting an intense moonlight glow over the yard.

'They do not look like fireworks,' said Noah, joining Mr Williamson at the window. 'The look like the sort of flares used to light a battle.'

And at that moment, there came a tremendous battering at the gates to the rear yard.

Noah and Mr Williamson exchanged a glance. Had their sanctuary been discovered?

As they looked out of the window, the gates swung open and a dozen uniformed policemen entered at a trot, Sir Richard Mayne following briskly behind them in the stark light of the flares. On nearing the steps to the building, the policemen formed a line and Sir Richard addressed the *façade* with a stentorian voice.

'George Williamson! George Williamson!'

In equal measure bemused and uneasy, Mr Williamson walked with Noah down the corridor and to the yard doors, which they opened to face the line of uniforms that were blue-black shadows in the false lunar illumination.

'What is all this about?' said Noah to the commissioner.

Sir Richard looked down at his feet and then back at the two standing in the doorway. 'George Williamson – I am here to arrest you for the murder of one Charlotte Dawson of Golden-square.'

FOURTEEN

EXTRAORDINARY EVIDENCE OF MURDER ON OXFORD-STREET

The traffic of Oxford-street was thrown into chaos yesterday afternoon when, shortly after three o'clock, a goods wagon drew up before the business of Goodall's gentlemen's attire and unloaded an object covered with a sheet of white cotton or linen.

On depositing the item at the corner of Princes-street and Regent-street (facing south-east into the swirl of Oxford-circus), the fellow who had lifted the object took off at a run northwards along Princes-street while the wagon driver turned immediately down Regent-street, almost causing a collision with an omnibus.

Within moments, and owing to the large number of pedestrians at that time, a crowd had soon formed around the draped object, whose form suggested that of a figure. Amidst the common clamour of interest, it was asserted by some that the object must be a sculpture or perhaps a model intended for the display of men's clothing at the shop immediately contiguous.

Presently, the proprietor of that concern, Mr Goodall Esq. himself, exited his shop to investigate the great agglomeration of personages thereabouts and beheld the draped object, which he stated was no business of his and which might well be removed as it was causing his premises to be blocked to passing custom.

By this time, the proliferating multitudes had quite spilled into the road and were hindering traffic, at which point a constable arrived to ascertain the reason. Appraised by the crowd of the recent curious delivery, the constable stated that the object should be moved out of the public thoroughfare until ownership could be decided, whereupon he pulled the sheet from the figure (better to take hold of it) and revealed the full horror of what lay beneath.

It was the body of a young girl that – though it bore all the hallmarks of a crudely executed effigy – wore the unmistakable veracity of a human form, albeit one cruelly malformed by its unnatural handling. A number of ladies present fainted immediately away, and the great shout of disgust that went up from those nearest brought still more people to the spot so that the whole of Oxford-circus was brought to as complete a standstill as Newgate on the Monday morning of an execution.

With much difficulty owing to the impenetrable roadway, the body was finally re-covered and transferred by police carriage to the station-house of Division D, Hermitage-street, for further examination.

Such was the report that appeared in *the Times* that day: a specimen of the penny-a-liner's art quite without rival if I might be permitted a degree of immodesty at the quality of my own work. Not a word did the editor cut, though the piece is quite larded with the tools of my trade: the superfluous parentheses, the artful tautology, the quasi-relevant detail, the supernumerary polysyllable, the lexical progenesis of the introductory subordinate clause and, yes, the dashed interjection. I used them all, each word adding pennies and shillings to my pocket. Naturally, it was also beneficial to my cause that I had been there on Oxford-street that afternoon. Or, at least, that is what I had told the editor. Need a witness actually see a thing to express it?

On the following morning, however, as that article was being bought and read, I was indeed on hand to see the arrival of the prisoner George Williamson at Marylebone police court, within whose jurisdiction the body had been discovered. And the scene thereabouts was more chaotic even than the previous day's *mêlée* at Oxford-circus.

On Paradise-street, on High-street, on Paddington-street, and within the reverberating confines of Grotto-passage, perhaps five thousand people swelled and jostled for a sight of the one arrested for the girl's murder. Shops remained shuttered to avoid shattered windows, and constables whirled rattles madly to make space for morning traffic. The mood was aggressive, with shouts of "Hang him!" ringing out, and a great ominous muttering about the monster soon to arrive.

'What manner of man could do what he had done to that girl?' they conjectured. What motivation could there have been to so brutally disfigure her beauty as he had? To look upon the face of this tormentor was surely to look deep into the darkest recesses of a man who had passed beyond sin. Perhaps seven in ten members of the crowd were females dressed in their finest attire.

When the arched roof of the carriage finally came into sight along High-street, the crowd gave a great convulsion of clamorous energy that rippled through the thoroughfares around and behind the court. *He* was surely coming among them. They pressed towards the place, elbowing each other aside and standing taller lest they miss a glimpse of his face appearing at the carriage's curtained panes.

But the driver did not attempt to reach the door at Grotto-passage. Rather, he stopped before the magistrate's private entrance on High-street and a phalanx of uniformed constables arrived to clear a truncheon-enforced passage for the prisoner to enter the building without being torn, Actaeon-like, by the baying hundreds around him.

The carriage door opened. A figure descended quickly, accompanied by constables. There was a glimpse of pale, pock-marked skin beneath a top hat, slim shoulders bowed by the obloquy raining upon them, and the merest glimpse of dark eyes that seemed quite dead to the world. Was this a murderer?

Inside, the court was almost as cacophonous. Every gallery was stuffed, every corridor and aperture filled by those who would observe or merely hear the proceedings. An official pushed back a gaggle of bellicose reporters whose applications for seats in the press gallery had been rejected. I on the other hand – as an official representative of Scotland Yard's Newspaper Office – had suffered no such misfortune and a lesser journalist had been ejected amid a splutter of expletives for me to take his seat.

Presently, at a given signal, the doors were barred to further access and the members of the bench entered to take their seats: Lord Montague, Mr Haynes, the magistrate Mr Etherington, and two churchwardens of Marylebone parish. With these in place, a nod was given to the officer of the court and the handcuffed prisoner was led in flanked by two officers.

Phrenzied chatter erupted immediately and continued as Mr Williamson was taken to the dock, his eyes downcast and his wrists clasped before him. In the public gallery, Noah Dyson and Mr John Cullen looked on with combined pity and anger.

'This examination will exonerate him, just you see,' said Mr Cullen. 'Then all these jeering fools will hang their heads in shame that they suspected him.'

'I hope you are right,' said Noah, 'though it would seem somebody has gone to a great deal of effort to effect this arrest. We must sit through the examination – parody that it is –and attempt to see the hand of our adversary behind it.'

'And if they find him guilty?'

'I was once found guilty of a crime I had not committed and he saw to it that I did not remain in gaol. He paid a price for that, and I owe him a debt.'

Mr Cullen looked from Noah's granite expression to the stooped figure of Mr Williamson. The magistrate was standing and indicating that the first witness should be brought.

'Now we will see,' said Noah.

The first witness took the stand and the court was called to order. When relative quiet had been attained, the magistrate – a spindly fellow with parsimonious features – stood to address him.

Mr Etherington – State your name and what you are.

Witness – My name is John Edwards, linen-draper of Guildford-street, Southwark.

Mr Etherington – Did you see the body delivered on Oxford-street?

Witness: That is right.

149

Mr Etherington – Tell the court what you saw.

Witness – Well, the wagon rolls up – it looked like any goods wagon but without any company's markings – and one of the men on the driver's seat gets into the bed of the wagon and lifts down this thing covered in a sheet. He sets it down just so, like it's supposed to be in a special place, but then he doesn't get back in the wagon. He just runs off down Prince's street and the wagon itself moves off.

Mr Etherington – Did you see the faces of either of these two men?

Witness – Aye – that is, only the one who did the lifting. Quite pale, he was, and his skin was kind of pimpled like he'd had the pox. My father had the same so I recognized it.

Mr Etherington – Do you see that same face in the courtroom here?

Witness – Yes, sir. He is sitting there in the dock.

A low hubbub swelled within the room as the witness pointed at Mr Williamson.

Mr Etherington – Are you quite certain it is the same man?

Witness – Yes, sir. I saw him clear as day. I remember particular that he seemed to show no emotion at all, like he was delivering potatoes or grain.

Mr Etherington – Very well. You may stand down. Call the next witness.

Two more witnesses were then called from the Oxford-street crowd, each of whom pointed to Mr Williamson as the man they had seen unloading the body from the wagon. The next was a matronly lady of significant girth who needed to be helped on to the stand.

Mr Etherington - State your name and what you are.

Witness – I am Margaret Hale of Golden-square. I am a widow.

Mr Etherington – Have you ever seen the prisoner before today?

Witness – I have.

Mr Etherington – In what capacity?

Witness – He has been a frequent visitor to the apartment below mine in recent months. I have seen him through the curtains on many occasions, either waiting on the street or entering the building.

Mr Etherington – Do you know why the prisoner might have reason to visit that address?

Witness – A girl lived there. She had many ... gentlemen visitors at all times of the day. *Many* gentlemen if you understand my meaning. The noises they would make! I could not sleep!

A knowing laughter here animated the court and the magistrate was forced to raise his voice.

Mr Etherington – Limit your answers to answering my questions if you please. Do you happen to know the girl who lives below you?

Witness – I know her by sight, and I know that her name is Charlotte – though I have also heard her called Mary by some.

Mr Etherington – Thank you. I will have need of your testimony again in a moment, but now we will take the next witness.

As the portly Mrs Hale was aided back to the witness gallery, her place was taken by a much more attractive female dressed in black lace finery that set the massed audience muttering at her likely profession.

Mr Etherington – What is your name and profession?

Witness – My name is Emma Jones. I am ... a milliner's girl.

At the euphemism, the muttering here swelled in volume.

Mr Etherington – Describe your relationship to Charlotte Dawson if you will.

Witness – We were friends. Occasionally we would work together if she needed assistance ... if one of her gentlemen friends had need of a milliner's girl.

The muttering became a chattering: an admixture of laughter and confected shock.

Mr Etherington – Silence in the court! Did Charlotte ever mention the name of George Williamson to you as one of her gentlemen visiters?

Witness – O yes, sir. She was particularly fond of him. She said that they talked of many things together, that he was a kind and honest man.

In the dock, Mr Williamson stared fixedly at the ground, unwilling to reveal his face lest his emotions be cheapened by the voracity of those who would consume his privacy as entertainment.

Mr Etherington – And do you know how Mr Williamson responded to the many other gentlemen visiters that Charlotte received? Did he know of them?

Witness – O yes, sir. It was a point of argument between them, you see. Mr Williamson did not like her to see the other gentleman. He offered to make an honest woman of her, but she declined. She was too young and she liked her liberty.

In the public gallery, Noah looked down upon his friend and silently shook his head at the hollow figure that seemed to diminish ever further into shadow as the statements proceeded. Somebody would pay for this assault.

Mr Etherington – Do you mean to say that Mr Williamson offered to *marry* Charlotte and that she rejected him, even as she accepted many other men into her home?

Witness – Yes, sir. It was her way. She liked Mr Williamson very much, but she did not love him.

Mr Etherington – Thank-you, Miss Jones. Please remain on the stand; we will now bring some evidence before you.

The magistrate gave a signal and the court officers left briefly, returning a few moments later pushing a figure upon a wheeled base: the body of Charlotte.

She who had appeared so flawlessly pretty to Noah just a few days previously was now reduced to a sorry travesty of that graceful form. Her pale skin, which had evidently been removed and replaced, covered a face that was misshapen with aberrant swells and hollows where the padding had been inexpertly applied. The lips were twisted, one glass eye seemed a different level to its twin, and the overall pose was more reminiscent of a broken hag than a beautiful girl in the full bounty of youth.

The courtroom reacted with a combination of groans, shrieks and *sotto voce* horror. A hundred and more pairs of eyes moved between the figure and the man accused of the crime against her.

As for Mr Williamson, gazing upon the abomination laid before him, his own expression was one of pity and shock, nausea and white-faced anger. His eyes glistened but refused any further precipitation.

And as the massed congregation watched in unblinking amazement, one of Charlotte's eyes began to weep – a pale pink tear rolling down her ruined cheek to the corner of her ravaged mouth.

'O my ___!' came a female voice from the public gallery. 'It is the "bier right" – see how the victim weeps blood in the presence of her murderer! It is a sign!'

This outburst brought even greater unrest and the members of the bench looked to the officers to remove the agitated lady who had initiated the latest outcry. The magistrate stepped forward once more.

Mr Etherington – That is enough! Silence in the court room. We will have no more shouted superstitions from the public gallery. No mere bloody seeping will convict a man in this modern court of justice. It is evidence that we seek, not heathen fancy. May I draw the witness's attention to the exhibit? Miss Jones – is this the person of Charlotte Dawson as you knew her?

Witness – It . . . she is utterly spoiled. Her face . . .'

Mr Etherington – The victim has indeed been brutally handled, but is this the body of your friend?

Witness – Yes . . . yes. It is the image of her. And they are her clothes also.

Mr Etherington – Very well. The witness may stand down. There is one more piece of evidence to present to the court. Call Constable Straw of Division D.

The constable took the stand, his top hat under his arm and his hair hastily combed.

Mr Etherington – PC Straw – you were the first to come upon the body and you saw to its transportation to the station house, is that correct?

Witness – Yes, sir.

Mr Etherington – Did you make any search of the body?

Witness – Yes, sir – in order to find any clue to her identity.

Mr Etherington – And what did you find?

Witness – A letter, partly concealed in the folds of her clothing.

Mr Etherington – I will ask you to read that letter to the court.

PC Straw cleared his throat and held the piece of paper at a distance so that he might focus correctly upon it.

My dear Charlotte

I cannot bear you to sully yourself with those other men. They do not, and cannot, love you as I do. If you will not accept my offer of a more honest and righteous existence with me, I must take action. I cannot allow you to bring shame upon yourself any longer. Forgive me.

Forever yours,

George Williamson

The court again erupted into an animated state and the magistrate was once more forced to shout for quiet. An officer was then charged with taking the note to Mr Williamson in the dock.

Mr Etherington – For the records of the court, will the prisoner state whether the writing in the letter is his own?

Mr Williamson looked at the writing and seemed to slump. He mumbled something, but the words were lost in the still susurrations of the crowd.

Mr Etherington – Quiet in the court, please! Will the prisoner please repeat his statement.

The prisoner – Her death is my responsibility. I have brought this upon her. I have killed her.

And now a sudden eerie silence descended upon the room. The magistrate looked to the bench. The reporters scribbled madly at their duplicating pads. The audience feasted upon the sight of a genuine murderer in their midst.

'He does not know what he's saying,' said Noah to Mr Cullen. 'The innocent fool thinks now is the time for absolution – or rather for the purgatory he wishes upon himself.'

'We must do something. He cannot be gaoled for this,' said Mr Cullen.

Noah stood and called out to the magistrate: 'Mr Etherington – may I address the court?'

Mr Etherington – Who spoke there? Who are you?

Noah – My name is Mr Dyson. I represent the prisoner in legal matters. I apologize for my lateness . . . the crowds.

Mr Etherington – You are a barrister? I trust you understand that this is not a criminal court.

Noah – I am his counsel. May I speak for the benefit of the court record?

Mr Etherington – This is somewhat irregular, but . . . does the prisoner consent? I see that you have no other representation.

Mr Williamson gave the slightest nod, his head remaining low and his gaze again downwards.

Mr Etherington – Let the court record that the prisoner consents. Very well, Mr Dyson – we will hear your comments if they contribute to the facts of the case.

Noah – My client disputes the identity of the effigy identified as Charlotte.

Mr Etherington – We have dealt with this already. Her friend has identified her.

Noah – I beg your pardon, sir, but it has been identified as a likeness only; the witness remarked that the face is much changed. And I maintain that we may legitimately doubt that we are looking at an actual human form. Has it organs? Has it blood? Has it a heart or a brain? In short, can a man be accused of murder if the body brought in evidence is not a body at all but an effigy in wadded cotton?

Mr Etherington – It is not the purpose of this court to try the prisoner – only to discern if there is sufficient evidence to proceed to trial.

Noah – Indeed, and that is why I would like to suggest that the court remands the prisoner until such time that the figure can be forensically proved to be the girl named Charlotte Dawson.

The magistrate paused here before turning to confer in hurried whispers with the members of the bench. As he did so, the audience had once again begun to rumble with comment.

Mr Etherington – It is the decision of this court that the prisoner will be remanded in the cells on the premises until eight o'clock tomorrow morning so that the identity of the body can be medically verified. Officers – please see that the room is cleared.

Noah sat heavily back into his seat.

'Well done!' said Mr Cullen.

'We have very little time to act. It almost certainly *is* her body and it will be easily proved. We need to make arrangements before tomorrow, for we will never save him if they move him to Newgate in anticipation of the next Criminal Court sessions.'

'What do you have in mind, Noah?'

'Something quick and something drastic. Listen . . .'

And as the scores of people flooded from Marylebone police court to spread the news of what they had heard and seen, I, too, set about my business of transmitting the story by newsprint, penny-broadsheet, paltry poem and popular song. It was a murder – no matter who the criminal – and therefore an opportunity for making money.

No doubt I would write a sanitary version of events for my temporary employers at Scotland Yard (ex-detective brings shame on the force *etc.*), but it would be the popular press, as always, for whom I would produce my best work. Every gruesome detail, every sordid allusion, every vicarious emotion and *faux*-guilty glimpse – I would report them all in language as rich as a Fortnum & Mason fruit pudding. And what I had not seen, I would make up.

FIFTEEN

Noah emerged from the public door in Grotto-passage amongst the noisy outpouring of contentedly scandalized people. Reporters who had been unable to gain access accosted the opinionated for second-hand stories, while the constables of Division D laboured to clear the streets so that normal business might resume.

The pressure of time quickened Noah's heart and he looked about the squalid passage for a sense of its possibilities. It was a poor quarter of the city, its buildings blackened, streets unswept and the whole of it permeated that day with the stench of the nearby burial ground, but his eye was drawn towards a faded wooden board just a few yards from where he stood: Paradise Juvenile Refuge. And an idea sprang fully formed to his mind.

A smell of dusty wood and damp masonry greeted him inside, though there was no guardian or warden to block his way. The only indication of life was an arrhythmic percussion tap-chattering through the ceiling beams – a sound that he recognized immediately from his own time as a parentless pirate of the street. So, too, did the musty, suffocating atmosphere evoke memories of forced scripture, of beatings and the adult hypocrisy of gentlemen blind with their own righteousness. It had been a lifetime ago, before he had seen the world, yet he carried it still.

Shaking off such traitorous thoughts, he took the twisting wooden staircase to the first floor and passed along a corridor to where he knew he would find the workroom. There, in that wide, bare space, sat perhaps forty boys at ranks of workbenches, applying themselves to the ceaseless labour of whatever the mercantile benefactors had set them. For some, it was wooden toys they would never own, for others it was hessian sacks to be sewn, and for the rest it appeared to be the finger-wracking work of weaving fishing nets.

The youngest of them might have been eleven and the oldest seventeen, all with the look of urgent emaciation and faded vigour.

They all looked up from their toil to see the stranger in the doorway. And in an instant, Noah again saw his younger self in their eager eyes – that boyish willingness for adventure no matter how unpleasant life may be.

'Where is your master?' he said to the room.

The boys looked at each other and Noah discerned that one boy in particular was receiving more looks than most: their leader. He was a pale, wiry thing with newly shorn hair and a sheen of uncomfortable cleanliness.

'You there,' said Noah to the lad. 'What is your name?

'Roger. I once saw a man killed.'

'Is that right? Speak for your fellows, Roger: is there no warden on duty here?'

'Old Warburton – 'e went to watch the prisoner at Marlybone. Prob'ly in the pub now.'

The other boys snickered at Roger's familiarity with Mr Warburton's name and Noah knew that he had found the right boy for his job.

'Who here knows the name of Napoleon?' said Noah.

Some hands were raised among the older boys, then emulated by the younger ones.

'Was a Frenchy king,' announced Roger with evident pride at his education.

'That is near enough. He was also a soldier and tactician: a leader of men. Is that you, Roger?'

'Ain't no Frenchy, me. Might be a "tack tishan" if it's a good thing.'

'I wonder if any of you has ever had a problem with a policeman? Perhaps they moved you on, or gave you a kick, or reported you to the parochial authorities as a candidate for the workhouse?'

An affirmative chatter went up from the entire room, work-worn fingers being pointed to bodily parts thus assaulted.

'How would you like the chance to strike back at the bluebottles? There is an adventure afoot and I need some soldiers. But you will have to defy your Mr Warburton. Rules will need to be broken. Are you game?'

The chatter became a clamour, but looks were still being cast at Roger by some of the younger boys.

'Will there be killin'?' said the lad in a tone that suggested he would participate whatever the answer.

'No killing. But a few constabulary ears might be boxed and the occasional shin kicked.'

'Then we're the soldiers for yer game,' said Roger. 'Rules don't mean nothin' to me. I once saw a gent killed.'

A cheer reverberated around the workroom.

'Very well,' said Noah, 'listen carefully and I will lay out the plan before your Mr Warburton returns. The action will proceed like this . . .'

Mr Cullen, meanwhile, had left *via* the High-street door with the details of the court's examination – and the humiliation of his mentor – buzzing in his mind. Clearly, the charge of murder was ludicrous to anyone who knew Mr Williamson, and yet the evidence cast him in a distinctly unfavourable light. Had that letter found on Charlotte's person been real? And could it really have been Mr Williamson that Ben had seen earlier that week so near to Oxford-street? Suddenly, that most predictable of men was offering surprises.

One thing, however, remained certain: Noah's insistence that more evidence be sought in order to exculpate their friend. With the revelation of Charlotte's crudely stuffed body, the lamentable figure of PC Taylor now had even greater significance, and whoever had fashioned that grim representation had to be found with all haste. Noah's instructions had been clear.

So it was that, after a hurried and covert return to the Fleet for evidence, Mr Cullen stood with some trepidation at the gravity of his task before the window of Baldock's Taxidermy Emporium on Wych-street. And even under the circumstances of his visit, he could not deny the wondrous oddity of the display there arranged. Hawks, owls, a parrot, ravens and the more common small birds of London were perched on twigs and branches against a painted backdrop of sky, while a carpet of moss below was home to such specimens as mice, a cat, a fox and some manner of sleek riverside mammal whose name or function was alien to this devoutly urban observer. Two dozen eyes of varying colour and size stared back at him with a vitreous vividness that quite unnerved, as if *he* were the exhibit and they the observers of the animated world.

With the ringing of the shop bell behind him, Mr Cullen saw that the interior was even more populous with suspended life. Here, though, were more exotic varieties collected from distant regions of desert and forest. A snake as thick as his arm was coiled immobile around a post, a large lizard squatted on a high shelf, and a fish with an enormous gaping mouth of triangular teeth hung from the roof beams on thin wire.

An elderly gentleman wearing a virulent scarlet waistcoat beneath a leather apron appeared behind the counter. His shirt sleeves were rolled back and there was a triangular needle in one hand. Seeing the direction of Mr Cullen's gaze, he nodded towards the fish: 'It was caught in the Channel, if you believe it. The fishermen brought it to me from Brighton, but would not pay when the time came to collect.'

'It is indeed a fearful thing,' said Mr Cullen.

'I suspect you are here about that girl on Oxford-street are you?' said the shopkeeper warily.

'Well, yes. What do you know about it?'

'Nothing whatsoever, but I knew as soon as I read the newspaper this morning that I would get visiters one way or the other. Are you a reporter? I have nothing to say because I have not seen the body.'

'I am not a reporter, but I do have questions about your particular art.'

'Are you a practitioner?' said the shopkeeper, doubtfully looking at his customer's great sausage fingers.

'I am not, but I . . . I recently came upon a piece of work that had been quite mauled to pieces by my dog and I am curious enough to want to know about the materials used in its manufacture. Perhaps it is foolish – and I do not wish to waste your time – but the process does fascinate me. For example, I see you have a triangular needle in your hand.'

The shopkeeper seemed to weigh the truth of what he had heard, noting that the fellow standing before him hardly seemed capable of guile. 'Well, I am always willing to share my art with a gentleman who yearns for knowledge. So few people understand the importance of it, you see. It is how anatomy was discovered. And, yes, this is actually a glover's needle, but it serves my purposes better than a surgeon's. What have you in your bag?'

Mr Cullen lifted some pieces of the unmortal remains of PC Taylor on to the counter. 'I would be most grateful if you could describe these items to me and explain their function.'

'Indeed, indeed. Well, this first is common enough: chopped flax to fill the cavities where muscles and organs are removed.'

'And the curious smell?'

'Ah, now that is more specialized.' The shopkeeper held the yellow-stained wad to his face and inhaled. 'Yes – I think you have a combination of preparations absorbed in this piece. There is a whiff of Bullock's preservative powder (it is camphor and musk you can smell), which is used to anoint and preserve the inside of the skin. And I suspect also some manner of glue using gum Arabic and hair starch: to hold the wadding in place.'

'Are these solutions quite common?'

'Indeed. I use them myself. Bécour's arsenical soap is also in widespread use, but I find the higher quantity of arsenic somewhat worrying.'

'What about these strands of twine?'

'Well, you have two sorts here. The pack thread is sturdy stuff used for binding joints, or wire to joints. It is coarse stuff unsuited to presentation, so that is why we use the other silk thread to sew the incisions afterwards. Some use cotton, but silk is preferred.'

'This is most fascinating. What about this wire?'

The shopkeeper twirled the coiled metal in his hands and looked at Mr Cullen with fresh suspicion. 'You say your dog attacked this specimen – but what animal was represented?'

'It was . . . a cat. I suppose that was why he went for it as he did.'

'You are lying to me now. The skin is of no feline, while the thickness of this wire suggests a joint – and therefore an animal – of much greater size and weight than a cat. Moreover, the diameter of the coil implies a bone almost as thick as a human bone. Do you, I wonder, even have a dog?'

'I . . . I will be frank. These materials come from the body of a man, a policeman, killed and left on the street. I am an investigator following the evidence of that crime, but I . . . I am not at liberty to reveal its fullest details.'

'I have heard rumours about that crime, but I thought they were the fancies of the common classes, like this so-called "masked man". What is your name? And why did you not introduce yourself as a police detective?'

'I am John Cullen, and the case is not a public one for reasons you might imagine. I need to discern from the remains who might have committed this crime and it seems you are the gentleman to help me do so. In fact, I will ask you outright: do you know of anyone in your profession who could, or would, prepare a human for taxidermical purposes?'

'Am I a suspect in this crime?'

'There are but a few men practising your art . . .'

'In a commercial capacity, perhaps – but there are scores of gentlemen – medical students, collectors, landowners – who practise at home. If they did not, I could not make a living from the sale of materials. Furthermore, since I am clearly the first man to be approached in the investigation, I would be a foolish criminal indeed to prepare him according to my profession.'

'I suppose so. All I know, sir, is that a man has been killed and stuffed. It is a hideous thing and I wish to bring the murderer to justice. If you can help me – if you can tell who might do such a thing and how – I would be in your debt.'

The shopkeeper pursed his lips and looked from the face of Mr Cullen to the wire coil still in his hand. As if making a decision, he then came around the counter and locked the street door, turning a card that proclaimed the business closed for lunch.

'Come to the preparation room,' he said to Mr Cullen. 'Bring your bag.'

Together, they went behind the counter and down a cramped corridor to a space at the rear of the premises that was quite powerfully scented with the taxidermist's pharmacopeia of burned alum, musk, camphor, tallow soap, tanner's bark and the residual aroma of boiled bones. A large workbench was neatly arrayed with the tools of the art: knives, scissors, pliers, needles and the apothecary's tools of sieve, gas burner, mortar and pestle. The carcase of a terrier also lay open there, its legs splayed and its cavities filled partially with flax.

'What is this white powder all about?' said Mr Cullen.

'Chalk. It is used to absorb liquids during preparation. What you must understand is that the materials you have shown me are all common enough. The solutions are perhaps mixed to different strengths, but only a chymist might prove it. No – the only way to identify a particular hand is in the minutiae of the execution: the modelling, the cuts, the choice and positioning of eyes. It is, after all, a form of sculpture.'

'I suppose you are right.'

'Tell me, detective Cullen – what is it about the preservation of a human form that so appals you. Is it the spectre of death? I speak not of unlawful killing, but simply the fact of mortality. Or is it the preparation of the mortal form? I might put it, rather, as a different question: is putrescing in a coffin preferable to a more aesthetic suspension of this too mutable matter we call flesh?'

'I . . . I am afraid you have rather lost me . . .'

164

'Mmm. Perhaps I might offer you a cup of tea. I fear the smells of the workshop are not appealing to the average person. Please, come this way.'

The shopkeeper led Mr Cullen through another door into what was evidently the kitchen of his own home. A young lady was sitting at the table with her back to the two gentlemen.

'Mr Cullen – may I introduce you to my wife Helen,' said the shopkeeper.

'I am pleased to meet you, madam,' said Mr Cullen.

She did not answer, of course. Neither did she turn or show the slightest movement of breath.

'Helen passed away three years ago,' said the shopkeeper. 'And you need not worry yourself about the legality of what you see. She died naturally and was pronounced dead by a physician prior to any of my procedures. Nor have I infringed any public health strictures concerning her burial – the perishable parts rest in the ground.'

Mr Cullen stared incredulously at the perfection of the woman's form. Her face seemed to glow with youthful vitality; her eyes shone with flecked colour; her hair had a vibrant sheen to make his own look dull, and her very figure seemed to mock her immobility, as if merely holding her breath rather than stilled for eternity.

'She is beautiful, is she not?' said the shopkeeper reverently.

'It . . . she is quite remarkable. I would not be surprized to see her blink. Indeed, I feel . . .'

'You feel awkward speaking about her – as if she could hear you?'

'Yes, that is exactly it.'

'That is why I wanted you to meet her. She is the very ideal of the taxidermist's art. I trust I am not being immodest when I say that no other practitioner could render her as loyally as I have done. In this way, every figure is an expression of the artist's higher sensibilities. Judge the maker by the work, I say.'

'Then how exactly am I to tell the particular hand of a practitioner from his work alone?' said Mr Cullen, taking out a pencil and small notebook. 'You said something about cuts?'

'Indeed. Look here at Helen's lips, for example. They are detached from the jaws during preparation and the incision must be quite precise. On sewing them back, the greatest care must be taken in retaining a natural shape because the very slightest distortion will be multiplied a dozen-fold in the eyes of the beholder. It is the same with the eyelids – if they are damaged in the cutting, they will never be the same again.'

'So the finest specimens of the art can be judged by these signs?'

'Not only the quality, but often the identity of the artist. The spacing between stitches, the kind of thread, the pattern of folds or the direction of cuts – all are specific to an individual technique. It is rather like a man's handwriting in that sense. I am sure I can recognize the work of many customers.'

Mr Cullen reached into the bag of PC Taylor pieces and felt for the swatch of skin that Mr Williamson had excised: a pale scrap with black hairs still attached. A row of holes appeared along one edge where the main cut down the chest had been sewn. 'Do you recognize this work?'

'Mmm. Well, it is a rather a small sample. An eyelid or ear would have been better ... but I can tell you that the practitioner is highly accomplished. See how the holes are quite evenly spaced and made with a narrow needle? This is a man who takes a pride in the appearance of his work. The hide is well and evenly seasoned with preservative. But I cannot say I recognize the hand. If I could see the whole body ...'

'As I said, it is dismantled. Not by a dog, in truth, but by a fellow detective. How long would it take to prepare a human specimen of this kind?'

'It rather depends. Perhaps eight or ten hours if one were in a hurry, but one must remember that the skin is elastic and retains moisture. If too hastily handled, it will stretch and warp. I believe I took a week over Helen, constantly applying the powdered chalk and arsenical soap to preserve her beautiful skin.' The shopkeeper stroked the figure's head affectionately.

'I . . . yes, I see,' said a somewhat discombobulated Mr Cullen.

'If you would like me to examine the girl who was found, I might be able to identify the work. At the very least, I could say something of the artist.'

'It is a kind offer and we may indeed make that request.'

'There is perhaps something else I could tell you that might be pertinent to your case. Mr Cullen. I did think it faintly odd at the time, but today's newspaper has given me reason to ponder it in a different light.'

'O yes?' Mr Cullen readied his pencil.

'Well, a chap came into the shop just a couple of days ago and purchased a large quantity of materials. That is not strange in itself – many country gentlemen do as much when they are in town – but it was made strange because the fellow did not seem to know what he was buying. He had a list and followed it blindly. Still, it was a considerable order and I was happy to take his money.'

'I suppose that does seem a little odd,' said Mr Cullen.

'And he was wearing a mask.'

The pencil paused, scoring a line in the paper. 'Pardon me – did you say a mask?'

'Indeed – and a very fine one. Had he not spoken from behind it, or if I had seen him in the street, I might never have guessed. The texture and colouring were excellent.'

'What manner of mask? A carnival sort?'

'Not at all. It appeared to be the face of a normal gentleman, albeit with pox-scarred skin. I have known gentlemen with leprotic complaints or burns to wear such contrivances, so I did not mention it to him.'

'Did . . . did the gentleman give a name?'

'He paid in cash. But he introduced himself all the same: a Mr George Williamson . . . I say . . . are you all right, Mr Cullen? You appear quite pale.'

Benjamin watched from inside the moist smokiness of a coffee house as the gas lamps of Marylebone police court's entrance were extinguished. Three men then exited the High-street door and went their separate ways, leaving the building a sombre *façade* of unlit windows. It was time for him to play his part in Noah's grand scheme.

Hatless, and dressed all in black, he was an animated shadow whose ghostly eye seemed to move disembodied through the enabling darkness of Grotto-passage. It was a matter of moments to gain access, for, as with Scotland Yard, security was paradoxically minimal in a building housing the machinery of justice. What criminal would be foolish enough to seek illicit access to a courtroom?

Inside, he attuned himself to a sense of the building. The smell and heat of the masses seemed to remain, while floors and ceilings ticked irregularly in repose from the footfalls of hundreds. Light from streetlamps cast angular strips across walls and furniture.

But the silence was not complete. Someone else was in the building – perhaps someone with the same urgent mission as Benjamin. He held his breath and sought out the other with his ears, hearing footsteps whose softness was nevertheless betrayed by the creaking old boards of the court. A lock rattled and a hinge whined.

Benjamin kept to the sides of the corridor where the boards were firmest, passing wraithlike towards the sounds and realising as he went that they emanated from precisely the room he himself would visit. A thief, perhaps. Or a competitor for the same prize.

A shadow flickered through the room's open doorway and across the corridor: a suggestion of a head and a shoulder. Benjamin approached with suspended breath and tilted his head so that his good eye might glimpse the room's interior.

A snatched impression: tables and chairs stacked against the walls – a storeroom. Another monocular glimpse: the unnatural figure of Charlotte, her face ghastly in a beam of gaslight from the street. Another urgent stare: a thin man in black kneeling to unfold a dark sheet of canvas, presumably with which to wrap and steal the body

In the corridor, Benjamin felt for the dagger secured at his hip. Was this the Italian whom Noah had once fought – that mysterious accomplice they had encountered once before on the smuggling case? Now was the time for retribution.

Benjamin leapt into the room with a celerity surprising for his size . . . and found the intruder waiting for him with an upraised blade.

The Italian's stiletto sliced a vicious arc at Benjamin's face, but the Negro was ready and blocked it with his own weapon. Metal clinked, and Benjamin turned his evasive sweep into a lunge that passed a mere hair's breadth from the neck of his assailant. The match was now on, and both men knew what they faced.

They circled like fighters in the prize ring: one unspeaking, the other tongueless. Benjamin held his knife blade-up in the style of the martial mariner; the Italian's meanwhile was a downward claw in the Neapolitan manner. Their eyes burned unblinking into each other.

The Italian made a feint and darted forward to pierce Benjamin's chest, but the latter (having fought continentals) had anticipated the strategy and leaned back to slash his double-edged dagger across his assailant's forearm. There was an intake of breath as the Italian whipped his arm back to examine the slashed fabric.

And Benjamin took advantage of this moment's inattention to make his own advance, bringing the weapon in a sweeping upwards wheel from his own thigh so that it appeared in the Italian's vision only as it crossed his forehead in a silvered flash. His eyes bulged in surprize, and the blood began immediately to run down the bridge of his nose.

Thinking quickly, the wounded man pulled down his woollen hat to stanch the flow and made an impassioned lurch at Benjamin, bringing his stiletto down like a swooping hawk upon the softness behind a collar bone. But Benjamin was quicker, grasping the descending wrist left-handed and twisting it with such taurine power that the cords and joints within it crunched.

The Italian let out a strangled yelp, his knife arm now dangling limp and ruined. He transferred the blade to his other and scowled through the pain. He looked to the doorway and saw it blocked by Benjamin's breadth. The only escape was through him.

A bloody smile came to the Italian's face and he returned his knife to a sheath at his waist. When the hand reappeared, it was holding a pistol. Evidently survival was now more important than silence. Aiming the muzzle at Benjamin's heart, the Italian began to move around his adversary, hoping, perhaps, to steer him away from the doorway under the baleful eye of the gun.

But Benjamin did not move. Neither man wanted to leave without the prize of Charlotte's body. And yet, even as they *manoeuvred* in that terpsichorean tension, they must have reflected that only one of them had two effective arms to remove the body. To fire the pistol might kill Benjamin, but it could also bring constables and result in a failed mission for the already disabled murderer.

Understanding as much, Benjamin stood aside to allow the Italian egress. The two glared at each other: a promise that the battle would be resumed. Then the Italian backed into the corridor and away in reverse, keeping Benjamin in sight all the way lest a dagger be aimed at his retreating back. At the first corner, he darted sideways and vanished.

Benjamin bent quickly to take advantage of the black canvas sheet left by his rival. He wrapped it around the standing figure of Charlotte and hoisted the surprisingly light effigy on to a broad shoulder. As he did so, a shot from the street shattered a window in the room – the Italian no doubt hoping to bring police to catch Benjamin at his crime.

Time was short. He set off at a run towards the darkness of Grotto-passage.

In his stone-vaulted cell below the building, Mr Williamson started at the distant sound of the gunshot. He had been lying awake in the impenetrable darkness, his mind a-swirl with thoughts of Charlotte's death, of Noah's courtroom intervention, of a fabricated constable and the possibility of the gallows. Between revenge and self-pity, humiliation and anger, escape and execution, he vacillated. A choice would come at the end of a rope, or at the hand of Noah Dyson.

SIXTEEN

Mr Newsome sat alone at a desk in the Newspaper Office. The painting of Her Majesty rested on the floor and the bricks that had been replaced by the Italian had been removed once more to reveal the neat hole in the wall. But the inspector was momentarily concerned with other matters, gazing distractedly at a version of himself reflected in a dusty mirror. Gas hissed, but the empty building was otherwise silent.

Having never before ventured into the office – or barely registered its existence – he had been led by his curious nature to take advantage of his sole access and to investigate what manner of work went on there. Inside one large cabinet, he had found numerous files listed under such titles as: "Politeness of Constables", "Notable Arrests", "Theatre Patrol", "Uniform Standards" and "Detective Force". This latter, he had discovered, contained a number of sub-files listing newspaper reports pertaining to the inspectors of that particular department and the men under its control.

Naturally enough, the one marked "Inspector Albert Newsome" was of particular interest. It was also the thickest and was quite stuffed with perhaps three years' worth of yellowing excerpts from the daily press. Scattered before him on the desk, they made for rather one-sided reading:

. . . then the detective, who had stated his name as Inspector Newsome, overturned the barrow of apples into the street to find what he believed was a hidden weapon. On not finding the item, he moved on without a care for the ruined stock or the clamour of outrage in his wake . . .

. . . whereupon a gentleman with curly red hair leapt forward to arrest the suspected criminal, proclaiming that he was a member of the Detective Force. When pressed for a name or rank, the policeman proceeded to ridicule the apprehended man with such coarse language that other men were heard to complain . . .

A glance at an archive file labelled with the name of "Sergeant George Williamson", though slimmer, told a quite different story in its choice of newsprint. Representative of the selection was:

Having observed the activities of the thief for some time, Sergeant Williamson was able to discern that the fellow would attempt his boldest robbery yet on the night of the full moon. Thus, when the criminal ventured to enter the building, he found the ingenious detective waiting for him with a pair of handcuffs.

Mr Newsome stared around the office with a bleak expression. Was this, then, how Sir Richard saw him? Through the eyes of those shabby fabulists, gossips and failed novelists who called themselves reporters? What of the many triumphs and seemingly impossible solutions that had marked his rapid career ascension? Where were *they* in the files of Scotland Yard? Between politics and police work, it seemed, he would always excel in only one.

He tossed the scraps of paper back into their respective files (feigning not to notice a few of his own slipping into Mr Williamson's) and focused again on the scene of the crime before him. Much had already been discovered.

The broken window in the water closet had been found first, while coal particles around its frame suggested the intruder had moved around the yard from the river. Whether dried muddy footprints around the landing stage had anything more to do with the intruder was still, however, open to debate.

In the Newspaper Office itself, fibres on and around the bricks had revealed the old cracksman's trick of using carpet to muffle the blows of the

173

chisel, while a stray thread caught on the lower door rim suggested a baffle to disguise the criminal's work light. In all, it was a thoroughly professional effort, made even more so by the revelation that no doors had been forced. Either they had all been picked, or the robber had used duplicates, the latter assumption being more likely since the existence of the secret well safe and its access points were evidently known in advance.

Regarding that improbable knowledge, Mr Newsome could only wonder at how the thief had known to penetrate the wall in the Newspaper Office. The only clue so far was a reference he had found in the *Police Gazette* concerning a burglary of Chubb's offices at St Paul's Churchyard a month or so previously. Only some small amount of cash had been taken, but the mess left by the burglars might conceivably have obfuscated the more serious intention of searching the lockmaker's records for the structural or manufacturing details of private commissions. Understandably, the company had not suggested this to the investigating officers.

Indeed, the facts of the Scotland Yard robbery – outrageous as they were – seemed less significant than its motivation. Was it the diary or the ledger that had been the goal? Or both? One had the power to potentially identify and convict its writer, while the other bestowed a fearful power upon its possessor. Whomsoever had that ledger controlled the will of many powerful men with a goad of ruinous humiliation.

But how to find a clue that would show the trail towards the criminal? There seemed an abundance of clues, but no clear pattern among them. Mr Newsome had punished his mind for answers. Might he approach some of the grand abbesses at London's most notorious houses of ill repute and enquire which of their lofty customers had suddenly stopped coming? These men would be likely victims of the blackmailer ... but how to approach them without revealing more than one should possibly know? Of course, one could follow them and hope to catch the blackmailer's accomplices, but such *surveillance* was precisely what had landed him back in uniform so recently.

Sighing, Mr Newsome reached for a piece of paper and a steel pen to scratch some ideas in the hope of releasing inspiration:

Criminal (and accomplices) – intelligent and highly skilled; not part of the usual thieves' community; seemingly unafraid of capture – a lunatic? Lucius Boyle?

Locations – Around Lincoln's-inn? Westminster, where the constable was taken? Within the police apparatus itself? (How does the criminal know what he knows?)

Clues so far – the masks from M Tussaud's: why? Mr Varney – no trace of him at his given address. The wax head in the coffin: proof of Boyle's continued existence. The stuffed body of PC Taylor? The stolen ledger and diary. The body of Charlotte?

Motives – revenge? Humiliation of the police? Personal attacks upon those represented by the masks I found?

And as he wrote the latter words, a sudden rush of thoughts came upon him. He scrabbled around on a desk for the most recent edition of *the Times,* hoping to understand more about the stories he had been hearing concerning the events at Marylebone police court.

What if this recent scandal concerning Mr Williamson and the stuffed whore was the villain's next step? Those inexplicable busts at Madame Tussaud's were obviously intended for some manner of illegality, and the use of a mask in Mr Williamson's current predicament would certainly explain much.

And the more he read, the more it seemed to make a convoluted sort of sense. All the witness evidence was against Mr Williamson, and those on Oxford-street must surely have mistaken one of those wax masks for the real man. If the letter found on Charlotte's person was not an outright fake, then it was almost certainly put there in a damning context by the killer who had prepared her corpse.

His mind racing now, Mr Newsome recalled with a jolt that, in fact, the stolen ledger did indeed contain a note relating to Mr Williamson's visit to the girl's house – a known *locale* of sin – in Golden-square. Was *this* the connection that had inspired the criminal's attempted ruination of the ex-detective?

Mr Newsome scanned *the Times* article again, a vague mental itch returning his attention to the opening lines. Yes – Lord Montague was sitting on the bench! *His* name featured abundantly in the ledger as one who sought the company of young boys at a certain house in St James. How curious that he – someone now so open to coercion – should be on the bench in a trial of dubious provenance. Perhaps even the magistrate Mr Etherington also had secrets to hide? Assuredly, it was no mere accident that the discovery of the body had fallen within the jurisdiction of Marylebone.

Then, of course, there was the parallel with the body of PC Taylor. Two such deaths in a single decade – let alone a single month – was too much to accept unless both were by the same hand – the kind of hand that would seek to inculpate and damn another. Especially if . . .

Mr Newsome felt another onrushing realisation that his earlier suspicions were indeed fact. He left the Newspaper Office at a half-run and ascended to Sir Richard's rooms, which had been left unlocked so that further evidence may be pursued overnight. But it was not the robbery that now occupied the inspector.

He surveyed the commissioner's desk and saw with a grim smile that it had been entirely cleared of matter: all papers safely locked in those sturdy oak drawers to dissuade the eyes of the over-curious. He could pick the locks, of course, but there would be minor marks and Sir Richard would certainly check. So Mr Newsome strode through the connecting door to the clerks' office and cast his eyes about the desk of the chief administrator.

And there, to the right, was the slim volume that Mr Newsome had glimpsed so often as Sir Richard conferred with his minions: the appointment book in which the days of the police commissioner were portioned into meetings, hearings, visits and the sundry political machinations that stood behind the uniforms on the street. He bent down to study it, gauging its exact position on the desk so that he might replace it without revealing his actions. Then he took it up greedily and turned to the pages of the last week or so.

The pages were almost full with times and names and places – all entries in the thin, spidery hand of the chief clerk. If he was hoping for something conspicuous, Mr Newsome was disappointed: the only notable entry was the date set for the Commons hearing on plain clothes policing, for which an entire day had been set aside. To learn more, it would be necessary to examine every single entry for ambiguity, obfuscation or code. Patience – that least abundant trait in his character – would be required. He sat with another sigh and applied himself to the hieroglyphics.

But within minutes he found the cobweb writing twitching and writhing illegibly before his tired eyes until he all but resigned himself to finding no proof here of his suspicions. Then a single line arrested his attention:

Wednesday – Fleet, Ludgate door. GW and ND

It was the word "Fleet" that had initially made him pause. There were no police offices on Fleet-street: no particular reason for a commissioner to be visiting the place in the middle of a busy schedule unless investigating the practices of a particular newspaper (something he would never have done in person). And how might a door on Ludgate possibly have anything to do with Fleet-street? The two were wholly bisected by the ceaseless circus where Farringdon and Bridge-street merged.

In fact, there was only one obvious interpretation of the reference. It must allude to the closed Fleet prison, which did indeed stand behind Ludgate and might conceivably be accessed from there. It did not take much longer for Mr Newsome to stare at those supplementary initials and read a world of meaning into the dumb pairings of accusatory letters. The questions that had rattled at the back of his scull for some days had now found their answers in those abbreviated names.

Where had Dyson and Williamson been living since their houses had been destroyed? Why had Sir Richard been so evasive in revealing who was investigating the PC Taylor case? Where was the body of that constable if not in a surgery at Scotland Yard? And why, now, was another stuffed body being used to accuse Mr Williamson of murder?

The conclusion seemed clear: Sir Richard was using that nefarious pair to investigate the PC Taylor crime.

Or, at least, that had been the commissioner's plan until their common adversary had played his checkmate with the body of Charlotte and the theft of the ledger. Success now lay in the hands of Mr Newsome alone – the one investigator who seemed to have so far escaped the particular attentions of their common enemy.

Not only success, but also the power, potentially, to exculpate the unfortunate Mr Williamson. Might not a more thorough investigation be made into the charges if Sir Richard knew of the masks and of Lord Montague's possible coercion?

On the other hand, what better opportunity to catch the true criminal than to allow his scheme to continue unhindered – especially if the criminal were Lucius Boyle seeking to continue what he had started with the fires. Perhaps the incarceration of Mr Williamson in Newgate would result in his death at the hands of another Boyle accomplice, which would in turn generate further clues. Clues were the thing – clues and further opportunities for the adversary to make a mistake.

Fairness, of course, did not come into it. Every investigator was in danger. Mr Newsome might have escaped attack thus far, but there was a mask featuring *his* face just as there had been one of Mr Williamson. Was it out on the streets at that very moment committing atrocities in the guise of its namesake? Had Boyle heard of his false grave being exhumed? Would there be a summons or an arrest warrant with the name of "Newsome" in the coming days? Time was short in this duplicitous game, and the fastest player would be the winner.

Mr Newsome replaced the appointment book exactly as he had found it and went to the window. The yard below was an angular darkness in which coal fragments glistened dimly like black ice. And as he stared through his reflection into the night, a sudden thought – or rather a single name – sprang to the forefront of his thoughts.

Noah Dyson.

The news of Mr Dyson's legal intervention had already been telegraphed around the constables and received in the corridors of Scotland Yard. He was not the kind of man to stand by as his friend was imprisoned, whether or not the conviction was just. Somewhere out there in the shadows, he and that demonic-looking Negro would be cogitating and conspiring to divert the path of justice and ruin Mr Newsome's hopes. An escape plan was likely already in motion.

Precautions had to be taken immediately. The cells of Marylebone police court might already be under siege. Mr Newsome quickly turned off the gas and concluded his investigations for the night, leaving just minutes later with his head hatless and his coat billowing in his wake.

Had he been in less of a hurry, he might have paid more attention to a subsequent entry in the appointment book: a single letter on a line of its own:

V.

In his haste, perhaps he had mistaken it for a Roman numeral or for a simple mark of separation in the text. But that truncated tick bespoke a greater meaning than any single number or letter.

Indeed, his sense of purpose on leaving the building was such that he paid no heed to the rather grubby street boy loitering at the end of Whitehall-place: a curious little fellow in what appeared to be an antiquated school uniform. The boy, however, took a greater interest.

SEVENTEEN

Dawn came to the environs of Paddington-street with an intimation of winter. A low mist, exhaled from the lungs of Hyde- and Regent's-park, had filled the streets of the west with the earthy perfume of fallen leaves and damp grass. Dew had settled heavily on rooftops and cobbles alike: a too-brief visitation of nature upon the blasted brickwork of the barren city's fabric. The mercury registered barely above freezing, and yet the air was a scented benediction at that fragile hour.

Few people stirred. The shops were still shuttered and the omnibuses would not begin running for an hour or so, but the sound of approaching hooves and wheels could be heard at the corner of High-street and Paddington-street: a police carriage bringing the reinforcements ordered by Inspector Newsome so that any attempt at escape might be dissuaded. The prisoner might have been safely locked in the cellars, but his friends were at liberty.

The carriage did not, however, approach the corner. Rather, it turned into Paradise-street and thence into the narrow Grotto-passage, which had less traffic and would therefore offer the best location for any escape attempt. Four sturdy constables from Division A sat within – their orders merely to remain on duty until the magistrate and attendants arrived to continue the previous day's examination. Thereafter, the constables would accompany the prisoner to his new accommodation at Newgate.

Steam plumed from the horses' nostrils and they clopped their hooves, perhaps in emulation of the beat constable who stamps to warm cold toes. The driver stepped down and wandered towards the main street in search of a tea vendor. Inside the carriage, the constables rubbed their hands and exchanged that particular currency of the uniformed man: gossip.

'I heard it was Newsome himself ordered this watch.'

'Newsome of the Detective Force? A rum one, he is. Did you hear about his work at the Thames division? Scandalous!'

'He's a fine investigator, I've heard. Sometimes a rule must be bent.'

'As fine as Williamson was? Did you know it is he who is on trial today?'

'George Williamson on trial? I have heard it but don't believe it. They say he was the best of the lot but had a funny turn and left the Force.'

'Aye, his wife died. Was murdered.'

'Did he catch the killer?'

'The fellow was found dead a while ago. Fell down the stairwell of the Monument from top to bottom, so they say.'

'That's what I call justice. If it were up to me, I'd—'

A sharp report on the roof of the carriage stopped the constable mid-sentiment. Then another much louder one.

'Some _____ is throwing stones,' said one of the men.

They each peered out of a window to glimpse the roofline of Grotto-passage, and what they saw there was quite unexpected.

Silhouetted against the milky mist of the sky was an array of ragged and diminutive figures pelting stones down upon the shining black exterior of the police carriage, inside which the noise was becoming quite unbearable. With a sharp crack, a window shattered, throwing shards across blue-uniformed knees. A boyish cheer went up from the gutters and parapets.

'Why, I will break some sculls!' said one of the constables, making to step down.

'Our orders are to remain within,' warned a colleague.

'Unless an escape is attempted,' replied the first. 'Perhaps this is it.'

All four men came out of the carriage with truncheons drawn. The one with a mind to break sculls shouted up to them: 'Be gone, you ragged scoundrels, or I will have you all in the workhouse!'

'I ain't afraid of *you* – I've seen a man killed!' came the response, followed by a swift *pirouette* and a drop of the trousers to reveal a cheeky *précis* of his opinion concerning the police. Laughter reverberated around the passage, accompanied by another hail of stones that claimed a further carriage window.

'Why, I will whip his hide until he can never sit again,' hissed the constable thus insulted. And without heeding his colleagues, he raced off in search of a stairway to the rooftops.

But there were now more boys and they seemed to be arriving into the passage from both ends. Though emaciated and grey of complexion, they were numerous, and there was mischief in every eye.

'Now then, boys,' warned a constable, truncheon upraised. 'I don't know your game, but it will end badly for you.'

There was a wink and a nod. Boys parted. A coil of rope was tossed from one to another and suddenly there was a multiplicitous whoop: a charge – some boys this way, some that way.

The remaining constables were momentarily distracted, not knowing where or who to strike. There seemed to be boys running in all directions.

A constable fell, his lower legs carried away by the rope strung between two racing boys. Another staggered blindly as a large hessian sack dropped over his shoulders from a young monkey atop the carriage. The third slipped and tripped as a juvenile whirlwind whipped a great length of fishing net about him.

Shouts and imprecations fought squeals and giggles while, up on the roof, an outraged adult yell was heard. And within minutes, the various constables had been quite trussed into immobility by the swarm of ragged youth.

The young lad called Roger appeared at ground level wearing a too-large constable's hat pushed back on his head. His troops reassembled, some of them with a trophy of truncheon or rattle or divisional lapel badge.

'Are you ready, boys?' said Roger.

The cheering response indicated an affirmative.

'Then let us invade!'

Mr Williamson regarded the woollen blanket that had lain folded at the foot of his bed throughout the cold night of his incarceration. Not using it had been the challenge he had set himself, preferring to pace the stone flags, stamp his feet and swing his arms when he felt the leaden chill numb fingers or toes. With his pocket watch taken from him, he could only estimate that daylight had reached the world outside.

He had not slept. Quite apart from the situation he found himself in, the damp masonry around him emitted its own unnerving influence. A woman prisoner had been infamously ruined by a senior policeman in this very cell not ten years since. Another fellow had hanged himself while on remand for forgery. How many others had occupied the space, their anguish absorbed into the very mortar over the years until a palpable atmosphere, an ominous sense of presence, made the cellars too dark for any gas to illuminate.

He had heard the rumble of the carriage arriving in Grotto-passage and assumed it was reinforcements. The curious mass of footsteps that followed shortly afterwards was more mysterious – perhaps the boys of the juvenile refuge leaving or arriving. Or, more likely, early arrivals for the carnival of public outrage that was certain to attend that day's continuation.

Mr Williamson sat on the edge of the iron-framed bed and rubbed his eyes. There had been no thoughts of escape. Somebody needed to take responsibility for the brutal murder and *post-mortem* humiliation of Charlotte. Somebody had to atone for her brief lifetime of sin now that she could not. Noah's intervention was thus merely a pause in the inevitable process.

Then came a shout and a clang of iron from the end of the corridor.

Mr Williamson stood and straightened his jacket. It seemed they would come for him early.

But the shouts continued, accompanied by the sounds of broken glass, crashing doors and the scuffle of many feet. A half-strangled cry was followed by a thud that rattled the door leading to the cells. A key scratched in the lock.

And a tatty youth sauntered into the cellar to stand before the prisoner. He wore a policeman's reinforced top hat pushed back on his shorn head and his eyes burned with the thrill of adventure.

'Are yer Mr George?' said the boy 'S'pose yer must be.'.

'What is going on here?' said Mr Williamson. 'Who are you?'

'Yer can call me Roger. I've come to get yer out. Hold on – I got a key on this ring.'

'This is a very serious crime you are committing.'

'Never fear, Mr George. I got a battalion with me. Yer'll be safe as 'er Majesty.' Roger examined the keys on the ring for a likely candidate.

'I should not leave,' said Mr Williamson. 'I . . . justice must be done. Is Mr Dyson with you?'

'He is the Napoleon what planned this lark.' Roger turned the key. 'Got it!'

Mr Williamson looked at the open bars and hesitated.

'Come on then, Mr George! We ain't got all day. They's boys with bloody noses for your sake! Will you see 'em hanged into the bargain?'

Noah's grand plan became clear. Had he himself appeared in the cell, a discussion would no doubt have ensued about legality and morality and guilt. No such eventuality could occur with this street pirate and his crew. There was simply a choice to be made: remain in the cell and see his rescuers quickly overpowered and taken into custody for eventual transportation, or accompany the child at the risk of adding to his own (already considerable) list of charges.

'Hmm. Hmm.'

'Mr Dyson said you might say that. Tole me to tell yer that he's got the body and yer got nothin' to worry about.'

'He has the body?'

'Are yer even listenin'? We got to get goin', and quick.'

Mr Williamson took his hat and followed the boy Roger up through a scene of general destruction that also featured two wriggling and rope-bound officers of the court. As he stared, a cohort of pale but excited boys seemed to coalesce protectively around him, steering him with grubby hands, elbows and shoulders through the building towards the Grotto-passage door.

Once outside, he beheld a police carriage with broken windows and its black varnish chipped in numerous places. Stones littered the area and three uniformed figures writhed beneath a tangle of rope or fishing net. The swarm of boys then nudged him in the direction of the carriage steps so that he was virtually carried inside with his sentinel Roger. On the banging of the door, a whistle blew and suddenly the swarm vanished – presumably back to the juvenile refuge from which they had originally fled.

Noah was waiting within. 'I was not sure that you would come, George.'

'Hmm. It seems you have gone to considerable effort.'

'You once did the same for me. And you have Captain Roger here to thank for your freedom.'

The boy grinned, revealing an incomplete set of yellowed teeth.

Mr Williamson appraised his rescuer. 'Have we met before, Roger? I feel that I have spoken to you in the past.'

'I saw a man killed. By the Fleet river. And I saw a demon – seven feet tall and black as night, with one eye. Tole me 'is 'ead was lopped off. Showed me the scars, even.'

The adults exchanged a glance.

'Hmm. What is this about you having a body in your possession, Noah?' said Mr Williamson

'It is Charlotte. Benjamin took her last night, and he was not the only one hoping to capture the evidence. The Italian was also there; they fought and Benjamin bested him.'

'The same Italian involved in the smuggling case? Why would *he* want the body?'

'I have no idea, but the fact of him wanting it is reason enough for us to have it. Whoever is attempting to inculpate you has evidently left a colossal clue in that body and I rather suspect they have realized it too late.'

'You think the Italian and his master are behind it?'

'I have a feeling they are.'

'Hmm. Where are we going now? We can no longer rely on the Fleet to house us now that you have effected my escape and stolen the body.'

'We must instead be fleet of foot, George. Our immediate destination is the one place where Sir Richard would not think to look.'

'Mr Cullen's house? I admit I have not the least idea where he lives.'

'No. We are approaching Charlotte's apartment at Golden-square. It is a crime scene, and she has returned to it.'

'To ... to Charlotte's ...?' Mr Williamson glanced out of the broken window and saw that it was so.

'There is probably evidence to be found concerning her death or abduction. And, as you say, the Fleet is no longer suitable.'

'Hmm. Hmm.'

''Oo's this Charlotte yer keep talkin' about?' said Roger, still wearing the absurdly large constable's hat.

'She is none of your concern,' said Noah. 'Indeed, it is time that you stepped down from the carriage. Your role in the war is over. Will you return to the refuge?'

'And be thrashed for a month by old Warburton? I 'ad enough of that from me father. No – I'm a man 'oo can look after 'imself.'

'Very well. Here is a sovereign for your upkeep. I wonder if you would like to continue your collaboration with us and earn more?'

'Eh?'

'Do you want to do some more work?'

'Aye – it seems I 'ave a taste for it. What yer got?'

'There is a policeman with red curly hair – a slim fellow who works out of Scotland Yard. His name is Inspector Newsome. If you can follow him and let me know what he does, you might earn another sovereign. But take care, he is not stupid and may see you.'

'I will be 'is very shadow.'

'Good lad. Let us meet at Dodgeley's butchers on Duke-street, Smithfield in two days to share information. I will buy you a meat pie there. At noon.'

'All right!'

With that, young Roger leapt down from the still-moving carriage, just another muddy droplet absorbed into the turbid stream of London.

Noah and Mr Williamson did not speak for the remainder of the journey, the latter looking drawn and contemplative from his night in the cells. But as they entered Golden-square, he seemed assailed by other emotions entirely.

'The carriage will stop around the corner,' said Noah. 'Your face is known hereabouts so I am afraid you must approach the house wearing this.'

Mr Williamson regarded the black theatrical beard with a derisory expression, but took it all the same. It was ready-gummed for immediate use and so he pressed it into place for a transformation that was remarkably effective. The worst of his distinctive complexion was now hidden and he might pass for an artist or retired eccentric.

'I will alight here,' said Noah. 'It is better that we do not enter together. The carriage will continue once you descend. We expect to see you in a few moments.'

And so it was that Mr Williamson approached Golden-square from the east as he so often had: a familiar route made strange by circumstance. He felt the same anticipation, the same dread, the same sadness as if she were alive – yet he knew that the girl who awaited him was now little more than flax wadding and wire, preservative powder and stitching.

Mr Cullen's face appeared briefly at the curtains and the door swung open in anticipation as Mr Williamson ascended the stairs into the sudden realisation that Charlotte's perfume remained in the narrow hallway: a betraying presence that brought to mind her laugh, her eyes, her skin, her physical heat. Breathing it made his throat catch.

Benjamin arrived to secure the door and stifled a grin at the sight of the beard. He laid a hand of wordless communion upon a slim shoulder and beckoned: come this way.

She stood in the centre of the parlour, starker and more horrible in the context of her own home than she had appeared in court. Her once luminous skin now appeared dry, her hair was unkempt and her clothes seemed to have been assembled by another's hand. Close to, the poor quality of the work was even more evident in the lumpen irregularity of her features and the unnatural curve to her back. Mr Williamson instinctively drew together the lace of her dress where it had fallen open to reveal an immodest degree of raggedly sewn *décolletage*. Evidently her re-dressing had been effected with none of the skill used in PC Taylor's body. When he turned, the other three were watching him as if gauging the equilibrium of his rational mind.

'Hmm. What else do we know about the circumstances of her death?' he said.

Noah seemed to catch Benjamin's eye and nod. 'All we know at present is what has been revealed in the newspapers and at the court hearing. Do you know if Charlotte was a "resident", or a "walker"?'

'She ... hmm, she would sometimes walk on Haymarket, but most of her ... "visiters" were at home. You are thinking that she was taken from here?'

'It would be most preferable for the killer, would it not? We have been careful to disturb nothing since we arrived. This room is exactly as we found it and may yield clues. One of us must also examine the body to—'

'I will do it,' said Mr Williamson. 'Nobody else will touch her. I will also examine the rooms since I ... I happen to know their customary arrangements.'

'Very well.' said Noah.

'I wonder if I might make an observation?' said Mr Cullen, half raising a hand.

The others looked to him expectantly.

189

'Well, I believe my recent interview with the taxidermist has given me some insight into these matters and I think I can state quite confidently that this body and the body of PC Taylor were fashioned by a different hand.'

Benjamin tossed an interrogative arabesque.

'Yes, Ben,' continued Mr Cullen. 'It is quite a different criminal. We are now searching for *two* killers.'

'I admit that there is a clear difference in finishing and pose,' said Noah, 'but might not these things be explained by haste alone? If the criminal was distracted, perhaps ...'

'Forgive me Noah, but it is simply not so,' said Mr Cullen. 'The abductor of PC Taylor was concerned with presentation. He took time and care with his work and its exhibition because he is by nature a meticulous fellow. He would rather not act than act in haste. This is also what Dr Hammerton suggested.'

'Proceed with your argument,' said an intent Mr Williamson.

'Well, it seems every taxidermist has a certain signature hand that can be seen in the way he executes a cut or a stitch. With practice, he does it the same way every time. Look at Charlotte's eyelids, or at her inner lips or at the backs of the ears. Do they look at all comparable with those of PC Taylor?'

Mr Williamson gently moved the dark hair and observed an ear. He delicately brushed the corner of her lips with a thumb. He leaned in closer to examine the eyelids, seeing in his mind not the muddy misplaced enamel orbs but rather the hot coffee hue of her living eyes. He held her face for the first time and it was cold in his palm.

Mr Cullen caught Noah's silent prompt to continue. '*Ahem* – and I have also noticed that the stitching along her breast is not only less disciplined than upon PC Taylor, but is also that of a left-handed man. See how the first hole is a different side? I maintain that even a man trying to disguise his hand could not do it so completely as this.'

Mr Williamson nodded slowly. 'Hmm. Hmm. This is good investigative work.'

Mr Cullen blinked at this benediction from his mentor and seemed to swell in stature. Benjamin flashed a secret wink.

'Do you really believe that we are dealing with two murderers, George?' said Noah. 'It seems a colossal coincidence.'

'I follow only the evidence, and the evidence suggests two separate hands. It is our task to prove or disprove it and thus make sense of it. Such is the detective's work.'

'I agree,' said Mr Cullen, standing beside Mr Williamson. 'Is it not possible that the body of Charlotte is in some way a *response* to the body of PC Taylor – an imitation, so to speak, which attempts to disorient investigators?'

'That is an interesting idea,' said Noah. 'Particularly since the details of PC Taylor's body are not widely known. If we are looking at an imitation, it is an imitation of a rumour rather than a direct copy, hence the mismatch of pose and finishing. Neither killer has seen the other's work. The principle intention was clearly to blacken George's name.'

'Hmm. Such suspicion can only have increased now that I have escaped from prison.'

'Then we must act quickly,' said Mr Cullen, 'so that we may present the true solution to the crime when Sir Richard finally discerns our whereabouts. We are all accomplices now, and we all stand to face punishment.'

'You are right, of course,' said Noah. 'But our avenues of investigation remain undefined. What do we know? The fact of the Italian attempting to steal Charlotte's body is a suggestion of the killer's identity in that instance, but the killer of PC Taylor could be anyone with a *penchant* for taxidermy. Where do we look?'

'I . . . I have an idea,' said Mr Cullen.

'There is no limitation on ideas,' said Mr Williamson. 'Out with it.'

'Well, there is a fellow who works at Scotland Yard: Mr Edward Figgs. He is called a pathognomist or physiognomist – I am not certain of the distinction – and his function is to assess men's fitness for duty by means of visual examination. The shape of one's head, the length of one's nose, the gestures one makes – all of these can apparently indicate a man's essential nature. Do you recall the fellow, Mr Williamson?'

'I have heard of him, but his so-called science is rather a new thing. I have not met him and know nothing of his skill.'

'How might he help us?' said Noah. 'We have no idea where to seek our killers, so how might he judge them. Do you intend, perhaps, that we describe the Italian to this Mr Figgs and be told he is a violent and cunning adversary?'

'No – of course not,' said Mr Cullen, blushing somewhat. 'What I suggest is a sort of reversed process. Rather than produce an analysis from a physical examination, we will produce a physical likeness from a character description. Do you see?'

The other men stared at Mr Cullen. Elucidation was clearly required.

'What I mean to say is this: Dr Hammerton has provided us with a detailed description of our man's mind. If I relate this detail to Mr Figgs, he may be able to tell us what physical characteristics such a person would have. For example, a meticulous nature combined with a violent temperament might equate with certain shape of scull. Then we simply take all of the detail provided by Mr Figgs and have a police artist sketch our possible suspect. Do you see?'

Again, his fellows studied him with expressions that might be read as either mild befuddlement or nascent respect.

'That is either genius or the wildest absurdity,' said Noah.

'I myself am dubious about these modern methods, but is worth trying under the circumstances,' said Mr Williamson. 'If it fails, we will be in no worse a position. However, I cannot see any of us walking into Scotland Yard to take advantage of Mr Figg's speciality, or to use a police artist. Every one of us has reason to avoid the police at present.'

'I will see to that element of the investigation,' said Noah.

Benjamin, who had been toying with the bandages on his arm, gestured that he might continue to trawl the streets in search of the urchin who had marked him. If the little fellow had a connection to either of the bodies, it would be another possible clue.

'You do that, Ben,' said Noah. 'And take Mr Cullen with you. The boy knows your face, but not his. Perhaps you can act as the lure and have Mr Cullen hook the slippery fish.'

Benjamin offered another wink to Mr Cullen and both grinned at the prospect of working together again.

'In the meantime,' said Mr Williamson with the faintest shadow of a smile, 'perhaps Mr Cullen will demonstrate his primary skill and make a pot of tea.'

EIGHTEEN

A single candle burned in that subterranean vault beneath the sediment, beneath the clay, beneath the river bed inside the Thames Tunnel. Too weak to illuminate the room, the frail flame instead cast a palette of darkness and distorting shadow in which all was indistinct. The cluttered work bench showed bowls of dried solutions, stray wads of cotton and pale accumulations of chalk among its crevices.

Breathing could be heard in the dimmest nether recesses of the space: a steady, glutinous sound that might have indicated sleep in another man, but which in this instance was a mark of crackling frustration. There was a rough scratch, a brief flare, and a Lucifer match momentarily lit the corner with flickering brevity until snuffed between the pinch of fire-calloused fingers to fall among two dozen others.

And with each brief burst of yellow-orange, the unmasked face seemed to twist and twitch, tighten and transform into a visage more hideous than any preying midnight incubus. Only the smoke-grey eyes bore any relation to a human, and they stared unblinking with madness upon an inner turmoil whose focus had a single name.

Noah Dyson.

The man was a thorn in the sole, sand in the eye: a mortal *deus ex machina* with the seeming ability to impede even the soundest inevitability. Had it not been the case since they had once – a lifetime and a world ago – shared a childhood on the streets that had ended in fire, capture and an oath of revenge? Had not each been the only one the other feared? Had they not faced each other across the city's gladiatorial perimeter for years, sufficiently matched that they would destroy each other before either could be victor? But now Noah had acquired his motley band of cohorts, and they were becoming quite intolerable. They, and that tenacious horse-fly Inspector Newsome who had so recently disinterred the deathless plot at Portugal-street burial ground. All would have to die.

Another match flared. The demoniac face contorted: a fire-writhing ember.

There was a knock at the door and he reflected with bleak mirth that even the knuckles rang false: a mock jocular tattoo designed to show that the visiter was not afraid. Perkin Mullender was paying a visit.

The mask slipped into place and he called out: 'Enter.'

The charlatan did as bidden, stepping with caution into the virtual blackness and immediately twitching his nose. There was a lingering smell of raw flesh that might have emanated from the masked man or from whatever unholy work he did in that plutonic sub-riverine cavity.

'It's rather dim in here,' said Perkin Mullender, unable to see the other man among the shadows. 'Shall we light a lamp?'

'No. I congratulate you on your recent work – the witnesses saw what I intended them to see.'

'It was a matter of the greatest simplicity for one such as I.'

'Quite. Do you have money for me?'

'O yes. I have it all here weighing down my pockets.'

'Did you have any problems? Did any of them balk and whine?'

'All paid will ill grace. Some offered mild threats. The bishop cried and offered a prayer for his own salvation.'

'And Montague?'

'He barely spoke, but he agreed all the same.'

'And you wore the mask for every collection – without exception?'

'The one with the broken nose, yes. Some asked me why I was wearing it and I replied that I would hardly show them my real face under the circumstances.'

'Good. I have another errand. You are to visit a manufactory in Rotherhithe and collect two barrels. The documentation is on the workbench there.'

'Chymicals?' said Perkin Mullender, squinting in the dimness to see the sales docket.

'Take the greatest care in their handling. Do not smoke or permit anyone else to smoke in their presence or you might find yourself airborne. And see that you do not spend any time with the barrels in a confined space. They will be thoroughly sealed, but the merest leak will have effects.'

'Very well. Will I bring them here?'

'Does this not qualify as a confined space? Have you listened to my words?'

'Yes, yes ... of course. I just like to be thorough.' A half dozen personalities twitched unbidden across those malleable features.

'You will take them to Westminster. The address is on the back of the docket. See that they are secure, and then never return to that place. Destroy the docket and any other evidence of your actions as soon as you are able.'

'Should I wear a mask for this?'

'The one with the curly red hair and the sly expression.'

'My favourite.'

"I cannot say I am surprized. There are also more letters for you to deliver. They are addressed and also to be found on the workbench. See that you hand them personally to the recipients and wait for their agreement.'

'Of course. I see that your Mediterranean friend has been in the wars. Been fighting, has he?'

'Mr Mullender – have I ever led you to believe that we are sufficiently acquainted to share small talk? I do not like questions – they suggest curiosity about my business.'

'I ... was just making conversation.'

'Do not. And do not dawdle talking to that imbecile card-seller before attending to your duties.'

196

'Yes.'

'Then go.'

But, of course, Perkin Mullender did stop to receive further unappreciated adulation and another card from young Jane. Had he not done so, he might not have glimpsed young Master Smalletts striding with juvenile vigour towards his own appointment with the masked man. Nor would he have had a somewhat unnerving encounter with the old fortune-telling crone just adjacent to the lower stairs.

'O! O! Fateful fellow!' she wailed as he passed.

And, though he never usually registered her histrionic patter, today he felt a certain thrill of amusement at the dubious kinship between one fraud and another. He stopped and turned to approach her stall, which was set out with such tawdry *accoutrements* of prognostication as a light-warping glass ball, chicken bones, well worn cards and the withered foot of some unfortunate minor mammal.

'What of my future, grandmother?' he enquired, eyebrows dancing, lips caught between mirth and derision, accent indeterminate. Whose future was he asking?

'Many men become one, quoth dark Hecate,' intoned the hag with an unearthly croak, her eyes rolled back to reveal blank orbs. 'He who multiplies in this realm is made whole in the next. Perish as another, perish as oneself. Beware the beasts of Apollo!'

'That's an impressive trick with the eyes,' said Perkin Mullender, allowing himself a genuine smile. 'The classical references lend it a certain vague authority. I applaud your performance.'

'Repent now afore ye perish, thou earthly Protean. You die less than one day hence!'

'Ah, now that's your downfall, grandmother. One should never be too specific in one's predictions. Ambiguity is the thing'

'O! Melancholy man!'

Perkin Mullender strolled away. It was only later, long after he had exited the tunnel, that a worrying notion struck him. At no point had the old woman asked him for her customary penny.

'A big black feller 'e was, but I weren't afraid. I guessed 'e'd be waitin' for me round the next corner and I 'ad the blade ready for 'im. Cut 'im good, I did, and 'e soon let go in an 'urry.'

The masked man regarded Master Smalletts with impassive wax emotion. 'You did well, Tobias – but you must learn to choose your battles. In this case you were lucky.'

'Weren't no luck – I bested 'im fair.'

'That may be so, but when an opponent is stronger, one does not challenge him in a trial of strength. One finds his weakness. Do you understand?'

'S'pose so.' The boy wrung his greasy cap, chastised.

'And you say that this Negro was simply walking about the town? He visited no particular addresses?'

'Just wanderin' about. Even passed the same spot a few times.'

'Interesting. I rather suspect he was looking for you, or someone like you.'

'Ain't no-one like Tobias.'

'Yes. What else have you seen? Any of those other gentlemen whose masks I showed you?'

'The red haired gent. 'E's a bluebottle, ain't he?'

'What makes you say so?'

'I followed 'im to Scotland Yard. 'E was collected by a constibble from a shop and spent most o' the night there, even after all the others'd gone 'ome.'

'From which shop did the constable collect him, Tobias?'

'Shop on 'olborn – sells models o' dead people and glass eyes.'

'Yes. Mr Schlöss's wax anatomy. I feel sure I know what he was asking about. Do you know where he went after he left Scotland Yard?'

'The old Fleet prison. Wandered about its walls for a while, tryin' to peer through where the doors and gates 'ave been boarded.'

'The Fleet, you say? Mmm. You are indeed a worthy agent, Tobias.'

''Ave you got another present for me?'

'I wonder if you know, Tobias, that I myself was once a boy such as you: roaming the streets of London, bereft of parental care. One must learn to be hard. One must learn the lessons of a more wild nature. As the rabbit is torn by the hound, so there are hunters and prey among men. Do you know why roosters attack each other?'

'What's a rooster?'

'They attack because they see a threat to their superiority. It is the guiding rule of all nature. One must seek dominance even if the battle for supremacy results in the death of both.'

Master Smalletts began to fidget where he stood, palpating the cap before him. The masked man no longer seemed to be addressing him, and yet he continued to speak with a distracted air.

'Yes, I was like you, Tobias. I was a soldier of the streets and I gathered more soldiers about me. Others challenged me, of course, but I did what was necessary to retain my power. One must sometimes befriend one's enemy in order to destroy him. And yet ... sometimes an enemy becomes stronger in defeat. He will not rest until he can exact revenge, though it takes a lifetime. That is a truly dangerous enemy. One might toy with him as a cat does with its prize, but eventually he must be quite thoroughly destroyed – he and anyone who may offer him succour. Yes ... yes ... thorough destruction is the only course ...'

The masked man slid the mask upwards to wipe a handkerchief across his brow. His eyes stared into the candle flame on the workbench. And Tobias suppressed a gasp at what he saw – at what he should not see. The raw, ruined face was like one of those anatomical exhibits so recently glimpsed in Mr Schlöss's shop window. And still he maintained the soliloquy of loathing.

'One must leave nothing to chance. One must never underestimate one's quarry. I have made that mistake too many times. Yes. Yes.'

The candle guttered but maintained its flame.

'Is . . . there another errand?' said Master Smalletts.

'What? Yes. I have further need of your talents.' The masked man seemed not to register that his ceroplastic guise had slipped. 'Do you like fireworks, Tobias? Do you attend the fires on the fifth?'

'I . . . I like the rockets and the serpents.'

'Of course you do. What boy does not? Well, there will be pyrotechnical enjoyment a-plenty this year. What do you think about this notice?'

The masked man leaned across the desk with a gaudily illustrated flyer:

REMARKABLE FIREWORKS DISPLAY

The residents of Westminster are invited on the night of the fifth of November to a fireworks show superior in magnitude to anything ever before seen in the city.

The show will begin at 11.00 p.m. on that evening, and will be accompanied by a number of barrels of spirits selected for their quality and strength.

No charge will be made for the show or refreshment.

Tobias, who could barely read, noted the array of fireworks illustrated there and nodded his mute approval.

'Your task is to distribute a quantity of these leaflets among the public houses located strictly on Duck-lane, Old Pye-street and Great St Anne-street. *Only* those places, do you understand?'

'Where mostly Irish drink,' observed Master Smalletts.

'Exactly that. You are a sharp one. I would like to make this gift specifically to the gentlemen and ladies of that nation – a mitigation, perhaps, on such an anti-Catholic evening. They live a harsh enough life in this metropolis, do they not? A free gin or whisky will be just the thing.'

'S'pose so,' said the boy, reflecting that in his experience the combination of free spirits and the Irish after dark was likely to result in a riot that would barely subside until dawn, particularly if the drink ran dry before they were satisfied.

'And I wonder if you would like to invite any of your acquaintances? Do you know any street-sweepers, boot-polishers or apprentice pickpockets who might enjoy the show? If so, advise them that they are welcome as your special guests – but only soldiers like you: wily and tough characters. You will be their leader.'

'I'll do it.'

'Very well. While you are in Westminster distributing these flyers, you will also visit an address that will be communicated to you. There, further instructions will be given and you will again visit the places featured in the maps we looked at together.'

'Aye.'

'Good boy. You may go. And see that you stay clear of that Negro fellow. He knows your face now and may be looking for you. You can collect the rest of those leaflets from our Neapolitan friend before you leave, and tell him to see me after he has done so.'

'Yes, gen'ral.'

Tobias Smalletts left in something of a daze, the fire-lit hideousness of that face imprinted upon his mind. Moments later, the door opened and the Italian stood silently at the threshold for instructions. His lacerated face showed no emotion.

'I want you to return to that house in Golden-square and see that there is nothing whatsoever that might be connected to us. They are moving closer and every care must be taken. Search it, then burn it for good measure. We can blame it on Mr Williamson and his accomplices now they are fugitives from the law. And if you encounter the Negro again, it would be my pleasure for you to exact your revenge to the fullest degree. It is his time.'

The gold earring glinted in the light from the anteroom and the Italian allowed himself a smile as thin and red as a razor slash before departing.

Alone again, Lucius Boyle removed the mask from the crown of his head and wiped its interior: an impression as blank and mendacious as the expression it showed. He laid it on a table at his side and rested his hand upon the ledger so recently taken from Scotland Yard. This, at least, was a prize to lighten his mood. It, and the unexpected bonus of the diary, would make his immediate plans much easier to accomplish.

NINETEEN

'One must not, of course, make the common error of assuming that aesthetics have any relation to the organic formation, and therefore the character. Were not both Socrates and Aesop known to be ugly men? Plato was corpulent and Voltaire no classic ideal of male beauty, but we could not possibly accuse any of those fellows of intellectual vulgarity.'

A flutter of polite laughter animated the small auditorium and Noah looked again at the other gentlemen who had gathered to hear the anthropometric wisdom of Mr Edward Figgs, advisor to the Metropolitan Police and recently the toast of science in London. Many earnest 'beards' were in attendance, along with a small number of fusty ladies and the odd medical student perhaps hoping to impress a professor with some new terminology. Pipe smoke hung thick in the air, wreathing the gas chandelier.

The stage was decorated with three large illustrations of human heads, and it was to one of these that Mr Figgs now made reference, using a conductor's baton to better describe an outline scull transected by various reference points.

'See here, for example, how the mesial line may be used as an indicator of general brain development, or how the sincipital development here denotes the animal region. When it is pronounced, we may read a greater degree of inhabitiveness, which, if combined with a narrow forehead, manifests the low intelligence of the idiot. Naturally, I am simplifying. A full diagnosis would require the reading of many, many inter-related signs.'

A gentleman with a greying efflorescence upon his chin raised a hand and waited for a nod of permission before speaking: 'Mr Figgs – I wonder if you might further clarify the difference between physiognomy and pathognomy? I, for one, believe I missed the niceties of it in your opening address.'

Mirth again touched the audience, its tone suggesting a certain relief that somebody else had asked what all were thinking.

'Indeed, indeed,' said Mr Figgs with a smile. 'Physiognomy is the study of the body's organic constitution: its shape and relative dimensions. There is a finite number of possible body shapes, just as there are a series of known individual features to the nose or fingers. Critically, all of these elements are necessarily connected within a single organic type so that a tall, thin man will not have a broad fat nose – unless, of course, he is of African descent. Phrenology, it need hardly be stated, also falls within the same discipline. Pathognomy, on the other hand, is the study rather of gesture and motion: the organic character manifested as a physical language, if you like. Thus, a thoughtful man gestures with grace, while the imbecile is spasmodic in gesticulation. Any skilled practitioner of the one discipline must master the other, since one's actions derive directly from the character as apples issue only from an apple tree.'

A mumble of approval met this latest oration and Mr Figgs made a modest bow. Another hand was raised and the speaker gestured with grace to receive the question.

'Yes, Mr Figgs. You have touched upon the science of phrenology, but I have also heard men speak of craniognomy. Is there a difference?'

'An excellent question – and one that surely needs to be answered more thoroughly. The first, of course, pertains specifically to the works of Dr Gall and the twenty-seven brain organs he has identified by which we might read a man's vanity, circumspection and benevolence *et cetera*. Craniognomy, however, is the cranial specialisation of physiognomy – relating to developmental shape rather than to Dr Gall's brain organs. Again, it is wise to be versed in both when making a diagnosis.'

Noah raised his hand. 'I see that you have an illustration of a Negro face as part of your lecture. Does not the powerful influence of racial origin affect your sciences?'

'Not at all, sir. The laws of science do not bend for the black man any more than for the Chinese or the American red Indian. Nevertheless, we may draw certain conclusions across racial categories. Note how this region on the Negro's scull denotes an especial appreciation of music – and are not the majority of those dusky fellows never happier than when playing a drum or singing? At the same time, note the inter-relation of the sagittal, sincipital and coronal regions that mean the black man is utterly ineducable. Books are mere toys to him, and written words are akin to the abstracts scratched with charcoal upon cave walls.'

Noah maintained his impassive expression with the greatest difficulty and nodded a curt acknowledgement. Other men in the audience were taking notes.

'Indeed, the gentleman's question leads me fortuitously on to the third of my illustrations,' continued Mr Figgs, adopting a more sombre tone. 'The anthropometric sciences are no mere parlour games for identifying a man's avarice or acuity. In the realm of police investigation, one might not only use these skills to select the most upstanding officers, but also to begin a classification of the murderous types. Our third image tonight is therefore of the infamous James Greenacre: a fascinating fellow by all accounts. I wonder if – now that I have outlined some elements of the science – anyone in the audience might try to identify a physical characteristic denoting the murderous urge?'

'His eyes are rather close together,' offered one young man.

'The cheekbones – they have an acute angle,' said a deep-voiced lady in tweeds.

'Interesting observations,' said Mr Figgs, 'but you focus too closely on the local at the expense of the whole. Many men might have closely set eyes, but not all are murderers. Indeed, it is a matter of mere folklore concerning that particular indication. Look instead here at the lower scull, whose slight swell shows an imbalance towards the animal instincts. A phrenological examination would reinforce the point with a raised organ of carnivorous instinct. His dark colouring further hints at a bilious temperament. And yet Greenacre was also something of a writer and thinker, as expressed in the lofty forehead.'

'Mr Figgs – I am afraid your observations are perhaps too subtle for the common practitioner,' said a fellow on the front row. 'Do you mean to say that you can truly recognize a murderer by these signs alone?'

'By a combination of signs – not by one or two in isolation. A bilious man is not necessarily a killer, but a man whose head, form and actions variously allude in that single direction is one who is more likely than another to kill. Imagine, for example, that one were a detective seeking an unknown murder suspect in a room full of people or on a crowded train carriage – would it not be invaluable to public safety if one could predict that such-and-such a fellow was the likeliest target?'

A mutter here went through the room: a nervous reaction to the figure of the anonymous murderer.

Noah took the opportunity to once again raise his hand. 'Mr Figgs – forgive me any impertinence, but might not a fellow disguise his true nature? I mean to say that a criminal who understands the elements of which you speak might adjust his posture accordingly, might modify his gestures and generally dissimulate the characteristics of another, less suspicious, type.'

Mr Figgs paused and seemed to stare with new interest at this particular audience member, perhaps applying the tenets of his combined sciences upon the questioner himself. It was the merest heartbeat of delay, but it was noted by all and urged an answer.

'You raise an interesting point,' said Mr Figgs. 'Of course it is possible for man to recognize the insistent marks of his organic nature and therefore change them. Witness the pickpocket at the races whose dress and manners allow him to assimilate himself among those he would rob. *Yet* – and let us be utterly clear on this point – the pickpocket *cannot* change the cerebral organs of acquisitiveness that impel his features to be thinner than average. Nor can he change the slimness of finger, the quickness of eye or the lighter colouring that bespeaks a sanguine temperament. No amount of dissimulation can completely hide one's essential character from the skilled anthropometrist.'

The defence was met with a broad murmur of approval and Noah nodded a curt acknowledgement. Thereafter, and for the rest of the presentation, Noah remained silent and used his time to study the audience rather than listen to any more of the quasi-science that painted Negros as ineducable. Everything in his experience told him that the springs of character were hidden darkly within a man's soul or were reactions to the stimuli of his circumstance, and yet here were dozens of apparently intelligent men nodding sagely at an image of an imaginary African who jigged to music like some humanoid ape. Might not any one of them turn murderer if their very survival were at stake, bumps and gestures be d_____?

Mr Cullen's idea, however, did have minor appeal. If there were even a grain of truth in the posturing of Mr Figgs, they might make a significant step forwards in their case by achieving some greater consensus in the description of their suspect. If not, at least it would prove that men like Mr Figgs and Dr Hammerton were nothing more than fabulists.

A thunder of stamping feet and applause stirred Noah from his reveries some time later and he got quickly to his feet that he might reach the stage to question the speaker more closely. But a *coterie* of fawners had already gathered about Mr Figgs to offer thanks or share their own insights (for does not every such gathering compel a few attendees to utilize the speaker as a mirror for their own self-perceived brilliance?) and so Noah dawdled until slow attrition finally left him alone with a perspiring anthropometrist.

'Your questions aided me greatly, sir,' said Mr Figgs with an extended hand. 'Naturally, I intended to cover them in my address, but one is always grateful when someone takes a particular interest. Are you a medical man yourself?'

'Perhaps you can tell *me*!' said Noah with a practised friendliness.

'Ah, you would turn my science into a test. Very well, then: I will take the bait on this occasion. Let me see ... mmm. Well, your general morphology suggests a combinatory sanguine-phlegmatic nature, which is to say you are thinker and a reader, a strategist with patience and tact. The slimness of your features, along with a clarity of eye, further implies an unusual degree of cunning ... which immediately makes me assess your economy of gesture and deduce that you might make a skilled thief if you so wished. Not any common robber, to be sure, but a cracksman or a trickster. I do not need to use any science to note the scars on your face and hands, but I dare say the strength written in your shoulders and arms can combine with that mild criminal bias to make you a violent man if provoked – although, I might add, only under circumstances of *extreme* provocation.'

Noah smiled. 'How do I know that you are not merely telling me what you believe I would like to hear? No doubt every clergyman you meet has an advanced sense of the divine and every lady an acute appreciation of beauty.'

'I see that you are not an adherent of my studies.'

'I have doubts that will be answered only with proof.'

'Then we are in complete agreement, for that is surely the credo of all scientists.'

'I wonder if, during your work with the police, you have had occasion to meet genuine killers?' said Noah.

'I cannot discuss such confidential matters, but let me say this: any man can recognize a murderer when a fellow is introduced to him as such. The skill is identifying one where no such suspicion exists. I have glimpsed men in the street and seen the nature of their crimes written in their very gait.'

'I wonder, Mr Figgs, if you might consent to participate in a minor experiment? I have undertaken a significant wager with a friend that your science is flawed. He maintains otherwise and has set this challenge: that you will be able to successfully describe the true features of a gentleman purely from a list of his character traits. I will detail them to you this evening and will later have them realized by a sketch artist. If the likeness is sufficiently accurate, I lose the wager.'

'This is hardly a matter for a man of—'

'Naturally, I will pay you for your trouble just as the police do. If the experiment proves unsuccessful, I assure you that nobody will ever know of your part in the wager. After all, you have promised nothing but a description.'

'In fact, I have promised nothing at all.'

'Five pounds, and ten minutes of your time.'

Mr Figgs looked at the money in Noah's hand. 'I will not have my name associated with this in any way, and will deny involvement if asked. There are no witnesses.'

Noah reassured himself that they were alone in the auditorium. 'As you wish.'

'Furthermore, you should know that the physical characteristics answering the temperamental traits you list will provide only a *type* – not the unique semblance of the fellow you seek. If you have it sketched or modelled, you will see only the face of any man possessing that particular combination of traits.'

'And if the characteristics themselves are quite rare? If their admixture makes them rarer still?'

'Then your image will certainly be more specific, albeit a likely caricature rather than a realistic human *visage*.'

'Do not such people exist, Mr Figgs?'

'Indeed they do, rarely, but we must differentiate between natural organic influence and deformity. Not every unfortunate with a birth defect or anatomical injury is necessarily a criminal type. Similarly, a man wearing the distinct hallmarks of a killer may have them partially erased if his countenance is changed by adverse events.'

'It rather sounds like there are more exceptions to your science than there are rules. Do you tell me these things by way of a disclaimer, as the fortune-teller prefaces her prognostications with a series of artful ambiguities?'

'Not at all. What I practice is as much art as science – but it is not magic and I will not provide you with an illustration from the spirit world. I say these things merely to refine your expectations.'

'Then I must accept these limits, Mr Figgs. Shall we proceed?'

'By all means. I hope I can dispel at least some of your scepticism.'

But let us here expedite the story by relating that Noah did indeed list every one of the characteristics identified by Dr Hammerton. Not only that, but he also added further of his own observations based upon investigations so far and upon his own shadowy suspicions concerning the faceless figure behind the fires and the cruel treatment of young Charlotte. It could hardly have been a more detailed catalogue of a man's inner workings, and Noah filled page after page of his notebook as each aberrant behaviour was answered with its physical partner in scull, face, limb and gesture.

And though nothing had yet been realized by an artist's hand, the effect upon the mind's lens was powerful. Every cranial swell, every dermal fold, every metrical specific and melanic mark combined to build an image whose multiple parts swam frustratingly as disparate motes in a sliver of objective light: hinting, suggesting, alluding, but never coalescing out of the darkness into a recognisable form. It could have been anyone, or no-one.

Thus it was that, on leaving the lecture hall, Noah passed with a striding purpose into the smoky coldness of the November night and made his way towards the anatomical emporium of Mr Schlöss, which at that time of the evening was a phantasmagoric vision framed in plate glass and brilliant gas flares.

As Noah approached, a group of street boys was giggling over an ophthalmic frogspawn of enamel eyes populating the lower display. The venerable Mr Schlöss had also bowed to the seasonal eccentricities of his adoptive culture and had attired one of his full-body ceroplastic studies in the guise of Guido Fawkes, a Lucifer match held in one skeletal hand and cartographic networks of veins showing beneath the dark drapery.

The shopkeeper was at the counter when Noah entered and looked up from his sales ledgers with a myopic stare that was soon remedied with an adjustment of his spectacles.

'Good evening to you, sir. You are fortunate – I was just about to close,' said Mr Schlöss.

'I am grateful you have not,' said Noah. 'I have a challenge that might be of some interest to you.'

'Ah, a challenge you say? Well, one does like a challenge. What have you? Is it a wax nose fitting? A replica hand to replace one lost to a whale in the Southern Oceans? Perhaps an enamel eye for a much-loved but wounded ratting terrier? I have seen them all and considered none a particular challenge.'

'I see I have found the right man for the job. What I seek is a ceroplastician who can fashion a head based on the precise instructions of the renowned physiognomist Mr Edward Figgs.'

'I have heard his name, of course, and I do not want to do myself out of the custom, but did you know that Madame Tussaud offers the same service to private clients for rather less money than I charge?'

'So I have heard, but I fear her modellers will not have your appreciation for the niceties of human anatomy. I need a hand that instinctively knows the difference between an occipital indentation or a sincipital occlusion. It is imperative that this work follows my instructions to the very letter.'

'Then I am indeed the right fellow for your order. Do you have the details with you?'

Noah handed the hastily written pages of his notebook across the counter and Mr Schlöss bent close to examine them with a series of "hmms". Finally, he looked to Noah again: 'The details are indeed specific and I believe I can make this head for you. Only, the description is incomplete in certain minor details. I will have to estimate inter-ocular dimension, rhinal flex and labial protuberance based on a harmony of the whole. It is not ideal, but . . .'

'I understand. Whatever you can make will be better than a mere sketch.'

'That is certainly true. But I . . . I wonder if I might enquire whether you are a detective?'

'The investigations of the Detective Force are strictly confidential. I could not say.'

'Of course, of course . . . it is just that I believe a colleague of yours was here just the other day asking about light grey eyes and I note that you are requesting the same. I cannot help wondering if the head he showed me is the head you wish made. It would be a shame if you were working at cross purposes . . .'

Mr Schlöss paused at the fixed glare and quite sudden pallor that had stricken his customer. Perhaps he had misjudged – as he occasionally did – the curious nature of the English in raising this singular coincidence.

'Did this other detective give his name?' said Noah with glacial phrasing.

'He did not introduce himself. A constable came to fetch him away and addressed him as Inspector something. I am afraid I cannot recall it now.'

'Did he have curly red hair? A man with rather a curt manner?'

'That is the fellow. Sharp eyes and a look of impatience about him.'

'Inspector Newsome.'

'Ah yes, that *is* what the constable called him. Is he working on the same case?'

'It may be. What did this other head look like – the one he showed you?'

'A curiously malformed thing. I first thought it a caricature, but he assured me it was taken from life. The appearance was quite nightmarish, as if the skin had been melted. Perhaps it was the result of a medical condition, or an accident.'

'A fire, possibly?'

'Indeed, though I would not imagine any man could survive such injuries. The inspector did not mention if the subject was still alive.'

Noah inhaled deeply and gripped the edge of counter with whitened knuckles. 'It seems you have indeed discovered a miscommunication between detectives. In fact, Mr Newsome has recently had an accident and is in a state of unconsciousness. He has been unable to pass on the details of his investigation and I am tasked with taking up his case. Whatever you can tell me will be of the greatest help.'

'O, I hope his accident is not too serious.'

'Not serious enough,' muttered Noah.

'I beg your pardon?'

'Not serious enough to endanger his life, I mean. What did he want to know about the eyes?'

'Well, the wax head he showed me had two light grey eyes that had been bought from this very shop and delivered, somewhat irregularly, to a fellow waiting on the steps of St Paul's. Wait a moment . . . here is the entry in the sales ledger.'

Noah drew his finger along the line and made a rapid computation concerning the date. The nagging rumour of Mr Newsome's recent disinterment activities rushed back upon him and his legs seemed momentarily to weaken.

'Do you feel unwell?' said Mr Schlöss. 'You seem quite . . .'

'It . . . it is nothing. Tell me – did the customer order these eyes in person?'

'Your Inspector Newsome asked the same thing and I told him that I received only a letter with part payment. I went to find the letter, but the inspector had gone when I returned. Perhaps I may show it to you instead?'

'Yes, please.'

Mr Schlöss produced the small piece of paper from a drawer beneath the counter and laid it flat for Noah's perusal. The writing was jerkily angular, as if written in great haste or great pain. It said nothing more than the requirements and the delivery address. No names, no initials, no salutations.

'May I?' Noah took the letter by a corner and raised it to his nose. There was a smell of mustiness and wood – the inside of a drawer, perhaps – but was there also the faintest scent of smoke combined with the sharp odour of sulphur and phosphorus? It was a *bouquet* to stir long-buried memories.

'In his haste, the inspector also left one of the eyes from the head,' said Mr Schlöss. 'Would you care to return it to him?'

'By all means.' Noah took the eye and held it in a clammy palm, the smoky iris rolling its dead enamel gaze back at him. 'I wonder – did the inspector say where he had procured the head?'

'No, and I did not ask.'

'Might you guess?'

'He told me that it had not been made by the Tussauds, but I could not say precisely where he found it. He carried it in a canvas sack and there were fragments of clothing adhering to the neck.'

'As if the head had been attached to a body?'

'Well, I suppose so. There were also a number of small splinters of wood embedded in the wax, as if it had been kept in a rough wooden box. And now I think about it, the hair did have a vague smell of damp about it – a rather foetid, earthy scent.'

'You have been exceptionally helpful, Mr Schlöss. I will ask you to make my order all the same so that we may compare it to the head you saw previously.'

'It will be my pleasure. I will ask you to pay a deposit now if you do not mind.'

'Of course.' Noah laid money on the counter, but noticed as he did so that the shopkeeper seemed suddenly transfixed by something on the other side of his display window. His mouth remained open and his finger rose limply to indicate what his voice could not articulate.

Noah turned ... and saw *himself* looking in from outside – not a reflection or a similar countenance, but the very same face down to the broken nose. There was the merest instant of mutual recognition; two pairs of

214

eyes widened incredulously, then the figure outside turned quickly into the flow of pedestrians.

'Did ... did you ... I swear, the selfsame face ...' said Mr Schlöss.

But Noah was already racing from the shop to stare madly about the swarming faceless multitudes. How far might the fellow have gone in those few seconds? And in what direction? Had a bus passed recently into which the man might have jumped? Was there someone looking quickly back to see if they were being followed? It was only people, people, people.

'Noah Dyson! Stop!' shouted Noah.

Some immediate passers-by stared at him, but the street continued upon its ceaseless flow, swallowing the imposter and the shouted name second by second deeper into its traffic-clogged artery. Noah issued a fricative-driven curse that drew further looks of disapproval and he stepped back into the shop.

'Did you see the fellow?' said Mr Schlöss.

'He has gone.'

'I have never seen anything like it. I have heard that two men may look alike, and I know that certain of the Roman emperors kept these, er, *doppelgangers* in their courts for amusement, but ...'

'It must have been a mask,' said Noah. 'The face was mine, but it showed emotion only in the eyes, which I believe were darker.'

'I did not see so closely, but perhaps you are correct.'

'If you see that fellow again, Mr Schlöss – if he enters your shop – I would be grateful if you could engage him in conversation and learn what you can. Do not reveal anything about the order for the head. He is clearly the grossest kind of imposter and must be captured.'

'Certainly I will do what I can to help the detectives.'

'Thank you. I will likely send colleagues to collect the finished head, which must remain utterly confidential. The security of the city may rest upon your discretion. Also, perhaps you will insert a pair of those same grey eyes into the finished article.'

And with that, Noah left the shop casting wary looks about him as he joined the crowds, for, in the space of the last half an hour, these streets had become significantly more dangerous. The cumulative implication of the evidence so far – no matter how incredible it may seem – pointed towards something Noah had feared in his darkest dreams. Could it be true that Lucius Boyle was indeed alive? That his death had been an illusion? That the burial had been a farce orchestrated by the man himself to earn eternal anonymity? Certainly, many of the unfortunate events of recent months could be explained by the fact of Boyle's continued existence, and proof that the incendiary still nurtured his vengeful enmity for one who had once been an equal – once a friend.

It may have been a lifetime ago, and Noah may have circumnavigated the globe many times since, but their connection had never been truly broken. Only the death of one adversary could effect such a break – not the rumour of death, nor the threat of death, nor the appearance of death. This time it would have to be personally delivered: hot-handed, remorseless and decisive.

But for now, there was an appointment to be kept at Dodgeley's butchers and visits to both Madame Tussaud's and Portugal-street burial ground.

TWENTY

The rooms at Regent-street presented quite a different aspect than they had the week before. Now, all of the books and newspapers, the old clothes and the wax fruit had evidently been packed into large leather-banded travelling trunks arrayed about the floor. The dagger that had been stabbed into the *escritoire* was also gone, leaving a neat diamond-shaped wound in the polished wood.

Sir Richard sat in the same chair he had occupied before and looked for the fourth time at his pocket watch. There had been not the merest sight of Vidocq since the ruffianly servant Jacques had admitted the commissioner some twenty minutes earlier. Rather, a series of increasingly immoral sounds had continued to issue from behind an oak-panelled door leading off from the room: girlish giggles and robust Gallic laughter that had descended into a silence punctuated by sounds Sir Richard cared not to interpret too closely.

After the sixth glance at his watch and a determination to seek his hat and coat, Sir Richard saw the connecting door finally open and a girl of perhaps twenty years emerge in a state of virtual *dishabille*, her face suffused with recent exertion. On seeing the unexpected visiter sitting straight-backed in his chair, she gave another giggle and nodded a flirtatious '*Monsieur*' before clopping quickly away in her high-buttoned boots.

Vidocq followed a few moments later, his habitual sardonic smile seemingly wider and his left eye shaded all around with a virulent yellow-purple bruising. He showed not the slightest indication of embarrassment in his handshake and address:

'Forgive me, Sir Richard – it seems that France has exported some of her finest talents to your city and I was reluctant to leave without a ... a *souvenir*.

Of course, I was also very curious when they told me that you wished personally to bid me goodbye.'

'Your eye, *monsieur* – have you had an accident?' said Sir Richard.

'It is nothing. I was visiting one of your rookeries one evening – Seven Dials, I think they call it – and a party of Irishmen took insult at our use of the French language. A violent debate resulted and the natives were persuaded of our linguistic merits. Nobody was killed.'

'What on earth were you doing in Seven Dials after dark?'

'Mere curiosity. I have seen the slums of Paris and wanted to compare. I must congratulate you – yours are certainly superior in squalor and depravity. Ha! But enough of this English chatter – will you have a cognac?'

Sir Richard sighed. 'I believe I will.'

'Bravo!' Vidocq clapped his hands and yelled into the hallway: 'Jacques! Cognac!'

'I see that you are packed for imminent departure, *monsieur* . . .'

'Bah! Let us not talk like ladies. Why did you really want to see me before I return to Paris, eh?'

'You assume that—'

'I assume nothing. I *know* many things.' Vidocq's eyed glistened with pleasure.

'Then perhaps we can dispense with the ludic element and you can tell me what you think you know.'

'Games are more fun, no? But I admit time is short. I have heard that you had a robbery at Scotland Yard . . . and before you interrupt, let us not talk about the origins of these things I know. Yes, you had a robbery: something very important, something that nobody knows of but you and your inspector Newsome. Something, indeed, so dangerous that you come to me on the pretext of bidding me *bon voyage*.'

Sir Richard merely stared, allowing Vidocq his pleasure. The servant Jacques arrived with two balloon glasses of cognac and left without a word.

'Then there is this fellow Mr Williamson accused of stuffing the whore Charlotte. He used to be one of yours, I understand: a fine detective by all accounts. Strange that he should be accused of a murder so similar to that of that constable, no? I have followed it in the papers. He is innocent of course – you must know that. I mean, your Williamson is innocent.'

Sir Richard took a sip of the cognac and noted grimly that it quite ridiculed the quality of the brandy served at his club. It tasted of history and southern sunsets.

Vidocq winked and continued: 'People – no matter which people – are saying privately that you have no ideas about this constable found near the burial ground and that your inspector Newsome is a lunatic – that a police force can have no authority when its own headquarters are robbed with impunity. Tell me – what was stolen?'

Sir Richard took another sip and watched Vidocq do the same.

'You may trust me,' added the Frenchman. 'I seek no personal advantage – only additional merit. One day I will die – we will both die – and they will search in vain for proof of this meeting. They will whisper that the great Vidocq conferred with the illustrious Sir Richard Mayne upon a delicate case at a secret *rendezvous*. These are the rumours that ensure immortality, no? Not the crimes solved publicly or the outrageous escape, but the case so notorious, so monumental, that it has been erased from the records – or not even entered! The imagination magnifies tenfold what in fact is often mediocre. *This* is why I ask you these things. Fame, *monsieur*! She touches few with her cool hand, and I stick my head above the crowd to get her attention, eh?'

'You are indeed a singular man, *monsieur*,' said Sir Richard.

Vidocq raised his glass in a toast of evident agreement.

'There was a fellow Parisian of yours: Inspector Marais,' said Sir Richard.

'Ah yes – a splendid fellow!'

'He was immoral and corrupt.'

'As you say: a fellow Parisian. But he was before my time.'

'He kept certain illicit files on notable people . . .'

'Aaaah!' The exclamation came slowly and spirit-scented. '*Now* I understand. But I thought the London police did not engage in such—'

'It does not. This was an aberration, a misjudgement masquerading as justice. A man has been punished. Now we face the cost.'

'So you have lost files listing the lecheries of your worthy citizens, eh? Is it a lengthy catalogue? Does it feature truly significant personages?'

'I have not read all of it, but what I have seen is shocking enough. I have no doubt the thief is already extorting his victims.'

'And you come to me now for advice? Because you have been driven into a corner by the criminal? It must have been difficult for you to make that decision.'

Sir Richard finished the last of the cognac and looked at Vidocq through the warping lens of the glass's bottom. He said nothing. He waited and watched the Frenchman's fleshy face work upon the problem: eyes narrowed, brows asymmetric, his mouth working at a *bolus* of thought.

'Your robber ... and the man who has turned the police upon your Mr Williamson with this Charlotte business ... it is the same fellow!'

'Why would you think that?' said Sir Richard.

'Because I think from the criminal's point of view. He seeks to ridicule the police. This Mr Williamson, I suppose, is working for you ... as an agent, eh? The criminal strikes at him perhaps to strike at you, no?'

'Continue.'

'I see that I have influenced the nature of your investigations after all! But Vidocq's methods are "*espionage*", are they not? The Metropolitan Police does not condone them, no?'

'*If* I have followed your suggestions at all, *monsieur,* they have led me to the position in which I now find myself. My "agents" as you call them have become fugitives from justice and I risk adverse public opinion on multiple fronts. Not only is an ex-detective accused of murder, he is then freed in a violent escape that leaves constables and magistrate red-faced.'

'Ah, but what an escape, eh? It was a beautiful thing: the boys, the stones, the nets!'

'How do you know such things, *monsieur*? Those details were not reported in the newspapers. I made sure that my Newspaper Office was quite vague in the official bulletins.'

Vidocq touched the side of his bountiful nose. 'It is my purpose to know such things. They come to me like bees to the flowers.'

'I see. Well, I would be most grateful if you might share some of your experience. I have made the mistake of playing by your rules and I have lost. I now find myself in an even more awkward situation. What have I done wrong?'

'You have not cheated! Did I not make clear to you before that the victor makes his own rules? If the criminal "cheats", you cheat. If your agents cheat you, cheat them in return. You must stop thinking like an Englishman! When the lake is muddy after the rain, one cannot see the fish – so one slaps the surface with a board and stuns them to the surface. Every peasant knows this.'

'I am not sure I follow . . .'

'Drastic measures, *monsieur* commissioner. Your quarry has the advantage of invisibility, but you have the advantage of visibility. You influence the newspapers, no? You have a thousand men at your command? You have many buildings, boats, carriages – you have more than I ever had in the *police de sureté*. And yet I arrested more criminals single-handedly in one year than does your entire Detective Force . . . Ah, do not raise your hands with the old lady's cry of "*espionage*"! The public cannot care what they know nothing about. You bicker in your parliament about "plain clothes" – I say wear the same clothes as your people. Did Christ wear a uniform to identify himself to his people?'

'That is blasphemy, sir, and I hardly think it an appropriate comparison.'

'Talk not of "appropriate", *monsieur*. Speak instead of "effective". Perhaps it is "appropriate" to chase the fox with hounds, but—'

'Please – not another rural analogy.'

Vidocq grinned at Sir Richard's irritation, thinking, perhaps, that with more cognac and argument the commissioner might even find his inner Frenchman. But not today. 'I asked you before if Inspector Newsome was investigating the case of the stuffed policeman and you told me he was not. That started me thinking "why not?" This Newsome is known to be a good man, if a little unpredictable. What are you not telling me? Is there another aspect to this case? Something to do with a coffin being exhumed, perhaps?'

'I . . . How long have you known this? And how?'

'It matters not. But if there is something you have not revealed, I cannot make better suggestions.'

'Very well. Very well. You know, of course, the name of Lucius Boyle.'

'Who does not? He was a great English murderer.'

'It seems . . . well, that is to say, there is a slight but indistinct possibility that he may not be dead after all. His burial plot contained only an effigy and there are . . . indications of certain . . . characteristic activity.'

Vidocq gave a low whistle and began immediately to radiate the pleasure of realisation. 'Of course! Now it all makes sense! The robbery, the exhumation, the sculpted constable . . .'

'I would not say that it makes sense – only that there may be connections. This does not help the investigation.'

'But it *does, monsieur*. You might not know his game, but if one knows the player, one can enter into competition with an advantage. You must gather all you know: everything from Inspector Newsome, everything from your agents, everything from your experience. You must take all this and make a strategy to beat your adversary. Bring together your best resources and you will be triumphant, no? I believe you have the answer in your hands, but you cannot see its every part.'

'What you describe is more difficult than you realize. There is a certain belligerent history between these various men – a history, I regret, of betrayal and distrust. Not only that, but one of them was a childhood fellow and lifelong enemy of Boyle. He would become quite deranged if he knew that the fact of his enemy's existence had been wilfully concealed from him.'

'You refer to Noah Dyson, I suppose? It is quite simple: you must lie to him.'

'What do you know of Mr Dyson?'

'Less than I know about Messrs Newsome and Williamson, whose deeds are largely a matter of public record. They are observed by a greater number. This Dyson, however, is like a shadow. Neither the police or the criminals seem to know him, which I suppose tells me all I need to know.'

'And what is that?'

'That he is exceptionally good: a true man of the city. I would like to meet him.

When I was active in Paris, they knew my name but they did not know my face. Your Mr Dyson is hardly known at all. You should always value a fellow like that. Use him – he is better than any policeman for your particular requirements.'

Sir Richard sighed.

'Truth or defeat, *monsieur*. The choice is yours. Think of the politicians to whom you answer. Do they stand before their peers and say truly what they think? Or do they say what they *think* the others would like to hear? Justice is compromise, Sir Richard. Yes, I employed ex-thieves in Paris; I associated with the lowest in society, drinking and swearing with them – but when the irons went about their wrist, justice was done and I had made the city safer. Choose your epitaph, *monsieur*: "He told no lies" or "He was true to justice".'

'You are something of a politician yourself,' said Sir Richard meditatively.

'Call me a thief and a scoundrel, but do not call me a politician!' laughed Vidocq.

'Even if I *were* to return to these men as you recommend, I have no idea where to locate them. Their houses are burned, their temporary refuge has been rendered unsafe and – as you have said – Mr Dyson knows the city like no other. Where would *you* look?'

'I need hardly tell you, Sir Richard, that a city is sometimes but a conglomeration of villages. The arrival of a stranger in either the poorest or the richest parts never goes unnoticed, so your men will likely be in one of those transient regions where people come and go, where apartments are left empty by international owners, or rented for short periods by people who are obliged to move up and down the social scale. Where do your common writers live in this city? Where are your minor diplomats and your higher-class prostitutes?'

Where – indeed – is the last place you would think to look for them? That is where they shall be if they are worthy of the name "agent".'

'I ... I believe you may have given me an idea, *monsieur*,' said Sir Richard.

'Bravo! Find these men and bring them together. Set them against each other if you must. As commissioner, you do not *play* the game; you *create* the game which others play. The rules are yours to change, as are the penalties and rewards. If the law is served in the end, all will be well.'

'*Monsieur* Vidocq – if only you had been born an Englishman. You would have been a great superintendent of the Metropolitan Police.'

'With all respect, I would rather be a French gutter-dweller than an English superintendent. Ha! Take my advice and you will see that I am right.'

'I trust that you will never reveal this matter, or even this meeting.'

'You have my word, Sir Richard. Indeed, let us make an agreement: I will send you a bottle of that excellent cognac, which you will open and savour *only* when you solve this case.'

'And if I do not solve the case?'

'Then your reputation will be soiled and your career over. You will want to drown your despair in the spirit of *la belle époque*. Ha! *Bonne chance, monsieur! Bonne chance!*'

TWENTY-ONE

Alone at Charlotte's house, Mr Williamson had struggled more with the lingering spirit of her life than with her obscene death effigy. Her perfume was more tortuous to him than the smell of any river-dredged corpse, and it seemed to saturate the very walls so that wherever he stood or sat was imbued with the feeling of her continued presence. Stray strands of her dark hair stroked his skin; pelvic indentations in cushions mocked him with a false promise of her corporeality; mirrors that had once feasted on her beauty now reflected only his averted gaze.

He had also been assaulted with an even greater sense of what these rooms had seen. The innocent sofa, the water closet, the bed – the bed – had all no doubt been sites of her innumerable ruinations, depravations, debasements and remunerative emunctions. There could hardly have been a space in that small apartment where she had *not* lain or knelt or otherwise dyspostured herself for another's pleasure.

He had also found her money hidden below a floorboard whose muffled rattle beneath a rug had betrayed its presence. The plain wooden box in that ratty cavity had contained almost three-hundred pounds – every coin of it a pollution of her purity, every note of it representing an act of lubricious dishonour too horrible to imagine yet too compelling to ignore. In Mr Williamson's hands lay the accumulated currency of sin that had once been in the palms of those many other men. They had bought her body, but they had never touched her mind.

If that had been the sum of all he had discovered, the investigation would have cooled. Fortunately, he had finally been able to face the body itself and to discern – without further disgracing her honour with unnecessary nudity –

that Mr Cullen's observations were sound. Quite apart from the obvious aesthetic disparities, the thread that bound her wounds was different; the stuffing was of a different texture and even the preservative chymicals had a vaguely different aroma than the figure of PC Taylor.

Furthermore, a cause of death had suggested itself. Applying the same meticulous examination he had used upon the constable's corpse, Mr Williamson had checked even within the folds and whorls of the ears, where he had discovered the merest accumulation of dried blood. A spike driven in through the ear to the brain, perhaps? Death would have been instantaneous and possibly without pain. And if she had been on her knees at the time ... The thought disturbed him greatly, but it seemed a logical enough manner for a stranger to buy her trust.

This assumption had suggested another, and half an hour of careful searching had led him to find her appointment book: another catalogue of lust whose populous pages gave name to the dozens of men who had filled her purse. It was also to some degree a diary in which young Charlotte had jotted reminders and observations about previous or expected clients. *'Prefers French'* was one recurrent note. *'Greek'* was less frequent, but regular enough.

And Mr Williamson was there, too: just another daily name preceded or succeeded by other men. He was described as "kind", as "gentle", as "naive". She had never intimated – why would she? – as they had sat talking, that the previous hour had been spent in a bestial tangle and that the next would be similarly passed forgetting his kind words amidst a phrensy of slapping flesh. It should have been obvious, of course, but only seeing it listed now made it humiliatingly so.

Again, however, the sorrow had been alloyed with evidence. In the days before her death, she had been visited by a "foreign-looking gentleman" who barely spoke but who merely indicated what he liked ("French"). Charlotte had described him as "mysterious and a little frightening" but had not noted any violence. The man had not made any appointments beyond the date when she must have been taken.

He was further considering the significance of this when he heard the rattle of a key in the street door. Evidently Noah or the burly pair had returned from their peregrinations about the city – most likely the former since silence indicated the absence of the garrulous Mr Cullen.

'Noah? I am in the parlour,' called Mr Williamson.

But the key kept rattling as if it were the wrong one. Could it be one of Charlotte's appointments, unaware of her recent demise?

Mr Williamson walked into the hallway and looked at the solid oak street door, which now began to rattle as force was exerted upon it from outside. He looked around him for a weapon and saw only a wood-handled umbrella standing in an earthenware pot.

'Noah? Is that you? Identify yourself!' he shouted.

The rattling stopped momentarily. Then it began with greater force. Mr Williamson took hold of the umbrella and held it above his head, ready to bring the thick handle on whomever's head might emerge.

The lock mechanism clicked and the door jerked open. The edge of a hat brim appeared and Mr Williamson swung at it with the force of a whole day's frustration.

'My G__!' came the cry of the victim as the curved umbrella handle crashed into the hat, knocking it off and continuing unimpeded to strike the nose. A thatch of curly red hair became apparent, followed by the furious face of Inspector Albert Newsome, blood now running freely over his lips and chin from his assaulted nose.

'_____ _____!' bellowed Mr Newsome, standing on the threshold and scrabbling furiously for a handkerchief.

'What on earth is happening?' came another familiar voice: Sir Richard Mayne, flanked by two constables in plain clothes.

Mr Williamson did not speak. The umbrella remained martially aloft.

'He has broken my _____ nose!' whined Mr Newsome from behind rapidly saturating cotton.

'Put down your weapon, George,' said Sir Richard calmly. 'We have not come to arrest you. We know – or least we strongly suspect – that you are not responsible for the murder of Charlotte. We are here to discuss who *is* and how, together, we might effect his capture.'

'How did you know to find me at this address?'

'A matter of deduction that is now irrelevant. May we enter?'

'Why must he be present?' said Mr Williamson, pointing the umbrella at a freely cursing Mr Newsome.

'It is perhaps regrettable, but the inspector has information that may be of use. Only by collaborating can we solve this crime. Now – will you permit us access before the whole street comes out to observe this *contretemps*?'

Mr Williamson thought quickly. He had little choice but to bid them enter, but Noah must be warned lest he walk blindly into the situation and risk possible arrest for his part in the escape from Marylebone police court. 'Will you position your constables unobtrusively outside?' he said. 'If you know of my whereabouts, perhaps others may also have discerned it.'

'Indeed,' said Sir Richard, nodding to his men outside on the steps and ushering Mr Newsome forward so that the door could be closed.

Mr Williamson lowered the umbrella and beckoned them to follow him into the parlour where they might be seated.

'Is Noah Dyson here, or any of those other gentlemen with whom you associate?' said Richard, taking a seat and noting with interest (but not surprize) the body of Charlotte standing to one side.

'So – another crime of which you are guilty,' muttered Mr Newsome, his eyes awash with pain but the sanguineous flow apparently stanched. 'Not only do you flee prison, but you steal evidence also.'

'We are not here for mutual accusations, Inspector,' said Sir Richard. 'We are here because there is a crime to be solved – a greater crime that touches us all.'

'To which crime do you refer?' said Mr Williamson, his mind still working rapidly to understand what this latest development might mean.

Much as he did not want to work with the police, he was homeless and at greater risk without the protection of Sir Richard – at least for the time being.

'Well, that is something I was hoping to discuss in the presence of Mr Dyson. Are you expecting him?'

'I am afraid I have no knowledge of his whereabouts.'

But at that very moment, there came a strangled grunt, a muffled bang against the street door and the sound of a heavy body hitting the ground.

'That will be him now,' muttered Mr Newsome.

And indeed a rattle of the key was followed by Noah's voice calling, 'George? Are you safe?' followed by the appearance of the man himself at the door of the parlour. On seeing the two policemen, he instinctively reached for his dagger and uttered a somewhat confused 'What?'

'Becalm yourself,' said Sir Richard. 'We are here on unofficial business. We know that George did not kill the girl.'

Noah glared at Mr Newsome, whose reciprocating gaze was no less unfriendly.

'I hope that we can be civil,' warned Sir Richard. 'I know that there are certain events in your shared pasts which may cause bad feeling—'

'He left two of my friends to drown in a flooded cell,' said Noah with his fists clenched tightly. 'He should be in gaol, not in the police force.'

'And by the same token, you left his unconscious body to the mercy of the river,' said Sir Richard. 'Discussing old animosities will do nothing to relieve the situation in which we find ourselves. I suspect that each of you knows things that can bring this case to a close – so let us close it.'

'Which case?' said Noah. 'There is the body of PC Taylor, there is the incendiarism of our houses, there is the murder of Charlotte . . . and there is the case of the body exhumed at Portugal-street burial ground a few days ago, which may have impelled all the others.'

The three listeners stared intently at Noah with an admixture of surprize, suspicion and shock. Nobody spoke for a few moments.

Finally, Sir Richard broke the silence. 'Very well. You have raised the subject of the exhumation, Mr Dyson, and so we must address it.'

'What?' protested Mr Newsome. 'That is my investigation and I will—'

'You will co-operate with this new investigation or you will face suspension,' said Sir Richard. 'We have been like men flailing variously at a fire when an engine to extinguish it stands fully loaded before us. What do you know about Portugal-street, Mr Dyson?'

'I know that Mr Newsome was disinterring a coffin there on the same night that PC Taylor was found. I also know that the plot held an unnamed body and that the Metropolitan Police uses the place for the occasional disposal of criminals. It seems there was an explosion – is that right, Mr Newsome?'

The inspector merely glowered, his reddened nose exaggerating the effect of displeasure.

'I ask rhetorically, of course,' continued Noah. 'I also know that following this exhumation, the inspector visited Madame Tussaud's and a certain shop on Holborn to investigate the provenance of the waxen effigy he had found in the coffin. The dates occurring in various records are suggestive if not specific. And it is strange, but the young man I spoke to at Tussaud's (at least, he called himself thus) seemed to be under the impression that the head he saw was a likeness of Lucius Boyle.'

'The loose-tongued _____!' muttered Mr Newsome, ardently hoping that young "Bill" had not also mentioned the fuss made about the masks.

'Why should we trust a word you say, commissioner,' said Noah, 'when you have concealed this from us? Lucius Boyle who devoutly wishes me dead – who engineered my transportation and who has tried to kill my friends – is apparently alive and at liberty in London. I have good reason to suspect that it is he who burned our houses and he that has attempted to have George imprisoned for the death of Charlotte.'

Noah's fists remained bone-white, though he controlled his voice. All the while, there was the trace of a smile about Mr Newsome's lips.

Sir Richard held his hands up. 'Now wait a moment, Mr Dyson. I . . . there are indeed certain people who believe Lucius Boyle may still be alive, but you were one of those who saw him dead – in fact, all three of you did so. How do you explain that?'

'I saw a badly burned man – that is all. It seemed at the time that there was no-one else in the balloon, but . . . but all the evidence before me now points to his continued existence. I believe he is still alive.'

Sir Richard thought briefly of his recent interview with Vidocq. Lying, it seemed, was going to prove ineffective with Noah Dyson after all. He turned instead to Mr Newsome and sighed his acquiescence: 'Tell them about the Frenchman Louis Chiveot, Inspector.'

'But my investigation is—!'

'Tell them. I will not warn you again.'

Mr Newsome's scowl was almost mask-like. He stared at his feet and spoke in a sing-song voice. 'There is a French detective working at Scotland Yard. He has been seeking a lad of his country who went missing that night at Vauxhall gardens – last seen in a balloon . . .'

'I knew it,' said Noah, and some dark emotion flamed across his aspect. 'It is the only explanation.'

'Hmm. How long have you suspected this, Sir Richard?' said Mr Williamson.

'I myself retain doubts, but the inspector here has unearthed some quite suggestive evidence that—'

'I saw him,' said Mr Newsome. 'In the warehouse beneath Frying Pan wharf as part of the smuggling case. I saw his face and recognized him. That is how I know he is alive. The other evidence is just a formality of juridical process.'

'And so you thought to keep this knowledge to yourself, for your own glory, while other men suffered the loss of their homes?' said Mr Williamson. 'How like you.'

'Are you a serving policeman – you and your gang of oddities – to be seeking criminals in the city?' countered Mr Newsome.

'That is enough!' said Sir Richard. 'I did not expect that bringing you together would be pleasant, but perhaps we can expedite the experience by remaining only with the facts as we know them. Inspector Newsome has revealed what he has found about the balloon ... and it seems Mr Dyson has discovered a number of details about the effigy found at Portugal-street. What else do you know?'

'Wait a moment' said Noah. 'I would like to know more about what was found in that coffin.'

'It was a sand-filled body with wax extremities,' said Sir Richard on behalf of his brooding inspector. 'Evidently the likeness was taken from a cast of the living face – a horribly burned face supplied with eyes as you have learned. Unfortunately, the specifics concerning the purchaser of the components and construction are too vague to investigate.'

'So there is not the least clue?' said Noah. 'Nothing further on the body or in the casket?'

Sir Richard fixed Mr Newsome with a piercing look of enquiry.

'There was a burned match inside the sand of the chest,' said the latter offhandedly. 'It is probably a mere piece of detritus ...'

'Burned entirely through, as if the flame had touched the fingers?' said Noah.

Mr Newsome hesitated then nodded grimly at his inadvertent revelation

'I found something similar at the launch site of the rocket that sparked the fire in my home – not a stray rocket, as was first suggested by some fire-engineers, but one with an explosive head. And the whole property was prepared with flammable materials to aid the conflagration. I also found this verse inscribed on the wall.'

Noah took the brittle Bible page from a pocket and handed it to Sir Richard, who scanned it and passed it to Mr Newsome.

'It is rather a heartfelt message if from a stranger,' continued Noah. 'I thought of Boyle as soon as I read it.'

'I see,' said the commissioner reflectively. 'This is precisely the kind of thing we need to be sharing with each other if we are to catch this criminal.'

'Do you *still* retain doubt as to his identity?' said Mr Newsome, brandishing the Bible leaf.

'Catching him will prove it,' said Sir Richard. 'What have we learned about the body of PC Taylor? We have, of course, found his disassembled remains at the Fleet prison, but . . .'

'Hmm. The fellow was thoroughly stuffed as we already knew,' said Mr Williamson. 'As for material clues, there are only two, neither of which is particularly helpful. The first is the unusually high quality of the work; the second is a minor trace of beeswax under one fingernail. Our investigations have not turned up any suspect – apparently the art is popular among many country gentlemen.'

'The question must surely be what connection this body has with the exhumation of Boyle,' said Noah. 'It seems too great a coincidence for them to be discovered on the same evening so close together. Could it be that Boyle received an intimation that Mr Newsome had been sniffing about the burial records and so placed the body there as a distraction? Wherever the man is hiding, he clearly has the privacy to engage in such practices.'

'Hmm. Hmm. There is a complicating factor that is perhaps misdirecting our investigations,' said Mr Williamson. 'I refer to the body of Charlotte, which was used to implicate me. My examination of both bodies (along with expert advice) makes for one undeniable conclusion: the two bodies were prepared by different hands.'

'Are you suggesting . . . that there are *two* such murderers at large in the city?' said Sir Richard.

'Either that or Boyle has gone to great lengths to disguise his work on the girl,' said Mr Newsome. 'Though I admit this would clearly frustrate his purposes if he was seeking to draw a parallel.'

'In that case,' said Noah, 'which of the bodies – if either – may be connected to Boyle? I submit that Charlotte's is the obvious choice since its use is a direct attack upon George. I never knew Boyle to have an interest in taxidermy, and the inexpert nature of the work suggests a hasty execution. My suspicion is that he was copying the murder of PC Taylor.'

'Then ... who is responsible for the death of PC Taylor ... and why?' said Sir Richard, attempting to keep a tone of increasing unease from his voice.

The others merely exchanged glances of enquiry.

'I agree with Noah,' said Mr Williamson. 'The death of Charlotte must be Boyle's work. We should focus on how it was orchestrated.'

'You certainly proved a willing participant with your courting of the whore,' said Mr Newsome with ill-disguised glee.

'Inspector ...' said Sir Richard in the manner of a man about to beat his dog.

'Hmm. I was referring to how the body was deposited on Oxford-street. Since the perpetrator was clearly not I, why did so many witnesses believe it was?'

'I believe I may be able to offer further insight into that matter,' said Noah. 'You recall, George, that Benjamin was sure he saw you on Holborn when you were actually at the Fleet? Well, Mr Cullen's investigation at the taxidermists's revealed another piece of infamy: a fellow fitting your description bought a quantity of materials shortly before Charlotte's body was discovered.'

'Hmm. Hmm. Why did neither of you mention it to me?'

'Because it was so patently absurd an idea, and because the shopkeeper identified the face as a mask rather than a real countenance.'

'A mask?' said Sir Richard.

'Indeed. Someone has been impersonating Mr Williamson. And this very day I have seen "myself" observing me through a shop window – an exact likeness that can only have been a mask.'

Mr Newsome remained assiduously silent and busied himself with a loose button on his jacket.

'If there are likenesses of you, Mr Dyson, and of Mr Williamson, one must wonder what other faces our criminal wears,' said Sir Richard. 'Enquiries should be made at whatever establishments manufacture these things. Madame Tussaud's, perhaps.'

'I will attend to that,' said Mr Newsome, somewhat precipitously. 'That is, I know a fellow there.'

'I do not believe it is Boyle himself who wears the masks,' said Noah. 'He has learned from hard experience that it is better to stay completely hidden. Rather, one of his accomplices must be the one.'

'You are thinking of the Italian?' said Mr Williamson. 'He who attempted to take the body of Charlotte from Marylebone police court?'

'He seems the likeliest candidate, but there may now be others,' said Noah.

'Wait a moment,' said Sir Richard. Are you referring to the "Italian" who was implicated in the smuggling case? He who was presumed dead but whose body vanished? And what is this about him attempting to take the body?'

'It is the same man,' said Noah. 'And he is patently not dead. The body of Charlotte that you see in this room was won through armed conflict and I think it is significant that he would want to gain possession of it.'

Mr Newsome had suddenly become once again attentive and willed Sir Richard not to turn to him with the next observation. But he willed in vain.

'Inspector Newsome – it seems we might now have a specific suspect in our recent robbery.'

'Ah yes,' said Noah. 'My sources tell me that the security of Scotland Yard has been breached of late and that Mr Newsome has been spending some time at the offices. What was stolen?'

'I am afraid that is—' began Sir Richard.

'That is precisely the kind of thing you should be telling us, since it likely has a bearing on our personal safety,' finished Noah.

'The diary,' said Mr Williamson. 'I found a diary during the smuggling case that proved the criminal – he who now appears to be Lucius Boyle – had been observing our every move. I left that diary in your care, Sir Richard, as part of an ongoing investigation. Where is it now?'

The commissioner looked to his inspector, who offered nothing in the way of help. 'I . . .'

'And was there, I wonder, not also some kind of illicit catalogue?' said Noah. 'Our Mr Cullen has spoken of a network of constables organized by Inspector Newsome – their aim being to gather information on the immoralities of highly-placed people. This information must have been stored somewhere.'

'That is a rather fanciful notion,' said Sir Richard without conviction.

'Perhaps,' said Noah, 'but such a document, if it existed, would no doubt feature Charlotte in its pages . . . as might the diary. If a man wanted to inculpate Mr Williamson, either one of those documents would be invaluable. So let us be frank – we have shared information with you and you may be withholding things that affect our personal safety.'

'Very well. Very well. You may assume that . . . that the information of which you speak is no longer in police hands."

Noah looked to Mr Williamson. Sir Richard did not look to Mr Newsome.

'Hmm. Hmm,' said Mr Williamson.

'Another repercussion of Inspector Newsome's boundless impetuosity?' said Noah.

'Recriminations are worthless now,' said Sir Richard. 'The situation is dire.'

'I suppose there is no useful evidence at the scene of the robbery?' said Mr Williamson.

'None, apart from the skill involved,' said Mr Newsome, 'and the suggestion that perhaps someone within may have provided key impressions. The locks are old – it could have happened at any time.'

'Well, the Italian is indeed a likely candidate for the robbery,' said Noah. 'He is one we would do well to capture. Unlike Boyle, he is probably at large on the city streets . . . if only we had the vaguest idea of where to look.'

Sir Richard seemed deep in thought, perhaps recalling once again his recent audience with Vidocq. 'I believe I may have a notion of how we might expedite our search. Mr Dyson – you are the one among us who has the most experience of this so-called Italian. Do you think that you might describe him to a police artist so that we might call upon the newspapers to do our work for us? It is, admittedly, rather a drastic measure and I do not want to cause a general alarm in the city.'

'His true deeds need not be described,' said Mr Newsome, apparently enthused by the idea. 'It is enough that his description is circulated and some manner of reward offered. No doubt we will need to make provision for some clerks to receive public reports, but it is an excellent idea.'

'Agreed,' said Noah.

'Hmm. I fear we are concentrating on the particulars at the risk of missing the larger view,' said Mr Williamson. 'The masks, Charlotte, the ledger and the diary – do they all form part of a grander strategy, or is Boyle merely toying with us? We have enough experience of the man to know that wherever he bids us look is very often a ruse: an illusionist's sleight of hand disguising his true action.'

'Very likely you are correct,' said Sir Richard, 'but, at present, we cannot fathom his deeds. Worse still, the possession of that ledger gives him an invisible power that even the Metropolitan Police cannot impede. Even if we were able to discern the targets of his extortion, we can hardly approach them – and they are unlikely to approach me.'

There was a flash of wordless communication between Mr Williamson and Noah.

'I believe I know someone who might help,' said the latter.

'Who?' said Mr Newsome.

'A person who would never deign to speak to one such as you, Inspector. I believe I may be able to obtain information from this source that no amount of police detection could discover.'

'Very well, Mr Dyson. I will ask you to meet that person with all haste,' said Sir Richard. 'Do you and Mr Williamson propose to use this building as your base? It is, of course, imperative that we stay in communication.'

'For the time being,' said Mr Williamson. 'If Charlotte was taken or killed here, it is a crime scene and may still yield some minor evidence. Also, it seems, I am still the major suspect in her murder and some members of the public know my face.'

'It is true you are considered a fugitive by the press,' said Sir Richard, 'but we may also assume that your face is known only to those who attended Marylebone police court: a matter of a hundred people or so in the whole city. I could, of course, make an announcement of your innocence, but I would prefer to catch the genuine criminal first.'

'Hmm. Hmm. So I must remain a prisoner here until the case is solved – a penalty hanging over my head as a means of persuasion,' said Mr Williamson. 'Is this what you call help?'

'I act in your best interests, George, but I must also—'

'No matter,' interrupted Noah. 'It is advantageous that someone remains at this property. The Italian might once more attempt to reclaim the body if he learns that we are here. If so, we will be waiting for him.'

'Well, well . . . take care,' said Sir Richard. 'These people have demonstrated that they have no compunctions about killing.'

'Are we not also forgetting the matter of PC Taylor?' said Mr Newsome. 'While we plot the pursuit of Lucius Boyle, it seems another murderer is free . . . if Mr Williamson's evidence is to be believed.'

'A good point, Inspector,' said Sir Richard. 'I am afraid, gentlemen, that this is something else we must address now that we have started the investigation. Did either of you, I wonder, speak to Dr Hammerton at Westminster hospital?'

'He was consulted and provided a description,' said Noah. 'Alas, the description was of any man who might commit this kind of murder: intelligent, meticulous, prone to violence.'

'I put no stock by these so-called sciences,' said Mr Newsome. 'One need not be a doctor to say that a murderer is a violent man.'

'Thank you, Inspector,' said Sir Richard. 'Your opinions on the matter are well known. The question, however, is whether the description you received might just as easily describe Lucius Boyle.'

'It would,' said Noah,' though the physical evidence would seem to suggest quite the opposite. Indeed, one might believe Boyle more capable of preparing PC Taylor than Charlotte. Such a thought, I admit, is not the least helpful.'

'There is only one way to be sure: catch Boyle and his men,' said Mr Newsome. 'Thereafter, all may be seen more clearly.'

'It seems Inspector Newsome is correct,' said Sir Richard. 'If the criminal is indeed preparing some greater outrage, we must act rapidly to forestall it and bring him to justice for all that he has so far wrought. For the purposes of general harmony, I will assume the lead in this investigation and will liaise with you separately. I trust that is agreeable?'

Glances of antipathy, but no words, flickered between Mr Newsome and the other two men.

'Very well. Let us proceed with all haste. Mr Dyson – I will send a police artist here this very evening to take your description and I will be in touch regarding our various investigations.'

Commissioner and inspector made to stand.

'And tell me, Sir Richard,' said Noah, 'Do you still intend to honour your promise of re-housing us? Whether or not Lucius Boyle is caught?'

'What is this . . .?' began Mr Newsome, but was waved to silence by the commissioner.

'The Metropolitan Police will see that those who are inconvenienced are adequately recompensed,' said Sir Richard gravely.

'Spoken like a true barrister,' said Noah. 'I will also request that the likeness discovered by Inspector Newsome in the coffin be made available for our examination. It is in all of our interests.'

'That evidence is—!' began Mr Newsome.

'—Is important to the case and will be made available,' finished Sir Richard with a raised hand indicating that no further discussion of the matter was required.

Mr Newsome's face – already fiery from the umbrella assault – seemed to move a shade darker towards apoplexy.

And with that, the two policemen left the apartment at Golden-square.

Inside, Noah and Mr Williamson discussed urgently what had just passed and what they had learned since last seeing each other. Outside, in a stationary cab, a fellow with long dark hair and a gold earring watched the property with narrowed eyes.

TWENTY-TWO

Tobias Smalletts felt himself suffocating against the vast puddingy bosom of the Irishwoman who was clutching him within a vice of plumply dimpled arms. Not only that, but he was now quite certain he was drunk and liable to vomit at any moment if he could not take air into his chest.

'Let the laddy go, Megan!' shouted one of the men who had forced whisky upon the boy. 'Ye're killin' 'im wit yeh udders!'

''Tis not a bad way to go!' offered another with spirit-glazed eyes.

'But he's so adorable in his liddle school suit,' cooed the woman named Megan, jerking the diminutive form of Master Smalletts against her abundant femininity until he was almost limp.

'Cnt brrth!' came the muffled yell.

'The lad can't breathe, for der love o' G__!' suggested the first gentleman.

And Tobias was finally released with a vermilion face and eyes staring madly for a whiff of air.

'Here, boy – this'll revive yeh,' said the barman, pushing a small glass of brandy across the drink-puddled marble.

'I muss be goin',' replied Tobias, his voice seeming to come to him some seconds after his brain had bidden it speak.

But the denizens of the County Cork public house had either not heard him or did not care. Since he had called at the first of Westminster's lower public houses with his bundle of flyers, he had been borne from one place to the next by the same cast of characters, all declaring that they must have a drink to celebrate the impending free fireworks and spirits. Now all the advertisements had been distributed and there were other errands to run, but the Irish would not let him go. A dramatic solution seemed the only choice.

'Ho! The lad has passed out!' shouted one of the patrons.

And, indeed, Tobias had fallen to the beery floor in an artificial faint. He felt dampness soaking through his clothes and smelled sour gin breath in his face.

'He's breathin' all right. Jus needs a bit o' air after being in Megan's teats so long!'

Arms lifted him and his stomach gurgled as they carried him out on to Old Pye-street to lay him on the cold stone flagging by a horse trough. Some muttered words were exchanged and then a thick, coppery finger was jabbed deep into the boy's throat so that a great gush of brown liquid erupted instinctively from within him.

'That'll see yeh right,' said a voice, and their footsteps returned to the smoky noise of the house.

He stood as soon as he thought they had gone and saw that his uniform, now reeking of tobacco and beer, had become yet more stained by his escape. Though still somewhat light-headed, he turned east and attempted to walk some strength back into his legs.

As ever, the Westminster slum presented one of the more scabrous aspects of the city. The soot-blackened, damp-blighted buildings retained a muddy high-water mark from the last flooding of the Thames and the very *façades* seemed to buckle under the weight of overpopulation. Low lodging houses, thieves' nests, brothels and public houses accounted for the majority of tenement space, while the filth-strewn streets were awash with the fishmongers, meat hawkers, kerb walkers and metropolitan flotsam to be found in any rookery.

Then, of course, there were the boys: the ragged, grime-smeared progeny of loveless copulation, who had learned early enough that their chances for survival were greater in the gutter than in the home of a slatternly mother or abusive father. Perhaps they instinctively recognized Master Smalletts as one

242

of their own. Certainly, he had attracted attention during his time in the area, and now small gatherings of boys were observing him from the ends of shadowy alleys. Was he an intruder to be thrashed and robbed, or was he an emissary from another parish, come to teach them illicit tricks or the arcane lore of thievery?

'Hoi! What yer doin' in our street?' shouted one of the bigger boys in a group.

He stopped and felt for the penknife in his trouser pocket. There was also a single remaining flyer concerning the impending firework display. It was the latter that he extracted.

'D'yer like _____ fireworks, lads?' said Master Smalletts, turning to face them with a showman's smile.

There was a mutter of general approval, which the big boy validated: 'Aye. What of it?'

'Are yer educatid? D'yer read? 'Ave a look at this.'

'Course I can read,' lied the big boy, snatching the offered flyer and noting the illustrations.

'Free fireworks and spirits, lads. Yer'll be me guests – all of yer – 'ere at eleven on the fifth. Tell all yer mates that Tobias Smalletts invites 'em. That's me.'

They looked at him anew, this boy who spoke his own name as if he were someone important and who wore an odd school uniform with a faded crest of ambiguous authority. Their animal instincts told them that one with such confidence must somehow warrant their trust.

'Aye, we might do that,' said the big boy.

Master Smalletts winked and sauntered off on whisky-warmed legs, turning with some relief down Great St Anne-street and on to the unofficial border of the rookery along Peter-street, which soon changed its name and appearance to become the more salubrious Wood-street. Here, the smell of the river was distinct and the fresh honey-hued masonry of the new parliament buildings stood like a theatrical backdrop against the smoky sky to his left.

Towards the northern end of Abingdon-street was a clutter of stonemasons' detritus where they were still cutting and dressing stone for the lofty gothic decorations above. Master Smalletts passed through the chips and shards and continued unnoticed around the building towards the south east corner, where an iron grate in the ground suggested a coal trap. It was, however, no such thing.

This was one of the many air intake shafts that formed Dr Reid's complex ventilation system for the Palace of Westminster. With a quick look around him, Master Smalletts lifted the plate and descended a shallow shaft leading to an aperture in the foundation walls. A lamp was waiting for him there and he lit it with a Lucifer match before hanging it round his neck on a cord. There were also a number of broad strips of thick hide, which he bound about his knees and palms before crawling through the space into the very bowels of the Parliament buildings.

It was a journey he had made a number of times, initially with maps provided by the masked man but subsequently with a growing understanding of the labyrinthine geography of the place. Despite its confined access, the first area was in fact a voluminous receiving chamber, which, though it was not quite tall enough to permit standing, was long and wide. Master Smalletts crawled on hands and knees through it towards an iron door that could be controlled from above to regulate the mixture of hot and cold air. The door, as expected, was open just sufficiently for him to squeeze through.

The next space was the mixing chamber, where fresh intake and heated air were allowed to combine before rising through regulator valves and perforated grilles into whatever spaces were above. It was much warmer here and the atmosphere was tainted with the scent of hot iron elements whose balmy draught seemed to move constantly about the stones, bringing with it occasional clues of its ramifying journey through vents and shafts, chimneys and valves. Sometimes it was the river's breath or the brewery's malted stew;

other times it was the tobacco smoke of some secret session, borne on echoing ripples of indistinct male voices. A barge carrying hides to Bermondsey might pass by on the river and, if the wind was just right, the smell would find its way to where Master Smalletts crawled among the dust and droppings below the government of the realm.

He passed on, moving between receiving chambers, mixing chambers and heat channels via the small iron doors until he could hear the wet aspiratory breath that told him he had arrived finally at the base of the Victoria tower, from whose summit was drawn the air for the palace's larger halls. Though he had seen it before, he stopped to watch the machines exhaling their jets of purifying mist through which the upper air was driven prior to its continuing between the serried particulate filters of diaphanous muslin. Unintelligible as it all was to the young man, it nevertheless had the novelty of modern science at work.

The next chamber was his destination – one that followed the same general structure as the others he had traversed, but which was considerably larger. Here, he positioned the lamp by his side and sat within its fragile purview to carefully unfold a hand-drawn plan of the very space he occupied. The reverse of the sheet showed a detailed diagram of the steam-filled heating apparatus, and it was towards this that he now made a move, familiarizing himself, as bidden, with its iron tubes and ribs.

'Must you wear that ridiculous mask? Show me your face that I might see the features of a true blackguard!'

Lord _____ was quite pale with outrage. Standing before him, Perkin Mullender stood calmly counting the blackmail money he had just collected.

'I say!' continued Lord _____ with empurpling cheeks, 'it is not enough that you extort me in my own home – but ignoring me is nothing less than a personal insult!'

Perkin Mullender smiled behind the mask which bore Mr Newsome's perpetual scowl. His voice was muffled through waxen lips: 'Sir – you might perhaps have considered morality more carefully when you last visited Mrs Percival's house for a whipping.'

'Well . . . well . . .!'

'Just remember the terms of my employer. If you do what has been asked, you may cease these payments. I will show myself to the street door if you don't mind.'

'I . . . I would rather you took the scullery door.'

'No – the street entrance suits my needs.'

And thus Perkin Mullender emerged at the top of the stairs on that street in the environs of stately Portman-square so that anyone observing might have seen a certain red-haired detective leaving the residence rather than the multi-faceted Mullender. As directed, he would remove the mask once out of sight around the next corner.

Or perhaps he would keep it on for just a little longer – just to the end of Orchard-street and possibly a mite further on to Oxford-street. For, was there not something wonderfully disingenuous, something deliciously duplicitous in strolling with a false face? Certainly, it was more effective in the open thoroughfare where pedestrians seldom looked one in the eye and where, after all, there was no need to reveal the inflexibility of his borrowed features in speech. With his hat and peruke in place, he *was* Inspector Albert Newsome. Even the walk – that impatient scuttle that was so particular to the detective, and which Perkin Mullender had studied – was faithful in its replication.

Irrepressible mirth writhed beneath the waxen carapace as he walked. There were flickered glances in the crowds, but none stared or gaped or noticed his lie. It was, indeed, invisibility of the finest variety: to appear and yet be unknown.

Engaged in such musings, however, he did not notice the shocked stare of a young boy approaching from the east with his governess. Nor did Perkin Mullender catch the perplexed impression of man with shoulder-supported boards fore and aft advertising Henderson's Hair Starch. Both were paradoxically sure they had seen the fellow with the curly red hair just moments previously in a different suit of clothes.

But as he continued, his fine sense of such things returned and he began to notice these looks with a growing realisation that he had to remove the mask with all haste. The real Inspector Newsome was evidently close at hand.

With nervous eyes under unmoving brows, he searched for a suitable doorway or alley to turn his back to the street and effect his transformation without attention, but Oxford-street was quite throbbing with people. If he could just reach the narrow confines of Bird-street . . .

Too late.

'You! Halt! You in the mask!'

The real Mr Newsome had paused on his way up into a cab and was pointing over the scores of bobbing heads to where Perkin Mullender had frozen immobile.

'You! Impostor! Do not move!'

The human tide formed a space around the masked man, all eyes now upon him.

Mr Newsome's gaze burned unblinking at what he could barely believe.

And Perkin Mullender bolted, darting through the people towards the traffic.

'Stop him!' shouted Mr Newsome.

But those assembled seemed quite stupefied by the doubled spectacle before them and merely stared at the sensation.

Perkin Mullender elbowed his way past the stationary horses of a goods wagon and careered madly towards the southern side of the street, casting rapid glances behind him to see if Mr Newsome was in pursuit. Had he not been so distracted, he might have noticed a laden dust cart bearing down upon him with its two giant horses in no mood to stop.

There was a shout, a cry, a collective gasp and a clatter of horseshoes. The dust cart lurched and passed over a hump of trodden, sodden clothing: the body of Perkin Mullender, lying now prostrate in the dung-carpeted road.

247

'Detective Inspector Newsome of Division A – let me through! Move aside, I say! Reverse that cab there! Give me space!'

The hooves and heavy wheels had done their worst. One leg was bent unnaturally under the torso and the other was mangled almost flat. The mask over the face had been partially crushed so that its fractured edge revealed half Inspector Newsome, half Perkin Mullender – one side flushed and staring madly in death, the other side placidly impassive but for a single startled eye and a smear of blood on the forehead.

Mr Newsome looked down at the remnants of his own face and saw that the impostor was quite dead, his backbone presumably snapped by the great wooden wheels or by a powerful hoof.

'Does anybody know this man?' he called.

It seemed that nobody did, but the remnants of the mask were already exciting attention. 'Masked Man' could be heard distinctly among the massed murmurs

A number of shopkeepers and their customers had flowed out into the street to witness the accident and Mr Newsome turned now to a man with a tape measure around his neck – evidently the proprietor of the tailor's shop immediately opposite. 'You, sir – does your shop have a yard at the rear?'

'Why, yes, but . . .'

Help me to drag this body there. It is evidence in a case.'

'I hardly think—'

'Police business. Help me now or face arrest. Everybody else, stand clear!'

The tailor muttered darkly and called for two of his apprentices to come. Together they simply lifted the corpse under the arms and dragged it as directed through the shop to a murky coal yard at the rear. When the crowd tried to follow, they were turned back by the tailor's outraged cries.

'Leave me here uninterrupted to examine the body,' said Mr Newsome to the apprentices. 'There is no need to call a constable, and if one arrives you should tell him that Inspector Newsome of the Detective Force has taken charge. Now go ... I said go back to your work and close the door behind you.'

The two did so, leaving him within the brickwork quad where the sky was a grey square and the noise of Oxford-street a distant thunder. Pigeons bickered unseen under sagging ceilings. There was not much time to search the body before the local superintendant arrived, demanding to know who was infringing his jurisdiction.

Mr Newsome crouched and removed the dead man's mask, pushing it hastily inside his coat as the primary piece of evidence. He then looked in the jacket pockets, where his first discovery was a very large quantity of money inside a drawstring leather bag and the second a number of sealed but unstamped envelopes addressed to sundry significant personages living around Mayfair. These, too, went into his own pockets unopened. There would be time later for closer examination.

Next came a couple of typical *souvenir* postcards from the Thames Tunnel. One of them was signed in pencil: "With love, your Jane." Mr Newsome examined the card closely, noting the corners remained undamaged, the scene had not faded, and the pencil strokes had not smudged. Evidently it was new – a memento perhaps acquired within the last day or two and therefore a crucial clue to the dead fellow's recent movements.

The inspector secreted the card inside his coat with the other evidence and was about to cease his search when he became aware of an alien odour: something akin to alcohol, but not redolent of any discernible spirit such as gin or brandy. Rather, it was more a chymical scent that one might smell on passing a manufactory. He looked around the filthy court for any sign of such industry but could see none. He sniffed the air and found that the body itself appeared to be the source – not the mouth as one might expect, but a portion of the coat, whose upper arm showed a small damp patch.

Mr Newsome squeezed the spot and rubbed the dampness between thumb and forefinger. It appeared to be a clear liquid with a faintly oily feel that left his fingertips dry. Had the goods wagon that had knocked down the fellow been carrying barrels of such stuff? Had the falling body rolled in a patch of the substance or been dragged through it to this court? Or had the fellow acquired the stain in the course of his illicit work?

Finally, he stood with cracking knees and started to approach the door into the shop. But as his hand touched the doorknob, he paused and looked back at the body. An idea had occurred to him of how he might at last gain the upper hand in the search for Lucius Boyle – an idea that would surely match, or even exceed, the diabolism of that demented foe.

Indeed, it was past midnight when, beneath the freezing weight of the Thames, Lucius Boyle waited in his dank arachnid cavity and looked for the countless time at his pocket watch. The hour of Perkin Mullender's appointment had long passed beyond the usual tardiness into the realms of concern. Had the vainglorious impostor finally gone too far in his fancies and been apprehended on his extortionate errands? Had one of the victims taken especial outrage and horsewhipped the money collector? Or had the fellow simply turned and taken a higher price? Such, after all, was the temperament of his curious *genus*.

There was a slight knock at the door – not the Italian's usual brisk double tap, but an altogether more timid sound that indicated bad news on the way.

'Enter.'

The Italian approached with an advance copy of that day's *Times* and laid it on the workbench. He had folded it open at the Police column, where a fine approximation of his own features had been printed alongside the following copy:

WANTED: DANGEROUS FOREIGN CRIMINAL

For questioning in connection with a number of crimes committed across the city. If you have seen this gentleman, who is of foreign – possibly Italian – extract, please report the particulars to the Enquiries Office of Scotland Yard. Make no attempt to address the man directly, as he is believed to be violent. A reward of ten pounds will be given for evidence that leads directly to his capture.

The newspaper crepitated in Lucius Boyle's hands. His fire-flayed face seemed to ripple and twitch with anger.

'So – you will not be venturing forth on to the streets as I had hoped,' he said with artificial calmness. 'At least, no longer in daylight hours and not with your own face. You must also rid yourself of that earring and long hair.'

The Italian stared.

'And you can no longer spend time here in the tunnel. The vendors must all know your face by now,' added Lucius Boyle. 'Find another place to stay. And sustain your fortitude – this game will soon end with my victory and their destruction. Now, leave me. But do not leave this place.'

The door closed and he looked again at the Police column in the newspaper. There was evidently much else in it to concern him.

TWENTY-THREE

As Noah reached towards the door knocker that next morning, he used the mirror in his gloved palm to check once again that he was not being observed from the street. He had not seen anything suspicious in his stroll along Park-lane and, indeed, nobody could have expected that he would be visiting this house. Nevertheless, its resident was as particular about privacy as he was, and information would be forthcoming only if he could assure absolute discretion.

A maid in pristine uniform opened the door and appraised Noah with a single sweeping gaze. Dressed in his finest clothes, he was not out of place on this most illustrious of thoroughfares.

'I am here to see the lady of the house,' he said.

'Which lady would that be, sir?'

He smiled and recognized that some manner of code should now be used to gain access. 'I wonder if you would tell her that I am the man from the British Museum reading room . . . and perhaps you will give her this gift.'

The maid looked at the pomegranate in his hand and back to his face, which appeared to be in earnest. 'The lady does not receive gifts at the door, sir.'

'Then consider it a calling card. I will stand here on the steps if she wishes to look down and verify my identity.'

'Please wait. I will return in a moment, sir.'

The door closed and Noah moved away so that he could be viewed from the grand *façade* of the building – the kind of property one might expect to be owned by a continental prince or a member of the English aristocracy. Such, at least, were the neighbours; the resident lady was one who lived from them.

There was a twitch of curtain on the second floor and Noah affected not to notice that he was being scrutinized. Rather, he looked once more to the street lest anyone was taking too much interest in his dawdling.

Moments later, the door opened and the maid beckoned him in. 'The lady has consented to see you, sir. This way, if you please.'

He was led up thickly carpeted stairs to a closed door on the second floor. Here, the maid rapped four times and then departed with a nod, passing silently back to her duties.

'Enter.'

The voice was calm rather than imperious: a modulation that managed to be both inviting and ambiguous in its two short syllables. He did as bidden.

And she had clearly arranged herself in anticipation of his entrance. Her pose on the *chaise longue* exhibited her Parisian dress of black silk to beauteous effect, allowing the shape of her legs to tantalize without offering any vulgar glimpse of flesh. Her long, dark hair was tied back in the elaborate fashion favoured by the Austrian royalty and held in place by a diamond pin that glittered perfectly in the light from the large windows to her side. Were Aphrodite to visit modern London, she would surely appear thus ... though this lady preferred another mythical name.

'Thank you for receiving me,' said Noah with a small bow. 'May I address you as Persephone?'

She smiled. 'You may call me that if you wish to stir memories of our previous acquaintance. I suggest, however, that Mary is more suited to the present occasion.'

'Then I am glad to see you healthy, Mary.'

'I suppose I have you to thank for that, Mr Dyson – you and your dark friend Benjamin. And how is the serious Mr Williamson? I have read some concern about his recent *travails*. He does not seem a man to be accused of such things'

'He is as serious as ever, and of course he *is* innocent. In fact, that unfortunate business with the girl Charlotte is partially why I have come to you.'

'I rather feared it might be the reason, but you must understand: my gratitude for your saving my life in that rather nasty incident last year is wholehearted. However, I believe all accounts have been settled. It is not appropriate for you to be here.'

'Nobody saw me enter.'

'You may think so, but some people always see.'

'That is why I have to come to you. You are perhaps the one person who can help us in a case that is quite mired in secrecy, reputation and power.'

'Mr Dyson – if I have any power at all, it is because secrecy is my promise. The husbands may call me *courtesan,* but their wives call me something else entirely. Neither should know who you are or that you have associations with the police.'

'I have no such associations.'

'That is not what I have heard.'

Noah smiled. 'Very well. I am already here – might I at least lay my case before you before I am ejected?'

Now it was her turn to be amused. Here was a man who knew how to speak to her, who was not obviously in awe of her beauty and who valued her intellect as a quality in itself. 'You may lay your case, Mr Dyson – but lay it gently and with *decorum.*'

'I will try, Mary. In fact, what I am hoping to discern is whether any strange effects have been felt within your world in recent days: any ripples, so to speak, disturbing the equilibrium of secrecy and confidence.'

'It is a broad question, Mr Dyson. There are always rumours and scandals that never reach the newspapers. How should I know in which you are interested?'

'I am thinking primarily of extortion.'

'Again, it is a common enough occurrence if one is not discreet. A butler or chambermaid may see something and believe a profit might be made. It happens all the time.'

'No – I refer to something more widespread and organized. The victims will be significant people who are approached anonymously and asked for large sums, or asked to exert their influence in underhand ways.'

'You understand, of course, that such victims do not freely admit to these things?'

'Indeed, but perhaps they tell a fellow at their club, and he mentions it to a lover while drunk or carnally satiated. I know enough of your world to know that you hear these things. They are currency to your worth. Tell me anything that seems odd, excessive or unprecedented – anything that cannot be immediately explained.'

She appraised him coolly, seeming to debate with herself what she might tell. All gossip could be traced back to its source with persistence, and so it could be nothing that she alone knew – at least, nothing that could damage her if revealed.

'There is one gentleman,' said Mary, 'who visits me weekly. Let us say he is known particularly for his horsemanship.'

'Viscount _____?'

'If you wish.' A smile. 'Well, he has cancelled his appointments for the foreseeable future on account of going away to the country, though I know for certain that he is still in town. Something else has persuaded him to be cautious.'

'His wife?'

'Not at all! She has her own stud stable and is well aware of his appetites. No, I suspect that something else has dissuaded him.'

'Blackmail, perhaps?'

'I could not say. It is possible.'

'I see. What else? Is there nothing being said in the judiciary, among the lords, at the House of Commons? You must hear of these things.'

'There was something ... but it hardly seemed ...'

'Tell me. It may be important.'

'Well, there are mere rumours, just *murmures de la chambre à coucher,* you understand, but it is said that some members have received letters advising them not to attend certain sessions. I do not know what manner of threat is made or enticement offered ... and such things are not entirely unknown. It is just that the *number* of instances seems odd.'

'Which members? Which sessions?'

'I really could not say for certain ... perhaps Sir _____ _____ is one of them. As for the sessions in question ... I know only these vaguest of details. As I say, such coercion is not unprecedented.'

'How are these men contacted – do you know?'

'There may have been something about a letter, but ... I really do not know. I could not say.'

'No matter. I wonder, Mary, if you have heard about the recent events at Scotland Yard?'

'Is there anyone who has not? They called it a water leak but the talk is of robbery.'

'Quite. I rather suspect, however, that you do not know what was taken.'

'Money? Something in the Lost Property Office? I cannot imagine there is much of value there.'

'What if I told you about the existence of a secret catalogue detailing the illicit letches of London's finer people – the addresses they visit and the acts in which they there engage?'

'I would be suspicious of such a rumour, Mr Dyson. I might believe it in Paris or Vienna – in fact, I know for a fact that such things exist there. But in London? Of course, it is well known that a certain Inspector Newsome would often canvass certain establishments for information, but I cannot conceive that the benign Metropolitan Police would go so far as to document it.'

'Not the police, certainly – but a single corrupt element within it.'

'The catalogue is real?'

'Apparently so. I have not seen it, but I know from the highest authority that it has been stolen.'

'I see now that I should have foreseen as much from the direction of your questions. Do you know if . . . if I am listed within it?'

'It seems likely that the address is even if your name is not. It was the victims who were followed rather than their passions.'

'This would certainly explain the behaviour of the viscount.'

'Indeed.'

'I suppose you do not know who took this catalogue.'

'That is why I am here. The only way to find the perpetrator is to seek the effects of his crimes. I am sure you appreciate the difficulty of approaching his victims.'

'Yes, yes – I see that.'

'Would it be possible, Mary, for you to learn more about these things we have discussed? Perhaps if these gentlemen knew that a private investigation was being undertaken . . .'

'I am not personally acquainted with these people. I—'

'But you know people who are acquainted with them. You have greater opportunities than I to see that they are made aware that help is available. If I could obtain one of these letters or be advised when a collection is to be made, I may be able to reclaim that catalogue and destroy it. It is to everybody's advantage.'

'I understand, Mr Dyson. But I wonder if you understand who I am and for what I stand. I am not a politician or a lady of court to simply address these people. I am necessarily invisible to them. They choose to see me only in these rooms.'

'I know, I know – but the men you see here know other men, and those men attend clubs with other men . . . Are they so timid – or so rich – that they will pay extortion money in perpetuity?'

'They have more to lose than you, Mr Dyson. Money may be something with which they are abundantly endowed, but reputation and honour come at a much higher price.'

'Of course.'

'I will think further on the matter. If an opportunity arises . . .'

'That is all I can ask, Mary. I am only sorry that I have come to you with such a distasteful purpose.'

'I trust that I myself am in no danger? Should I be hoping for another visit from the silent Benjamin?'

'I am sure Ben would be delighted to be of service, but the criminal in question has nothing to gain from exposing you. Promise me only one thing, however: if you become aware or an Italian-looking fellow in the area, see that you send word to me. I suppose I need not tell you where to find me.'

'Very well. I will find you if necessary. You are an interesting man, Mr Dyson – and I flatter myself that I am a good judge of the subject. Some men are vain, some are cruel, some hide their weaknesses with intelligence – and most are selfish. You do not look at me as other men do. I recognize desire in a man's eyes just as I recognize contempt, and yet I see neither in yours.'

'What *do* you see?'

She smiled sadly. 'Loss.'

Noah looked down at the ornate Oriental rug at their feet. 'A pseudo-scientific gentlemen recently told me from my features that I had a "combinatory sanguine-phlegmatic nature".'

'Then perhaps he was more "pseudo" than "scientific".'

Noah now smiled and stood. He took her extended hand and touched it briefly to his lips. 'I offer my sincere gratitude for this audience with the goddess Persephone. No doubt you will contact me if you hear more.'

'Perhaps, Mr Dyson. Perhaps. But do not forget your mythology: Persephone ruled only in the Underworld, as the consort of Hades. A deity she may have been, but she was also a prisoner.'

'I still cannot believe it,' said Mr Cullen as the cab in which he and Benjamin sat made jerky progress east along Oxford-street. 'Lucius Boyle still alive! Imagine Noah's feelings on the matter.'

Benjamin indicated that his friend had indeed been much preoccupied since having his recent suspicions finally confirmed. It was clearly a worrying state of affairs.

'But how could anyone have known?' said Mr Cullen. 'The man was seen dead by three witnesses, was buried and became quite invisible to the world. And yet he was there all along, watching, plotting, waiting. It is enough to give one nightmares.'

Benjamin merely nodded, concerned, perhaps, that those years of corrosive revenge in Noah's blood would now return to consume him again unless the criminal could be captured or killed with certainty

'What do you think, Ben? Will this wax head be the image of Boyle? Do you believe in the science of Dr Hammerton and Mr Figgs? I have a strange sense that we will soon be gazing upon the face of a murderer.'

Benjamin shrugged. The only face he wanted to see was the cold, dead face of the real Boyle, ideally lying at his feet.

'Well, here we are! Let us see what Mr Schlöss has to show us.'

The two disembarked and stepped quickly into the shop while the cab provided some degree of cover from the other side of the road. Inside, the shopkeeper was at the counter examining a newly-arrived wax nose ordered from France by a fellow who had taken a catastrophic tumble down a flight of metal steps. One look at the ghostly eye of Benjamin suggested that here, finally, was a customer rather another investigator.

'Good afternoon, gentlemen,' he said. 'I perceive that you are looking for something in the ocular department.'

'In fact we are here to collect an order for Mr Dyson,' said Mr Cullen. 'He may have said we would come in his stead.'

'Mr Dyson . . .? O, yes – the business with wax head. Perhaps you will accompany me to the workshop for added privacy. You must forgive the mess – I have just had a large delivery of raw materials.'

And the small room behind the counter was indeed a clutter of packages about the floor and tables. Mr Cullen noted a stack of white blocks like oversized bars of soap and smelled the distinct aroma of hot beeswax.

'I am preparing a large batch of pigmented wax for a full-body model,' said Mr Schlöss gesturing towards a formidable metal vat of redness that bubbled thickly at its molten centre. 'Take care not to burn yourself. Now – Mr Dyson's order is just here. I have wrapped it for collection.'

'May we look at it before we pay?' said Mr Cullen. 'Just to be sure that it is the right one.'

'Of course, of course. I have not added hair or colouring, though I could do so if required.'

Mr Schlöss began to unfold the brown paper where it had been tucked under the neck, his hands seeming to work with infuriating slowness as Benjamin and Mr Cullen leaned closer for the first glimpse of their enemy.

'There, gentlemen!' said the proprietor with a terse Germanic flourish. 'Is that your likeness?'

The blank white face was a cipher: its cheeks pale, its brow unlined, its chin hairless and its scull a featureless sheen. It might almost have been a pedimental Greek hero, but for a certain vague malevolence that would not be defined by any single feature. Only the incongruous eyes, with their glassy grey stare, suggested any trace of identity.

'You look disappointed, gentlemen,' said Mr Schlöss. 'Is this not the fellow you seek? I will ask you to remember that pigment and hair can make a significant difference. Also, the instructions I was given do not account for scars, ageing, poor health *et cetera*. This might be the face of your man as a youth, for example, or in his purest form before the vicissitudes of life changed him with the lines we all acquire. Perhaps your real gentleman has a beard. I can attach one if you like. There is no way I could know these things – I have made what was detailed in Mr Dyson's notes.'

'I am sure it is exactly what was specified,' said Mr Cullen, still studying the thing for any trace of recognition. He turned to Ben, who seemed similarly unimpressed. 'Perhaps if I can hold it and look at it from different angles . . .'

'By all means.' Mr Schlöss passed it over.

He head was cool to the touch and much lighter than expected, though the natural wax made it something more that a mere object. Mr Cullen held it to his own face so that he was staring into the deadness of its enamel gaze. Still, there was no spark. Would Noah be disappointed?

'Here, Ben – you try. Your hands are more sensitive.'

But as he handed the head to his right, the exposed skin of his wrist caught an extremity of the great bubbling vat of wax. He exclaimed. He jerked. The head toppled inside.

'Quickly! We must get it out or it will be ruined!' shouted Mr Schlöss. 'Those tongs – use those large tongs there!'

Benjamin unhooked what looked like a huge pair of scissors from the wall and rapidly dipped the spooned ends into the vat to grasp the bobbing white head. And as he lifted it clear of the rim, Mr Cullen gave a sharp intake of breath.

'My G__, Ben! Look at it!'

The lower portion of the head had been stained a virulent red from the pigment so that the outline of the jaw was distinctly delineated as a solid block of colour. The rest of the face, meanwhile, was variously streaked and spattered as if with gore. What had moments ago been a bland anatomical study was now a thing of disembodied horror.

Benjamin's operative eye glared at the object and his jaw muscles worked.

'I say – that reminds me rather of the head that the inspector showed me,' said Mr Schlöss. 'I simply did not see it before. It is the colouring, perhaps . . . the jaw is quite distinctive is it not . . .'

'I believe there is no other like it,' said Mr Cullen sombrely.

It was easier to see the room objectively now that the sense of her had been partially erased by the presence of Messrs Newsome and Mayne. Before that rude intrusion, she had seemed to whisper to him in the gas flames and breathe cold mortality upon his skin from the window draughts – but now her spirit had evidently moved on, leaving just a shell of flesh and a murder scene to study. It was almost as if Charlotte had understood, acquiesced and ceased to torture a mind that could not function amid such confusion.

With this enhanced clarity did Mr Williamson assess the apartment that evening while the other gentlemen were about their various errands. If this truly was the scene of her abduction, it had apparently been effected without struggle, for Noah had found no sign of disruption on first entering. True – the criminal may have carefully returned everything to its original position and attempted to dispose of any incriminating evidence, but even the most punctilious intruder will tend to miss a minor detail: the indentation in a carpet where a table leg stood, the sliver of glass where once a mirror hung, the subtle marks on wood or carpet pile of a body dragged from room to room. None of these were apparent at Golden-square.

And yet the Italian had apparently been most eager to reclaim the body from Marylebone police court. There must be some clue upon or within it that might lead investigators back to a culpable place or person.

In fact, Mr Williamson's earlier sense of *decorum* had betrayed him. In not fully undressing the body (as he had done with PC Taylor), he had not had the opportunity of closely examining the interior of Charlotte's clothing, which may have harboured clues as to the site of her ruination. Looking again at the travesty still standing in the parlour, he now understood his error and offered a silent apology – he would have to strip her.

It was easier if he did not look at her face, which, though its beauty was gone, retained the rudiments of humanity and might stimulate feelings of pity or anguish or pain. Rather, he worked only with the garments, cutting them from the rigid form with scissors so that he might lay each out on the floor for a closer examination of lacework, seams and contact points at elbow or shoulder.

Within minutes, he discovered what the Italian had perhaps sought to destroy: various minute mineral traces within the garment linings that suggested they had been hastily pulled inside-out from the body and left upon a dirty surface as the unspeakable incisions had been made. One of these grainy deposits had the unmistakable smell and granular texture of gunpowder; another offered the distinctive olfactory character of sulphur. There were others, which were likely pyrotechnical adjuncts such as antinomy, camphor or copper shavings, but the overall implication seemed clear enough: the body had been prepared in a fireworks manufactory or a storehouse of such elements.

He was considering the direction of this evidence when his eyes alighted upon the quite naked form of Charlotte: a deformed insult against her living beauty that now sagged and swelled aberrantly. Soon she would rest in the ground and live in his memory as the woman she had been rather than the . . .

A sound fractured Mr Williamson's thoughts.

It was not the street door, but a scratching that emanated from the rear of the property. He gripped the scissors and began to move towards it, compelled not by curiosity or fear, but by a rising fury directed at any who would further desecrate this already broken place.

A shadow moved across the hallway ahead and Mr Williamson raised the scissors. Holding his breath, he stepped silently closer to the room whose door was ajar, knowing that whoever was trying to enter must surely know from the lights that someone was resident. Such recklessness forewarned violence.

There was a slight scrape, a soft footfall and a creaking board from within the room. The shadow loomed closer and the door began to open . . .

'So – you must be the Italian,' said Mr Williamson without surprize.

He thus addressed – garbed all in black as he had been at Scotland Yard – paused where he stood. A bloody cut marked his forehead where Benjamin had slashed him. There was a dagger in his hand and a malicious cast to his features.

'Hmm. Hmm. I suppose you have come for her,' said Mr Williamson. 'Well, you shall not have her. Her mistreatment at your hands is over. I have discovered what you sought to hide.'

The Italian began to advance, his stiletto seeking blood.

But at that moment – as the malevolent silence tautened intolerably between them – a key rattled into the street door and male voices could be heard.

The Italian paused. His eyes showed a flicker of fear.

'That will be Benjamin and Mr Cullen coming to beat you quite senseless,' said Mr Williamson.

With no further hesitation, the Italian turned and ran whence he had emerged.

'Here! Here! The Italian is in the apartment!' shouted Mr Williamson as his two burly acquaintances arrived through the street door. 'This way – take him!'

Benjamin was first, dropping the bag he was carrying and thundering down the hall to dart into the room after his quarry. Mr Cullen was but a heartbeat behind, his enormous fists balled for action.

Mr Williamson followed and saw the Italian struggling to climb out of the window even as Benjamin gripped a leg to haul him in. A blade scythed in the dim light and slashed scarlet across Ben's wrist. He grunted in response and twisted the Italian's leg with such ferocious might that Mr Williamson heard cartilage crunch from the doorway. There was a scream.

Mr Cullen took hold of the leg higher up and together they struggled to pull the Italian back into the room, but his darting knife was threatening to quite shred their hands into slivers.

'Let him go! He will maim you!' shouted Mr Williamson despite his ardent wish for capture.

Mr Cullen obeyed instantly, looking with evident concern at the lacerations upon his hands. Benjamin fought on until a particularly brutal swipe caused him to leap back sucking at the wound.

There was the sound of a falling body and a gasp of pain, followed by a limping, scraping gait, the crack of a whip and hooves racing away.

For a while, there was only panting.

'I would dearly like to meet him again,' said Mr Cullen.

Benjamin's sticky red fingers described a more violent sentiment of similar implication. He slammed a fist wetly into a palm.

'His time will come, gentlemen,' said Mr Williamson gravely. 'Now – what were you carrying in that bag when you entered?'

TWENTY-FOUR

'Have we met before? I have the distinct impression I know your face.'

Thus had Mr Newsome stood at the door of the reopened Newspaper Office the previous evening following his encounter with Perkin Mullender. Mr Parker and his clerks had long since "*vacated the premises*", leaving me temporarily resident should any urgent communications be requested before *the Times* went to print. And, naturally, I was using the opportunity to comb covertly through the files for stories that might sustain me after my references were inevitably discovered to be false.

Looking up from my crime, I smiled at the inspector and remarked that I did not believe I had met him before, but that I knew him by reputation.

'Well, I do not easily forget a face,' he said. 'Perhaps I have seen you in the street. Are you new in this office? Can you help me with a press request?'

I admitted that I was new, and that my "*superior*" had left me here for just such an eventuality.

'That suits me perfectly,' said Mr Newsome with a half-smirk. 'I require you to write and send a police report to *the Times* with all haste. I have the details with me now and can dictate them to you. Is that within your capabilities?'

Here, I mumbled with sufficient subservience that Mr Parker was supposed to check all outgoing reports and that Sir Richard also needed to authorize them, but, even as I spoke, my hands were preparing pencil and paper with such enthused alacrity that I thought my glee would be detected. This was, after all, the dream of every penny-a-liner: the exclusive story.

And I was not disappointed. The story related to me by that detective was so new that it had not actually occurred. Or rather, the true facts of the matter were quite different and would not be revealed until some hours later. Nevertheless, it was necessary to submit the copy that very hour to be sure of publication.

So it was that, mere hours later, the newspaper that Lucius Boyle had read in the Thames Tunnel was the same as the copy deposited on Sir Richard Mayne's desk later that morning was the work of my own humble pen – another instalment in the rabid public fascination with unnatural murder:

EXTRAORDINARY SECOND BODY FOUND AT WESTMINSTER

Last evening, another shocking discovery of a human effigy was made on the corner of Princess-street and Queen-street, Westminster.

The figure – now being held at the Division A station house, Gardener-lane – has been described as that of a man aged 30-35 with brown (glass) eyes and dark hair. Witnesses have reported that the effigy's singular pose had it conspicuously holding a single burned Lucifer match and looking towards the east.

Within hours of the discovery, a large and clamorous crowd had gathered outside the station house on Gardener-lane, demanding to satisfy their curiosity by viewing the body. Such requests were refused and additional constables were brought from Scotland Yard to disperse the unruly congregation.

No further particulars have been released by the police, and there is no indication at this juncture whether the body has any connection with the recently discovered body of the unfortunate Charlotte Dawson, which is still unaccounted for after the scandalous robber of the Marylebone police court (and whose alleged murderer, Mr George Williamson, remains a fugitive). Nevertheless, unsubstantiated reports have been heard to the effect that this latest figure appears to have been much better executed than the body of the girl.

A statement is expected imminently from Scotland Yard on the investigation of this latest grisly find.

One might barely imagine the consternation experienced by Sir Richard on seeing the news. No doubt he urgently re-read the divisional occurrence reports of the previous evening, searching in vain among the notices of Division A for news of another body. No doubt he remonstrated with the sententious Mr Parker, who would have legitimately denied all knowledge of preparing such a report for the newspapers. No doubt he would then have snatched his coat and made directly for Gardener-lane to verify with his own eyes what appeared to be a mere figment of the press.

Once there – having witnessed for himself the considerable crowds waiting outside – he encountered Mr Newsome in the station's receiving office

'What on earth is going on, Inspector?' said Sir Richard. 'Have you read the newspapers? Is this a hoax? I can find no corroboration of this thing actually occurring, and yet it is all over the city. The Newspaper Office has no records of an official statement.'

'Perhaps we should examine the body, sir,' said Mr Newsome, gesturing towards the private quarters of the station inspector, Mr York.

The two were led to the sitting room, where a fire crackled in the grate and where the figure of Perkin Mullender stood bearing all the signs of life except the circulation of blood. Unlike the figure of Charlotte, it had been executed with such artistry that one might have expected the limbs to move or the frozen face to smile at any moment, as if it had all been something of a lark.

'My G__', said Sir Richard. 'It is surely the work of him who killed PC Taylor.'

'Not quite, sir,' said Mr Newsome. 'The nostrils have been prepared in a slightly different manner and the ears are cut in a different place . . . but I agree the work is superlative.'

'Have you already examined the body, Inspector? You seem to know rather a lot about its finer detail. Did you see an early edition of the newspaper?'

'Sir – I know for a fact that the taxidermist responsible for this body is not the same as he who made PC Taylor.'

'You are being worryingly evasive, Inspector. How do you know this?'

'Because, sir . . . well, the truth is that I myself commissioned this piece of work from a taxidermist on Wych-street.'

Sir Richard blinked. Had he misheard? His mouth opened to speak, but he found his throat momentarily clenched. His face became a mask of almost apoplectic incredulity.

'No law has been broken,' said Mr Newsome, taking rapid opportunity of Sir Richard's speechlessness. 'The fellow was quite dead before the procedure, and his innards have been respectfully – albeit cheaply – interred. It is a mere anatomical study rather than a corpse . . .'

'Have you gone *quite insane?*' exploded Sir Richard. 'What were you thinking? Do you realize what you have done . . .? Was it *you* who issued the report to *the Times* against all official procedures? What were you thinking, Inspector?'

'Sir – if you will becalm yourself for a moment . . .'

'Becalm myself? I . . . I am quite beside myself. Can you imagine what will happen if news of this escapes? Can you imagine what people will say about the police? Inspector Newsome – you have utterly surpassed your previous efforts at insubordination.'

'Nobody knows the facts, sir – only you and I, and a fellow in the Newspaper Office who is unlikely to speak if he wants to preserve his position. The policemen at this station know only that the body was delivered here in my name earlier this morning and that it was found nearby in Westminster. Nobody could possibly suspect the truth.'

'And what is the truth?'

'Well, sir—'

Mr Newsome was interrupted by a knock at the sitting room door, which opened to reveal the duty clerk:

'Sorry to bother you, but there are two gentlemen here to see the Commissioner.'

'Tell them to go away – they will likely be reporters,' said Sir Richard irritably.

'Yes, sir.'

'Wait a moment . . . Did they give their names?'

'Yes, sir. It is a Mr Dyson and a fellow calling himself Mr Smith, sir. They are quite insistent about seeing you.'

'Why do you doubt the name of this fellow Smith?' said Mr Newsome with a glance at Sir Richard.

'He is the very image of Sergeant George Williamson, sir. I knew him, you see. Only it cannot be he because I know Mr Williamson is a fugitive from justice . . .'

'They must have seen my carriage,' muttered Sir Richard. 'Or deduced I would rush here.'

'They should not see this,' said Mr Newsome.

'Why not? They have seen worse and know more. What disadvantage is there in them seeing this also? Clerk – tell them they may enter. And do not share your observation with anyone else that this Smith looks like ex-sergeant Williamson, who is indeed a fugitive and cannot therefore be here.'

The two gentlemen entered moments later and beheld the figure of Perkin Mullender. Speechless greetings were nodded, and old antipathies exchanged.

'You take a considerable risk walking about in public, Mr Williamson,' said Sir Richard. 'You could be—'

'What happened?' said Noah, pointing to the body. 'Who is the victim and what does this mean? It looks like the work of PC Taylor's killer.'

'The inspector was just about to explain himself when you arrived,' said Sir Richard. 'Perhaps he will continue now that he has an audience.'

Mr Newsome scowled, but recognized he was the sole focus of attention. He adopted a more oratorical demeanour: 'Well, I was travelling along

Oxford-street to enquire at Tussaud's about the masks when, quite by accident, I saw a man with my own face: a masked man. I chased him, he was run down by a wagon and I took the body into my care.'

'You call *this* care?' said Noah, indicating the figure.

'Hmm. I am afraid I do not understand,' said Mr Williamson. 'Do you mean to say that he was *not* stuffed when you saw him? What was he doing, this fellow with your face?'

'He was strolling along with an air of perfect self-satisfaction,' said Mr Newsome. 'There was no furtiveness to his imposture whatsoever.'

'But why did you subject him to this ... this unnatural procedure?' said Sir Richard.

'I—'

'Wait,' said Noah with a disbelieving glance at Mr Williamson. 'Did I hear correctly? The *inspector* is responsible for this effigy?'

'If you will just let me finish!' said Mr Newsome. I searched the body and was about to leave it where it lay when an idea occurred to me. Is it not the case that we have been run quite ragged by Boyle? That he has frustrated our purposes at every turn, humiliated us before the public and used our own institutions against us? Is it not time that we employed a different sort of strategy in our search for the man? One that takes the initiative and draws him out of his cover? We have chased the quarry for too long without even knowing where he lurks.'

'It is an interesting oration, Inspector, but you have not answered my question,' said Sir Richard. 'Why have the fellow stuffed?'

'Because the evidence suggests that he is an agent of Boyle's and—'

'What evidence?' said Noah.

'Certain evidence that I have discovered ...'

'Inspector ...' warned Sir Richard. 'We are all working on the same case.'

'Well, the fact of his wearing a mask is highly suggestive when we consider the masks of Mr Dyson and Mr Williamson.'

'Hmm. But this is not in itself persuasive evidence of Lucius Boyle's personal involvement,' said Mr Williamson. 'You must have more.'

'Very well, very well.' said Mr Newsome irritably. 'I also discovered a large quantity of money on the body and a number of letters addressed to important people about the city ... people, that is, who are known to frequent certain immoral houses.'

'Blackmail,' said Sir Richard. 'I assume you have opened and read the letters?'

'Indeed. I have a specimen here – they are all written after the same model but with names and dates varying.'

Mr Newsome took one of the letters from his breast pocket and handed it to Sir Richard, who scanned it with an expression of distaste and passed it to Noah.

Your Honour

You do not know me, but I know you. Or rather, I know you enjoy a penchant for the criminally younger gentleman, which you indulge from time to time at the address of Mr Jarrow, Grosvenor-square. Indeed, it appears that you go there regularly on Thursdays and Tuesdays.

I cast no moral judgement on your proclivities, though I suspect that others might. It hardly seems fitting that a man of your position has such dark and unpleasant secrets, but, fortunately for you, I am willing to keep my counsel on receipt of ten pounds to be collected from your home every second Wednesday from this day forth.

If you go to the police, I will reveal this much and more. If you abuse or challenge my agent, I will see to it that you or your property comes to some harm. If you refuse to pay the money ... well, let us say that you have more to lose than I.

Yours in trust

'Evidently the money you found is indeed the proceeds of extortion, and this fellow the collection agent,' said Noah. 'Was there no other clue on his person to identify him or his origins?'

'Nothing indicative of anything in particular,' said Mr Newsome.

'Hmm. Do you mean to say you did not find the merest clue upon his clothing or his shoes to suggest his previous movements?' said Mr Williamson. 'A good detective would always look.'

'I did look, and as I say: nothing indicative. The pockets were empty apart from the letters and money. There was a patch of alcohol upon his sleeve that he must have acquired when he fell. Nothing more. He was quite covered in filth from the road.'

'Do we have a name?' said Noah.

'One or two constables here at the station say they recognize his face. It seems he has been convicted on a number of counts of fraud, deception, forgery and coining. The names given were different every time – it could be one of half a dozen possibilities.'

'That is how such fellows are,' said Mr Williamson. 'Had you followed him instead of chasing him under a wagon, we might now have Lucius Boyle in custody.'

'At least I have taken a forward step rather than chasing my own tail!'

'Gentlemen!' said Sir Richard. 'Let us proceed with what we have rather than what we do not. Mr Dyson – you were to visit an acquaintance of yours to investigate this suspected extortion. Did you discover anything more?'

'Only that there is doubtlessly some apparent unease within that privileged community. People are changing long-held habits. There are rumours of letters being received.'

'Rather vague,' said Mr Newsome dismissively. 'I have discovered more.'

'But I did not have to kill anyone to discover what *I* know,' said Noah. 'I have further learned that certain Members of Parliament have been warned not to attend certain sessions. The names are unspecified, but Sir _____

_____ may be one of them. Of course, we now have some further names and addresses.'

'Which sessions?' said Sir Richard.

'I am afraid my source does not know. There is no indication that it is the work of Lucius Boyle– but it is highly suggestive.'

'Sir _____ _____ attends my club,' said Sir Richard. 'I was not aware that he is involved in anything illicit.'

'Hmm. One seldom knows one's fellows,' said Mr Williamson with a pointed glance at Mr Newsome.

'Do any of the letters you found refer to Commons sessions?' said Sir Richard to Mr Newsome.

'No, sir. All are simple requests for money.'

'Perhaps I will try to find a way of learning more about Sir _____

_____,' said Sir Richard. 'In the meantime, I believe, Inspector, that you were about to tell us why you took the body to a taxidermist when a trip to the police surgeon would have been more appropriate.'

'Yes, sir. It occurred to me that Boyle cannot venture on to the streets if his face is indeed as hideous as the coffin model would suggest. Certainly, he might wear a mask, and we have seen how masked men seem to be proliferating at present, but he must surely rely on agents such as this fellow and the one referred to as the "Italian" to do his work about the city.'

'Yes, yes – but why have the fellow *stuffed*, Inspector?' said Sir Richard with some exasperation.

'It is something of a gamble, but my reasoning is this: the report in *the Times* makes no mention of the new body's identity, and yet Boyle will, by now, be missing an agent. Knowing that the body was found in the area where he had sent his man to deliver letters, he may assume the body is the same fellow. Moreover, if Boyle is indeed the perpetrator of Charlotte's unnatural death, he cannot fail to be struck by the occurrence of another such incident. Perhaps he will assume that the killer of PC Taylor is responsible. In short, I seek to agitate our adversary into making an appearance. One of his agents is unmasked and another is killed. He will be confused, wrong-footed . . .'

'It is a strange process of thought, but I still cannot perceive a clear advantage for our investigation,' said Sir Richard. 'What do you propose we do with this body you have had manufactured?'

'It is simple, sir. We will arrange for this body to be exhibited somewhere public. We will do this on some pretext or other – for example that the identity of the dead man is unknown and we are seeking someone who knows him. Might not Boyle or his Italian attend such a viewing to verify that it is *their* man who is dead? They must, after all, be consumed with curiosity about how he came to meet the same fate at Charlotte. Additionally, they will hardly suspect the police of such a ruse.'

'That latter observation, at least, is true,' said Sir Richard. 'This is the strategy of a lunatic.'

'One must think like a lunatic to catch one, sir.'

'I am averse to your way of thinking, Inspector, but recent experiences suggest you may be correct. What do you other gentlemen think of this madness?'

As Mr Newsome had been speaking, Noah and Mr Williamson had been exchanging glances of combined surprize and reluctant approval.

'Much as I am loath to admit it, I see some advantage in this plan,' said Noah. 'But I believe I know a way to make it even more effective.'

'Then speak freely,' said Sir Richard. 'It seems the Rubicon has already been crossed.'

'Let us remember this one critical fact,' said Noah. 'It would appear that neither killer – of PC Taylor or of Charlotte – has actually seen other's work. The differences in their methods suggest as much. Might it not be the case that the killer of PC Taylor may also attend an exhibition of the body to examine the work? He, too, must be intensely curious.'

'You fail to recognize that we have no idea who the second killer is,' said Mr Newsome. 'Even if he did attend, how would we recognise him?'

'That is the masterstroke of my conception,' said Noah. 'We will organize the exhibition in such a way that all those who observe the exhibit will themselves be observed by a panel of experts who are tasked with assessing their behaviour.'

'I am not sure I understand,' said Sir Richard. 'To what manner of experts might you be referring?'

'You have a gentleman working at Scotland Yard called Figgs.'

'What of him?'

'Well, it seems he is something of an authority on human appearance. If his science has any basis to it, might he not be able to spot a murderer in a crowd – especially if that murderer stands in clear sight looking at his own victim?'

'I suppose he might,' said Sir Richard uncertainly.

'But Mr Figgs will not be the only one,' continued Noah. 'We will also employ the taxidermist Mr Baldock of Wych-street, who presumably made this figure. More than any other man, he will be able to recognize a fellow taxidermist by the way he examines a nostril or ear or finger. These people are quite particular in their art.'

'Hmm. It is true,' added Mr Williamson to pre-empt more doubt from the commissioner. 'Go to Madame Tussaud's and you will see that the common visiter does not actually study the figures. Rather, they judge the effigies purely on the superficialities of perceived faithfulness to the original, or the effect of any horror being sought. The finer details quite pass them by.'

'And this is why we must also employ a ceroplastician on our panel of experts,' said Noah. 'Both of our killers have resorted to the use of artificial features in bodies prepared specifically for exhibition, so might they not take a particular interest in the eyes or the pose of this gentleman Mr Newsome has procured?'

'Not only that,' said Mr Williamson, 'but such a person might also be more adept at seeing a mask in the general crowds.'

Sir Richard assessed the expression of the three investigators before him, all of whom seemed quite earnest about this eccentric endeavour. What would Vidocq have said about such a scheme?

'It seems to me,' said Mr Newsome, 'that the most effective system would be for these experts to make some manner of vote on likely candidates. If the taxidermist believes he has seen a certain kind of observation, he will confer with Mr Figgs and the wax-worker will add any further comment. If all express a similar suspicion, that particular member of the public will be taken aside for questioning.'

'I wonder if you gentlemen realize what kind of a sensation this is likely to create?' said Sir Richard. 'You know how the discovery of Charlotte has galvanized the public. Such an exhibition as you propose would draw many hundreds and would need to occur in an open space – a park perhaps.'

'St James's park is nearest,' said Mr Newsome. 'We might organize it during the common working period to minimize the crowds. After all, our suspects are unlikely to be dissuaded by the hour – their curiosity will overcome them.'

'There is one more thing to consider,' said Mr Williamson. 'We three investigators must be conspicuously not present at the exhibition. It already looks like a trap, so we must seek to distance ourselves from it if we are to entice the prey.'

'I have an idea how that might be effected,' said Noah. 'You may leave it to me. Perhaps I will also enquire at Madame Tussaud's about the masks of ourselves since Inspector Newsome has not yet managed that part of the investigation.'

'No – I will do it!' said Mr Newsome with rather an excess of emphasis.

'Try to remain composed, Inspector,' said Noah with a smile. 'Why not toss a coin for the privilege?'

And with this, Noah took a gold coin from his trouser pocket: a sovereign, but one not of this century, or even of the one before. It was in fact an Elizabethan piece that Noah now turned to glint in the light so that the inspector might perceive what it was.

'That . . . that is *my* coin!' said Mr Newsome.

'I think not. Did you not just see me take it from my own pocket?'

'I found it . . . in the sewers on that last case . . . it was in *my* pocket as I was struck by the Italian's bullet . . .'

'A coincidence, then. I found it at Frying Pan wharf.'

'Yes – in my pocket!'

'Well, let us not argue. I will toss for the coin and for the right to question androgynous Bill at Tussaud's. I call tails . . . and tails it is. Bad luck, Inspector.'

Mr Newsome smouldered and looked ready to leap at Noah's throat. Mr Williamson found himself smiling openly at the spectacle.

'Perhaps it is time for us to each embark on our respective duties,' said Sir Richard.

'I will have Mr Cullen investigate what is known of this stuffed fellow around Westminster,' said Mr Williamson. 'No doubt his acquaintances will not speak freely to a known constable in uniform.'

'Very well,' said Sir Richard. 'I have much to organize and many enquiries to make. May I stress that we must all act with the greatest discretion at this time. Our adversary will be most dangerous now that he has lost a man.'

'And I would still like to see the likeness of Boyle that was disinterred,' said Noah. 'If it is indeed taken from life, our safety might depend of recognising the man as he now appears.'

'That makes sense,' said Sir Richard.' I will see that it is brought to you at Golden-square. Do you feel that the address remains safe? The longer you stay, the more likely it is that he will find you.'

'Let him find us,' said Noah. 'I would rather he or his agents came to us than that we persist in this interminable pursuit.'

'Remember, Mr Dyson, that our aim is to take the fellow into custody that we might try him,' said Sir Richard. 'If he dies at your hand, you become the murderer and you will be tried.'

Mr Newsome looked as if he was about to speak, but swallowed his words and instead brooded mutely.

There came a knock at the door.

'We are not to be disturbed!' said Sir Richard.

'It is something that may concern you, sir,' came the muffled voice of the clerk.

'Then enter,' sighed the commissioner.

'My apologies, gentlemen,' said the clerk. 'You must all be aware, I suppose, that the unfortunate PC Taylor was a constable at this station?'

'The question is not worthy of the interruption,' muttered Mr Newsome.

'I mean to say, rather ... that is ... a second policeman now appears to have gone missing.'

The four gentlemen simply stared in response.

'He has not returned from his beat,' said the clerk. 'It seems he has vanished utterly.'

TWENTY-FIVE

Mr Cullen had been the only man not wearing uniform in the stuffy confines of the Gardener-street wardroom. The other men – constables all – had regarded him with an admixture of suspicion and respect while remaining mindful of the fact that their station inspector had told them this fellow was a representative of the Detective Force on a special mission for Sir Richard Mayne himself. At the same time, there had also been much muttering that the more pressing matter at hand was the disappearance of one of their own. Surely that was more important than the provenance of a tawdry local charlatan?

For his part, Mr Cullen had vacillated between diffidence and immense pride on adopting the temporary designation of "detective". These men in blue were the same doughty stock from which he himself had sprung, but from which he had been propelled to the ethereal heights of association with the very police commissioner.

'So, gentlemen,' he had said with a deeper voice than was customary. 'You have all seen the effigy and I have heard that some of you recognize it. I need to know from you what names he went by and where I might find his associates in these streets.'

'He's been arrested by me as "Harry Dobbs"' said one constable.

'I've known him as "John Tavistock"' said another.

'He is a trickster and cheat,' said a third, older man. 'You will likely not locate his colleagues using those other names because he uses them only with his victims or with the authorities. I believe he is known . . . was known to his peers as "Mullender" – although I don't know if that is a surname or a Christian name.'

'Very good,' said Mr Cullen, jotting these facts into a notebook as detectives will. 'Do we know where his fellows might drink? Did he have a girl among these streets? Did he have family?'

'He might have been from here, but I believe he had long since left,' said the older constable. 'No man of success stays in the rookery by choice. You might, however, ask after him in the public house on Old Pye-street: the Sign of the Cross. I understand he used to be a patron there.'

'An Irish pub is it?' said Mr Cullen.

'Rather not. The name is from the time of the plague. It seems that a number of local residents barricaded themselves within to survive the pest. They painted the holy sign upon the door to keep people out, though it is probably best not to imagine what they ate during that long quarantine. Certainly, fewer emerged once the horror had passed.'

The other constables had laughed heartily at this, making comments to the effect that the story well exemplified the spirit and history of this black spot on their portion of London.

Mr Cullen had then thanked them and ventured alone down King-street and on to Tothill-street in search of that ill-named hostelry. They had, of course, warned him against his solitary excursion; they had suggested that an early morning attempt would have been safer; they had offered uniformed support – but time was short, Lucius Boyle was at large, and he knew from experience that a thief would never speak of a colleague to a policeman. Moreover, this was his personal test, his chance, his apprenticeship piece. Noah could have done it. Mr Williamson could have done it. No doubt Benjamin would also have welcomed the challenge if he had a tongue.

The thing was to walk with confidence. He was, after all, a big man and broad. And yet there was something about a rookery – particularly at night – that could make the bravest and most rational of men afraid. Perhaps it was the primitive reek of vegetable detritus or the stench of massed humanity crammed into low lodging houses. In the case of Westminster, it was possibly also the case of its being below river level so that the rains of recent days had rendered the place a virtual quagmire of muddy puddles, flooded gutters and great standing pools of steaming effluvia. One might almost have been walking two centuries into the past.

Then there was the bestial populace of such places: poor, hungry, gin-addled and alert for the slightest possibility of illicit or immoral gain. They huddled in groups, whispered in alleys and stared at his good wool coat as a street boy stares through the misted window of the pie shop. Muttered speculation followed him like a shadow: was he one of those writers come to document their poverty? Was he a clergyman with a pocketful of promises for the next life? Was he a receiver come to collect his weekly due from his gang of pickpockets? Or was he a detective with his military bearing and his heavy-booted march? Certainly, he was a stranger.

As expected, the Sign of the Cross was a raucous place that spilled light and music across the putrid cobbles. Despite the grimness of its name – depicted as a sanguinary double daub upon the swinging sign outside – it was clearly one of the few places in that desperate locale where joy might be found. Mr Cullen took a breath and entered.

Inside, the air was opaque with smoke, heat and the fumes of drink. There was laughter, shouting, and a number of discussions whose chief subject seemed to be the forthcoming spectacle in St James's park, to which, it seemed, everyone was planning to go.

'What'll yer 'ave, big feller?' said a large, red-faced lady behind the bar.

'Gin,' said Mr Cullen.

'Lost are yer?' said the barmaid, pouring his drink. 'We don't get too many tourists in this part o' the City.'

'I am looking for someone.'

'Copper are yer?' She assessed him with a suspicious gaze but seemed to think not. 'Yer won't find nobody round here if yer a copper. Ooever it is, 'e ain't 'ere.'

'I seek justice – but not the kind a magistrate might hand down. A man has cheated me and I will have my revenge.'

'Well, yer in the right place. Here's yer drink. Aye – revenge, regret and ruin are what yer'll find at the Cross any evenin' yer like. Got a blade, 'ave yer? Jus' don't be killin' anyone in 'ere. I don't need the mess of it.'

Mr Cullen felt the sheathed dagger lying heavy in his inside jacket pocket. Noah had made him carry it after the Italian's attempt at Golden-square. 'It is a fellow called Mullender I seek – a dark-eyed chap. Fancy in his attire. He passed himself off as a shipping clerk and made away with my cargo. They tell me he might be known in this part of Westminster.'

'"Mullender", yer say? Name rings a bell. I bet Eddy'll know. Eddy knows 'em all. Hoi, Eddy! Come 'ere a minute!'

A man in the latter stages of dissipation looked up from his argument at a corner table and stood to stagger towards the bar. Drunk and dishevelled he may have been, but the eyes in his puffy face were sharp as he looked at Mr Cullen.

'This feller's lookin' for a chap called Mullender,' said the barmaid. 'Dark-eyed feller. Know 'im?'

'You a copper?' said Eddy, spitting on the floor for emphasis.

'He cheated me,' said Mr Cullen. 'I would like to meet him again and . . . discuss the matter with him in private.'

The man called Eddy squinted at the seemingly guileless face before him, thinking perhaps that the stranger did not have the sly swagger of a detective. 'Can't 'elp you, mate,' he said, finally. 'Mullender used to spend time round 'ere, but he moved on to better things. Too good for the likes of us. B_____ liar – can't believe a word 'e says. Touched in the 'ead, as well: talks to 'imself.'

'Have you spoken to him recently? Do you know where he might be found?'

'Sure you're not a copper?' Another gobbet of saliva joined the first.

'Does a policeman go armed?' said Mr Cullen, opening his jacket so that Eddy might see the dagger's stag handle.

'Aye, well … Mullender deserves a blade in 'is back more than most. It's one thing to take a man's wallet, but another to go in his 'ouse or trick the money from 'is pocket. There's no honour in it.'

'Where can I find him?'

'No idea, mate. Last I 'eard, he was workin' for a feller out east. All very secret. Was even tryin' to tell me that *'e* was the Masked Man everyone's been talkin' about. Can you imagine? The man is full of ____.'

'Mullender claimed *he* was the Masked Man?'

'Aye, that's what I said.'

'When was the last time you saw him?'

'Must've been a couple of weeks past, near the new Parliament buildin's. Saw 'im standin' there and the _____ pretended not to know me! Then, when I stopped 'im, 'e showed me a load of money in 'is pocket – tryin' to prove 'ow flash 'e was.'

Mr Cullen nodded meditatively, though it was all mere corroboration of what they had surmised. 'Did Mullender say where he was going or where he had been? Where was he living? I want to find the man.'

'And show 'im your dagger, eh? Sorry – but I've no idea, mate.'

'You said it was near the Palace of Westminster. Where exactly?'

'Bottom of the Victoria tower – round there.'

'By the Office of the Lord Great Chamberlain, perhaps? The place where one buys tickets for admission?'

'Aye, I suppose it was thereabouts. There *was* a queue of people.'

'Thank you. This might help me,' said Mr Cullen.

'So will you buy me a drink?' said Eddy.

Mr Cullen indicated that the slattern behind the bar should give the fellow whatever was his pleasure ("Gin, with a brandy and water to see it down") and stepped out into the street, whose dank chill was preferable to the smoky fug of the house. A firework hissed its pale scar across the sky as he stood breathing steam, and something at his feet caught his attention.

A muddy footprint had overlaid the printing, but the title and most of the text of flyer was still legible:

REMARKABLE FIREWORKS DISPLAY

He was about to throw the paper back to the ground with disinterest when an idea occurred to him. Or rather, it was one of those connective flashes of the investigator's mind when the question "What if . . . ?" sets forth a chain of supposition that leads irresistibly to a realisation.

Had he not been so preoccupied with such thoughts, he might have noticed the occasional billow of smoke emanating from a nearby alley, where a grubby lad in a curious uniform chewed a clay pipe and watched the burly fellow stroll back towards Gardener's-lane station.

And as one investigator returned to his base, another was venturing out. Mr Newsome walked almost in a cogitative trance. A cab would undoubtedly have been faster, and a steam ferry quicker still, but the metronome of his feet upon the sodden city streets was a balm to his fevered experience. Through bustling thoroughfares he strode, an automaton of thought undistracted by the flash and pop of sporadic fireworks or the relentless rattle of wheels and hooves all around. In his head, a mathematical calm was sorting the pieces of the case. In his pockets, the tools of his investigative intent rattled metallically.

This latest development of the second missing constable had indeed been unexpected. However, it bore not the least connection to any other line of enquiry except the strange death of PC Taylor, which in itself was a distraction from the true prize of capturing Lucius Boyle. Mr Williamson and his band of oddities were welcome to that incidental part of the investigation if it meant that he, Inspector Newsome, would move rapidly closer to his personal adversary.

Of some concern, admittedly, was the knowledge that Noah Dyson had probably already learned from the androgyne "Bill" Smith that the various mysterious masks had been made at Tussaud's. Further reprimands from Sir Richard would follow in due course, but by then the business of the grisly exhibition in St James's park would hopefully be the main focus of attention.

More immediately important was what Mr Newsome had not revealed to the others at the Gardener-lane meeting concerning his discovery of the postcard on Perkin Mullender's person – a direct link to a person who had known the man and a place where his reputation may be sought. Thus it was that Mr Newsome walked on and on through the gas-flare reflections and glistening precipitation of that early November night towards his goal: the Thames Tunnel.

In retrospect, one had to admit it was the perfect place to seek Lucius Boyle or his accomplices – a space neither here nor there, a space both under water and under land, a furtive space whose span one might not see and where no beat policeman walked on account of its being private property. Then there was its reputation, which metamorphosed after dusk from the tedious tourist novelty of its diurnal incarnation to the less salubrious connotations of its nocturnal life. Like a moral drain, it received a flow of sin each night.

It was this Thames Tunnel that Mr Newsome approached, paying his penny and clanking through the gate to enter a less jovial, less welcoming shaft of staircases. Gone was the organ music and festive air of familial wonder. Gone was the echoing chatter and the welcoming smells of coffee, cake and candle. Most of those gaudy vendors were now departing or had already left until dawn, leaving a cavern of hissing gas and illicit whispers, of the homeless and of strictly commercial assignations conducted in the shadows.

Not all of the hawkers and charlatans had yet vacated the tunnel, however, and as he reached the bottom of the stairs Mr Newsome noted that the fortune-telling hag remained at her stall, staring blank-eyed across the open space before the tunnel openings. She seemed at first not to have noticed him, but then let forth an otherworldly moan as he walked briskly past her.

'Go not so quickly to your doom!' she intoned.

Mr Newsome waved a hand in her direction as if at an irritating fly and continued on his trajectory.

'Some old, some new – thou hast old sin upon thy soul,' droned the would-be witch.

He stopped. Had she used his surname, or had it merely been an impression of her garbled words? 'Do you know me?' he said across the hall.

'Not I, not I, but the eye of vengeful Tisiphone seeks its due. You walk in Justice but leave bloody footprints. Go not in water – no! – for your guilty soul stains streams incarnadine.'

'Deranged old lunatic,' mumbled Mr Newsome, resuming his progress towards the tunnel shaft itself.

One might not have known the hour from the illumination therein. Only the scarcity of people and the silent shuttered stalls indicated that darkness reigned above. Nevertheless, he was relieved to see that he had not missed one of the pretty girls who sold postcards. She was in the process of locking her wares into a trunk beneath the stall when he approached.

'Good evening to you miss . . . Jane, is it?' he said.

She turned with a smile that seemed brighter than one would expect from a girl who spent most of her waking hours below ground. 'Do I know you, sir?'

'I believe not, but I wondered if you might perhaps help me. I found a pocket book in the street and I would like to return it to the gentleman who must have dropped it. This postcard was within. It is signed, as you see, and I was hoping . . .'

'O, it is Mr Winchester! He's a handsome fellow: witty and kind.'

'I did not see him, only his pocket book on the street.'

'He's down at the tunnel often, sir. Give *me* the pocket book if you like and I'll see that he gets it.'

'Alas, I do not have it with me. Do you know where he might live?'

'No, sir. He talks to me whenever he's down and I save the best cards for him, but I haven't yet had the pleasure of meeting him outside.'

'He must think highly of you to carry your card so close to his heart.'

The girl blushed and failed utterly to control the smile saturating her features.

'Perhaps you can tell me, Jane – what does he do when he comes down here so often?'

'He says he comes for the exercise, sir. He walks down the left-hand tunnel to Rotherhithe and comes back along the right.'

'How long does that normally take?'

'It rather varies, sir. I suppose some days he's brisker than others. Sometimes he seems to take an awful long time, but there're many people during the day. Perhaps they slow his progress.'

'Yes, that must be it. Have you seen him meet anyone in particular down here?'

'Not at all. He speaks only to me.'

'Then have you noticed anyone suspicious in the tunnel at the same time?'

'O, do you think Mr Winchester might be in danger? I wonder … I wonder if you are thinking of the "foreign criminal" described in the newspapers.'

'What do you mean? Have you seen that fellow here?'

'Why, we've all seen him. As soon as we saw that picture in the papers, we all said to each other that he's down here almost every day. At least four of the girls have gone to Scotland Yard to report it.'

'Have they indeed?' Mr Newsome ground his jaw, imagining the stacks of unread witness reports sitting on a desk somewhere at Whitehall-place as the true villain escaped.

'Yes, sir. But the odd thing is that he hasn't been seen since the article appeared.'

'That is indeed odd.'

'Has this something to do with Mr Winchester?'

Nothing at all. If you see him, tell him that I have left his pocket book at Scotland Yard and it may be collected from the Lost Property office there. No doubt he will be relieved.'

'Thank you, sir. I'm sure he will. I'm leaving now, but I'll look for him tomorrow. And do take care if you plan to stroll – it's not so nice at night.'

Mr Newsome tipped his hat to the girl and turned to continue his walk into the tunnel, musing ruefully that if young Jane were not so busy selling cards, she might visit St James's park and see her beloved Mr Winchester stuffed full of flax, his dark eyes made cold enamel. Later, she might discover the truth about his eternal corpse and learn that such are the vagaries of fate – one day in love, the next day broken, betrayed or bereft.

Evidently, a darker mood had begun to descend. Perhaps it was the enwombing masonry about him, or perhaps it was the palpably foetid smell of the river, but, as he walked deeper under the city, he could not help but recall those grim, desperate days he had so recently spent trapped in the sewers. Without sleep, without food, and with only the dimmest glimmer of light, he had stumbled in filth until he thought his own reverberating screams would drive him insane. They were memories that had not yet left his sleep, and they swarmed into his waking mind even now.

At this hour, people were sensed more readily than seen. One caught sideways glimpses of entangled bodies in the alcoves; one heard the drunk's atonal roar; one stepped between reeking rags and tried to avoid the challenging stares of strangers. Amid such stimuli, Mr Newsome looked about for the slightest clue of what the Italian and his stuffed colleague might have been doing here. Had they met Boyle in these anonymous depths? Had they exchanged messages and strategy out of sight of the police? Was there perhaps some manner of drop site where they might leave each other the materials of their crimes?

He had passed the halfway point when he stopped to analyse something that had registered latently on his perception. The empty alcoves that had accompanied him thus far on his right now appeared to have been replaced by *trompe l'œil* images stretching for about ten yards. He studied the painting and tried to recall a newspaper report of a year or so ago in which he had read that the twin tunnels had originally been constructed with a solid wall between them and the alcoves knocked through later. If that was so, might not some other space have been inserted?

Within minutes he found what he sought: a rusting iron door let into the side of the last alcove before the painted section. He bent to study the ground and saw the directional scuffs that suggested footsteps and a scraping door. Was this the place?

Mr Newsome withdrew a pistol (whose discovery would surely see him ejected from the force) and tried the door knob. Discovering it closed, he rapped on it with the pistol butt and pressed his ear to the cold metal to listen.

Nothing.

With a furtive look into the tunnel shafts each side of him, he next took a hammer and a thin, pointed chisel from his coat pockets and directed a tremendous blow into the lock mechanism, by which means he aimed to knock off the back plate. Three such impacts resulted in the desired clatter of metal within and he was able to agitate the door open with a scrape.

It was the smell that told him he must have found his quarry: the sour stench of confined men, consumed oil and a compost of other scents that seemed to suggest chymicals and old blood. A single Davy lamp burned within the room and Mr Newsome's heart jumped as he saw the many Chubb Patent Detector lock mechanisms laid out on a bench. The place was a veritable trove of evidence.

His fingers now throbbing with excitement, he sorted quickly through the chaos of papers on the bench. There was hand-drawn interior plan of

Scotland Yard, a ripped-out *Times* advertisement for Baldock's Taxidermy Emporium, a stack of order sheets marked with the name of Chubb, and a copy of *Mogg's Stranger's Map of London* with circles drawn variously at Golden-square, Blackfriars, Lambeth and Westminster. Crumpled beneath the bench was also a flyer for a fireworks display, the back of which bore a scribbled note: *"x200 for Tobias".*

Mr Newsome's mind whirred. He should immediately send for Sir Richard . . . and yet, had there not already been ample proof of how slow police administration had been concerning witness reports of the Italian? No – the best course was to gather all evidence himself and take the next steps personally to apprehend the criminals. That way lay glory and promotion which neither Noah or Mr Williamson could frustrate.

It was only now that he noticed the other door in the gloom and stepped quickly to enter that room. Again, the smell was the first indication of its significance: a sharp aroma of sulphur and phosphorus, of gunpowder and of some lingering organic taint reminiscent of a butcher's shop. Then there was the workbench, which was perhaps even richer in incriminating evidence.

Even in the poor light from the other room, the tools for firework manufacture were obvious enough. Mr Newsome examined an explosive metal head as used in a Congreve rocket and dropped it in his jacket pocket. Next, he turned two aromatic tubs whose labels proclaimed them to be *Bécour's Arsenical French Soap* and *Sheikh's Superior Gum Arabic.* A fine white powder had additionally worked its way into the crevices of the wood and could be seen on undisturbed sections of the floor. Mr Newsome rubbed it between fingers and smelled it. He had a distinct sense of something horrific having occurred in this space.

Putting such emotions from his thoughts, he continued to examine the workbench and read the spines on a number of volumes. The first was William Swainson's *Taxidermy: Bibliography and Biography.* The second was Dr Reid's *Treatise on the Benefits of Ventilation.* The third was *A Treatise on Poisons* by

Robert Christison M.D., in which a scrap of paper marked a page. He opened the book to see a section underlined in black ink:

An interesting case has been published which proves that nitric ether in vapour is a dangerous poison when too freely and too long inhaled. A druggist's maid-servant was found one morning dead in bed, and death had evidently arisen from the air of her apartment having been accidentally loaded with vapour of nitric ether, from the breaking of a three-gallon jar of the spiritus etheris nitrici. She was found lying on her side, with her arms folded across the chest, the countenance and posture composed, and the whole appearance like a person in deep sleep.

The passage could not help but stir in Mr Newsome the memory of how Lucius Boyle had once before used noxious vapours to effect an ingenious murder. Was there to be something similar? Was it in progress at this very moment?

Mr Newsome's breath now came in snatches. Frustration distracted him. The clues were abundant, and yet the story to connect them would take too long to piece together. He snatched at a large architectural plan and unfolded it to see the new Palace of Westminster, upon which a number of pencil marks had been made. Sundry other sheets thereabouts showed indistinct structures that may have been pipes or tunnels or chambers. Whatever reason Boyle might have for needing these, it could not possibly be a good one.

Another realization flashed across his fevered thoughts: might not the stolen ledger also be in this foetid sett? He searched beneath and around the workbench. He ventured behind a screen where consumed matches littered the floor. He lifted a tarpaulin under which squatted an iron-banded lock box. This was surely the place. He reached for the pointed chisel in his pocket . . .

Then his heart seemed to freeze. The iron door from the tunnel had just scraped.

Mr Newsome struggled to withdraw his pistol and stood pointing it at the doorway in anticipation of an immediate assault. He heard somebody kick the pieces of the destroyed lock to one side ... then silence as the intruder evidently looked around to see what had been disturbed.

Footsteps approached and a shadow fell across the crack between door and jamb. A gloved hand pushed the gap wider and a figure appeared. Partially *silhouetted*, it seemed calm and confident.

Mr Newsome felt the weapon heavy in his extended arm and squinted to see the face beneath the top hat. Confusion flickered in his resolve and he half-lowered the pistol.

'Sir Richard?' he said.

The figure reached wordlessly to take off his hat. Then, with a similar gesture, he removed the wax carapace likeness of the Police Commissioner. In the side-slanting shadow from the outer room, the revealed face now seemed to spasm hideously – a countenance hewn raw from living flesh.

'Boyle!' hissed Mr Newsome.

'Inspector,' said Lucius Boyle in even, unperturbed tones. There was a glutinous sucking to the pronunciation. 'Your persistence is enough to make one turn in one's grave.'

TWENTY-SIX

Were one to possess the omniscience of an Argus Panoptes and be able simultaneously to see every street, lane and alley in our great ashen metropolis, one would have witnessed that next morning a singularly curious phenomenon of multiplicity.

Anyone who recognized Noah, for example, might have met him walking casually east along Oxford-street accompanied by a lofty Negro with an eye-patch who was almost – but not quite – the image of Benjamin. And yet the same pedestrian, on continuing west, might be more than a little surprised to see the identical pair on Baker-street, although this incarnation of Benjamin was admittedly slightly shorter and wider than the original. Nor was this the only such reflection, for a similar pair was also to be seen standing contemporaneously on the steps of St Paul's for the entire world to see.

As for Mr Williamson, three of his likenesses were additionally abroad in the city with a series of facsimile Mr Cullens strolling the Strand, browsing on Regent-street and crossing the various bridges on an endless circuit of the most prominent streets. It was almost as if this alleged fugitive from justice was seeking a witness to his freedom, and indeed at least one of the Williamsons would later be stopped for questioning by a sharp-eyed constable who knew the ex-detective by sight and who was utterly perplexed to see that the fellow he stopped was nothing more than an impostor in a mask.

Regarding the owners of the real faces, they were to be found (with the exception of Benjamin) at 4 Whitehall-place, where they were standing in sombre silence in the office of Sir Richard Mayne. Arrayed before them on the broad oak desk were seven wax representations.

The head recovered from the coffin at Portugal-street was the most lifelike, and it was at this that Noah stared with a melting intensity. Also present were the four heads Noah had recently obtained from young Bill at Madame Tussaud's, namely: himself, Mr Williamson, Mr Newsome and Mr Cullen. These, being unpainted and bereft of hair, offered only the pale, eyeless features of antiquity, suggesting the oddest sense of familiar foreignness. Next to these, the partial mask recovered from the mangled Perkin Mullender made a sorry semi-exhibit, whose principal worth was that it represented the only mask actually to be captured by the investigators.

But perhaps the most horrible of all was the head made by Mr Schlöss to Noah's order and dyed by Mr Cullen's clumsiness. Though it was hardly representative of Lucius Boyle's true countenance as revealed in the first head, it was somehow the most indicative of his baleful spirit – a stark caricature of crimson and white that was simultaneously a parody and an encapsulation of the universal murderer. It was, one might almost have said, the face of evil itself.

Sir Richard turned from the grim exhibition with a look of distaste. 'I cannot say that I am entirely surprized that Inspector Newsome kept the fact of these other heads from us. I am only disappointed that he did. At least now we have some justification for the odd sightings you have variously reported. You may be assured that the inspector will be reprimanded.'

'Do we not know his current whereabouts?' said Noah. 'I have made arrangements for various impostors to lay a false scent as far as we are concerned, but those efforts will be wasted if he arrives conspicuously at St James's park to scare away our quarry.'

'He was supposed to be here for this meeting,' said Sir Richard. 'I can only assume he is engaged upon the case and that he will be there at the park. I think we can trust him to be discreet.'

'Hmm. Hmm,' said Mr Williamson.

'Mr Dyson – I wonder if may I ask you where is your Negro?' said Sir Richard.

'He is not *my* Negro. He is a free man named Benjamin and he remains on guard at Golden-square lest Boyle or his accomplices smell the trap and attempt a strike in that direction. If so, Ben will be ready for them. Might I ask *you*, Commissioner, if anything further has been discovered about this missing constable from Gardiner-street station?'

'Investigations have begun, but all we know at present is that he vanished shortly before the relief of his beat. There is not the least indication of violence, but neither was there in the disappearance of PC Taylor. Do you suspect the same abductor?'

'It seems likely,' said Mr Williamson, 'but I think we have learned never to anticipate what our criminal might do. I cannot see any better strategy at the moment than to proceed with our plans with Perkin Mullender. If they come to nought, we will have to wait for the next body to appear.'

'We apparently have no other choice,' said Sir Richard.

'Were you able to speak to Sir _____ _____ concerning the rumours about him?' said Noah. 'I believe you mentioned he was a member of your club.'

'Indeed, but he told me nothing suspicious. I discovered that he is listed to attend the hearing on plain clothes policemen this evening and I asked him if he still planned to come. He said that he was now unable to do so on account of a sudden bereavement in his family.'

'Hmm. I suspect the only thing that has passed away is his honour,' said Mr Williamson.

'He is a fine man,' said Sir Richard. 'I hope that you are wrong in suspecting him. But it now remains only to adjourn to St James's park and to proceed with this ridiculous pantomime. I have heard that crowds are already considerable. You have no conception what it was like to explain the plan to the Home Secretary and to secure the requisite authority.'

'Hmm. It is no more outrageous than the mass spectacle of the gallows outside Newgate,' said Mr Williamson.

'And I am sure the Home Secretary will be glad to take the credit if we are successful,' said Noah. 'It might even support your case for the use of plain-clothes policemen.'

'Perhaps, perhaps,' said Sir Richard, averting his eyes. 'I myself will not attend. I have much work to do.'

'Preparing your speech about the use of plainclothes policeman for this evening's hearing, perhaps?' said Noah.

The commissioner was unamused. 'Each of you should make his own way to St James's as discussed. On arrival, you should present these letters of introduction to the Division A inspector who is orchestrating the event.'

Sir Richard handed the sealed letters to Noah, Mr Williamson and to Mr Cullen. 'Now – make haste before this spectacle becomes a disaster. I wish you luck.'

Evidently, the plan to display Perkin Mullender's remains when more people were engaged in employment had done little to abate the crowds. Whitehall itself was discernibly busier and there was almost a carnival atmosphere as a ceaseless flow of spectators from the east commingled with the more well-to-do *voyeurs* of the west. Meanwhile, a hawker in Charing Cross stood to make himself wealthy with a barrow full of unnerving stuffed *homunculi* fashioned from pale vellum and sold, according to his patter, as "*Souvenirs* of the times – buy 'em while they last!"

The park itself quite swarmed with humanity, which, though not as populous as a gallows crowd, nevertheless seemed to swell to the very perimeters of that stately space where lofty mansion *façades* and the blank edifices of government cast disapproving looks upon the scene. People had long since spilled beyond the gravel paths on to mud-churned turf, all pressing towards the large tent that had been erected at the eastern extremity of the Serpentine. And the most fanciful supposition was animating that murmuring multitude:

'They say he is a hunchback with only one eye!' said a governess with her wide-eyed young charge by her side.

'I bet it's my Harold. He's been missing for days now,' said a bent old woman walking with sticks.

'Of course, a man's soul does not fully leave his carcase until a week after his death,' opined an earnest young student with his fellows.

For all of them, nothing less than the nourishing state of actual physical proximity would suffice. They had read about this body, talked about this body, imagined this body – now they must *see* it, but a fence of policemen was preventing them access until the allotted hour.

And within that yearned-for tent, the likeness of Perkin Mullender remained impassive in its suspended state. Standing on a *dais* and lit brilliantly by gas, it seemed to look into the distance as if in thought, its once agitated multiplicity of personalities now becalmed into one dead expression.

The inspector of Gardener-lane station stood below the effigy and addressed a small audience consisting of the "experts" gathered to curate the event and the "agents" charged with catching the criminal. He cleared his throat for attention:

'*Ahem* – the public will be given access in a moment so let us clarify for the final time how we will proceed. They will enter *here,* pass in single file around the figure *here* and pass out of the tent *there.* Constables Harewood, Abbey and Frost will see that the line continues to move at a steady pace so that we allow access to as many as possible. At the same time, each entrant will be marked on the back of their right hand with indelible ink so that nobody may return for a second viewing. The experts will be situated just *there* behind that sheet of gauze. The hidden chamber is unlit, so you will be able to observe the line without yourselves being observed.'

The experts nodded their understanding, but seemed somewhat ill at ease with the task ahead. The elderly taxidermist Mr Baldock may have seemed composed, but was betrayed by the hand fiddling at the buttons of his scarlet waistcoat. The anatomical ceroplastician and prosthetical supplier Mr Schlöss was becoming increasingly confused about which detective was which and where the investigation was going. Mr Figgs, meanwhile, had already expressed confidence in his ability to spot the murderer, but appeared more perturbed in the presence of the German fellow who very likely knew more about the actual science of the cranium. All could not help but be unnerved by the great sonorous drone from the waiting masses – a storm gathering in distant treetops.

'Any member of the public who believes they recognize the body – which is, after all, the ostensible reason of this display – will be directed to give the particulars to constables on exiting,' continued the inspector. 'As for our true purpose, the experts in their covert chamber will relate to Mr Williamson who they collectively believe may be a suspect. Mr Williamson will then pass this information on to Mr Cullen, who will work with my constables to extract those persons at the exit and sequester them for questioning. Mr Dyson will be stationed outside to observe the crowds around the tent. Are there any questions?'

'I was led to understand that Inspector Newsome of the Detective Force would be here,' said Mr Figgs. 'I am not sure I feel comfortable proceeding without the presence of a senior detective – a genuine detective.'

'I was told he had had an accident,' offered Mr Schlöss.

'We are here under the *aegis* of Commissioner Sir Richard Mayne himself,' said Noah, 'and this action has been authorized by the Home Secretary. If Mr Newsome is not here, it is because he is unprofessional. Furthermore, Mr Figgs, you are alone among our experts in being paid a considerable fee for your aid, so your discomfort is therefore irrelevant.'

The anthropometrist pursed his lips and nodded curtly. 'Let us continue.'

'Very well – will everyone take their stations?' said the inspector. 'Let us attempt to complete our task as quickly and efficiently as possible.'

There was a general movement in sundry directions and within minutes a whistle was blown to signal that the tent should be opened to the public. This in turn prompted a convulsion that rippled outwards through the park and an eruption of excited chatter that sounded quite fearful from within.

'They will tear the place to pieces if they don't get a good look at the body,' said Mr Schlöss, who had seen enough of the English mob to know its capabilities. He tried to gauge the thickness of the gauze between them and the body to see if it truly would hide their presence. Through it, the whole scene had something of a misty, dreamlike quality.

'Fear not,' said Mr Baldock. 'It is only the curiosity of novelty they seek. Once they see he is just a man – not deformed, not horrific – they will simply pass through, disappointed, and word will go out that the show is not worth the wait. Only a true enthusiast will bother to queue.'

'Let us hope you are right, sir,' said Mr Figgs, 'or we might be here past nightfall.'

'Concentrate, if you please,' said Mr Williamson, standing behind them. 'Here they come.'

Indeed, the opening of the tent had heralded the first rush of people, channelled by ropes and steered by policeman so that they looped around the raised figure of Perkin Mullender, their eyes wide to consume this spectacle that had been so magnified in their expectations.

'Do you see?' said Mr Baldock. 'They look at it, but they have no idea what they seek in it. They merely ask themselves "Is it realistic?" "Does it bear the obvious marks of murder?" That is the extent of their experience, as when a common man looks at a painting by a great master. He sees not the technique, only what is depicted. A Grecian temple or rustic scene means nothing to the tailor or watchmaker.'

And it was precisely as the taxidermist had said: the shuffling line of people gazed, but did so as one gazes in a gallery or zoological garden – seeing, but feeling nothing more than disappointed curiosity. They did not know this fellow, who might as easily have been fashioned from wax as human skin and who was little more to them than a curious statue. Only his notoriety made him anything more – that and the fact of his being an apparent murder victim. The Room of Horrors at Tussaud's was far more engaging.

'There! Did you see that?' said Mr Baldock. 'The fellow in the top hat . . . he with the moustache: he made a particular study of the fingers.'

'Mr Figgs? Your opinion please,' said Mr Williamson, who had seen the act.

'Well, the occipital zone is suggestive . . . his colouring and features bespeak general intelligence . . . but I see no homicidal urge in his morphology. Perhaps he is merely an amateur taxidermist.'

'We will take him all the same,' said Mr Williamson, moving to a curtain and opening it to advise Mr Cullen which fellow should be removed from the outgoing queue.

'I wonder if we will truly see the criminal today,' said Mr Schlöss. 'There are so many people, and they all look the same after a while.'

'Nonsense,' said Mr Figgs. 'Every man carries his judgement in his own features. One cannot hide one's true nature, which can be read as easily as a book if one is literate in the relevant arts.'

'I cannot agree,' said Mr Baldock. 'The propensities you think you see in a man's appearance cannot speak of his individual thoughts. *They* are hidden and revealed only in action.'

'Hmm. Please pay attention to the queue,' said the returning Mr Williamson. 'There is likely a murderer here before us.'

And, as grains through an hourglass, the people flowed without pause.

Outside, Noah had metamorphosed. His good suit of clothes had been replaced by a rather ragged outfit of corduroy and his top hat by a too large cloth cap whose front quite concealed his eyes. A false moustache completed the transformation from investigator to common costermonger.

It was in this guise that he moved invisibly among the crowds, scanning their faces, watching their movements and looking out for the merest trace of the Italian or the strange boy who had cut Benjamin. Admittedly, it did seem possible that, following the incident at Golden-square, the Italian may be too injured to attend, but Boyle's hand must be forced one way or another.

Noah might almost have been a spirit amidst the shifting masses, who seemed to follow some primal instinct for congregation. On Oxford-street, at the theatre, at an execution or at a warehouse fire– wherever one's personal existence could temporarily be assimilated by the collective – the people of the city became a different organism altogether: moving together as a flock, adopting a common mood and speaking with one Babel voice. In the crowd, one no longer existed individually, but rather sought the individual *outside*.

Thus was it possible for Noah to more readily view those around him, watching for an anomaly in the herd: someone, like himself, whose gaze was not directed irresistibly towards the tent and who was also alert to the enmeshing group itself. They might perhaps be found on the periphery, or at a more elevated position where they could observe the police and potential escape routes. Wherever they lurked, the advantage would go to whoever saw his quarry first.

And there was indeed another keen observer in that undulating sea of heads – a bent-backed beggar with a walking cane who was similarly examining the faces about him. Closer inspection of the fellow would have shown that the grey hair beneath his hat was not his own and that the ragged clothing masked a body both powerful and lithe. One sallow earlobe bore a half-healed hole where an earring must recently have been, and the dark eyes were as alert as any circling hawk . . .

The fellow with the moustache had, after all, been nothing more than a gentleman in town for the week who had taken the opportunity to view the stuffed body. Taxidermy was indeed one of his hobbies and he had been outraged at the suggestion of any murderous act on his part. Mr Cullen's faith in the whole *charade* had begun to falter as early as that.

But subsequent events had become stranger yet. On the expert panel's say-so, four more people had been extracted from the interminable flow for special questioning – four people whose stories one might not have imagined, but which nevertheless represented the true diversity of the London masses.

The first was clearly a lunatic living among the common populace: a fellow of shabby appearance maintaining with all seriousness that he had been sent personally by the queen to examine the body and to report his findings to her. On being questioned further, he had admitted to being Her Majesty's secret consort (after which revelation he was taken away in the care of a surgeon).

The second had freely admitted that he was the famed Masked Man being sought by the whole city and that he had murdered the figure exhibited there that day. He was, however, unable to provide even a single *alias* of Perkin Mullender or any detail whatsoever on the subject of taxidermy. A third man, following about forty minutes later, made similar claims of murder without offering a fibre of evidence. Both were duly arrested for wasting the time of the police and were taken directly before a magistrate.

As for the fourth – a young man with a wild look to his eyes and an unhealthy damp pallor – he had broken into sobs immediately on being taken from the crowd and had admitted, without prompting, to strangling his young bride at a cheap lodging house nearby on Marsham-street. Mr Cullen made him tea while two constables were sent to verify the story, and the young man was promptly arrested for murder when they returned. Why, asked an astounded Mr Cullen, had the fellow decided to attend the spectacle in James's park while his wife's still-warm body lay blue-lipped upon a bed? Because he had read about it in the papers and everyone was talking about it, replied the fellow. When his wife had not wanted to go, they had argued.

At least the so-called science of Mr Figgs appeared to be showing some minor validity if this small sample was to be believed. One had to reflect with grim irony that if they did not manage to catch their murderer that day, they had nevertheless discovered a different one. As for the purported purpose of the exhibition, more than fifty names had already been collected regarding the supposed identity of the taxidermied body – only one of them being "Perkin Mullender".

And still the people filed through, undissuaded by the wait or the mud. Indeed, the reports flickering through the crowd were evidently embellished with a fancy born of disappointment. No matter that the figure of Perkin Mullender was utterly unremarkable, the whispers were rather that his body was a Frankenstein's monster of disparate parts: a dermatological patchwork wrought by some maniacal seamstress. There was even a rumour of a man selling spirit alcohol on sponges so that people might remove the indelible ink and visit again.

Mr Cullen peeped through a fold in the tent and sighed at the field of heads: unending, undiminished, undeterred.

'What about that tall fellow?' said Mr Schlöss. 'Did he look slightly longer at the eyes?'

'He may have done . . .' ventured Mr Baldock with a sigh.

'No matter if he did,' said Mr Figgs. 'He is clearly the most benign sort of man. How much longer must we tolerate this, Mr Williamson?'

'Hmm. A little longer.' His tone seemed equally fatigued.

The people moved through, each one following a now predictable pattern. From the entrance, they peered excitedly for a clear view; in the shuffling line, they evinced an enthusiastic expectation of horror to come; close to, the looked blankly at a man no different to the one next to them, albeit dead, filled with flax and marginally more handsome; on exiting, they looked back as if perhaps they had missed something, and began immediately to reshape the memory into something better.

'See there – the old fellow with the cane,' said Mr Schlöss.

'What about him?' said Mr Figgs.

'Something in his physiognomy is not right, do you see? His leg may be genuinely injured – he rests heavily on the cane rather than putting weight upon the limb – but he hunches his shoulders merely as an affectation.'

'What are you implying?' said Mr Williamson, taking a fresh interest. 'That he is not as old as he pretends?'

'I ... cannot be sure. It was just something in the way he moved – something incongruous.'

'Watch him as he approaches the body ... watch his every reaction,' said Mr Williamson. 'Can any of you discern a scar on his forehead?'

'The cap is pulled too low,' said Mr Baldock,' and he *is* rather hirsute about the forehead in any case.'

'Hmm. Very convenient.'

'Did you see that?' said Mr Schlöss.

They had all seen it: the very slightest blink from the "old man" on seeing the figure of Perkin Mullender at close quarters. A blink of surprize? A blink of recognition?

'He is looking closely at the burned match in the figure's hand,' said Mr Baldock.

'Mr Figgs – your opinion please,' said Mr Williamson with great restraint.

'It is difficult to see much of him what with the hat and the exaggerated posture ...'

'Hmm. Where is your "science" now?'

'Wait ... there is something in the set of his jaw ...'

The old fellow was now passing out of the tent, his head down so that his face was now quite hidden. But as he approached the exit, the person in front of him paused to turn for one last look. They collided and the old man reacted quickly by withdrawing his forearm quickly as if it was injured ... as if it had been wounded in a knife fight at Marylebone police court ...

'Stop that man!' shouted Mr Williamson.

A mass of heads towards the masking gauze of their hidden chamber. The constables in the main room jerked alert.

'The old man! Stop him.'

The fellow with the cane was moving again, yet there were at least three other men present who might have fitted the hastily yelled description. Constables looked about them in frustration.

Mr Williamson withdrew a knife from his belt in an ecstasy of urgency and slashed madly at the gauze so that a great flap fell away to reveal the seated panel. He pointed the blade at the escaping old man as if it were a pistol.

'Him! The one with the cane at the exit!'

At that moment, the object of the chase attempted to quicken his pace, but he had not reckoned on one unseen element.

Noah Dyson was standing just outside the exit wielding a long stave of wood. He brought this down in a slashing arc upon the already wounded knee of the Italian, who buckled with a cry. In the same movement, Noah stepped in to hammer the heel of his palm into the temple of the falling man.

'Police! Police! He has attacked the old man!' came a female cry.

Noah reached down to the unconscious form and grabbed a handful of cap. It came away with a grey peruke, revealing the newly shorn head of the Italian.

Mr Williamson and Mr Cullen arrived simultaneously to witness the unmasking.

'I was lucky – I saw him just as he was entering,' said Noah. 'I knew I would get him on the way out if you did not spot him first.'

'Is he dead?' said Mr Cullen.

'Not yet,' said Noah.

'Hmm,' said Mr Williamson. 'What do you suggest we do with him?'

'Certainly, we should not put him in the hands of the Metropolitan Police,' said Noah. 'They will incarcerate him, try him and then execute him before he will reveal the whereabouts of his master. If we are to learn the information we need, we must make haste in removing this body immediately to a place where we can extract what he knows.'

'Hmm. Hmm – despite all he has done, I am not sure I can condone the torture of this man.'

'Then you need not be present, George. Besides, mere violence alone will not persuade him to speak. Something altogether more subtle is required.'

'The station inspector is coming,' said Mr Cullen.

'Then let us act quickly and take the body,' said Noah. 'There is a carriage waiting for us on Birdcage-walk. Mr Cullen – you stay here and tell the inspector that we have taken the injured fellow to Westminster hospital.'

'And the exhibition of Mr Mullender's body?' said Mr Cullen.

'Let it continue – until midnight if it so pleases the people. We have what we want, and the experts may now take their leave. Or rather, I believe we will take Mr Baldock with us.'

TWENTY-SEVEN

Mr Newsome had willed the pistol not to shake in his outstretched hand. At the same time, he had fought to control conflicting urges within him. Just the slightest pressure of his finger and this notorious murderer would be no more – a year of frustration cancelled in a single explosion. Or, with a modicum of self-control, he might compel the villain to reveal enough to see him hanged before a jeering multitude.

'It is difficult, is it not?' said Lucius Boyle, seemingly unconcerned at his situation. 'One dreams of killing a man. One imagines the satisfaction of his end, and yet the will is often lacking when the time for action comes.'

'Quiet, Boyle!'

'I wonder if you *could* kill me? If I made my escape now, could you shoot me in the back and become a murderer yourself? Could you sleep peacefully with that knowledge?'

'You may believe it.'

Something in the inspector's tone clearly gave Lucius Boyle reason to pause. In the half-light his face seemed to glisten and seep. 'But I forget – you have already taken a life, Inspector.'

'What? What are you talking about? Quiet, I say!'

'O, I know it is hardly common knowledge. No charges were brought on account of its being an "accident" – but I am beginning to think it was no accident. Is that weapon becoming too heavy for you, Inspector?'

The pistol had indeed begun to quiver, despite Mr Newsome's best efforts. His mind flashed dark and light: shoot him . . . question him . . . shoot him . . . question him . . .

He willed extra strength into his arm. 'Is that valve on the wall supplied with gas?'

'Of course,' said Lucius Boyle, 'But I prefer to use a lamp. My eyes—'

'Light the valve ... slowly!' Mr Newsome held the pistol with two hands now and pointed it with deadly intent as his adversary reached with theatrical slowness into a coat pocket and withdrew a box of Lucifer matches. Striking one of these, he held it to the brass nozzle and – with a discernable flinch – turned the key so that a tongue of pale fire hissed into life.

The room was now revealed in more detail, as was the terrible countenance of Lucius Boyle himself. What had previously been only a shadowy suggestion of horror was now shown to be an irremovable mask more grisly than any theatrical wax-worker might imagine – worse, even, than the effigy head in the coffin. In fact, the face itself seemed to have melted and sagged as wax does. The eyes had no lids, but were startled circles of flesh that might have been shaped by a child with scissors. The mouth was askew, the lips not quite meeting. The notorious red birthmark on the man's jaw remained, only even more aggravatedly pronounced. Mr Newsome could not hide his distaste.

'I am, I admit, a thing of no beauty,' said Lucius Boyle. His mouth moved in what may have once been a smile.

'Sit down – there at the work bench ... keep your hands above it! You may clasp them before you.'

Mr Newsome remained standing and lowered the pistol to his side with evident relief, its emotionless eye still pointed directly at the enemy.

'What now, Inspector? An interrogation here beneath the river? I reveal all you wish to know and am rewarded with the gallows? I see little advantage in it for me.'

Indecision persisted. There was surely sufficient evidence in the room to see Boyle hanged. And yet a pistol shot would be faster. The murderer would die in any event, whether here or at Newgate ...

'There is money in this room,' said Lucius Boyle, perhaps perceiving the imminent danger. 'Many hundreds of pounds. Take it. Say I escaped. By all means, continue your search for me thereafter, but do so as a rich man. I believe old policemen are not well provided for.'

'Quiet! I saw you – I saw you at Frying Pan wharf. I know that you were behind the smuggling case. And I know all about the balloon theft at Vauxhall Gardens. I have been the only one . . . all the others thought you dead.'

'Do you seek my congratulations?'

'I presume also that you have heard about the exhumation I conducted at Portugal-street. There is no use denying it.'

'I deny nothing. Indeed, I had anticipated it long before the idea occurred to you. I can only surmise that the powder charge was made too moist by the burial.'

'A man was maimed in that explosion.'

Lucius Boyle shrugged insouciantly. 'What kind of man disinters the body of another? It is an insult against the sanctity of death.'

'I have proof concerning the body of Louis Chiveot.'

'Who?'

'The young man you assaulted in the balloon to make your escape – he whose body you draped over the basket to stand for your own. He was a young Frenchman.'

Again, the shrug: 'Do you intend to narrate the whole of your investigation to this point, Inspector Newsome? I am not Sir Richard Mayne to laud your efforts. I take no pleasure in them. It is said in certain circles that you have become insane – perhaps I can believe as much.'

'We have your man in custody.'

Lucius Boyle did not blink.

'No doubt you are wondering which one?' continued Mr Newsome. 'The Italian fellow with the long hair and earring, or the handsome deceiver who collected your blackmail. Well, the latter is currently on display at St James's park. We were hoping you would attend, but I feel sure your Italian has been sent there to verify your fears. He is most certainly in custody as we speak. As are you, Lucius Boyle.'

'The *police* orchestrated this pantomime with the body?' The voice showed surprize as the face could not. 'I would never have expected such a strategy from Sir Richard . . . assuming that he actually knows of it.'

'He knows. Finally, it seems, he realized that different methods were necessary.'

'I must say that I am impressed. Well, Inspector – what now?'

'You will accompany me to Scotland Yard, from where you will be immediately taken before a magistrate to be charged.'

'Charged with what? Where is your evidence?

'It abounds, as I have said. The lock mechanisms and plans of Scotland Yard in this bolthole are suggestive of the recent robbery even if I have yet to locate the actual ledger.'

'Yes – the ledger. But whose is the crime there, Inspector? It was *you* who collated that catalogue of sin – not I. You are the criminal in that case and I cannot see it being brought before any magistrate if the stolen goods are themselves illicit. I must admit that I was delighted when it fell into my hands. I applaud your slyness in conceiving such a thing.'

'So you admit you have it. There is additionally the book on taxidermy and the taxidermical materials hereabouts, suggesting strongly that the girl Charlotte was prepared in this very room. Further evidence will not be difficult to find. That is murder.'

'A suggestion is not a conviction, Inspector. Who is to say I have not been preparing pigeons?'

'What do you know about PC Taylor of Division A?'

'Nothing at all. This is becoming rather a tiresome conversation . . .'

'I have seen a map in the other room there featuring circles around sites of known incendiary fires and the home of the dead girl. More than coincidence, would you not say?'

'Might not any man take an interest in local incidents and mark its occurrences on a map after the fact?'

Mr Newsome felt his hand tightening on the pistol grip. He fought a powerful urge to pull the trigger. 'Why were you wearing a mask of Sir Richard's face when you arrived here?'

Boyle hesitated, his glibness momentarily failing him. 'Well, I can hardly venture forth from this place with my own face, can I?'

'Sir Richard is not planning to be at Scotland Yard for much of today. He is speaking at the House of Commons tomorrow evening and will likely spend much time in the library there.'

'Is that so?'

'If you have planned some new outrage, you may mitigate your sentence by telling me now.'

'Mitigate a hanging, Inspector? Will a silken rope be used instead of hemp?'

'I have seen that you have plans of the Palace of Westminster. Why? What do the marks upon it represent?'

Lucius Boyle folded his arms, apparently drawing a conclusion to his participation thus far.

'And what is this book I have seen on poisons – ether, specifically? It is a powerful and dangerous vapour.'

Beneath his folded arms, Lucius Boyle's hand worked slowly towards a pocket. He said nothing. His unblinking eyes glared.

'We also have Tobias in custody. We know about the fireworks display,' said Mr Newsome: a gambit to test his interrogatee.

There was a twitch of recognition, or perhaps of concern in Lucius Boyle.

'Yes – he did not want to talk, but I persuaded him to tell us many interesting things about his work in Westminster. For his aid, we have promised him transportation rather than death.'

Lucius Boyle's eyes glistened and his tortured features rippled with some subcutaneous emotion. Anger? Suspicion? Frustration? Sorrow? Then the scarred flesh showed what may have been a smile. 'You do not have Tobias, and if you do he has not revealed what he knows. If he had, you would not be asking me all these other questions. You would not be in this place at all.'

Mr Newsome made to stand, the pistol briefly moving away from its target's heart. 'Very well – if you will not speak here, we will go to Scotland—'

Lucius Boyle's hand flashed from the pocket where it had so gradually moved. In it was a quantity of loose gunpowder, which he cast forcefully into the twisting flame of the gas flare.

There was an orange flash and a tremendous explosive crack. The pistol fired a mere fraction of a second later, finding no target but the wall.

Mr Newsome staggered away from the workbench with a forearm covering his blackened face. His eyes stung, his face burned and his hearing was mere muffled numbness. He swept his arms blindly about for Boyle's throat.

But Lucius Boyle had turned his back at the moment of combustion, suffering nothing more that a smoking coat and similarly stunned ears. His lidless eyes now smarting, he grabbed a stone pestle from the workbench and crashed it into the temple of his flailing assailant.

Mr Newsome grunted and fell insensible to the thick stone flags

Lucius Boyle looked down upon him with contempt. His gaze returned to the workbench and the sharp glint of a surgeon's knife. Its metal was cool in his fingers. It offered little resistance when he jabbed it into Mr Newsome's chest.

And there the victim had lain, stunned, weakened, bleeding and unconscious through the long subterranean night, through the remarkable events at St James's park the following day and towards a new darkness. Whether he would wake at all for the pyrotechnical events of the fifth of November was a matter for time and fate.

Darkness had long fallen, but the London sky was alight with the pops, bangs and fizzes of fireworks. The low cloud that hung heavy over the city reflected the orange light of innumerable fires, and the smell of wood smoke commingled with that of the coal-stacked hearths of a million households. Already, the streets were populated with men wearing grotesque theatrical masks and gangs of boys parading their effigies of Guido Fawkes.

The gentlemen gathered in an upper storey cell at the Fleet prison paid little attention to the show, however. Rather, they sat in tense conference on an assortment of chairs dragged into the room by old Adam. Benjamin, whose hands were heavily bandaged, was expressing himself in his particular fashion as the others looked on with varying degrees of incomprehension.

'I agree, Ben,' said Noah. 'I myself would like nothing better than to beat the information out of him, but do you really believe it would work? Would *you* give up your secrets to a fellow who beat you? No – you would welcome the blow that offered the gift of oblivion. This Italian is a tough one. We must use other methods.'

'Hmm. Do we even know that he speaks English?' said Mr Williamson. 'Or even Italian for that matter. I do not believe that any of us has heard his voice.'

'I feel sure that Lucius Boyle does not speak other languages,' said Noah. 'They must have their ways to communicate. The important thing is that we must ask the right questions. Time is short. When Sir Richard hears that we have disappeared with this body, he will send men to Golden-square and here. We must have answers with which to defend our actions.'

'Then there is the question of Inspector Newsome,' said Mr Cullen. 'Since he was not at St James's park, might we assume he is pursuing Boyle alone?'

'That is very likely,' said Mr Williamson.

'So – what are the levers with which to pry open the Italian's resolve?' said Noah. 'What do we know that he does not know we know? And what do we need to know?'

'We need to know the whereabouts of the ledger in order to stop the blackmail,' said Mr Cullen.

'Hmm,' said Mr Williamson. 'I rather feel that men who engage in sinful activities earn the risk of blackmail.'

Noah looked with amusement at his friend and withheld a comment. 'Perhaps, George – but where we find the ledger, we also find Lucius Boyle. That must be the priority in our interrogation.'

Benjamin coughed for attention and expressed through his bandages the opinion that their prisoner would never willingly reveal that fact.

'A man will reveal anything if asked properly,' said Noah. 'It is only a matter of time and method. Alas, we do not have the former.'

'What about Perkin Mullender?' said Mr Cullen.

'What about him?' said Mr Williamson.

'Well, I mean to say that he and the Italian appear to have been accomplices of Boyle. Might not we attempt to discover from the Italian what Mullender was doing and what his aim was in blackmailing those members of the house? That might in turn lead us to Boyle.'

'Hmm. It is an interesting question,' said Mr Williamson. 'You told us that this Mullender was seen loitering outside the office of the Lord Great Chamberlain where tickets of admission are purchased. Then we learn that Sir _____ _____ has been compelled not to attend a session. Am I the only one who finds that coincidence worrying?'

'I did have an idea . . .' said Mr Cullen, somewhat tentatively.

'Do not be shy' said Noah.

'Well, I found a flyer for a fireworks show at Westminster and it occurred to me that today is the fifth of November . . .'

'Hmm. You have certainly learned much of the detective arts,' said Mr Williamson.

'I mean to say . . . if I were an incendiary with a mania for ridiculing the police . . . and if the commissioner of the police were speaking at the house on the matter of plain clothes investigators . . . and if that hearing were to fall on a day commemorating an attempt to bring down the very government . . . might not a similar attempt be quite within my character?'

The other men looked at each other for a reaction. Fanciful as the notion may have seemed, nobody had actually laughed.

'Hmm. That would surely be a step too far even for Lucius Boyle,' said Mr Williamson, albeit with a doubtful rather than a definitive tone.

'It is indeed a stretch of credibility,' said Noah, stroking his chin. 'Though it might explain why Boyle would want a wealthy blackmail victim such as Sir _____ _____ to be absent from the chamber on this day.'

Each man pondered further on Mr Cullen's suggestion. If they were not unsettled by the thought, they were at least giving it due consideration.

'Then there is PC Taylor,' said Mr Cullen. 'I realize that we have no idea who abducted or stuffed him, but the area around the Palace of Westminster was on his beat. What if he saw something he should not have? What if the wax under his fingernail was from the mask he tried to pull from his assailant's face before he was rendered unconscious with a pad of ether or chloroform? What if that mask belonged to Perkin Mullender?'

'That is a lot of "What ifs",' said Mr Williamson, himself a firm believer in the question.

'Perkin Mullender's sleeve was soaked with a stain that smelled of alcohol,' said Noah. 'Ether smells much like alcohol, does it not?'

'Hmm. Such a stain would have long evaporated since the abduction of PC Taylor . . . unless the substance has recently been used again on another missing policeman. I think it is time we spoke to our prisoner,' said Mr Williamson.

The gentlemen stood and walked along the stone flags of the corridor to a room at the end. Old Adam was standing guard, looking occasionally through the half-open door to ensure that the prisoner had not managed to escape his formidable bonds.

'Perhaps it would be best if you retired for the evening,' said Noah to that elderly denizen of the gaol, and Adam merely nodded before shuffling towards his quarters, one hand tracing along the wall as he went.

Benjamin pushed open the door to reveal what must once have been a mortuary or infirmary. The Italian was roped prostrate to a stone plinth about waist height and was unceasing in his writhing to be free despite the thick hemp that bound him. His eyes glared, his teeth were bared and his face shone with perspiration at his efforts. On seeing the four gentlemen enter, he spat viciously in their direction.

'I fear he will not be co-operative,' said Mr Cullen.

Benjamin, meanwhile, was rolling his sleeves and approaching the plinth with a menacing expression. Mr Williamson looked concerned and seemed ready to restrain the burly Negro.

'Wait!' said Noah (who had rehearsed this much with Benjamin beforehand). 'Let us try to be reasonable with this fellow.'

The Italian stared madly from Benjamin to Noah.

'We are not policemen,' said Noah. 'Do you understand? It makes no difference to us if you die here today. Nor is it any of our concern if you walk free on telling us what we want to know. Naturally, you will want to flee, and we will let you. But first we have some questions.'

The Italian spat again, his saliva hitting Benjamin.

The bandages around Benjamin's hands ripped audibly as his colossal fists clenched in self restraint. If he felt pain in those fresh wounds, he did not show it.

'Are you so loyal to Lucius Boyle?' said Mr Williamson. 'The worst he can do is kill you, and you face that same threat here and now. Tell us where we may find him and you may go.'

The Italian screamed something in his own language, but with such ferocity that not a word could be understood.

Noah looked to Mr Williamson, who nodded his assent. They would proceed with their other plan.

317

'I will fetch Mr Baldock,' said Mr Cullen.

Moments later, the taxidermist of Wych-street walked into the room accompanied by Mr Cullen. Between them, they carried a large wicker basket and three large hessian sacks that they took to an old stone sink by the exterior wall.

The Italian strained at his bonds, watching the show with commingled curiosity and dread.

Mr Baldock began to remove the contents of the baskets, laying them out along the work surface so that the Italian may turn his head and see the array of pots, brushes, bowls and sacks. As he did so, the taxidermist kept up a steady description for the benefit of the prisoner: "Chopped flax . . . binding wire . . . gum Arabic . . . powdered chalk . . .'

By now, the Italian had realized the significance of what he was seeing and had begun to mumble rapidly to himself in prayer or condemnation, occasionally breaking from these solecisms to turn his head and yell incomprehensibly at his captors.

Once the basket had bee emptied, Noah gestured to the Italian: 'Mr Baldock – please proceed.'

The taxidermist selected a large pair of scissors and applied them to the hem of the Italian's left trouser leg. Immediately, the captive attempted to thrash free, but could manage only the slightest movement beneath the ropes. Benjamin leaned with both hands on the knee that he had earlier twisted. The Italian screamed and Mr Baldock began to cut the trousers away.

Mr Williamson turned sharply to Noah and hissed *sotto voce*: 'You said we would not have to go through with it!'

Noah flashed a warning expression: wait and see.

The yelling and writhing had now made the Italian's body quite shine with perspiration. With the trousers gone, Mr Baldock set to work upon the jacket and shirt as Benjamin aided with unforgiving downward pressure.

Soon, the body was all but naked, sleeves left partially on the arms where the ropes made it difficult to remove them and scraps hanging about the ankles. A swatch of material had been left to protect the Italian's modesty but his humiliation was otherwise complete.

'Are you ready to talk now?' said Noah.

The Italian stared. His energy seemed utterly depleted and yet his jaw remained clamped in mute refusal.

'Very well, Mr Baldock – you may go on with the full procedure,' said Noah.

Mr Williamson glared at Noah and walked briskly from the room. Mr Cullen hesitated briefly and offered an apologetic glance at Noah before following quickly behind.

The taxidermist asked Benjamin to tie a large leather apron around him and took a curved blade from his selection of tools on the work surface. Next, he put on a pair of spectacles with large lenses made of plain glass.

'You may want to step back,' said Mr Baldock to Benjamin. 'This is going to be rather messy.'

The blade was positioned slightly above the *pubis* and Mr Baldock held the cold metal just above the Italian's skin.

'We will leave you to it, Mr Baldock' said Noah, beckoning Benjamin to accompany him. 'Call us when he is fully stuffed and mounted.'

The blade's edge pressed on to the skin and the Italian screamed: '*Basta!* I speak, I speak, I speak!'

Noah tried to disguise his sigh. Benjamin gave a secret wink.

TWENTY-EIGHT

Whether it was the novelty of attending a hearing in the new Houses of Parliament, or whether it was the subject at hand that had attracted so many people, the area around St Stephen's staircase was quite clogged with people trying to gain access that evening. Naturally, more tickets had been issued than there were places in the public gallery, so there was a palpable air of excitement that was only exacerbated by the hectic, colour-bursting sky above the building's gothic *silhouette*.

I was among them: guaranteed entry under the auspices of Scotland Yard's Newspaper Office. Thus, when the doors were opened and the crowd surged forward, I was at its vanguard, rushing into lofty halls whose masonry, mosaics, woodwork and towering plate glass had yet to attain the illustrious patina of history and which instead smelled of the mortar, varnish and fresh stone of recent construction. No matter – all who enter here (save the politicians themselves) cannot help but be awed at the *accoutrements* of authority: the colossal brass *chandeliers*, the lofty ceilings, the pristine marble statues, the sturdy oaken doors through which one might occasionally glimpse the ranked leathern spines of a library, their gilt titles glinting by the light of a healthy hearth.

But such impressions were fleeting as our footsteps echoed *en masse* through massive St Stephen's Hall towards the even more impressive Central Hall, where a veritable vortex of people seemed to swirl into surrounding corridors. Compelled by the flow, we churned left into the narrow Commons Corridor which, like a cataract, accelerated our velocity and tossed us forth into the lobby, where the noise of hundreds threatened to carry away the doors that blocked our entry.

Such a congregation could be contained no longer and, at a signal from the sergeant-at-arms, the great oaken barriers were swung aside so that the august House of Commons itself might be entered. And it was indeed a sight to calm that onrush of humanity.

Many of the members and speakers were already occupying their places as the public shuffled into the upper gallery: swallowed into the hush-inducing *gravitas* of the oak-panelled, green-leather-upholstered chamber. In whispers now, they noted to each other the *totems* of government. There was the speaker in powdered wig and black silks; there was the Commissioner of Police seated beside the Home Secretary; there was the illustrious mace that would soon signal the start of proceedings; and there was Sir Robert Peel himself: Prime Minister and originator of the modern police. Meanwhile, clerks moved like phantoms in black, carrying ribbon-bound sheaves of paper and boxes of evidence for the hearing.

Then the vast doors were heard to close upon a chorus of frustrated public pleas and the sergeant-at-arms took his place there as guardian of the session. A battery of coughs sounded around the space in anticipation of the commencement. A crepitating silence descended gradually upon the room. Clerks bustled into place and it was announced by the speaker that a petition was to be heard from a representative of the parish of St George, Middlesex: a windy looking gentlemen with white side-whiskers and a face reddened by heat or indignation. Hush settled as he stood.

'It will not have escaped the House's attention,' he began,' that there has been much recent comment in the newspapers concerning the use of plain or "coloured" clothes by police constables and detectives alike. But this is not a new phenomenon! No! Perhaps the Right Honourable Prime Minister will remember being present at a similar petition some eleven years ago in which the appearance of plain clothes policemen at certain clubs and meetings was raised – not as keepers of the peace, but as agents of state *espionage* . . .'

It may be understood that the fellow continued at some considerable length in this vein. His points were no doubt cogently, if sententiously, argued

– but what none of those august gentlemen could have known was what greater concern lay beneath their very feet at that moment.

In fact, below the woven haircloth carpet, below the perforated iron panels, and below the equalising chamber with its numerous disperser valves, a figure of seeming demoniac appearance laboured in the stifling heat of the ventilation mixing chamber. Small in stature, the creature wore a specially-made smoke suit fashioned from supple leather and fitted with two green glass eye pieces through which all appeared an undersea realm. A thin tube from the rear of the hooded head extended for many yards around the subterranean maze to an iron grate blessed with pure night air

Tobias Smalletts had no fear of smoke, however. The danger to his young lungs rather came from the vapour created by the mix of liquid ether and chloroform that he was painting onto to the hot metal of the substantial heating elements before him. Not hot enough to ignite the volatile stuff, they were nevertheless of sufficient heat to evaporate the liquid as quickly as he could daub it on, filling the chamber slowly but certainly with that invisible soporific vapour. At least, drowsiness would be only the first symptom.

Inside the suit, Master Smalletts sweated freely, blinking repeatedly and cursing that he could not wipe his seeping brow. The masked man's warnings had been emphatic enough: remove the hood and you will die. So he kept on dipping the brush and splashing the liquid over the elements. As soon as he had finished, he could leave and watch the fireworks.

Mr Newsome awoke to complete darkness. The cold stone floor had chilled his limbs and his hearing was little better than a smothered crackling. He had no conception of how long he had lain unconscious. Certainly, he could not have imagined that he had missed the entire exhibition at St James and passed into a new night.

On attempting to sit, he felt the point of the knife in his chest and realized that he had been bleeding into his clothes. He tugged the weapon free and tossed it to one side, mindful that his life had probably been saved by the woven hemp *gilet* he had opted to wear beneath his coat that previous evening. The military supplier at Woolwich had promised him it would stop small shot at a distance, but they had not reckoned on a knife in their discussions.

A ripple of nausea washed through him as he rested a palm on the gritty ground and tried to stand, realising only now that it was not the darkness that so impaired his vision. He was blind – unable to see even his own hand before his face. Either the combustion of the powder had cast lacerating particulate into his eyes, or the blow from some blunt object to his temple had shocked his brain into sightless stupor.

He groped for a seat and wobbled his weight on to it with a groan. But there was no scrape of its legs on the stone floor and he realized now that he must also be virtually deaf – deaf and blind in this masonry chamber deep beneath the cold black flow of the river. A stench of sulphuretted gas and excremental slime came to him from a recess of memory: a bubble of recollection associated with fear and frustration. His enemy was free in the city while he, the pursuer, was trapped in the stygian depths.

But his mind was active. As long as he could think, he could investigate.

He tried to remember what he had so phrenziedly examined on the workbench before Lucius Boyle had arrived: that puzzle of clues that must, when ordered correctly, tell the story of their ill intentions. Those flyers advertising a fireworks show, for example. What possible advantage could there be for Boyle in attending such a thing? Could it be that the incendiary merely enjoyed such shows – that this day above all was a kind of holy day for him? It seemed likely enough. Or had he organised the show himself and distributed two-hundred copies as the scribbled note suggested?.

Then there was the treatise on ventilation. No doubt this sub-riverine hole required its own specific airflow to remain habitable ... but was not the author of that book the illustrious Scotsman Dr Reid? He who had been commissioned to provide a consistent supply of clean air for the new Palace of Westminster? Mr Newsome now recalled reading a piece in a journal on the ingenious filtration system ...

And the pieces of the puzzle began to move of their own accord: the plan of the palace, the passage concerning ether vapour in the book on poisons, those mysterious plans of some sub-architectural labyrinth, the mask of Sir Richard ... and now the sudden recollection of something Boyle had said before throwing the powder – something like, 'If you had Tobias, you would not be here.'

Mr Newsome felt a renewed sense of purpose course through his limbs. He might not have the entire solution, but he knew what he must do.

With shuffling steps, he felt his way towards the other room and followed the smell of the tunnel to the iron door whose lock he had broken and whose parts clattered now at his feet. Somehow, inconceivably, he would have to make his way sightless and silent back to Wapping, where he must find a beat constable in a locale notorious for its nocturnal threat – a locale, moreover, where his face was known and disliked.

Walking with one hand along the stonework, he was impelled by the contradictory forces of urgency and hesitation. Too fast and his impaired senses would see him fall; too slowly and the expected catastrophe would go ahead before he could prevent it.

He paused. There had been a distant whispering, a tinny intimation of a voice through his ruined ears: someone near him in the tunnel. A friend or an enemy?

'Is somebody there?' he said boldly to the darkness. 'I am Detective Inspector Albert Newsome. I have been blinded and need to get quickly to the Wapping side. A serious crime is about to take place.'

A blow to his face knocked him to the ground and rough hands searched his pockets. He bellowed in frustration but the robbery was quick and efficient. He stood only when he felt they had gone, dabbing at his bleeding nose and continuing doggedly towards the surface.

Sir Richard was now on his feet and speaking with confidence: '... and let us not forget that one of Sir Robert Peel's original and founding rules of policing was that "The test of police efficiency is the absence of crime and disorder, not the *visible evidence* of police action in dealing with it." The truth is that, since its inception, the Metropolitan Police has been regarded with suspicion and accused of *espionage*, whether in uniform or out of it. But I ask the house: how is one to observe and capture the habitual criminal if the policeman is made so conspicuous by his rigid military appearance and behaviour? Why, the very dictionary definition of a detective is: "A policeman employed secretly to detect crime" – so I must put it to the petitioners: where is the secret if he is in uniform? How can one expect the criminal to be caught when he cannot be observed?'

A low murmur of approbation or dissent rumbled around the chamber. In the hour since the session had begun, the initial excitement had settled into the comfortable progress of the long debate, with various members adopting postures of such informal relaxation that some in the public gallery were shocked. The member for _____, for example, was resting his feet on the bench in front, while the elderly Sir James _____ snored softly on one of the higher opposition rows.

In fact, it seemed that the temperature within was causing drowsiness among many and so the sergeant-at-arms was discreetly signalled at the main doors. He then communicated the request to the assistant on ventilation, who exited through the north-west door to see that the warm air shutters below were narrowed and the outlet valve opened above.

And still the debate continued. The original petitioner was again addressing the space, but in an odd, distracted manner that seemed to suggest he was either tired or drunk: '. . . in connection with . . . er, with the recent case in Yeovil where, er . . . where a boy was placed in an adjoining cell to elicit the prisoner's secrets. I cannot express this better than in the words of the press, *viz*: *"The tiger that has once lapped blood is never sated with the taste of it. The spy, er . . . who has been once employed for hire will invent the discourse which he cannot hear; and when he finds his fictions can be turned to profit will concoct them, er . . . concoct them without scruple.'*

A shout came from the public gallery: *'Espionage!'*

Unrest rippled briefly through the chamber and the speaker called for order, but the muttering and shuffling ignited into outright clamour when one of the clerks seated by the speaker toppled from his seat as if utterly lifeless and lay unmoving on the floor.

Three other clerks immediately rushed to his aid, whereupon one of them, on bending to examine the unconscious man, joined his colleague in immediate loose-limbed oblivion.

'It is too hot in here!' called a member.

'Those wigs and silks – they have become overheated,' another was heard to say.

'Is somebody seeing to the ventilation?' shouted the speaker to the sergeant-at-arms.

At that moment, the assistant on ventilation returned from his errand with a concerned look and walked briskly to whisper in the ear of the sergeant-at-arms. On hearing this news, the former seemed to remonstrate with the other fellow in a dumb-show watched by hundreds of spectators. The mood in the chamber was now becoming unruly.

'What is it? What is happening?' said the speaker over the rising noise.

But even as he spoke, one of the older members on the front row leaned forwards and vomited copiously on to the carpet before tumbling onto his face and half-rolling on his side to lie quite still.

'What is that smell?' said one of the clerks to the speaker. 'Do you not smell it? Something like alcohol.'

'Gas leak! Check the pipes! Ventilation!' was now the common call.

The sergeant-at-arms marched towards the speaker to relay the facts of the situation, namely that some inexplicable blockage was preventing the correct mechanisms from adjusting the ventilation. Somebody would have to venture beneath the chamber to rectify the problem.

'Well, see it to it quickly!' said the speaker, leaning suddenly amid a fit of dizziness.

Sir Richard clenched his jaw in consternation and turned to the Home Secretary sitting next to him: 'It appears we will have to adjourn . . .'

The Home Secretary, however, sat slumped and insensible, his head lolling back and his mouth open.

Sir Richard felt a chill of dread. Something terrible was surely afoot.

And still more men were falling from the benches or drowsing where they sat on the lowest rows. There was a sound of vomiting and a growing hubbub of concern. The strange alcohol smell was now clearly discernable in the higher rows.

'Open the doors!' screamed a voice from the public gallery, where many were now standing and attempting to leave the chamber.

The sergeant-at-arms looked for a signal from the speaker and made to unbar the great doors, but his legs seemed to buckle even as he did so. He leaned against the oak panels and tried to support himself with a hand before sliding ineluctably to the ground.

Sir Richard stood, wobbling with an unaccountable nausea, and began to shout: 'Everybody to the doors! Open all the doors to the lobbies . . .'

Blackness had begun to narrow his vision. The desire to sit and to sleep came powerfully upon him even as a persistent thought prickled within his fading consciousness: might not this mysterious vapour have a point of volatility, and might it not soon be reached, to be ignited by the gas lights and to explode the entire chamber into fragments?

'Everybody to the doors! Flee now!' he cried, but the voice existed only in the dwindling spark of his consciousness, and the floor had somehow come to rest on his cheek . . .

A number of people had gathered on the Palace of Westminster embankment to watch the fireworks flash brilliance upon river and sky: one a black glass mirror, the other a cloud-raked and smoky infinity. But the gasps and pointed fingers soon turned earthwards when the shuffling figure approached from the north.

Groups parted, voices muttered in commingled shock and distaste, and Inspector Newsome made his eyeless way beneath the shadowy parliament walls. A constable guided his arm, but the inspector seemed impelled by some powerful inner vision despite the undoubted *travails* experienced between Wapping and Westminster. In addition to the injuries sustained at Lucius Boyle's hand, his hat had gone, his jacket was torn, an open wound glistened on his cheek and the wild red hair seemed matted with grime.

'What do you see, constable?' he said.

'Just people, sir. They are gathered to watch the fire—'

'No! You must look for signs of suspicious activity. Look at the base of the walls and at the windows. The pencil marks I saw on the plan – they were hereabouts. There must be an air inlet – I am sure of it!'

'There is nothing, sir. Just . . . O, wait a minute . . .'

'What is it? Describe it to me!'

'I think I see a fellow's head . . . there is a metal grille in the ground and he is emerging . . . in the darkness: there where the masonry protrudes.'

'Take me to the place. Quickly!'

The constable half led and half followed Mr Newsome. There was a scrape of iron against stone as they approached, as if the grille were being moved.

'Police! Stop!' yelled Mr Newsome. 'Constable – what do you see? Constable?'

But the constable had become quite dumb with fear at the sight of the formidable Negro who had materialized from the shadows of the buttress to bar their way. A pale filmy eye fixed him with a glare that said 'Go no further.'

'Constable? Speak to me, d___ you!'

Another man appeared head and shoulders from the gloom beneath the grille and beheld the scene that was unfolding, much to the general confusion of those who had come to watch the sky.

'That is no way to speak to a man in uniform, Inspector,' said Noah from the pit.

328

'Noah Dyson? What in the name of G___ are you doing here?' said Mr Newsome.

'The same as you, it would appear – only with more success. Are you injured?'

'Never mind that! What have you found? Where is Mr Williamson?'

'He has gone with Mr Cullen to follow a clue that we uncovered.'

'To the Thames Tunnel?'

Noah glanced at Benjamin. 'Why do you ask about the tunnel?'

'I come directly from there. I discovered plans. I believe there is a plot to destroy the palace. I discovered plans—'

'Lucius Boyle – was he there?'

'He escaped me. He blinded me with gunpowder. I was robbed and assaulted . . . but what have *you* found?'

'Where? Where did Boyle go?'

'He was not kind enough to tell me as he knocked me unconscious and thrust a knife into my chest. Tell me – *what have you found?*'

Noah looked with fresh attention at the condition of the inspector and tried to gauge if he was hearing – or should tell – the truth. He sighed. He held up the leathern smoke suit, which, in its diminutively vacated state, appeared to be nothing less than a freshly sloughed dermis complete with two vitreous green eyes. 'It is merely the *pupa* of the criminal.'

'What? What is it?' said Mr Newsome grasping at the unseen air between them.

'It is a sign that something toxic to humans has been handled below,' said Noah, guiding the outfit into the inspector's grabbing hands. 'And judging from its smell, I would guess it to be ether, though that chymical is not so very volatile in its liquid state. A strange choice for—'

'The ventilation!' said Mr Newsome. 'Boyle had plans . . . a book by Dr Reid . . . the vapour must pass into . . . we must get inside immediately!'

Noah looked doubtfully at Benjamin. Under a lengthy interrogation, the Italian had revealed only that chymicals were being stored under the Palace of Westminster, implying that they were to be used as explosives.

The inspector was already being led around the building.

'What did Boyle look like?' shouted Noah, caught suddenly between desires. 'Was his face the same as the grave effigy?'

'He has a mask: Sir Richard's face!' came the fading response.

'Then perhaps he is close . . .' said Noah to himself.

Benjamin described a digitolocutionary sentence: a question. Should they chase a phantom, or help prevent a massacre.

Noah regarded the night. The air smelled of smoke. Lucius Boyle was out there amidst it.

But even as he pictured that hideous face, there was a great reverberating explosion – louder and more violent than any thunder – from the other side of the palace. The warehouses and manufactories of Lambeth glowed momentarily orange in a reflected infernal glow.

'That must be him,' said Noah.

Again, more forcefully, Ben raised the question.

'Very well, very well – let us aid the Inspector in his attempt on the fortress. We will secure the genuine Sir Richard, and then the next commissioner we see after that, we kill.'

Together, they began to run.

Mr Williamson stirred from insensibility as the wagon passed over a particularly rough patch of road, jarring his body against the rough-rattling planks. He was bound tightly around his lower legs and knees. A broad wooden beam had evidently been pushed through his sleeves and across his back so that his arms were forcibly extended then lashed so securely at the wrists that he could barely feel his hands. A mask had been tied to his face, but one without eye holes. He had not the slightest idea of where he was, how he had got there or who he might appear to be.

'Mr Cullen – are you there?'

His voice returned to him inside the imprisoning wax, muffled and distorted. There was no reply.

It was apparently still the same evening, for the sky was now alive with the explosions and fizzles and pops of fireworks. The air was thick with smoke. The occasional boyish beggar chants of *'Please to remember Guy Fawkes!'* or *'A penny for Pope's Day!'* could be heard. And though the streets around were clearly clogged with people, he lay there trussed and powerless and seemingly – he realized with a lurch of nausea – bound for a pyre.

TWENTY-NINE

'Do you not understand? The palace must be evacuated – there is imminent danger!'

Mr Newsome's voice had become hoarse with shouting in the few moments it had taken Noah and Benjamin to join him at the public entrance. The deputy sergeant on duty, however, was quite adamant:

'There is a session in progress. No public admittance is permitted until the next recess.'

'I am Detective Inspector Newsome – I am not a member of the public!'

'That is all very well, sir, but nobody may enter during a session unless he is a member. All of you gentlemen must stand back – you are blocking the doorway and—'

His sentence was truncated by a blow from Noah's fist that sent him to his knees and thence to the floor, unconscious.

'I think we might agree later that that was accidental,' said Noah, pushing open the doors.

'Indeed,' said Mr Newsome, who in any case could legitimately deny having seen it.

Noah and Benjamin then rushed with echoing footfalls through the lofty halls that, at this hour, were now all but deserted. At their rear, Mr Newsome strode energetically beside the constable and shouted ahead:

'Turn left at the central hall then down through the Commons corridor and lobby!'

The great oaken doors to the chamber were predictably closed, but Noah maintained his momentum and ran at them to land a resounding kick. It was quite ineffective. Together, they pressed ears to the wood and attempted to hear the proceedings within.

'What is happening?' said Mr Newsome, arriving at the scene.

'We cannot force these doors from outside,' said Noah. 'There are too few of us. I cannot hear anything inside – the chamber might as well be empty.'

'It is not empty,' said Mr Newsome. 'We must find another way. There is access to the Commons from the east and west division lobbies. Come – there is not a moment to lose!'

They rushed to their right and into the empty east division lobby, whose reverberating dimness was illuminated only by the dark windows onto Commons court.

'Here!' called Noah, pointing to a smaller and less formidable door. It was not locked. Nor was it entirely possible to open, for as Noah pushed against it, a human body on the other side impeded its movement. A head and shoulder was visible through the crack, along with a jumble of other inert limbs about the space. A powerful smell of ether wafted out of the chamber.

'Cover your faces. Try not to breathe,' said Noah, pulling off his coat and wrapping it around his lower face. 'Ben – we must get inside and open all available doors. Inspector Newsome – it is not safe for you to enter. You must see that as many doors as possible are opened and that any gas flames along those corridors are extinguished. Is that clear? Smash windows if need be – fresh air is required.'

'What about utilizing the ventilation system?' said Mr Newsome. 'It will be faster.'

'It has clearly been disabled, and even if it had not been, the chimney for mephitic air is likely aided by a coal-fired flue. We might ignite the whole palace if all the vapour rushes to that spot.'

'Very well. I understand.'

'One more thing, Inspector: we need people – many people – to help us drag these gentlemen out of the chamber. If they do not soon inhale clean air, their unconsciousness will lead to death.'

Mr Newsome bustled away with his constable.

'Are you ready, Ben?' said Noah as the footsteps receded.

Benjamin tightened his own coat around his nose and mouth and offered an affirmative thumb.

'If you begin to feel faint, get out. Right – deep breath – help me push open the door . . .'

Together, they forced the weight of the body out of the way and entered the Commons chamber to behold a scene of quite staggering magnitude.

Most were insensible: scores of men slumped in peaceful repose where they sat, or lying in various postures about the floor and stairways as if they had simply dropped where they stood. Some hung over benches and many more lay tangled in the approaches towards the main doors. Evidently, their attempts to escape had been too late. On the upper tiers of seating, there were still signs of life: men drowsing with extreme lethargy as they fought to escape the heaviness of sleep.

Benjamin clicked his fingers and pointed towards the speaker's seat where the distinct countenance of Sir Richard Mayne, pale and open-mouthed, stared lifelessly up from the carpet. Noah nodded and indicated that Benjamin should clear the main doors where the body of the sergeant at arms was surrounded by others. Then he took the commissioner under the arms and dragged him over other bodies through the door into the west division lobby.

There, Noah leaned on his knees and took his first breath since entering the poisoned chamber. Aid was too long in arriving. If more men could not be similarly dragged free, they would pass into everlasting sleep. In frustration, he looked about him and picked up a heavy mahogany chair, which he swung with great force and released at the windows looking out onto the Star Chamber court.

There was a cascade of jagged glass onto the floor and cool, smoky air seemed immediately to pour into the lobby. He retrieved the chair and threw it again and again until the glazing was reduced to so many fragments. Presently, through the holes, he heard the blessed sound of outrage and raised voices. Mr Newsome must have reached his goal. Somebody was finally coming to their aid.

And yet, as Noah looked up at the rectangle of sky outside, he could not help but think that the evening's drama was far from over. The very heavens beyond glowed red amid vast clouds of billowing smoke. A colossal conflagration appeared to be raging through the Westminster rookery.

Mr Williamson had tried in vain to twist free of his bonds, but it was quite futile. He had tried shouting also, but the noise of the streets and the rattle of the wheels and the muffling wax mask over his face had conspired to reduce all such exclamations to nought. Even if anyone could see him, he was just another one of many effigies on its way to a fire: the stuffed likeness of Popish conspirator Guido Fawkes soon to be consumed in flame.

How had he come to this? He remembered the headlong rush to the tunnel with Mr Cullen. He remembered descending the stairs and seeing the face of Sir Richard Mayne seemingly ascending towards them, impossible though that should have been. But then that pseudo-commissioner, on noting their presence, had suddenly turned to retrace his steps. It could only have been Boyle.

They had given chase and discovered, after some minutes, the broken door to the hidden chamber so rich in evidence. They had noted the bloodstain where Mr Newsome had lain. Then, as Mr Cullen had ventured to search the anteroom, there had been a scuffle of feet, a grunt, a falling body. Mr Williamson had rushed there in response . . . only to wake up lashed to a beam in the back of a wagon. As for Mr Cullen, his whereabouts were utterly unknown.

Evidently, the cart was now leaving the main streets that ran parallel to the river, for the traffic noise was lessening and there was a brief, earthy scent of composted leaves that suggested they had gone west towards the parks. The smell was soon replaced by something ranker: rotting vegetables, decayed housing, cess pits and the stagnant water of blocked gutters. It could be no other than the Westminster slums, where PC Taylor had gone missing and where Perkin Mullender had begun his criminal journey.

There was also a quite fearful noise to be heard in that locality: not only the raucous cacophony of streets full of roaming drunks, the continuous explosion of fireworks and the chatter of boys, but also the great groaning roar of a huge fire. Indeed, Mr Williamson could smell its breath from where he lay – not, it seemed, a single bonfire, but more likely a burning structure whose windows could be heard shattering under the assault of heat or stones.

The wagon stopped. Footsteps approached. Mr Williamson began to kick blindly with his bound feet in anticipation of an attack.

'This one's a bit lively for a straw man,' said a gruff voice.

'Gen'ral sez not to ask no questions,' said another. 'Sez just toss 'im on the fire when the time comes. Sez we can 'it 'im if we need to make 'im still. Feller's a bluebottle – it don't matter none.'

'I am not a policeman! Release me!' cried Mr Williamson from beneath the mask. But the painted face said nothing, and went impassively to its fate as clubs rendered the body violently pliable.

Dozens of windows had been broken and numerous bodies now lay in ranks upon the damp ground of the Commons court, dragged there by Noah, Benjamin and all other able persons whom Mr Newsome had been able to rally. Some of the stupefied members were stirring – others lay quite immobile as doctors moved urgently between them to monitor breathing and pulse. At least five of the older gentlemen had been carried with great haste to Westminster hospital – two fume-bemused rescuers among them – though none had yet died. Sir Richard himself remained unconscious yet stable.

Noah, wiping the sweat of effort from his brow, caught Benjamin's attention and signalled in their cryptic language that they should leave this place and travel to the Thames Tunnel forthwith. Not only might Mr Williamson need their help, but it was the surest strategy to finding Lucius Boyle.

'Noah Dyson! Where are you going?' said Mr Newsome (who had anticipated such an errand and asked his constable to inform him of the attempt).

'What concern is it of yours?' said Noah.

'I hope you do not think you are going to the Thames Tunnel. I have designated it a scene of crime and it is for the police to investigate.'

'I understood that the tunnel is private property.'

'And I feel sure that its owners would not like it repeated abroad that the girl Charlotte was skinned there. Discreet arrangements will be made. It is work for a detective. If you try to go against my orders, I must have you both arrested.'

'Inspector – I have just personally saved the life of the police commissioner.'

'No doubt he will thank you for it later, but one good deed does not permit an ill one.'

Noah looked with malice at the squinting and dishevelled Mr Newsome. Benjamin held his friend's arm in anticipation of an imminent strike.

A palace watchman appeared at the doorway where the *impasse* was taking place: 'Is one of you gentlemen called Mr Dyson?'

'I am he,' said Noah. 'What is it?'

'A fellow is asking for you quite urgently at the public entrance.'

'Did he give his name as Mr Williamson?'

'No, sir – it is a Mr John Cullen. His message is that your Mr Williamson has gone missing.'

Noah pushed immediately past the watchman and began to run, joined a heartbeat later by Benjamin.

337

'Wait! Wait! This is a police matter,' called Mr Newsome, his voice vanishing into heedless halls. 'D____ them all!'

Mr Cullen was waiting impatiently at St Stephen's staircase when they arrived. His hat was missing and there was a bloodied spot at the hairline near his left temple.

'What happened? What did you find? Where is George? Are you injured?' said Noah.

'It is nothing – I was hit on the head. We found a chamber in the tunnel ... it was certainly Boyle's hiding place ... but I was hit and was alone when I awoke. There was no trace of Mr Williamson.'

'Was it Boyle who struck you?'

'I did not see who did it, but we thought we saw Sir Richard at the tunnel. It must have been a mask, I suppose, since the Commissioner was supposed to be here.'

'He is here. He is alive, but unconscious.'

'Are you sure, Noah? About the unconsciousness, I mean ... because I thought I saw him just a moment ago ...'

Noah's eyes burned into Mr Cullen's. Benjamin, too, seemed to have become more alert.

'Where?' said Noah. 'Where do you think you saw him, and when?'

'When I was approaching the palace along Margaret-street, perhaps ten minutes ago ... I thought I saw him cross Old Palace-yard towards Abingdon-street. He was alone. I thought of shouting to him, but ...'

'Can you be sure it was *his* face?'

'It was quite a distance ... but my first thought was that it was he – at least, it was the same face I saw at the Thames Tunnel.'

Benjamin offered a conjectural arabesque: where might this incarnation of Sir Richard be heading? South to cross the river at Vauxhall, or west into the rookery?

And as they paused in momentary indecision, a phalanx of police reinforcements came hob-nailing down Margaret-street from the Gardinerlane station, each armed with a bullseye lamp and a drawn truncheon. Mr Cullen hailed the inspector at the head of the group:

'Ho! What is happening? Where are you going?'

'Riot in the rookery!' shouted the inspector without pausing. 'The Irish gathered for a firework show and free spirits but received none – or not enough. Now they have started burning buildings!'

The policemen clattered without pause along Abingdon-street towards the corner of College-street. In a moment, they could only be heard.

The three men exchanged looks.

'It is the event I learned about previously,' said Mr Cullen. 'I found another such advertisement at the tunnel. It promised fireworks and free spirits. Do you think Boyle went in that direction?'

'You realize, of course,' said Noah, 'that a riot in the rookery is an ideal diversion of police manpower at a time when the Palace of Westminster is under silent attack. What could be better for agitating the Irish than withholding the promise of a drink – and on an anti-Catholic commemoration into the bargain? Mr Cullen – you will head towards Vauxhall-bridge with all haste while Ben and I will visit the slums. Be on your guard. And if you find Boyle, render him insensible. Go!'

'Yes, Noah!' said Mr Cullen, taking off at pace.

Noah now turned to look westwards, where the sky swirled still with orange-tinted smoke lit sporadically by the flash of coloured gunpowder.

'Ready, Ben? Tonight we must finally get him.'

Ben showed a determined fist and they followed briskly in the footsteps of the police reinforcements. They could hardly have imagined what a chaotic scene they were to enter.

Rounding the corner on to College-street, they found themselves running towards the boiling centre of that depraved quarter, whose streets were now quite swarming with pyrophiliac celebrants. There were boys with their effigies, vendors with their billowing charcoal burners, mobs of drunkards, hordes of magdalenes driven Dionysiac – and many wearing the horrible masks traditional to the occasion: horned demons, anonymous highwaymen, the sinister *medico della peste* with his long beak and red eyes. Meanwhile, clouds of sparks gusted between buildings on infernal winds so that one might almost have strayed into the final Judgement. Certainly, it was a night for a masked man, a violent man, an incendiary, to be out on the streets as freely as any other.

'We need masks,' said Noah as they approached Smith-street and paused for breath. 'We are conspicuous here for being ourselves, and he knows our faces. There – the old woman vendor with the barrow full of faces.'

Noah thus became a red-faced fire demon, while Benjamin adopted a pirate's grimace with a convenient patch to hide his deathly eye.

'We must go separately to save time, Ben. Look for Sir Richard's face wherever you see a building burning. Perhaps George is here also – stay alert!'

To Mr Williamson, blind and voiceless beneath the mask, the noise of his surroundings seemed more greatly amplified than it might otherwise have done. The voices of hundreds appeared to throng about him, and the *fusillade* of detonations was maddeningly ceaseless.

They had hoisted him into an elevated position – that much was clear. He had felt and heard the rope tauten, felt his weight leave the ground and felt the beam through his sleeves being hooked onto some contrivance that now held him aloft. Moreover, the massed voices were discernibly below him and the tenor of their baying was unambiguous:

'Light it! Burn the Guy!'

'Spark it up, then! Let's see 'im roast.'

'Oo 'as a Lucifer? I'll start it meself!'

The latter voice was a youthful one, although Mr Williamson could not have recognized it as a certain Tobias Smalletts, fresh from his burrowing at the Palace of Westminster and keen for a spectacle. A number of local boys had also joined him, no doubt impressed by his bravado, and were similarly chanting for a flame.

But somebody *had* noted that boyish cry and recognized it with the clarity of a biting blade. Benjamin strode across the narrow area of Stretton-ground, looking sharply towards the group around the large pyre and seeing that the lad in the uniform was indeed among them. And there was something else – something curiously disturbing.

It was not the smart attire of the effigy atop the pyre that first attracted Benjamin's attention. Rather it was the impression, then the certainty, that the figure was actually moving. Bound rigidly, it nevertheless seemed to twitch on its makeshift perch, its head moving from side to side and the legs shaking. Its mask was one of simple, unadorned wax – a cipher to stand for any man. Had nobody in the crowd noticed the signs of life? Or did they simply not care in this most godless of metropolitan regions?

Benjamin moved closer, secure in his piratical anonymity, until he was within striking distance of young Master Smalletts. It was then that he heard the muffled cries from the effigy – almost too faint to hear above the general hubbub, and certainly too distant for coherent words to be heard . . . and yet there was a familiarity in the tone, a resonance in the syllables, a note of outrage that might have been reduced to that most distinctive of verbal mannerisms:

'*Hmm! Hmm! Hmm!*'

Benjamin did not hesitate. He took the nearest piece of wood in the pyre and brought it down with stupefying force upon the head and back of the would-be incendiary Tobias Smalletts. The boy pitched forward, senseless, on to his face and Benjamin began to toss aside the makings of the fire so that he might reach and free the captive effigy.

The gathered masses were not, however, in agreement.

'Oi – what yer doin' to the fire – lay off!'

'Why d'yer belt the lad, yer bully?'

'Get the pirate!'

They descended upon the burly interloper as a pack of dogs, and though he assailed their sculls with blows, the very weight of men upon him soon drove him to his knees. A multitude of fists and feet thudded into him. His mask came free. There was a recoil of shock. The mob renewed its violent vigour.

He might have died there that night under the massed onslaught of drunks, but fortune proved contrary and there came another event so monumental, so unignorable and so appealing to the massed spectators that his beating immediately became an irrelevance. It began with an explosion that shook the very ground and filled the sky with a hail of lethal masonry.

Everyone paused. A distant cry was heard: 'The manufactory is a-fire! Mottram's fireworks manufactory is burning!'

In an instant, Benjamin's cheering persecutors fled *en masse* towards that site, leaving Stretton-ground a sudden wasteland of litter and smoke. Finally, it seemed, they would get the show they had been promised.

Noah started at the sound of the explosion, recognising it as the sound of igniting gunpowder. A great billow of fire swelled into the darkness above, followed by a surging urgency in the crowds. Here was a spectacle worth seeing – the kind of destructive vision that delighted men and could mesmerize an incendiary.

He ran with them towards the heart of the slum and beheld a scene more apocalyptic than any so far. Here, amid the festering, decrepit *façades*, roared a battle between the constables of Division A and the rookery crooks: truncheons swinging, fists flying, women screeching, dogs yapping, bodies unconscious, glass glinting on cobbles and non-combatants leaning from windows to scream support. Evidently news of the manufactory fire had not yet interrupted the Irish – who prefer a fight to a fire – and so the rush towards Mottram's merely flowed around them, Noah as flotsam among it.

Dozens were already gathered beneath the squat-square chimney of the manufactory, kept back from its walls by fear and heat. A section of roof had gone completely in the explosion, its ragged hole belching angry vortices of smoke. The windows, too, were gone, each vomiting fire, and the stores of combustibles were producing their show: the red glare of antinomy, saltpetre flashes of yellow, camphor white and sulphur blue, *sal ammoniac* green with electrum glinting brass and steel. Their volatile perfume filled the air, erupting to a percussion of squibs and crests, rockets and serpents, hisses and pops *ricocheting* madly within the confining walls.

Noah was glad of the fire demon mask protecting his nose and mouth from the toxic clouds, though his eyes stung with their smoke. On the crowd's periphery, he squinted at the congregated faces for a sign of a waxen Sir Richard. Where might his adversary be?

If Lucius Boyle was here, he was unlikely to be among the throng itself, where an inadvertent jostle might loose his mask and reveal the true horror beneath. Rather, he would have found himself a vantage from which he could enjoy the show and escape if need be. An upper window? An street lamp's cross bar? The driver's platform of an abandoned cab? None appeared to betray his presence.

The bell of an approaching fire-engine sounded above the moaning flames and within minutes a brigade of uniformed engineers appeared in martial formation. Disappointment flickered through the audience, expressed in catcalls of 'Let it burn, won't yer?'

'Everybody must move to safety!' shouted the helmeted engineer. 'There are powder stores in the cellar and they will take the whole street with them! Stand back! Get away! Don't you understand?'

But the crowd was not to be denied, and though they retreated sufficiently to allow the engine to approach, they would not forego the spectacle of hose and water doing battle with the multi-hued elemental flames

Noah searched the masses with growing frustration. Visibility was becoming worse amid the rain of sparks and drifting smoke, yet more and more were being drawn by the bells to that place to watch the manufactory burn. Was Lucius Boyle even here at all? Or had he escaped towards Vauxhall as his grand diversion drew everyone awry?

Noah vacillated. Should he go after Mr Cullen? Should he head for the Thames Tunnel and more proof of Boyle's movements? Should he look for Benjamin and learn what he had discovered?

He was thus distracted when he became aware of a set of eyes upon him – a feeling rather than an identifiable stare. He cast a furious gaze across the hellish scene but saw no mask directed at him: no discernable observer. Had it merely been a reveller drawn briefly to the theatricality of his devil's mask?

Then Noah caught the glassy flash: two round green discs reflecting the flames – a smoke suited engineer with a truncated tube hanging from his obscene hood of leather. The same kind of suit found at Westminster Palace. The same kind of suit seen emerging faceless from the burning house at Blackfriars.

Noah returned the stare. He raised his arm slowly and pointed: you! He pushed back his mask so that the green-eyed thing might see him true. And the creature turned to flee.

Lucius Boyle?

Noah began to push through the people around him.

Mr Cullen had been able to run no more. No passers-by had seen a masked gentleman run that way. Either Boyle had adopted another face, or he had never ventured that way at all.

It was the explosion from Westminster and its great orange blossom against the darkness that had determined Mr Cullen to return and aid the others. Clearly all the night's activity was occurring in that *locale*.

He was walking quickly along Wood-street, his mind churning with supposition about his fellows, when his cogitations were disturbed by something down John-street to his left: a grunting sound that might have been a man attempting to move something heavy. A cargo wagon was waiting there in the shadows, a fellow in the back labouring to cover his wares with a tarpaulin.

But as the man looked up from his work, Mr Cullen saw a face that was unmoved by its efforts – a still, expressionless face that had the dullness of a mask. The street was otherwise quite empty at that hour, and there was surely no reason for a man to wear a mask as he worked in the dark. A thief, perhaps, stealing coal? A cracksman robbing the house of people who had gone out to attend a fire?

'You there! What are you doing?' called Mr Cullen.

The man jerked his attention towards the voice and jumped quickly into the driver's seat of the wagon, whipping the pair of horses into action and directing the vehicle to where Mr Cullen stood.

The latter paused indecisively at the wagon's approach and reflected that he was no longer a policeman. If a thief *had* been at work, it was hardly his business . . . and yet the mask did seem to hold some dubious significance in light of recent developments. He moved into the centre of the narrow street and held up his hand for the driver to stop.

In response, the wide-eyed bridling pair came straight at him. A whip lashed across his cheek and he leaped to the side to avoid being run down. He caught a flash of impassive wax and a burning human stare.

'Hoi! Stop!' called Mr Cullen to the back of the wagon, his eyes telescoping in sudden shocked realisation upon a protuberance emerging from the ill-secured tarpaulin: two stiffened legs seemingly attached to a board.

His own legs seemed to lose vitality as the enormity of the vision assailed him. Was this the Masked Man of popular myth? Was this the killer of PC Tatylor discovered near Portugal-street? Was he even now transporting the latest Gardener-street abductee to its place of exhibition under the cover of darkness?

'Stop that wagon!' he yelled in futility. Not a soul was there to hear him.

He had to act. Blood coursed in his limbs and he began his pursuit as the wagon headed with growing speed towards Great Peter-street. There would soon be crowds and people who might help.

'Stop! Stop that wagon!'

And still it rattled on unimpeded, Mr Cullen giving chase on legs that had already given their best.

'Hoi! Somebody! Anybody! Stop the murderer!'

The distance between him and the wagon was growing inexorably. He shouted until hoarse, but the few people populating the streets thereabouts looked with mere curiosity at the hectic scene. It was none of their business. A group of boys seemed to flee screaming at its approach.

Or rather, they were fleeing from a squib they had left sparking in the thoroughfare, rushing gleefully beyond its blast. And explode it did . . . immediately before the hooves of the racing horses.

They shied, they whinnied, they jerked to the side. The wagon twisted, tipped and fell so that driver and cargo were thrown to the cobbles.

Mr Cullen arrived within moments and breathlessly beheld the grim taxidermied form of a policeman laid out on the road: perfectly preserved and mounted as PC Taylor had been. Some yards away, the driver groaned semi-conscious and face down, one leg evidently snapped by the crash. Meanwhile, people had begun to arrive, drawn by another spectacle of violence.

'Everybody stand back!' said Mr Cullen, approaching the writhing masked man and employing a rough kick to turn him over.

Only half of the anonymous wax mask remained, but the other half was one Mr Cullen knew well.

'My G___! It is *you*!'

'It was not within my will to decide!' pleaded the murderer. 'I was doomed to it by my very face – I was fated to kill by Nature herself, do you not see!'

Noah struggled to get through the crowd that was growing denser every moment around the manufactory walls. Fortunately, the smoke-suited quarry was facing the same problem and could not easily flee without becoming trapped among them.

'Hold that man! He in the smoke hood – he is a murderer!' called Noah, but his voice was insignificant against the roaring flames and cheering throng. Some people turned to look, but soon refocused on the show. 'Out of my way in the name of C____! A murderer is going free!'

The villain had hesitated, gauging the distance between the edge of the crowd and Noah. The glass eyes of the hood flickered viridian-red in the conflagration's reflection. And he bolted towards the manufactory itself, though great gouts of fire spewed from the shattered windows and the interior was quite impenetrable with smoke.

'*No! Do not enter!*' screamed a helmeted engineer.

But the fleeing figure charged heedless into that writhing Gehenna and was swallowed instantly by its fury.

Noah attempted to pursue, but was blasted back by the heat and smoke.

The engineer grabbed his arm and tugged him away. 'Are you insane? That other fellow will be dead in seconds, even with the smoke hood.'

'So he is not one of your men?' said Noah, his eyes smarting from the flames.

'No – it is the St James's engine that has the nearest smoke suit and their brigade is not yet here.'

'Is there another door to the manufactory? A yard at the rear for deliveries, perhaps?'

'I suspect so, but I tell you: that man is already dead. You should not attempt—'

'Stop him if he emerges – he is a murderer.'

And Noah ran, sprinting alongside the blazing, blackened *silhouette* of Mottram's to the corner, then along the long windowless wall of its side towards the next corner where he hoped to find a gate and a yard and his prey emerging phoenix-like from the destruction.

It was not to be.

Even as he rounded the corner and darted towards the gates of the yard, there was a cataclysmic eruption. The sky became fire. Windows were shattered across Westminster, Chelsea and St James's. Flaming debris soared quaquaversally to rain just moments later as fractured masonry, smoking timbers and the gritty particulate of ground metal.

Noah had been knocked from his feet by one of the sturdy wooden gates that had ripped clean away from its post in the blast. He now struggled from under it and stared in dumb frustration at the site of destruction before him – a vast vaporous pile of bricks, beams and smaller fires that showed not the slightest sign of human life.

His face blackened and his clothes grimy, he walked as near as he could to the rubble pile and tried to make out any sign of the leather smoke hood, a charred limb, a smear of blood. But there was nothing – nothing at all.

THIRTY

CONFESSION

Written and signed by my own hand in the presence of witnesses

I, Edward Figgs, do herewith admit to the abduction, murder and unnatural taxidermical transformation of PC James Taylor and another constable of that station (whose name I do not know). That is to say, I did knowingly and purposefully disable them with a wad of flax soaked in ether while they were on their beat in Westminster, thereafter transporting them by wagon to my home in John-street for preparation. To hide my Judas face in these acts, I wore a mask of wax.

Following my work on PC Taylor, I did purposefully deposit him on Clements-lane, Lincoln's-inn, where he was discovered that very same night by the purest coincidence. I had chosen the place for its quiet streets and had not the least awareness of Inspector Albert Newsome's nearby activities. The second body I had intended to exhibit somewhere similarly quiet, but was frustrated in this attempt while leaving Westminster.

I offer no defence for my actions but that I was chosen by fate for such horrible crimes, coming to realize as much only when I became ensconced in my studies of anthropometry. For the unbearable truth is this: my own scull, features and anatomy mark me out as a born murderer.

You may be sure that I sought every avenue to disprove it and that I consulted every learned work for a mitigation of Nature's sentence upon me, but a body cannot lie. The signs may be read in my eyes, in my basilar formation, my sagittal depressions, my peculiar occipital protuberance. They may be read in my quickness of gaze, the curve of my fingers and the very timbre of my voice so that every mirror became a curse and a reminder of what I must necessarily one day do. My will was

not in question; I had no choice. It was merely a matter of how long I could delude
myself into believing otherwise.

Why taxidermy? Alas, the refinement of my science told me that I would never
be a phrenzied killer. No hammer, knife or rope would be my tool. Just as a man
lives, so he murders. My nature is drawn to careful preparation, to ritual and
harmonious appearance, so naturally I enjoy aesthetic pursuits. Yet my organic
impulse is to kill, so I employ a lethal methodology most fitting to my nature:
taxidermy. It is clean, it is organised; I let the victim's blood while he is
unconscious and skinless so that no ugliness remains.

Nothing in human behaviour is random, and so my choices of victim were also
driven by physiology. There was never malice in my selections. Rather, it is perhaps
a curiosity of coincidence that one of my duties is – or was – to examine men for
temperamental fitness in their work for the Metropolitan Police. In such a way, I
spent many hours studying them and saw men who were born to be victims – men
who were weak, men who bore the precise opposite traits to my own and whose
existence in some ways required the mortal equilibrium my own. For as they were
born to die, I was born to slay them and exhibit them as the perfect forms they were.
I will not appeal to God or to Justice for mercy, for I have no faith in either. I have
been created evil, and it seems fitting that I will find my place in Hell.

Sir Richard appeared pale, but otherwise healthy after his experience at the
House of Commons. Mr Newsome, however, looked as if he would have
been better accommodated in a hospital, with his face still burned from the
powder flash, his many injuries still raw and his eyes squinting to manage the
sight that was only now returning to him. The two gentlemen were sitting by
the fire in Sir Richard's office at Scotland Yard.

'I can still barely believe it,' said Sir Richard, putting down the
confession. 'The man was a respected member of the scientific community.
He was an expert who was trusted and who worked within these very walls.
Yet . . . he is clearly a sophisticated form of lunatic.'

'Respect and trust are often misplaced, sir.'

'I know that you never held his methods in high regard, Inspector.'

'That is true, sir, but evidently *he* took them seriously enough.'

'Yes, well – he will now hang for them. It is a pity when an intelligent man goes that way. It is a great pity. Had he confessed his secret fears, we might have sought treatment. There are places – private asylums.'

'Yes, sir. I suppose so.'

'It seems that the fellow who apprehended Mr Figgs was once a constable in Lambeth. Were you aware of that?'

'Mr John Cullen, sir. I have worked with him in the past. He was briefly in the Detective Force but was considered unsuitable.'

'Really? It rather seems he has improved since then, does it not?'

'Sir – he is one of those who goes about with Mr Dyson and Mr Williamson and that fearsome Negro. He and those others are virtually outlaws and . . . well, you know my feelings on those gentlemen.'

'Indeed.'

'I wonder, sir, on that particular matter, if I might offer the opinion that the use of such people has been proven to be ineffective. I perceive that they have been involved in these recent events, but with what success?'

'What exactly do you mean to say, Inspector?'

'Only that employing such "agents" is an embarrassment to the good men of the Detective Force and that, ultimately, their benefits have been scant. Lucius Boyle has, it appears, once again slipped beyond our grasp, while Mr Figgs was apprehended by the purest coincidence – *anybody* might have noticed those legs sticking out of the wagon. As for the most important clue – the Thames Tunnel chamber and all of its evidence – it was I who discovered it, not they.'

'You discovered it by withholding the evidence of that postcard from me and from them, Inspector. That is not good police work, but selfishness in the name of self-aggrandizement. Furthermore, you went there alone and were almost killed. How would that have contributed to the case?'

'With respect, I was not killed.'

351

'Not this time. There are additional examples: the mask models you discovered at Madame Tussaud's which you omitted to tell anybody about, the ridiculous business with the body of Perkin Mullender, your use of the Newspaper Office without my consent . . . and, I might also add, that illicit ledger of your ill-judged creation. It is still missing.'

'Are . . . you sure, sir? There was a locked box in the chamber at the Thames Tunnel . . . I felt sure it would be found there . . .'

'The constables you sent to secure the evidence after that terrible riot in Westminster discovered the box as you had described it, but it had been forced open and the contents taken.'

'I do not understand . . .'

'Quite. You concentrate only on your own part of the investigation without considering the wider circumstances. It seems that Mr Williamson and this Mr Cullen were in the tunnel shortly after you left in blind pursuit – perhaps you even crossed paths in different tunnels. They witnessed a fellow wearing a mask of *my* likeness.'

'Lucius Boyle?'

'Perhaps. We will probably never know. It would certainly make sense for him to secure that ledger as his only means of retaining power and money. Perhaps he was disturbed in his work by the arrival of those other two and rendered them unconscious. At least, that is what I understand so far. Fortunately, all of the other evidence remained and, as you have said, seems strongly to suggest that he was responsible for the robbery here and the murder of the girl.'

'May I ask where these other "investigators" are now, sir?'

'It is not your business to know, Inspector.'

'Then might you at least tell me if you still intend to house them as you once promised? It seems a misappropriation of official budget to—'

'A promise must be kept if made, Inspector. You need not concern yourself with how such things are effected.'

'Yes, sir . . . but my understanding is that Noah Dyson is nowhere to be found. He was at the rookery pursuing Boyle and now both are missing. He was at the exhibition in St James's park and, it seems, disappeared with a suspect. Where is that suspect? Is Dyson beyond the law? Do such things not concern you?'

'What concerns me is how close we came to a slaughter at the Palace of Westminster. It seems I have Mr Dyson to thank for my life.'

'I was unable . . . I was blinded at the time . . .'

'You were blinded by your own selfish ambition, Inspector. And let us not forget that this outrage in the Commons was made partially possible by your illicit ledger. It appears that the sergeant-at-arms was compromised by his immoral activities listed therein and agreed, much against his better judgement, to adjust the ventilation valves accordingly. You must learn that there are consequences to your recklessness, whether they are immediate or more delayed in their fruition.'

'Sir, I . . . Have you managed to discover more about Sir _____ _____ or any of those others who were advised not to attend?'

'That fellow is now quite contrite. He was indeed being blackmailed and obeyed the villain in staying away from the hearing. He must live with that shame. As for the others, all I can do is see that suspicion falls upon them. It is a lesson for many, is it not, Inspector?'

Mr Newsome made to speak, but seemed to think better of it. Instead, he clenched his jaw and stared into the fire. The two men passed a few moments in such silent contemplation.

'I wonder if, after all that has happened, you still give so much credence to the so-called sciences of detection?' said Mr Newsome.

'Mr Figgs may have been unbalanced, but that does not mean all branches of anthropometry are false, Inspector. We must look to the future in our fight against crime.'

'Yes, sir . . . but I cannot think of a single instance where these "experts" have aided the investigation. From what I understand, Dr

Hammerton's opinions were no more precise than the ramblings of that necromantic hag at the Thames Tunnel. Between all of them – Figgs, Hammerton, Schlöss – they managed to produce only an anonymous wax head: a blank cipher that could have been any man at all.'

Sir Richard smiled. 'Is it not the case that any man, ultimately, can be a murderer? Have you not considered that the head suggested by those various methodologies is in fact an everyman of murder? Paint the jaw red and it is Lucius Boyle. Add a red peruke and it is Inspector Albert Newsome.'

'I am not a murderer!'

'A mere example. As long as science is able to aid me, I will use it.

Mr Newsome seethed. The flames crackled in the grate.

But the quiet was short-lived. A shout came from the yard outside. Then another. Then a clatter of boots that increased in volume.

Sir Richard looked to Mr Newsome with a mild interrogative gaze.

'It is probably the coal-whippers fighting again, sir,' said the inspector. 'There has not been a fight for some months and perhaps they are due one.'

Yet the volume was still increasing and the noise was not the raucous rabble of battle. Rather, it was akin to a mob at a spectacle: an urgent murmur, a thrill of novelty.

Mr Newsome stood and walked to the window, where he saw a number of people running from shops and the public house towards the river. It was not clear what they sought.

'A ferry crash, possibly?' said Sir Richard, joining his inspector at the window.

There came a knock at the door.

'Enter,' said Sir Richard.

'Commissioner, Inspector – you might want to come down to the yard,' said a rather flushed and panting man in uniform.

'What is happening, constable?' said Mr Newsome.

'Two bodies, sir.'

'We need hardly concern the Commissioner with bodies dragged out of the river.'

'O, they are not dead, sir – nor pulled from the water. They are quite alive. It is said to be ... to be ... well, they are saying it is the murderer Lucius Boyle.'

Mr Newsome flashed a glance at Sir Richard – a moment of doubt that became a flicker of hope. In an instant, they were leaving the office to follow the constable downstairs.

Upwards of fifty people had gathered by the muddy river's edge: the vendors and workers of Scotland Yard, along with a number drawn from Whitehall by the growing clamour. Their mood seemed a combination of jocular and galvanic fascination as Mr Newsome pushed through to the front.

'Make way there! Make way for the police!'

The people parted and, suddenly, the remarkable spectacle presented itself.

Mr Newsome became quite rooted in shock and felt instinctively for the truncheon he was not carrying. Sir Richard simply gaped in wonder at what his eyes could not accept.

Two filthy figures lay struggling on the mud as if dropped there from a river-plying lighter. Each was securely bound with rope at ankle, knee and wrist, and each bore numerous signs of bodily injury beneath the slatherings of reeking mud. Even in their begrimed condition, their identities were clear enough.

Lucius Boyle's face in the flat, objective daylight was a truly hideous sight, its melted skin, patchy hair, lidless eyes and notorious red jaw expressing the fury of humiliated frustration. The Italian, meanwhile, looked a beaten man – his head shorn, his face bruised and his spirit evidently broken. The intensity in *his* eyes was merely that of the cornered animal. As the spectators increased, both captives continued to struggle quite uselessly against their bonds.

Mr Newsome remained stupefied at the spectacle. 'What ... how did these men come to be here?' he said to the crowd at large.

'Lighter just pulled in and dropped 'em o'erboard wi' a rope,' said a coal-faced labourer. 'I were standin' right 'ere smokin' when they done it.'

'What did they look like, these men on the boat?'

'Jus' like any lumpers. One were a black man – had a funny eye.'

Mr Newsome looked to Sir Richard, who seemed equally stunned by the turn of events. How had Lucius Boyle been captured and how had he come to be here in Scotland Yard? Where had he and his associate the Italian been in the intervening hours? If Noah and the Negro Benjamin were indeed behind this, where were they now?

'This gathering is becoming unmanageable,' said Sir Richard. 'I think it is time you did your duty, Inspector, so that we may find some answers.'

Mr Newsome turned again to the trussed and writhing figures before him. A beatific glow of satisfaction now suffused his face. He raised his voice so that all could hear: 'Lucius Boyle – I am placing you and your accomplice under arrest on the charges of murder, extortion and smuggling. I am sure I will think of more before you see the magistrate.'

The villain did not speak, but glared with the vitriol of pure hatred.

And as Mr Newsome arranged for the pair to be taken away by constables, Sir Richard returned somewhat dazed to his office, where he was to experience one final surprize.

On opening the door, his attention was taken almost immediately by an object placed in the centre of his desk – an object that had most definitely not been there when he had rushed from the room not twenty minutes previously. It was a bottle of evident antiquity, coated with dust and featuring a yellowing label in the French language. Not one of the clerks could account for how it had arrived there. Indeed, it was only when Sir Richard examined the bottle that he found, with a rueful smile, the small note stuck to the base:

V.

Later that day, across town and in the very shadow of St Paul's, four men sat close to the fire in the dense smoky warmth of the Cathedral coffee house. They were indeed an interesting group, even by the standards of a place popularly frequented by rather desperate looking writers.

Mr Williamson sighed. 'Give it no further thought, Noah. Your course of action was the right one. Now Lucius Boyle will face the trial and execution he deserves.'

'I thought that you were against execution as a tool of justice,' said Noah.

'Hmm. Ordinarily, I am. But his crimes unfit him to live among civilized men.'

'I had the chance . . . I could have killed him just as easily as snapping my fingers.'

'And it is to your credit that you did not. Restraint is what separates us from the animals.'

'No, you misunderstand me, George – I mean that killing was, in the end, too good for him. When I rushed from Westminster to the Thames Tunnel, I was hoping that he was still alive, that he would return there as his one last refuge and that I would be waiting for him – to kill him. And as I waited there in that chamber for an hour or more, it seemed he would never come and that I would be cheated once again in my hopes to release myself from a lifetime of vengeful hatred. But . . . but when he did arrive, he was a pitiful sight: half roasted in the Mottram's fire and coughing like a consumptive. It was no effort at all to overpower him.'

'So you felt pity, Noah. There is no shame in it.'

Pity? No. I felt that stabbing him through the heart would be too easy. It would have been almost a relief to him – certainly better than the coldness of the condemned cell, the ridicule of the Newgate crowd and the hemp around his throat. I could not grant him that escape. I never thought I would believe it, but justice proved to be the more worthy fate.'

'Hmm. Hmm. I am sure the lawmakers do not see it in quite the terms you describe.'

Mr Cullen – still benefitting greatly from the acclaim of discovering a murderer – slapped Benjamin on the back and attempted to lighten the tone: 'But we showed them, did we not? Can you imagine Inspector Newsome's face when he saw how we had bound the villains and delivered them to Scotland Yard?'

'He will know well enough who performed that task,' said Noah. 'To him, the most important thing would have been making the arrest. He will be happy enough with the outcome.'

'What about Sir Richard's promise to re-house you both?' said Mr Cullen. 'He can hardly retract it now that you have captured Boyle *and* saved his life, Noah.'

'To be frank, I feel that I have had too much connection with the Metropolitan Police in recent times,' said Noah. 'Let us imagine for a moment that the commissioner did provide houses for us – what other "favours" might he then ask once we were indebted to him?'

'You make a valid point,' said Mr Williamson, 'but how else are we to be housed? I am not wealthy or young. I cannot live on the streets or move from place to place. I will not reside in a prison or live the fugitive's life for the rest of my time.'

'I believe I may have a solution,' said Noah.

Benjamin began to laugh and returned Mr Cullen's back slap as if to say, 'Wait for this!'

Noah reached under his chair and brought out a well worn leather bag.

'Hmm. I was wondering about that,' said Mr Williamson.

With a quick look around the coffee house, Noah opened a the flap and pulled out a large black ledger, lying it on the table between them.

'Hmm. Hmm. Is it what I think it is?'

'Indeed it is,' said Noah with barely concealed enjoyment. 'I found it in a lock box in that cobwebby nook beneath the river. I have been reading it, and I am sure that it will provide us with all we need for a comfortable future.'

'Noah – I hope you are not suggesting that we profit from extortion.'

'George – you have little idea what activities are detailed in this catalogue. A fellow who will buy an apartment and stables in Mayfair so he can keep a courtesan is certainly wealthy enough, and immoral enough, to come to an agreement with us. We will not be greedy. One moderate payment from each of the richest listed here will be quite enough. Let these men who flout the laws of decency pay for our recovery.'

Mr Williamson stared darkly at the ledger. Was he perhaps thinking of one particular address therein? An address in Golden-square? No doubt there were lists of men who had visited, men who had paid to use her and who kept her in that life of sin from which she had never been able to escape. 'Hmm.'

'I was hoping you would say that,' smiled Noah.

Benjamin let forth his *basso* laugh and offered a gesticulatory sentence.

'I agree,' said Mr Cullen with enthusiasm. 'Four meat pies and another round of coffee.'

'Actually,' said Mr Williamson, resting his hand on the ledger, 'I believe I will have a brandy on this occasion.'

As for myself, I was not too far from the scenes so described. In fact, I was sitting near the opaque and dripping window in that selfsame coffee house and watching them covertly from my table.

Superficially, I had little to celebrate. Mr Parker at the Newspaper Office had, inevitably, discovered that my references were fabricated and discharged me, though it was the constant leaks of police business to the private presses that had first set them sniffing for the rat among their ranks. Nor had my role in helping Mr Newsome perpetrate his scheme with Perkin Mullender gone unnoticed (particularly since my words had found themselves sent simultaneously to – and printed in – *all* of the other city newspapers.) But I remained philosophical; I had made a significant profit from my brief association with the police.

And, of course, the case of Lucius Boyle was once again setting the newspapers ablaze with scandal. He had died, then he had been heretically resurrected in the flames of Mottram's manufactory. Never before had Fleet-street's editors enjoyed the opportunity to sell a murderer's story *twice*, and they were quite insatiable in their greed for facts. Who better than I to supply them? I who had followed the monster from his very beginnings and observed the investigators' pursuit from within the corridors of Scotland Yard itself. I was the one with the facts and the contacts – and what I did not know, I could imagine.

Thus was it that I raised a covert glass to those gentlemen by the fire, and, yes, to the absent Inspector Newsome whose idiosyncrasies make any story colourful. I would soon be leaving the warmth of the coffee house to visit Newgate gaol, where, at the bidding of *the Times*, I was to approach the condemned cells and observe the killers themselves awaiting their date with the noose: that sullen Italian and the seething Lucius Boyle, secure within double-barred windows and many feet of imprisoning brick. Perhaps they would speak – perhaps not. I did not know then, of course, how subsequent events would surprise us all.

There are others, too, that I might mention before taking my leave – mere stragglers in the piece. Charlotte was laid to rest with due dignity under the name she had chosen. None of her past lovers attended, but the coffin was the finest available specimen, paid for anonymously by a certain lady of Park-lane – one of the sisterhood, it might be said.

Perkin Mullender could boast of a lesser fate, accommodated in a dark cellar cupboard beneath Scotland Yard with the other forgotten curiosities of London's criminal history. There, amid the evidence of past murders and the secrets nobody wanted to know, he gathered dust and cobwebs until quite grey: a deathless ageing upon a changeless face. He may still be there, for all I know.

And as for the living, there was one, at least, who had escaped to thieve another day. Let us observe him as he saunters along Holborn with his greasy hat, his dirty face and his uniform of accumulated filth. It is Master Tobias Smalletts – biding his time at present, but with certain ideas on how his future might develop. Was he not, after all, the boy who had almost brought down the government?

He pauses now, to peer through a large plate glass window of a shop selling attire for the finest schoolboys in the land: uniforms of such cut and fabric and gaudy crests that his young eyes cannot help but feast upon them. He mutters something: an expression, perhaps, of summary awe and reflection – a fitting epitaph, indeed, for our story as a whole:

'_____ _____!'

Acknowledgements

Moniczka – moje słodkie kochanie

Neil Fletcher – for the question

Rahil Sheikh – Maecenas to my Horace

Thomas Peckett Prest – casualty of art

Adam (www.copypasterepeat.com) – for the cover

About the Author

James McCreet was born in Sheffield. He taught English abroad for several years before returning to the UK to become a journalist and copywriter. This is his fourth novel in this series.

For more information: www.jamesmccreet.co.uk

Also in this series

THE

MASKED

ADVERSARY

James McCreet

2

Printed in Great Britain
by Amazon